Kristi—
May your arrow
fly true!

VORODIN'S LAIR

VORODIN'S LAIR

Book Two of the Warminster Series

J. V. Hilliard

Paperback ISBN 978-1-77400-052-6
Ebook ISBN 978-1-77400-053-3

Printed on Acid Free Paper

DragonMoonPress.com

ACKNOWLEDGEMENTS

WRITING ACKNOWLEDGEMENTS FOR ONE'S novel is possibly the most rewarding part of this process. Most think that a writer is an island, adrift in a sea of obscurity, pounding away at a keyboard or tucked away in their study or favorite coffee shop. But in truth, writing a novel requires a team, some working with you on the project daily; others contributing from the sidelines and in some cases, unaware of how much they've meant to the final product.

First, let me reiterate this point from my debut novel—I will never be able sufficiently express my eternal gratitude to my family and friends for their continued support and encouragement. Andrea, you have sacrificed so much to let me chase down this dream. For that, I say again and again, I love you.

Secondly, I need to thank the rest of my Warminster team for helping make the series a success. To Dane Cobain, my literary compass; Andrew Jackson, my mentor; Shai Shaffer, Abigail Linhardt and Brianna Toth, my development sherpas; Larch Gallagher, my champion illustrator; Phil Athans and Pam Harris, my fantasy wordsmiths; Victor Bevine the voice of Warminster; Jan and Susan Dickler, my media giants; Ann Howley, Leah Pileggi and Maria Simbra, my JAM session members; Auggie Tagabunlang, my social media guru; Hannah Nathanson, my poetess extraordinaire; Emily's World of Design for my family tree and cartography; all of my "Professor Howley" classmates; and of course my Dungeons & Dragons group, Brent Burich, Joey Davis, Chris Niziol, Markus Rauhecker, James Stefanyak, Jim Stillwagner and Kent Szalla. And yes, you Maureen Kelly and Sheila Kirk for giving me the idea for the Ophidian.

Lastly, of course to you, my readers. I hope you've enjoyed your second trip into the Realm of Warminster, and I hope you continue your journey throughout the series.

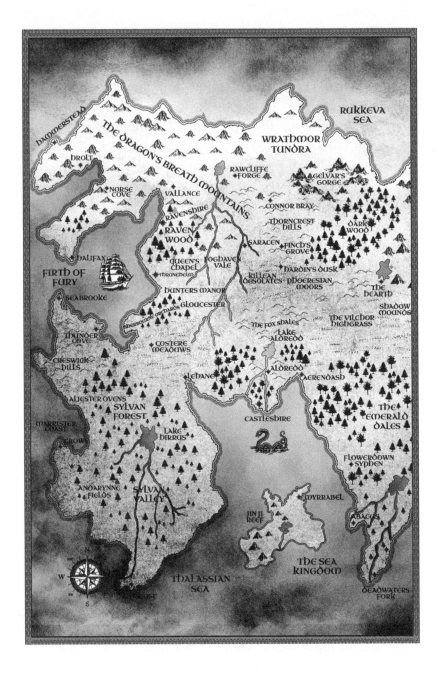

The Seven Baronies of Warminster

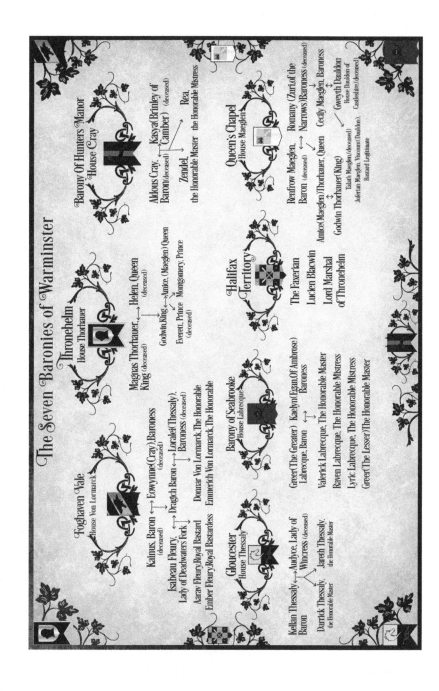

Thronehelm
House Thorhauer

Magnus Thorhauer, → Helen, Queen (deceased)
King (deceased)
→ Godwin, King ↔ Amice, (Maeglen) Queen
   → Everett, Prince Montgomery, Prince
      (deceased)

Barony Of Hunters Manor
House Cray

Aldous Cray, ↔ Kasyat (Brinley of
Baron (deceased) Camber) (deceased)
   → Zendel Rea,
      the Honorable Master the Honorable Mistress

Queen's Chapel
House Maeglen

Renfrow Maeglen, ↔ Romany (Zurf of the
Baron (deceased) Narrows)/Baroness (deceased)

Amice (Maeglen)/Thorhauer, Queen Cecily Maeglen, Baroness
   ↕
Godwin Thorhauer King) → Gweyth Dauldon
Talaith Maeglen (deceased), Viscount (Dauldon), House Dauldon of
Jolertan Maeglen, Castleshire (deceased)
Bastard Legitimate

Foghaven Vale
House Von Lormarck

Kalnus, Baron ↔ Eowynne (Cray), Baroness
   (deceased)
→ Isabeau Fleury, ↔ Dragoth Baron ↔ Loraleif (Thessaly),
   Lady of Deadwaters Fork Baroness (deceased)
      → Aarav Fleury, Royal Bastard Donnar Von Lormarck, The Honorable
         Ember Fleury, Royal Bastardless Emmerich Von Lormarck, The Honorable

Halifax Territory

The Faxerian
Lucien Blacwin
Lord Marshal
of Thronehelm

Barony of Seabrooke
House Labreque

Greer (The Greater) ↔ Kaelyn (Egan Of Ambrose)
Labreque, Baron Baroness
   → Valerick Labreque, The Honorable Master
      Raven Labreque, The Honorable Mistress
      Lyric Labreque, The Honorable Mistress
      Greer (The Lesser) The Honorable Master

Gloucester
House Thessaly

Kellan Thessaly, ↔ Audyce, Lady of
Baron Wincress (deceased)
→ Darrick Thessaly, ↔ Jareth Thessaly,
   the Honorable Master the Honorable Master

PROLOGUE

*"Divine mother, the most honored of beasts,
I beseech thee. Return to our side."*
—Zamiel of the Moor Bog

SHADOWS HAD LONG SINCE filled the temple, swallowing the barest echo of holiness. Any innocent or foolhardy trespasser would have turned away, if not for the lateness of the hour and the darkness of the main hall then for the tell-tale stench of carrion and the generations of old stains marking the altar.

But the man sitting before the altar, still as death, was no corpse. Like any high priest, it was simply his due to take periods of fasting and prayer before a sacrament.

Zamiel, for that was his name, paid little mind to the tallow candle that flickered in front of him. He'd grown insensible to the smell and the sensation of hunger. His cassock was dirty and badly stained, and his withered form was hardly that of a fat and prosperous city priest, for he'd abandoned any aspirations of dignity or wealth. His goal was far grander.

He didn't know exactly how long he'd been sitting there; time seemed to pass in uneven waves, first in a slow haze and then as a lightning bolt. His attention stayed fixed on the object of his meditation: Threnody, the Ancient of Death, she of the dark wings and the sudden doom. Mercurial, but of all the Ancients the most familiar to him, as well as the most beloved. For what seemed like the hundred-thousandth time, Zamiel exalted her name, seven times and then seven times again. He prayed for focus.

The loud toll of the Harkening Bell marked the end of his prayer. Zamiel drew a long, rattling breath and watched the fat drip from the candle.

"Holy Father," a familiar voice called from behind him. It was Gwyllion, his most trusted attendant. "It's time."

Zamiel nodded, lowering the cowl of his cloak. After a moment, he heard Gwyllion exit. He took a second to gather his thoughts and then stood slowly, reaching for the staff he'd kept close to him. It was hewn from bone, the mighty femur of an honored beast long gone, and thus was adequate as a convenient crutch when one needed to address a congregation after fasting for three days.

And it was a more than adequate weapon.

He left the main room of the temple and took the old route down to the caves, hunching under the low tunnel ceiling, the presence of the Ancients swimming in his head. They'd listened, they'd rewarded him as they always did; the prayer had worked.

The tunnel opened out into the covenstead, sparsely illuminated by a few weak torches ensconced on the walls of the cavern. Before him stood the hooded ranks of the Moor Bog, with Gwyllion alongside them. At Zamiel's entry, she waved a hand and the muttering of prayers ceased. He moved among them, the faithful parting at his passage, until he stood at the center of the encircled throng. There was silence as they waited for him to speak.

"I, your Black Vicar, have spoken to the Ancients tonight," Zamiel proclaimed. His voice came out strong and steady, fortified by the divine presence, though incongruous with his emaciated frame. "The prophecy has been confirmed. Our journey begins now, sons and daughters."

His followers exulted softly, some of them falling to their knees, others bowing their heads. One or two of the youngest even dared to smile at him.

"This sacred cave is the birthplace of our divine mother,"

he reminded them, leaning ceremoniously on his staff. "The time of her return is near. What will take place tonight is the first step, after a millennium of work by our order, toward restoring her to her rightful throne. This I tell thee, sons and daughters. We will all bear witness to her glory in our lifetime."

Gwyllion, sensing the end of the oration, raised her arms to signal the Harkener. From somewhere in the underground labyrinth, the low reverberations of the bell tolled twice.

"Bring forth the honored beast," she intoned.

The sea of dark robes rippled, making room for their inhuman guest to enter. From the darkness on the far side of the covenstead, a figure crept toward the assembled masses. It was faceless, seemed almost boneless, and stood at the height of a human, with wings like a gargoyle. All of those in attendance, and even the Black Vicar himself, bowed in its presence.

"Tell us, most honored beast," he said to it, "what sacrifice should we offer you in return for your service?"

The creature's empty face began to bubble as if mired in a primordial sludge, slowly mirroring the familiar features of Gwyllion.

"Well chosen," Zamiel replied, without hesitation. "Your choice will be honored."

The beast's face morphed again, this time taking on the countenance of Zamiel himself.

"This choice, too, will be honored," the Black Vicar said, hiding a moment of surprise. "We'll both be yours this night."

The skin-stealer abandoned its imitation and bowed deeply to him, awaiting his reciprocal demands.

"*Endre,*" Zamiel incanted, "*stjele, ansiktet.*"

At his words, a man, bound and gagged, appeared on the cavern floor. Gwyllion moved forward dutifully, grabbing the man by his hair and dragging him to the creature. A weak moan was all that escaped the captive, who was evidently too drugged to put up a fight.

The beast bent toward the helpless figure at its feet, drew a deep breath, and then seized him with both hands.

The man tried to scream, his eyes widening in terror and pain, as the skin-stealer's hands and then its arms melted into a pool of bloody mud, penetrating his flesh.

The creature wasted little time with its transformation. Like a plague, it spread throughout the man's carcass, eating him from within, climbing into every limb and diffusing itself through his torso. The man's form ceased shaking, momentarily paralyzed, and then his eyelids flickered and opened.

The skin-stealer looked out at the Moor Bog through human eyes, its expression mild.

Zamiel felt a rush of intense awe and sublime terror. He'd never before witnessed the honored beast's transformation with his own eyes, and it was a sight he would never be able to forget—nor, he felt, would he wish to. It put into his mind the dark beauty of his own divine mother.

The shackled figure sat up, and Zamiel motioned for Gwyllion to undo its restraints. Within moments, the not-man was free, and the masses muttered again in adulation.

"You need no longer address me as 'honored beast,'" said the skin-stealer, "for I now possess the form that you have chosen. What would you have me do?"

Zamiel fought to remain calm in the face of his anticipation. "Return to Castle Thronehelm and wait for my command," he told it. "You'll be called upon in a day and a night. But first, tell me who you are."

The skin-stealer smiled, subconsciously rubbing its moustache. "I'm Meeks Crowley, trusted servant of King

Godwin and Queen Amice Thorhauer. I must return home before I'm missed."

Zamiel nodded in approval.

"You'll honor our arrangement," the creature stated, a note of warning in its tone. It didn't need to repeat its choice of sacrifices, but Zamiel knew it had sensed his surprise earlier and that it would not forgive an attempt to recant the promise.

"Of course," he agreed.

With that, Gwyllion signaled the Harkener and the bell tolled thrice.

THAT SAME NIGHT, ACCOMPANIED by twelve of his followers, the Black Vicar left the covenstead. It was time, after too many decades of waiting, for the prophecy of the Moor Bog to come to pass. He knew, deep in his bones, that they wouldn't fail.

The thirteen made their way through the crags of the Dragon's Breath Mountains and down into the dense surrounding forests at an impossible pace, ushered along by the Ancients' gifts of speed. An hour before dawn, they came to an open field, far from civilization and only set apart by its curious strain of grass, which was said to appear blue in moonlight. The meadow was unique, and to Zamiel's knowledge it was the only possible place the prophecy could have described. The field was quiet under the starlight, and the Moor Bog took up their position just inside a nearby tree line.

"Pray, my children," Zamiel said to them. "When the time comes, don't follow me." His congregants knelt and waited, hidden among the trees of the Ravenwood.

Zamiel stood alone in the clearing and quieted his soul, seeking the voices of the Ancients. Time seemed to slow, and a magnificent animal emerged from the eastern stretches of the forest, its pitch-black coat almost invisible under the cover of night. Even from a distance he felt its magic thickening the air like a cloud. This was a tetrine, a singular creature that was rarely sighted. Even then, it was usually mistaken for a unicorn, despite being almost double their usual size and possessing more powerful magics. As the fallen Keeper had foretold, it was alone.

Zamiel held his breath, suddenly feeling much younger than his years. Was it really he who was destined to do this? How could he dare to approach such a magnificent cryptid and keep his life?

"*Sjarm hest magi*," he muttered, trying to control himself. This was no time for fear. The Ancients were with him, as was his flock.

He pointed the sharpened end of his staff at the beast and watched as a magical web fell around it, holding it in place. The creature's muscles tensed visibly, but it couldn't run. Zamiel remembered that the tetrine were said to have an innate respect for those with the power to capture them, but he had no idea if that was true. He and his entourage had enough magic between them to trap it, but nothing could stop it from smiting him where he stood.

Zamiel forced his muscles into motion, growing ever wearier after the frenzied journey and the days without food or sleep. This was what it came down to, what would set everything in place. As he drew nearer to the tetrine, its enormous size became more obvious, and he registered in the back of his mind that if the animal did decide to kill him, it wouldn't need magic to do so. He was a tall man, but it towered so mightily over him that it could have ended his life with one kick.

The tetrine only waited, watching.

Zamiel was close enough to touch it, if he dared. His hand half-reached out, then stopped.

"I ask you to come with me," Zamiel said, his voice no stronger than a whisper. The power of the Ancients was leaving him, their brief blessing fading away. *Did the tetrine know? Would it care?* "We have much to learn from each other," he tried. "I can offer you *things* in return. Will you come?"

The tetrine tilted its head and leaned into his hand, then followed the Black Vicar into Ravenwood.

CHAPTER ONE

"Never wish to do less than what your duty requires."
—Annals From Halifan Military Academy

ADDILYN THOUGHT IT LOOKED like old blood. The embassy courtyard was a sea of earth tones, bathed in the rays of the setting sun. The crowd of Vermilion in attendance, adorned in dark reds and near-blacks, numbered a quarter of Castleshire's full population of elves. There Addilyn stood, at one end of an eight-pointed star formed by rows of her father's attendants.

It shouldn't feel real now, she thought. It should have felt real then. When she had been sitting by his body, having watched his life drain away in front of her eyes, having heard his final words. It should have felt real when the red she couldn't stop staring at had really been blood. But something about the chill in the air, the thin shoulders of the local temple attendant who had been called on to perform the rites, the somber faces of her countrymen, and Ritter at her side, kept ringing in her head like a bell.

Real.

This wasn't even the formal ceremony. The proper one would be happening back home in Eldwal, with his body, with the coronelle and all their sparse family and multitude of friends and admirers in attendance. It would have a poetry reading, and maybe a dance, things her father would have liked. This was cursory, just a quick ritual farewell from his colleagues and acquaintances in the city who had been shocked by Dacre's murder at the hands of the Bone elf assassin. She shouldn't cry at these rites, at the voice of the strange templar, at these unfamiliar and unbeloved surroundings and unknown people.

"The hands of the Ancients have taken him up," assured the priest, and a small sound escaped Addilyn's throat when she failed to fully suppress her cry. No one looked up, except Ritter.

"The hands of Melexis have covered him," recited the others standing in the star. Addilyn muttered along, her vision blurring and then clearing as tears gathered and fell.

Damn Melexis's hands. Damn all the Ancients' hands. Damn her own hands and the hands of her dutiful guard, Jessamy. Too slow. Damn her cursed, stupid father's hands, which should have been on her shoulders right now, should have been braiding her hair like he used to when she was little and still did when she got upset. He would never touch her hair, ever again. Every braid she ever put in it now would be...

Addilyn closed her eyes and struggled to breathe without sobbing. Silently, Ritter took her hand, and she gripped it hard, leaning her shoulder so subtly into his and hiding their entwined fingers in her long, wide sleeve.

"I don't think I know how to be me anymore," she whispered under the recitation of the priest, the words slipping out unbidden almost before she thought them. Words that had sunk like silt to the bottom of her heart and lain there undisturbed since she'd watched him die. Every piece of her felt untethered now, like she was drifting apart. The princess she was because of her father. The mage she had become to make him proud. The diplomat she had learned to be, meant to follow in his footsteps. Everything she was had been tied to that one stake in the ground.

Daughter.

And it had been pulled up.

Ritter, too wise to attempt any kind of reply, only squeezed her hand.

"YOU OUGHT TO LIE down."

Faux glanced up from her seated position on the floor. Arjun was looking at her, his hooded blue eyes exhausted but filled with concern.

She didn't move. "It's not as though I would be able to sleep anyway."

Her friend sighed. It was true that they'd been awaiting the executioner's axe for what felt like years, in more ways than one. The walls of the dank cell around them seemed only to solidify the prison Faux had taken with her when she'd left home with Arjun so long ago, making it difficult to gauge how long it had been. To her, it could have been hours or days since Daemus had interrupted the Caveat's proceedings with the Sight.

Faux shook her head. "We should have never come home." She had been muddling through her own feelings on the subject since they'd spoken to Kester, Daemus's uncle, and agreed to escort the Alaric heir back to Castleshire safely. She was caught somewhere between anger, fear, melancholy, and a vague, wavering nostalgia. It seemed her emotions shifted by the second if she thought too hard.

Arjun made a noncommittal noise. "This isn't home. It doesn't mean much to me—other than the sentence of death, of course."

Faux looked at him before understanding lit her gaze. "I don't know how I forgot. You're not from here, you're from Abacus."

His blue eyes sharpened. "That's not home either."

"Well, you talk about it little enough." She didn't want to admit it, but she was nettled by his refusal to discuss it with her. Upon learning in her late childhood that he wasn't from Castleshire as she had thought, Faux had tried to bring up his home city to him but had stopped asking questions when he only ever gave evasive answers. It was just a week ago when she finally learned more of his hidden past, his love of a fellow soldier named Anoki. But it took their stand against Clan Blood Axe at Homm Hill to evoke the tale. It was in his moment of greatest vulnerability when he confided in her, and even then, it had been a war story, told in front of their entire group.

A tense silence ensued. Arjun looked at his battle-scarred hands, while Faux looked at him.

"Sorry," she said at last, leaning her head back against the wall with a sigh. "I think you're probably right. Not a good time to talk about things like this."

The guardsman half-shrugged.

Faux smiled a humorless grin then sat up, her ears catching the faint sound of booted footsteps down the corridor. As she listened, the footfalls grew louder until the familiar face of Zayd Nephale, Castleshire's jailor, peered into their cell.

"Is it the executioner's block for us, then?" Faux asked, the finality of the inevitable settling in her guts.

The man cringed. "Not just yet." The jailor twisted his waxed moustache in a slight pause. "I'm to take you to speak to Lord Darcy."

"The same Lord Darcy who's left us to stew in a cell for uncounted hours with no last meal, only to think about the blade of an axe?" Arjun spat.

"He sends his apologies," Nephale snorted, looking genuinely chagrined. "The Caveat needed to confer for a time. Please come now."

Faux pulled herself to her feet and offered a hand to Arjun to help him up, which he took with an indulgent air. Nephale unlocked the door and affixed their shackles together, then the trio walked in silence through the labyrinthine halls, save for the sounds of the dragging chains at their feet. She noted their surroundings gradually became cleaner and more polished until at length they reached a large door, upon which Nephale knocked.

A voice called from within, and the jailor ushered them inside. Lord Darcy, the head of the Caveat's Regent Council who had read them their sentence, looked up at their entry and directed Nephale to stand outside before clearing his throat.

As they stepped through the door, Faux noticed both Jaxtyn Faircloth and Ranaulf Alaric sitting to the side of Lord Darcy. Her heart fluttered in hope while her mind fogged in confusion.

Lord Darcy wasted little time. "After some reflection—" he paused and looked at Faux, his metered voice remaining neutral, "—we decided this conversation was probably best to have in private quarters, as opposed to in front of the entirety of the Caveat."

Faux shifted and glanced to the floor. *What did this mean?*

Darcy sniffed and raised his head as Arjun stirred. "Arjun Ezekyle, you are personally acquainted with the Athabasica of Abacus. Is this correct?"

Faux's head whipped around. Arjun's posture stiffened, his expression blank but a touch stricken by the question.

After a brief pause, he responded. "Anoki? I knew her... once."

Darcy's left eyebrow lifted slightly. "Good to know Master Faircloth was correct. In that case, in the wisdom of this council and at the urging of both Lord Alaric and Master Faircloth here, the Regency has decided to offer you a choice, one that will commute your sentence if you succeed."

"Go on," Faux urged, her glance catching Jaxtyn's blue eyes smiling at her.

"This... *Athabasica* has refused to communicate with the Regency in any manner since she assumed the office several years ago. And with the display of Erudian Sight manifested by Daemus Alaric, it appears we have no recourse other than to directly her ask for her help, however…"

"What do you require of us?" Arjun asked.

"According to Master Daemus, you told him that you and the Athabasica were soldiers together at the High Aldin? She saved your life at the first battle of Homm Hill? Is this correct?"

Arjun's eyes widened.

"Captain?" Darcy prodded.

"As I said, I know Anoki," Arjun whispered. "But I haven't—"

"Excellent, Captain," Darcy interrupted. "You and your companion will deliver Daemus Alaric and Princess Addilyn Elspeth of the Vermilion nation to the safety of Abacus and introduce them to the Athabasica, extending the Caveat's request for her assistance."

"No execution?" Faux blurted before considering her situation.

"And in exchange," Darcy said at length, "you will both be granted clemency. If you survive the journey… and Captain Ezekyle is successful in securing her support."

Faux bristled at Darcy's brusque and presumptuous manner but turned to Jaxtyn to see him give a subtle nod. At a look from Arjun, however, she barely swallowed a rude reply. This was no time for pride.

Arjun bowed. "We accept."

Darcy's face eased infinitesimally. "Good. You and Lady Dauldon will leave in the morning for Abacus. I will assure the Caveat of your good faith." Then he looked up, as if just remembering something. "Oh… I'm sure you are aware that the princess has been troubled by assassins of late."

"A Vermilion princess?" Faux replied, not quite succeeding in controlling her tone. "No, we weren't."

Darcy straightened his shirtsleeves, unconcerned. "That

will be all. The Caveat thanks you for your cooperation. Rest assured that if you perish on the journey, your service will be… remembered."

"And our names cleared?" asked Faux, chasing a morbid curiosity.

"Of course," Darcy mumbled through a thin smile. "Presuming that you are not so careless as to reappear elsewhere after your *untimely demise*. Master Faircloth, their irons, sir?"

Faux tracked Darcy's eyes across the room to Jaxtyn, who stepped toward her, her freedom in his hands. Trapped somewhere between love and gratitude, she could only respond with tenderness and a tear in her eye. Her hopeful stare met his countenance, where she found a smile.

He took her hands in his and with a gentle turn of the jailor's key, unchained her wrists, then her ankles.

"Thank you," she managed to whisper.

"Have faith," he replied. "Let's get you out of here."

———✦———

BLUE CONNEY FELT LIKE death.

The shock of the nightmarish event outside the castle gates hadn't really set in until what remained of their party had set foot in the Alaric house, where the family had agreed upon the request of the Caveat to put them up until Faux and Arjun's legal proceedings were completed. The light in the suite of rooms they had been given was poor, but Blue hardly knew whether to see that as a slight or not; it had started raining outside and he was just glad to have a roof over their heads. Marquiss was sitting on a rickety chair in the corner, taking off his boots. Both were too exhausted to be much for talking. Jericho lay on the floor, his big head resting on Blue's bag.

The noise of an arriving carriage was soon followed by muffled conversation in the foyer.

"I hear Lord Alaric." Marquiss's elven ears perked up through his mint green hair. "They are here."

A knock at the door soon followed, and Blue sat up from his seat on one of the beds. Arjun and Faux entered, looking almost as bedraggled as he felt. The dog whuffed softly in greeting.

"Out already?" Blue joked, his exhausted tone too flat for effect. But the springheel jumped from the bed and embraced his friends one after another. "Glad to see you still have your heads. Seems that you have friends in high places after all."

Arjun shook his head. "We are not free."

Marquiss's expression contorted. "No?"

"Nay. The Caveat made us a private offer. We'll be tasked with escorting Daemus and a Vermilion princess to Abacus. If you two want to come...?"

Marquiss raised his head and shot an incredulous glance at his half-sister, who had yet to say anything. "*If?* Arjun!" he protested. "Of course, we're going!"

Blue nodded, more from duty than from want. In truth he wasn't exactly thrilled with the idea of heading out on another voyage just now, but he hated the idea of not being there for his comrades even more. "You'll be needin' us. Obviously, we're goin'. And Jericho too." He bent and petted the war dog's head.

Faux seemed to come back to life and met his eyes with a slight frown. "You sound concerned, Blue. Something we should know?" Her tone was a little sharp, but Blue knew better than to take offense; she was the prickliest of them when tired, and this was nowhere close to her worst.

"Yes," Blue grumbled. "We have a problem."

"Aye," groaned Marquiss, putting a hand over his face. "The beast."

"What?" snapped Faux.

"There's some kind of monster outside the city walls," Blue explained, stretching his legs in exaggerated height and raising his arms as far as they'd go. "Marquiss and I had a bit o' a brush with it during our sweep when you went into the city. Nearly had us."

"It's the one from Daemus's dreams," Marquiss added.

"How can you be sure?" Arjun's hands rose to his hips, and he shook his head.

"The goat legs, the scarred chest," Marquiss continued. "Even the skeletal head with antlers. I've seen nothing like it, from here to the Eternal Forest."

"And Arjun," Blue added, his tone serious for once. "It's fast, strong. Can't be taken down like a beast or a man, I don't think. The kind of thing that can hold its own against a group of men."

"How big a group?" inquired Faux, her eyes intent.

Marquiss lifted one shoulder. "Couldn't say. We didn't try much to fight it. Were too busy running."

"It moved like a tracker," put in Blue. "Smellin' 'round, like Jericho does. Best guess is, it was lookin' fer somethin', and I'm thinkin' that's Daemus. If I'm right, we might be havin' some trouble on the road to Abacus."

"We'll handle it." Faux's face tightened around her eyes and mouth. "No choice."

"A little choice, maybe," Marquiss's voice piqued, but he closed his mouth when Faux glared at him.

"Nothing worrying can fix." Arjun began putting down his things. "But some planning can. Time for us all to get some rest. We leave tomorrow."

Blue nodded, then looked at Faux. That prickle behind her eyes was still there. Knowing she wouldn't appreciate a wish of sweet dreams, he prayed once for her to the Ancients for a peaceful night and once for himself to Flerick, the patron Ancient of his huldrefolk. Shortly after, he fell into the darkness of an uneasy sleep.

CHAPTER TWO

*"Fear not the Ancient of death, for her song calls for all
of us. Her four sons ride the stars to bring us home."*
—Graytorris the Mad

PRINCE MONTGOMERY THORHAUER SAT in silence
beside Viscount Joferian Maeglen. The early morning sun
shone through the windows and warmed their backs, but
Montgomery hardly felt it. He stared at the undisturbed
contents of his breakfast plate, vaguely registering the
tantalizing smell of bacon and fresh eggs. It had been two
days since the Bone elf had taken both his and Joferian's
brothers from them.

Admiral Valerick LaBrecque sat across from the prince along
with Master Zendel Cray of Hunter's Manor and the twergish
First Keeper of Castleshire, Aliferis Makai. The Lighthouse Inn
was full of wealthy patrons, and the silence at their table went
unnoticed by many. Until the front doors flew open.

"Valerick LaBrecque!" a gruff voice boomed from the
doorway. "Or do I need to call ye 'Admiral' these days, ye
mermaid's fart?"

The dramatic entrance drew the attention of all the
patrons, including the Lighthouse's owner, Greyson Calder,
who reached for the old sword that hung above the bar.

"Aye." LaBrecque raised his head, his back to the voice in
the doorway. "It's 'Lord Admiral' to you, kraken dung."

Montgomery reached for his own sword and saw Joferian
do the same.

"Not again, LaBrecque," Calder growled.

There was a pregnant pause throughout the inn as the
customers waited for the drama to begin. The man in the

25

doorway belly-laughed and threw his arms in the air.

"C'mere, me boy!"

The two made their way past several tables of confused patrons and embraced one another. There was a collective sigh, which relieved the tension in the air. Calder shook his head and mumbled something, but Montgomery was too far away to hear what it was. He didn't care, either. The prince returned to his untouched food, barely hearing the conversation occurring in front of him.

"Captain," LaBrecque began, "thank you for coming so early and at such short notice."

"Anything for the Seawolf."

"No need for introductions, m'lords, First Keeper." The man placed his hand on Prince Montgomery's shoulder, signaling for him to stay seated. "I know everyone here, at least by reputation. Please accept my condolences for the tragedies that have befallen all o' ye."

Montgomery managed a nod.

"So, you must be Captain Halford?" Joferian asked.

"Dorian Halford at yer service, sir." The captain saluted and tipped his cap. He made a respectful bow then took an empty seat and without asking, began to fill his plate.

"Captain Halford," Montgomery started, not wanting to speak, but needing to. "As you know, *Doom's Wake* was damaged two days ago in the battle in the harbor. She can't sail, and the viscount and I need to return to Thronehelm. I asked Admiral LaBrecque to find a dependable ship and a trustworthy captain. Are you that man?"

"Aye," Halford said, his brogue muffled by a mouth half-full of his first bite of breakfast. "I'm yer man. The *Sundowner* is provisioned and ready to hit the seas as early as this morn'. She's not a warship, but she's fast and we can defend ourselves if need be."

"And her crew?" Montgomery inquired. "The admiral's mariners are staying here while the *Wake* is refitted."

"Aye." Halford turned from the prince and flashed a brace of wooden teeth at LaBrecque as he slapped the admiral on the shoulder with his paw. "And what a crew it is."

"Raynor?" LaBrecque inquired.

"Of course," Halford smiled. "And Hallowell. That elf hasn't left the seas in m'lifetime."

"Well then." LaBrecque pursed his lips in approval. "It looks like we're in good hands. What of payment?"

"Yer money's no good, Lord Admiral."

"Thank you for your kindness," Montgomery offered. He recognized the man's generosity and perhaps duty for what it was, but the gesture only reminded him of his dead brother and cousin. "It won't be forgotten."

"Nay," Halford scowled and pointed a thumb at LaBrecque. "I mean *his* money's no good. The man's a scallywag."

LaBrecque and Halford laughed, but the rest of the table's occupants were too preoccupied to engage in friendly banter. Halford rose, putting his hand on his scimitar and bowing. "We'll await ye at the harbor. We leave at yer convenience, m'lords."

As he left, silence recaptured the table and Monty's frown returned.

"Halford is a man without a home," LaBrecque remarked of the captain, attempting to dispel the tension. "He prefers to take to the sea."

"How do you know him?" Cray asked.

"He's been a friend to Seabrooke and Thronehelm for years." LaBrecque took a swig of his morning wine and turned his attention to the food in front of him. "As has his crew. Declan Raynor is a master navigator and shipwright. He and Birch Hallowell have an interesting story."

"How so?"

"Birch is a Dale elf who hails from the Crown Islands and *not* the Eternal Forest," LaBrecque explained, pausing between sentences to swallow his food. "He's sailed the seas for nearly a hundred years. He's a healer, a fisherman and a privateer. I remember sitting on deck with Hallowell and Raynor through all hours of the night, listening to their sailing stories from across the realm. Tales of mermaids, sea monsters and hurricane squalls on the high seas."

Joferian cracked a forced smile. "He sounds like a great storyteller."

LaBrecque nodded. "Aye, but unlike most, his stories are all true."

THE MEN DEPARTED THE Lighthouse Inn after saying farewell to Tribune Calder, who watched from his private perch atop the old lighthouse's stack as they made their way to the docks. As the men boarded the *Sundowner*, LaBrecque broke from the group to look for Hallowell and Raynor.

The remaining quartet of Montgomery, Joferian, Makai, and Zendel Cray stood at the planks, waiting for their precious cargo. Montgomery watched as the crew carefully hoisted Everett's coffin aboard and placed it in the hold. His blood still boiled. His adrenaline pumped as though still in the heat of battle.

He produced the dagger the assassin had left in Everett's side. The pommel, which was carved into the form of a black rose, stared back at him. Everett's blood still stained the blade. He'd lost track of how long he'd been staring at it before his cousin Joferian nudged him.

"Monty, let's go below." Joferian rested his hand on his cousin's shoulder. "We should find our quarters. Staring at the coffin will do nothing."

"We need to find them." Monty sheathed the bloody dagger. "The Bone elf *and* his benefactor. They must both face the wrath of Warminster."

"I agree." Joferian frowned. "And that quest begins when we sail for home."

"Home," Monty groaned. *How will I ever face my father?* he thought. *How could Joferian not understand?* Monty could count on one hand the times he and his younger brother had been truly separated. It was his job as the eldest to watch out for Everett. To protect him.

Joferian had no response.

"What fools we were," Montgomery continued. "The price of victory—"

"Victory?" Joferian interrupted. "What *victory*?"

Montgomery glared, turning away from Joferian, not used to being corrected, let alone by his younger cousin. But there was an undeniable truth to Joferian's assertion.

"You're right," Montgomery conceded. "The only victory was survival."

"The days at Halifax…" Joferian paused and looked to the sky. "They seem so far away. Do you remember the games we played? Everett was a natural, the best of all of us."

"Aye." Montgomery nodded and allowed himself a small smile as he recalled the memory. At least Joferian wasn't pretending to be made of stone. Reminiscing would help. "And Talath was the smartest of our class, and a skilled fighter. There's a reason why his name was carved onto the rolls of valor at Halifax by the Faxerian." He averted his eyes down. "A lot of good it did him."

"My brother was a better man than I," Joferian murmured. He sighed. "He had better luck with the ladies, too. I fear that my mother will think the wrong son died."

That pierced Monty's heart and he hurt for his cousin. "I fear my mother will go mad with grief," he managed. "My father will thirst for revenge. He won't rest until he has it." Perhaps Monty would join him on this journey for vengeance. That would satisfy this grief, surely.

"And what of Camber?" Joferian asked. The question was sudden, and his face curled with the question. "Lady Thessica Camber of *the Kingdom of Foghaven Vale*?" He mocked her title when she spoke on the floor of the Caveat against them.

Monty stared at him, his face reddening. "She grew up with us, cousin. How could those words ever leave her lips? Was her offer of help even sincere?"

"Treason," Joferian responded, his face remaining stoic. "Nothing short of it. The same with the Thessalys. Gloucester leaving Warminster is… inconceivable."

"But it happened."

"Aye, but how are these plots knitted together?" Joferian asked. "It seems we're still at a disadvantage."

Montgomery paused in thought for a moment, staring at the mariners and the cargo they loaded. To his left, Cray and Makai spoke in hushed monotones. Montgomery could hear the words, but he couldn't process them. With Everett dead, they didn't matter. *Nothing* mattered.

He glanced at Joferian, who gazed morosely at the sky. He couldn't read his cousin's somber face. He had to be feeling the same pain.

"I… I'm sorry we have nothing but Talath's sword to return to your family." Montgomery paused. "He, House Maeglen, and all of Queen's Chapel, deserve better."

"As did Everett," Joferian acknowledged with a stiff nod. He looked away from the skies and down at his boots, then took a deep breath. "May I confide in you, cousin?"

"Of course," Monty agreed, his heart lightening.

"I wish she were here."

Monty took in Joferian's pained face. "Your mother?"

"No," Joferian shook his head. "Ember. I miss—"

Monty felt something in his head snap. Like a lit match in a keg of silver flake, his right arm flew to his pommel, which he gripped so hard the veins stood out from his knuckles. His left arm arced through the air and hit Joferian on the chin, knocking him a step backward. Joferian stumbled and, shaken, knocked him near the rail of the *Sundowner* and close to the water. There was an audible click as his teeth snapped together from the blow. Joferian's hand flew to his nose and came away bloody. His eyes widened in a whirlwind of fear, confusion, and hurt.

"Monty, I—"

"Viscount Maeglen," Montgomery growled, using his cousin's title, and gripping his pommel still to steady himself. "Hold your tongue. You have no right to fret over a treasonous bastardess while your brother lies at the bottom of the sea and mine lies not three yards from us in his coffin."

Cray and Makai ceased their whispered conversation and rushed forward to stand between Montgomery and Joferian, though neither was armed. Cray shouted for LaBrecque, who emerged from inside the ship and started across the gangplank toward them. Monty had no intention of moving forward for another blow, but Makai held his hands out to the prince to stay him should he try.

"Talath is dead, Joferian!" Monty cried, his voice quaking with unhinged emotion.

With that outburst, Makai did lay his hands on Monty, only to have them swatted away with a savage cry.

"Boys, boys," LaBrecque began.

"I was a boy when I left Thronehelm," Montgomery spat, panting. "It took my brother's death to make me a man and to understand the ways of this world."

"A man can tell his friends from his enemies," Cray murmured.

Montgomery turned his head to glare at him and Cray took a step backward, almost spilling off the dock and into the water. Monty still gripped his sword.

"Enough!" LaBrecque bellowed, stepping forward into the gap between Monty and Joferian and spreading out his powerful arms to put some distance between them. "Let us focus our vengeance on those who've earned it."

"The assassin," Montgomery grumbled, his tone flat, dropping his hand off his pommel. "And what of him?"

"They still haven't found the body of the Bone elf or that damned creature he controls," LaBrecque replied.

"If we must be caught between grief and vengeance," Joferian said, "I choose grief."

"Will the bastardess alleviate your grief?" Monty growled.

Joferian turned stony and impersonal again. He raised his head high. "Their bodies will be found."

Thinks he's taking the high ground, Monty thought bitterly. Joferian could condescend to him all he liked, but he knew he was right. Joferian wasn't thinking of his brother, his mother... he only thought of himself.

Joferian finished, "I saw Ritter down the creature with Silencer. I wish it was different, cousin. I wish one of us could have delivered the killing blow."

He reached out his hand for Montgomery to take it.

Monty glared harder, his eyes blurring with burning, unshed tears. He scowled and slapped Joferian's hand away. Spitting on the deck, he retreated astern, away from the judgment of all the eyes watching him.

CHAPTER THREE

"A true teacher neither commands nor counsels. They merely present knowledge and let the student decide."
—Anoki, Athabasica the Poet

DAEMUS, ONE HAND WORRYING at his horse's mane, watched as Faux said her goodbyes to Jaxtyn near the gate. Their posture was tense, the interaction perhaps a bit awkward or run through with unspoken feeling. They were leaning toward one another. When they moved to kiss, Daemus looked away.

"Ready to be on the road?" inquired a voice at his shoulder. Daemus turned; it was Delling, the Disciple of the Watch who had offered to accompany them. His brown eyes were gentle.

Daemus started to shake his head, then stopped. "I don't know," he said, surprised a little at his own honesty. "Right now, it feels as though I'm just being… swept along. Time doesn't feel the same anymore. Things just keep happening." Struggling to explain himself, he glanced at Delling, but the man only looked sympathetic rather than confused as Daemus had expected.

"You feel like you're not really here," Delling replied, and Daemus blinked in surprise.

"Yes. Like someone else is controlling everything I do."

"I've never had the Sight." Delling turned, looking back at the young lovers, who were separating at last. "But I've heard stories of what such knowledge can do to the gifted. They can start to feel as though their every action is pre-determined, as though their body moves on its own, their mouth sometimes speaking before their thoughts can catch up."

"How do I learn to deal with it?" Daemus asked, a little desperation in his voice.

Delling half-shrugged. "No single way. I know a few tricks that might help, though. Kind of things that keep you present and thinking when you're in the middle of a battle, or when you're running around on no sleep." Daemus started to thank him but was interrupted by Faux, who was riding up now, her expression difficult to read.

"Let's be on our way, then," she signaled to the group. "I don't think it's wise to linger outside the gate when your cryptid friend is afoot."

Daemus tightened his grip on his reins. He knew it didn't make sense, but it felt as though talking about the Antlered Man would summon it straight out of his nightmares. Before much longer, the party were on their way.

They traveled at pace but with caution, keeping watch at all hours of day and night, with Blue and his war dog Jericho at the rear of the party and Ritter and Storm, his war falcon, at the front. They hoped the animals' keen senses would be able to grant them some additional warning if the Antlered Man or some other trouble drew near, but everyone knew there was no real safety to be had with such a cryptid on their tale.

Daemus kept close to Delling, finding an odd but quick camaraderie with him. He felt safe with the man that gave him a modicum of peace during the long rides and their short, tense campfire conversations. Delling reminded him a little of Kester, his uncle. They had the same way about them when talking, listening before offering rational, clear-headed advice, although Delling's manner was a little more serious than Kester's had ever been.

Two days into the journey along the road known as Harbinger's Run, things had gone as planned. Daemus knew they had nearly two more weeks ahead of them to Abacus. The golden reeds of high grass swayed like a sea, ebbing and flowing in the wind as they rode. On occasion, a defiant tree rose on the plains, but the Run was a glorified trail at this distance from Castleshire. It had been a day since they'd seen the last caravan of merchants passing them by on their way to the capital.

They'd trekked northeast to a region travelers referred to as the Turn. The Turn represented a quick change in direction for the Run, heading from northeast to southeast around an oblique bend in the topography. It also represented the start of the longest stretch of their march.

They rested and kept their fires low to avoid the supernatural senses of the Antlered Man, and Daemus found himself sitting with Delling by the campfire. It was a little while, after most of the others had started going off to sleep, Delling asked Daemus about his eyes.

"I was born blind." Daemus began with some hesitancy. "Or so I'm told. I was too young to remember any of it, but my uncle told me the story when I was older."

"Did you see a healer?" asked Delling, frowning. "I've never heard of one who could cure inborn blindness, something not caused by an injury."

Daemus shook his head. "My family is… wealthy." His voice sounded dispassionate to his own ears. It was still odd for him to talk about his family's resources, when he had seen so little benefit from them. "My parents sent word far and wide asking for help. They knew the same thing you do, that some things can't be healed. But they still tried." He blinked. "No son of the Alaric house could be allowed to remain so." That had certainly been drilled into him enough. *What a burden you are. How much we've done for you. But we had no choice. And neither do you.*

Delling said nothing, but his gaze turned somber.

"From what my uncle said, an intruder appeared one night in the nursery where I slept. I was asleep in my crib, and the nurse saw a figure standing over me, reaching in. She said the visitor touched my eyes while I slept… I'm not sure if that's true, since she said it was dark." He shifted uncomfortably. "She screamed and called for my parents, and it woke me up. I started crying. My father came running."

"Not your mother?"

Daemus didn't look at him, and Delling fell silent. "When he reached me, there was no one there. And he said when he entered the room and picked me up, I stopped crying, and that was when he noticed I was looking at his face." He offered a slight smile and glanced at Delling. "That's all there is to the story. No one ever saw the visitor enter or leave, no doors or windows were broken or damaged. I was blessed with sight, and nothing else happened afterward."

"Other than the visions," Delling commented.

Daemus's smile fell. "Yes. I think the first day they realized my dreams were coming true was the day they truly believed they had lost me."

"How do you mean?"

"Well, when I was blind, there was always the possibility, however remote, that they would find some healer or sorcerer that could bring me sight. But the true Sight isn't something that goes away, is it."

"Until it does," Delling pointed out, his eyes sharp. Daemus thought of the Keepers and closed his mouth. How had he forgotten that their gift had all but disappeared? His departure from the cathedral felt like years ago.

"How did you come to join the Disciples of the Watch?" Daemus asked, not wishing to talk any more about the Sight or visions.

Delling pursed his lips. "Wasn't always a proud warrior of Erud," he admitted, his tone light. "I grew up a petty thief, a swindler and thug to be honest. Had to struggle hard to survive. When I was old enough, I joined the army, hoping to make a living for myself, but I had no faith in the power of the state. The first time I saw my fellows looting a civilian home, I deserted. Didn't want to be part of more of the same that I'd grown up seeing, people trodden on."

His expression had turned grim but Daemus kept listening.

"I became a drifter, trying to make my way without stealing from other folk poor as I was, but there's only so far your strength of will takes you when you're starving. One day, I spotted a man I thought was wealthy and I tried stealing from him. He was a follower of Erud. No one important." His eyes were soft. "Not like the Keepers in the cathedral. Only a lowly archivist. But he took pity on me, fed me, and taught me to read.

"I learned faith from him, faith in people, but most of all faith in knowledge, the power of knowledge. I wanted to be an archivist at first, asked to become his apprentice, but I ended up deciding to use what I'd learned of combat and the streets to protect the followers of Erud, my fellow Keepers of knowledge. So, I became a Disciple of the Watch."

"Why didn't you become an archivist?" Daemus asked. Delling tilted his head back and forth, thinking.

"Just wasn't what I was good at, I guess. At first, I thought what I wanted was to be just like Gyurisin—that's my friend who taught me to read. But I eventually realized that what I really wanted was to believe in things the way he did. Being a Disciple, I could do that, too. Didn't have to just be around books." He smiled. "That's when I started forming closer bonds with people. I'd learned as a child that people try to take care of each other, but they often just end up hurting each other.

But as a Disciple I learned something different, that people can take care of each other when they have all they need."

"I wish I'd had those. Bonds," Daemus remarked without much thought.

Delling gave him a sharp look, but then paused and seemed to revise what he was going to say.

Daemus realized how ungrateful he sounded for things Delling had lived without for most of his life.

"Yes. Seems you had money, and little else. Poverty of the soul, eh?"

Daemus swallowed down his shame, grateful Delling hadn't pressed him on his words.

"I had my uncle, Kester," Daemus replied. "It wasn't so bad." As it left his mouth, he registered the lie. From his expression, so did Delling. Kester had been his single oasis of companionship, but his uncle hadn't been around for much of his life. He'd been off on his own business often, leaving Daemus to remain shut away within the walls of the Alaric house. The botched heir, no birthright, no purpose, no place.

"The Divine Protectorate of Erud is different these days than it was when I was a young man," Delling offered, a little abruptly. "A lot of things aren't the same as they used to be. They've lost Erud's favor now, but things were going wrong long before that happened."

"How do you mean?" asked Daemus, surprised. He'd had no idea there had been anything amiss in the cathedral until he'd realized he was the only one still having visions.

Delling heaved a sigh. "People losing faith," he said at last. "People losing... that sense I came into the Disciples looking for, of being part of something larger than myself. Of not being selfish. I don't know. I started feeling a long time ago that the culture among the followers was starting to change.

People stopped knowing things they used to know."

ON THAT EVENING, DAEMUS sat next to Ritter, watching the hunter gut then tine a run rabbit over the fire. Run rabbits were the size of dogs and a hunter's nightmare on the trail, as they often attacked predators with their sharp teeth and forepaws. They could leap great distances, even further than the springheel Blue Conney, and they traveled in small packs, feeding on flesh and fruit alike. Ritter had harvested one on each of the three nights on the trail and seemed to prefer hunting his food to eating his rations.

"Another, Sir Ritter?" Marquiss asked, after returning from sweeping the trail behind them.

"It was the bull," Ritter commented. Daemus had no idea what Ritter meant, but he didn't mind the taste of the roasted beast over his salted venison. Marquiss didn't argue, but a hush blanketed the camp again, save for the crackling of the fire Ritter attended. He carved a slice of meat from the Run rabbit and gave it to Daemus to taste.

"It's done," the young Keeper murmured.

"When morning comes," Ritter mumbled over a slice, "Arjun and I will teach you how to cover our scent with aniseed and harsh pepper. The Antlered Man tracks well, according to Blue and Marquiss, and possesses a better nose than a horsehound. That means we must stay downwind and use well-marked trails. The pepper and aniseed should also cover our campsites, where we'll leave the greatest imprint."

Daemus nodded. The chore was a small one, but he liked to learn from Ritter. He had no older brother and had been a stranger to the woods as a child. He was fascinated by Ritter's knowledge of the forests.

"Ah, Marquiss, you are back." Arjun was returning from a

sweep of his own. "Anything?"

"Nay," Marquiss replied. "Conney's dog and Ritter's falcon will alert us if it changes." He plopped down next to the fire and removed the sword and dagger from his belt.

Daemus shot a glance at the old captain, who seemed settled by the news after being preoccupied during their journey. For the first two days after leaving Castleshire, he barely spoke. He seemed to grow more distant the further they got from the capital.

As the group settled around the camp, Daemus watched Marquiss, at the urging of Blue Conney, trying to flirt with Jessamy Aberdeen. He wasn't the only one to notice; Ritter nudged him and nodded at them with a knowing smile.

The two, so different in their pursuits in life, were a poor fit, but Blue had been pushing Marquiss to approach the swordswoman ever since they'd left Castleshire. It was more of a dare between friends than anything else, but the whole camp was aware of the unspoken game, including Jessamy.

The two men watched Marquiss approach Jessamy. They were out of earshot, but they knew her answer. With a blurry whirl, she flipped around and drew her sword, knocking Marquiss over and sending Blue into paroxysms of laughter.

Marquiss got the message loud and clear and reached his hands up to the sky, seeking mercy from the swordswoman. Jessamy sheathed her sword and Marquiss reached for a helping hand from her. The raven elf stared at him before turning and walking away, leaving him on the ground. Blue belly-laughed again, and Ritter and Daemus shared in the laughter.

"Enough of that," Marquiss said to them, pulling himself from the ground. Daemus looked back at Jessamy to see a thin smile appear on her face.

DAEMUS WAS TRYING TO sleep, but his eyes didn't want to close. He was afraid of his dreams.

"How are you feeling?" he heard, a little distance away behind him. After a moment of trying to place the voice, Daemus identified it as Ritter.

"I don't know," said another, softer voice—the princess, Daemus registered with surprise. "During the daytime I am able to go about things as normal. I like talking to Faux."

"But nighttime is hard," Ritter finished in a gentle tone. "I understand."

Addilyn exhaled softly. "I know your watch is coming up soon," she said instead of replying.

When she spoke again, she seemed to struggle a little. "But… would you stay here, just until I fall asleep?"

The ranger was silent a moment. "What about Jessamy?"

"I don't care." The elf's voice was flat. "She cannot dictate whom I spend my time with." There was a short pause. "Besides, if she was really my friend, she would understand."

"I think she means well," Ritter said. "And she's meant to stay with you for a long time, isn't she? Wouldn't you rather get along with her?"

"I wish you could be my champion instead," the princess whispered, so quietly that Daemus realized he was straining to hear her and felt embarrassed at his eavesdropping. Resolving that he could handle dreams better than Addilyn could handle a stranger listening to her private conversations, he closed his eyes and before long dropped off to sleep.

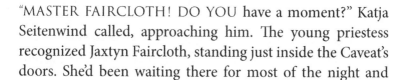

"MASTER FAIRCLOTH! DO YOU have a moment?" Katja Seitenwind called, approaching him. The young priestess recognized Jaxtyn Faircloth, standing just inside the Caveat's doors. She'd been waiting there for most of the night and early morning to find him. Her sect, the healers of the Temple of Ssolantress had gathered the evening before when they heard the clap of thunder that cracked the dome of the fabled building. She and the other priests and priestesses of the temple grabbed their supplies and ran for the Caveat, and into the chaos of the last evening. Thankfully, no one was hurt, but many were shaken from the event.

Jaxtyn bowed his head. "A moment of my time is the least I could do for a lady of Ssolantress. Thank you for coming to our aid last night. What can I do for you, Priestess?"

Katja cast a glance around and, sensing her need for privacy, Jaxtyn gestured to the Caveat doors. Once inside the foyer, Katja continued in a hushed tone. "I wonder if I could speak with Daemus Alaric. It's rather urgent."

"I'm afraid that's not possible, as Daemus and a few others have departed for Abacus this morning."

"Already?" She stopped and thought for a moment. "Perhaps I could speak with the Alarics in his stead. Daemus's public display of his powers here isn't the only example of his strength. The night he arrived in Forecastle, I was summoned to help him and his group of injured adventurers, who were fresh from the road."

"And?"

"It was there that I met Daemus," Katja said. "He took an interest in the goddess Ssolantress and I told him of our most sacred place, a divine pool of water known as the Crystal Well. It's the most holy place in all of Warminster. It's where our goddess last stood before leaving for the Hall of the Ancients. It has many powers of healing."

"I see," Jaxtyn said, leaning in. "What does this have to do with Daemus?"

"Daemus had a dream of the Crystal Well," she explained. "A dream where the well was polluted by the man who's chasing him in his dreams. If his visions are as powerful as they seem, I need to warn my matron mother, Persephone Rhowan. She guards the well and grants visitations to those who need its powers."

"I've heard of your well and its whereabouts. It belongs to the Silvercroft Mountains, does it not?"

"It does," she agreed, "and Daemus's family is from the Silvercrofts. Their lands are there."

"And you need my help getting a message to your matron mother?"

"I do," she replied.

"Well," Jaxtyn said, "I suggest we pay a visit to the Alarics. I'm sure they're sending messages and goods back and forth to the Silvercrofts. With their help, we should be able to deliver your message."

"Thank you, Master Faircloth," Katja said. "That would be most helpful."

"No thanks are needed," he replied. "The Alarics should be able to get word to your Matron Mother faster than any resource that I have."

KATJA WAITED PATIENTLY ALONGSIDE Jaxtyn as the two arrived at the doors of the Alaric family stronghold. Well-poised for her years, Katja feared little when it came to social engagements. Her calling lay beyond the trivialities of station.

The door opened, and Katja watched Jaxtyn have a whispered conversation with a guard attending the gates before waving for her to approach. They were escorted into a hexagonal, two-story foyer. Made of decorative marble, it had a glass dome above it that brightened the room from all angles.

"Thank you, Ellissio," Jaxtyn said to the chamberlain, who hustled off in search of the masters of the house. Moments later, a balding man of substantial size entered the room with a middle-aged woman in tow. They were dressed impeccably and looked the part of Shirian nobles.

"Katja," Jaxtyn began. "This is Lord Ranaulf and Lady Mercia Alaric of the Silvercroft Mountains."

"It's a pleasure to meet you, Priestess." Mercia's countenance was bright. "During his brief time at home, Daemus told us much about you. I understand that we have you to thank for our son's condition? Allow us to donate to the Temple of Ssolantress for your troubles. Daemus couldn't stop talking about you before he left. Despite everything he had on his shoulders, he was still thinking of you."

"No money is required, my lady." Katja blushed before recovering. "That's not why I'm here."

"Then what brings you to our home?"

"As I told Master Faircloth this morning, I need to get a warning to my matron mother in the Silvercroft Mountains. She watches over our Crystal Well."

"We know of it," Ranaulf acknowledged. "It's a godsend to our people."

"Daemus warned of a man in his dreams who wishes to destroy the well," Katja said. "I, myself, have been having troubling dreams. Though the Ancients have not blessed me with Daemus's ability to gaze into the future, I feel they were a sign to seek help through you. I need to get that warning to her."

"We know of your matron mother," Mercia said, "and we're happy to send word through our messengers. You're in luck. By mounted rider, our messages take at least a month to arrive, but we have a longtime friend and merchant of hoar fox pelts who's traveling there tonight. His name is Phineas Silvera and he, by some magical means, travels back and forth much more quickly. He takes our most urgent messages."

"How much will that cost?"

"Fifty gold palmettes."

"Thank you for the offer, my lady." Katja's eyes turned down and she looked at her feet. "But I'll have to decline it. I don't have that kind of gold."

"Nonsense, girl." Mercia shook her head. "We'll bear the cost for you... and Daemus."

"Your generosity is too much."

"It's the least we can do." Ranaulf replied. "We'll send your message tonight."

"Thank you for your kindness." Katja offered a slight bow. "I'm sure that my note will help to prepare my matron mother."

"Excellent," Mercia said. "Oh, and one more thing."

"Yes, my lady?"

"Please visit more often." Mercia smiled. "You're a welcome guest at our home."

Katja grinned. "It would be my pleasure."

CHAPTER FOUR

"Two may keep a secret if one of them is dead."
—Precept Radu of the Divine Protectorate of Erud

PRECEPT RADU STEPPED AMONG the Knights of the Maelstrom as they and the rest of the deacons and Disciples aided in removing the larger detritus from the cathedral's halls and outer properties. Amongst the stronger Knights, his old frame felt weak. But he hadn't been blind to the tension and caution surrounding the Knight as he moved about the campus. They were uneasy. Wary.

He himself had done little more than walk amongst the wreckage and pray to Erud since the Tome was stolen. At night, he could still hear the fiery hail raining down, and the exploding destruction of the blessed observatory. Tails of blackened embers still flickered orange in the dusty wind, giving way to a grey pallor that hung over the Cathedral of the Watchful Eye.

Every now and then, a tear tracked down his face and he would turn from passersby, trying to maintain an air of calm, but inside, his guts churned in nervous anticipation. Without the Sight, the Keepers were all but useless to not just the Divine Protectorate of Erud, but to the leaders of all of Warminster. They could not *see*. They could not calm those they had been instructed to guide. The full weight of the attack crushed at his heart.

The courtyard brimmed with activity as the whole of the protectorate worked to recover from the carnage. Radu stopped outside Quehm's Hallow at the far end of the campus, the only building left untouched by the falling stars. He watched one Knight work with a group, trying to dislodge a boulder from the courtyard when a shadow passed from above. For a moment, his heart leapt into his throat, and he turned to the skies. The Knight shared his gaze up, not nearly as afraid.

"Danton Hague," the Knight offered to Radu, stepping away from the boulder and dusting off his hands. "I hope he brings news."

Radu tracked Hague and his hippogryph mount as they circled the campus, then descended toward his position. *Any news would be welcome,* he thought.

The pair touched down and came to a slight gallop only yards from Radu. The Knight slid from his gryph, landing hard on his feet. His knees buckled in fatigue.

"Easy, girl." Danton Hague petted the neck of his steed. "I know you sense it too."

Radu approached Hague with a hug and forced smile. "Welcome back, Captain."

"It's good to see you too, Precept." Hague turned from his friend and looked to the Knight beside Radu. "Lorraine, how is the recovery coming? Have you been able to keep the peace in my absence?"

Lieutenant Rutger Lorraine approached his captain, offering a fatigued salute. "Captain, let me gather the men so that you may address them all directly."

"And what of my question?"

Lorraine turned, leaving it unanswered. Hague stood in confusion, looking cockeyed at his lieutenant as he strolled to an open spot in the courtyard and waved to the Knights on the wall. They sounded the horns and within moments, Hague's corps rallied to him. Lorraine stayed at a distance until the whole of the corps had reported, his face contorted in unspoken words.

"You seem uneasy, Captain," Radu prompted, hoping to get Hague talking and impart any news he had.

An unsure grimace appeared on Hague's countenance as he tightened his riding glove, but his eyes remained on Lorraine. "My lieutenant is a crafty veteran," he whispered to Radu, "a worthy champion for the Knights of the Maelstrom. But the man can't bluff. Something's amiss."

"I know the lieutenant was passed over for captain when you were promoted," Radu murmured, noting Lorraine's rank. "We must all honor the decisions made by Nasyr, even in her death," he said as kindly as he could. "There is much out of balance."

Hague nodded then stepped forward and turned to his men. "Knights, I return with news from Castleshire. I met with the full Caveat and our First Keeper Aliferis Makai. There is hope."

Radu expected this news to bring relief to the tension, but all it did was further tie his stomach into knots. He didn't quite know what to think anymore. An old precept like him should have answers, be able to make decisions. But he'd felt lost in the days since the attack.

"Where's Makai?" Lorraine asked, interrupting Hague.

Radu noted the absence of protocol for Hague's rank and turned to peer into the captain's face.

"'Where's Makai, *Captain*?'" Hague corrected Lorraine.

A momentary pause passed between them as the two shared unrelenting stares.

"Where's First Keeper Makai, *Captain*?" Lorraine answered in his baritone voice. "Shouldn't he have returned with you, as First Keeper Amoss ordered?"

"Sir, there are rumors that the First Keepers have all returned to the cathedral," one of the nervous Knights interrupted from the ranks. "Is that true?"

Radu stepped in to quell any emotion before it got too high. "Yes, it is, soldier. They're returning to choose a new Great Keeper from amongst their number."

Lorraine stared at this and glanced at Radu. As the only precept nearby, Radu nodded solemnly. "Then *The Tome of Enlightenment* no longer chooses for us?" the lieutenant sounded worried, as though he was afraid to ask the heretical question aloud.

Hague sighed and fidgeted with his glove again. "The Tome is missing," Hague reminded the corps while staring down Lorraine. "Until it's recovered, the First Keepers will guide us. We must have faith in them and our leadership. These are unprecedented times for all of us."

"Were you waylaid, sir? What took you so long to return?" another Knight called from the rear of the ranks.

"I was gone for four days, soldier," Hague's face contorted, surprised by the question. "Castleshire isn't an easy place to have a simple conversation. They often debate the mere meanings of words in the Caveat."

"Sir," the private continued, "while you were away, there's been talk that the Keepers shouldn't hold that right anymore. Some say the Disciples of the Watch should assume command until the Tome is found."

Hague flashed his eyes to Radu. The precept swallowed the lump in his throat and met the captain's questioning gaze.

"We must hold a council," Radu offered as calmly as he could. "We have much to discuss. Many have a voice and want to be heard." He stopped there. He didn't dare speak for the Keepers or First Keeper Amoss.

Hague's eyes danced back and forth between images Radu could not see. He quickly scanned his warriors, who were usually tight and poised.

Radu looked them over too. The uncertain strain evident in their faces made him cautious.

"Precept, there's an encroaching paranoia about the campus," Lorraine offered from the rear of the ranks, glancing at Radu.

"And growing tension between the Keepers and the Disciples."
Then he walked through the ranks and approached Hague. "No
one knows who to trust and there was no clear direction in your
absence on how the Knights of the Maelstrom should defend
the cathedral. Seems like we now follow orders from everyone."

"I was counting on your honesty surfacing, Lorraine,"
Hague said as a matter of fact. Then he shot a reassuring glance
to Radu. "You take your orders from me, Lieutenant. And
only me."

"And from whom do you take orders, *sir*?" Lorraine asked,
causing heads to turn. Radu held his tongue.

"The Keepers have always been our leaders," Hague replied.
"I'll follow First Keeper Amoss until a new Great Keeper is
chosen from among them. As will you, Lieutenant."

Lorraine rested his hands on his hips, neither confirming
nor denying Hague's assertion.

"Is that clear?" Hague's brow dropped and his lips
straightened. Lorraine nodded, but Hague persisted. "I want
to hear you say it, Lieutenant."

"You're our captain, sir," Lorraine replied.

"Good," Hague nodded. "Now, back to your post." He
turned to Radu. "Take me inside."

AFTER DANTON HAGUE ADDRESSED his troops, Radu
pulled him aside and led him across the campus to Quehm's
Hallow at the rear of the cathedral's grounds. "We have
a conclave of the Keepers of the Forbidden in a matter of
moments, Captain," he offered. "Once the internment
ceremony is completed."

Before them, the Keepers formed a private processional
for their sect and laid the fallen Great Keeper, Nasyr, in her
final resting place.

With a respectful pause, Hague waited until the ceremony had ended to reply. "I understand Amoss is in command," he said at length, as the last of the Keepers filed out of the mausoleum. He eyed them one at a time, taking in their ranks. Radu shook his head. "Amoss would not presume to step into the role of Great Keeper." Radu cleared his throat to dislodge some of the tension there. "This has never happened before, Captain. The Tome always imparted to us the name of the next Great Keeper. It was ordained by our Ancient, Erud, themself."

Hague didn't respond right away, and the two men walked discretely away from the others. Radu sensed the captain wanted to ask what they intended to do, but he held his tongue. Radu appreciated it. He'd been with the cathedral longer than almost anyone, but even he had doubts about how to proceed. He prayed Amoss would have sound counsel. Radu broke the tense silence. "Tell me the truth of Castleshire."

"It's in chaos," Hague confided, glad to be speaking as they traversed the campus. "But one of the Keepers still holds the Sight."

Radu glanced sideways at Hague, curious.

"The Alaric boy," Hague almost whispered. "He shared his visions on the floor of the Caveat. His voice cracked the dome of the great hall."

Radu stopped walking and looked at Hague, confirming the truth in his eyes.

"I've never seen anything like it," Hague remarked. "He silenced a room that couldn't be silenced."

Radu looked up to the darkening sky, amazed, relieved, and frightened all at once.

"The plot runs deeper," Hague replied. "There's a Vermilion princess with him. They've ridden from behind the walls of Eldwal."

Radu stared at him, waiting for more.

"Aye," Hague confirmed and cocked his head sideways. "It's the damnedest thing. It's as if Daemus and the Vermilion princess were called together at *that* time and in *that* moment."

An awkward half-smile appeared on Radu's face. "Erud teaches us many things, one of which is humility. We'll never understand the Ancients, no matter how hard we try. We need to return the Sight to the cathedral. Without it, the Keepers are adrift. The others—your Knights, the Watch, and even the Low Keeper—may think we lied to them. Kept our waning Sight a secret."

"Did you?" Hague pressed.

"Welcome back, Captain," the voice of First Keeper Amoss interrupted. The portly man waddled toward them.

"First Keeper, it is good to be back." Hague reached out to embrace him. "I see I missed the burial. I'm sorry for that, Great Keeper."

Amoss shook his head. "I'm not the Great Keeper. Please don't address me as such. The meeting of the First Keepers will determine who bears that lodestone."

"Of course, sir."

"I may be old, but I am not deaf," Amoss assured. "Now, if Daemus has the Sight as you say, why did he not return with you? And where is First Keeper Makai?"

"Daemus is riding for Abacus, and First Keeper Makai is off to Thronehelm. They are in need of a Keeper since the suspicious passing of our old friend Samuels."

"Abacus? What for? He belongs here, so that we may rebuild. Perhaps he may divine which of us should be Great Keeper?" Amoss stared at his feet, his hands scratching at his balding scalp. "Captain, this Low Keeper is our *only* connection to Erud. We must protect him."

"Aye," Hague confirmed, a nervous laugh escaping him.

"It seems that Erud and the Vermilion goddess, Melexis, have placed us on the same path," Amoss surmised. "But I know not for what purpose. I'll pray on it. Come, Danton. Radu. We have a conclave to attend to."

"Of course, First Keeper," Radu stepped alongside him.

Hague stopped and turned. "I'll post the ceremonial guards as we discussed and then meet you inside."

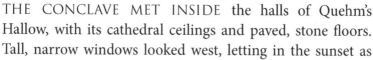

THE CONCLAVE MET INSIDE the halls of Quehm's Hallow, with its cathedral ceilings and paved, stone floors. Tall, narrow windows looked west, letting in the sunset as the day drew to a close. Wooden chairs and benches lined the Hallow and were filled with every Keeper from around the realm who had been summoned home. Radu sat among them, eyes on Amoss as he filed in and took his seat. The First Keeper's voice of wisdom was sorely needed in this moment. Radu took in the others, feeling their anxious spirits matched with his own. For the first time in his long life, they would not be following the lead of a Great Keeper picked by Erud.

"First Keepers and defenders of our faith," Amoss began, gaveling the conclave of First Keepers to order. "Thank you for returning to Solemnity at such short notice. It's with a heavy heart that this unique gathering must take place, under circumstances that our order has never before been forced to contemplate."

He spoke from the center of a square consisting of four long tables that had been pushed together to accommodate the large gathering. Among the other Keepers were a diverse group of humans, elves, twergs, lardals, huldrefolk and trollborn from all four corners of Warminster. Radu watched the towering wooden doors, knowing full well more would be joining them.

"We laid our Great Keeper and friend to rest this afternoon," he continued. "And tonight, we gather to choose her successor.

This charge is new to the Keepers of the Forbidden, as in the millennia since Erud left this terrestrial plane for the Hall of the Ancients, the ascension of a Great Keeper has always been a formality, written for us in the Great Tome by Erud as the pages turned."

Amoss stopped and breathed before continuing. The weight of what he was about to say lay on them all and Radu felt it in his heart.

"Now, that responsibility falls to us," the First Keeper of the cathedral went on. "I know with prayer and the wisdom of Erud, we'll make the right choice. As this is a new practice, I've asked Captain Danton Hague to join us as sergeant-at-arms and as a witness of our great conclave. He has no vote here."

Radu met Hague's eyes and nodded to him. *So, Hague was not here to give counsel, only to witness? Good. Then at least there would be an impartial third-party to the conclave. Someone neutral who could defend what was about to unfold.*

Amoss stood to move the proceedings along when an unexpected banging at the Hallow's locked double doors echoed through the room. A few of the First Keepers exchanged glances. Amoss looked up, catching Radu's eyes. He'd thought others from the protectorate may come.

Should I have said something to Amoss before?

"Captain," Amoss said, reading Radu's face. "Quell that noise. We're not to be disturbed."

Radu watched Hague open the arched doors. The dark alcove filled with torchlight from outside.

Hague growled, "You're disturbing this honorable conclave—"

"Let me in, Captain," a familiar voice snapped back. "I have as much of a right to be present as you do."

Radu walked to the door and peered over Hague's armored shoulder. The courtyard was full of disciples and deacons, led by Volcifar Obexx, the High Watcher of the Disciples of the Watch. His followers stood behind him with only the crackling of their torchlight interrupting the silence.

"Volcifar," Radu said, loud enough for Amoss to hear and understand. "I was unaware that you'd arrived. We haven't seen you for months."

The befuddled murmurings of the other First Keepers, equally confused to his presence, filled in the doorway behind him.

"I should be present," Obexx demanded, glaring at Radu and Amoss in turn over Hague's armored shoulder. "If Hague can join—"

"Only as sergeant-at-arms," Radu interrupted. "He has no role beyond that."

"I'm the High Watcher," Obexx pressed, "and I ask not for a vote—but to be heard. Why did you not reach out to the Watch?" His eyes flittered to Amoss. "We are all part of the Divine Protectorate. This is uncharted territory for us, is it not, Amoss? And our order must be represented as well."

"The conclave is for the Keepers," Amoss retorted. "As for your blustery entrance…"

The crowd supporting the High Watcher from the courtyard booed and hissed in an act of public defiance. Radu braced himself behind Hague, ready for the onslaught of pressing bodies. Amoss turned his gaze back to Obexx, who held his tongue.

"Very well," Amoss agreed, after a brief pause to contemplate. "You may attend but will have no vote, like Captain Hague."

Volcifar Obexx smirked. "Agreed," he said coyly, pushing past Radu to enter the Hallow.

Radu shared a glance with Hague before they returned to their seats. All eyes were on them until they sat back down.

"This is most unprecedented," one of the gathered Keepers

complained. "This is a duty for *our* order. For the Keepers alone."

"Did you read that in the Great Tome?" Volcifar snapped. "Last I heard, the Tome was missing. Stolen from under *your* protection."

"Sacrilege!" the Keeper spluttered. "Mind your tongue, High Watcher."

The room erupted with raised protests from the Keepers.

"Or what?" Obexx said, snidely. "Will you order the good captain to arrest me for stating the truth?"

Amoss gaveled the gathering back to order and the group took their seats, including Obexx, who sat away from the table of agitated Keepers.

"I bring this conclave of First Keepers to order," Amoss reiterated. "We have a solemn duty to choose the next Great Keeper from our ranks. The decision may be as critical, in time, as any other that we've made in the history of our order."

"May I be heard, First Keeper?" Obexx asked, raising his hand.

"We must get down to our business, High Watcher," Amoss groaned. "Your interruptions are keeping us from that."

Obexx stood, his eyes fiery with hurt and insult.

"If I may, First Keeper," Obexx continued, "it's not my interruptions that led us into this dire predicament. I spent these past months toiling away in the field for the good of our order, only to return to a ruined cathedral. I find your indignation misplaced."

"Sacrilege!" someone screamed. "Blasphemy!"

"How dare you?" Radu muttered, glaring at Obexx. He watched as Obexx boiled with contempt. He glanced to Amoss, whose lips were pressed together, knowing he had to let Obexx speak or else the conclave would spin out of control.

"Enough!" Amoss yelled, above the hustle and bustle of the crowd. "You've come here with something on your mind,

Volcifar. Let's have it."

Many of the Keepers rapped their knuckles on the tables in agreement. Radu stood silent, waiting to hear what the High Watcher had to say.

"Thank you, First Keeper," Obexx responded, stepping to the fore. "The great men and women of the Disciples of the Watch feel that, in the absence of *The Tome of Enlightenment*, we should have a say in choosing the next Great Keeper. There's never been a more critical time than now."

Radu shook his head. "That isn't a decision for your sect to make."

"But is it yours?" Obexx interrupted, flinging his arms wide to indicate the entire room. "How does this group of withered, 'blind' Keepers expect to do the right thing? Without *The Tome of Enlightenment*, you have no vision! You and yours have been too dependent on divine intervention to interpret our futures and the future of the protectorate without it."

The conclave erupted in jeers and threats.

Radu stood up. "You've gone too far, Watcher." He saw Amoss raise his hand to stay him, so he didn't go on.

"The truth stings, Precept," Obexx taunted.

Danton Hague rose from his position near the Hallow's doors to stop the outrage, but Amoss waved a careful hand, ordering him to stand down.

"Peace, Radu, Hague," Amoss said as calmly as he could. His steady eyes met Obexx's gaze. "The chamber will hear High Watcher Obexx." Amoss banged his gavel on the table. "We'll do so out of respect for his office as High Watcher. But this is an order built on tradition, and in the absence of the Tome, you need to understand that we, the Keepers of the Forbidden, are in charge."

"Agreed," Obexx said, his voice calming. He

remained standing.

Hague picked up his chair and moved it over to sit beside Obexx, staring him down. Obexx ignored him.

"The floor is yours, High Watcher," Amoss waved. "Speak your mind."

"Thank you," Obexx began, and he stepped to the fore once again. He was more subdued in his manner, but no less stark. "This is no time to rest on the traditions of the past. The Disciples of the Watch and the Divine Protectorate of Erud have depended on the wisdom of this chamber and the Great Tome for a millennium. But your order's authority is dwindling, and you've failed in your promise to keep and defend our faith. You've done neither. And you lied to us."

Amoss reached for his gavel as the room fell apart again in raised voices and anger. Obexx's comments cut like a knife, their truth acting as a whetstone. The Keepers had failed. Obexx stood quietly with a smirk on his face.

Amoss rose and silenced the crowd with an extended hand. He took a moment to pause and gather his thoughts.

"High Watcher," he began. "This falls outside the traditions and sacraments that Erud, our Ancient, has provided. These are traditions that have been maintained throughout the centuries. Even with the Tome gone, it's still a tradition that we, the Keepers, make the final decision. Why do you present this good council with the possibility of a cold civil war between our sects? Now of all times?"

"There's nothing *cold* about it," Obexx replied, ominously. He pointed to the closed doors of the Hallow and the torchlight shining through the painted glass. "What I've said is true. And with your powers dwindling… perhaps it's time for something new."

Hague rose, grabbing at the pommel of his sword in the

face of Obexx's hubris, but Amoss steadied him again. This time, the Keeper needed no gavel.

Radu's chest tightened in fright. *Has Obexx come to fight?*

"Volcifar," Amoss tried in an appeasing voice, "we agree that these are unprecedented times, but we need to act rationally and not rashly."

"Come now." Obexx's face curled. "How long has the Sight been fading from this collective's eyes? And you kept this knowledge from the other orders, did you not?"

The room was silent.

"A Keeper shall keep no secrets, brother," Obexx admonished. He looked as steady as ever, but contempt dripped from his tongue. "Knowledge must be shared. I am here simply to bring us together. Make us stronger." He gave a false grimace. "Don't turn away from me, First Keeper. What else do you know? Who would have ordered such an attack on the Cathedral of the Watchful Eye?"

Amoss held his head low and turned to Obexx. "We believe it was Graytorris the Mad, returned from exile to take vengeance. He's the one who stole the Tome."

Obexx laughed and shook his head in disdain.

"Why do you mock us?" Amoss asked.

"So," Obexx sighed and began to pace. "The hallowed Keepers of our faith allowed a crippled, blind man, long thought dead, to steal our god's most treasured gift to the realm? And they did so while hiding that their Sight had dwindled from the other three sects? And now you ask the Knights of the Maelstrom, who've bled for this order, to fall victim to your deceit? You ask it of the brothers and sisters of the protectorate, who have toiled across the realm for this order? And of the Disciples of the Watch, the influencers of nations for our order? Perhaps that's why Erud abandoned you!" His voice rose as he lectured the gathering before him. "Perhaps your misinterpretation of Erudian signs has caused this calamity. Perhaps by blinding your order and allowing Graytorris to re-emerge, Erud is showing us all how far we've fallen from our path? You are blind to the change that is needed, First Keeper. You and the Keepers have lost the favor of Erud, and consequently, the powers of the Sight."

The Hallow stood in silence again until Danton Hague rose from his chair. Radu's heart leapt as he read Hague's intentions before he spoke.

"There's one Keeper among us who still sees," Hague supplied. "I was sent to Castleshire to deliver the news of this calamity. It was there that I saw Daemus Alaric speaking on the floor of the Caveat, his eyes aglow with Erudian Sight."

"You mean the boy that your order expelled a month ago?" Obexx mocked. "He, too, hid his visions from the rest of us, did he not? I'm not sure whether I can believe anything that's been said in this chamber tonight. We won't fall for your skullduggery, Captain."

Hague responded with words instead of by reaching for his blade.

"The boy's powers of Sight were immense," Hague insisted. "And his prophecy was spoken in a tongue that no one understood. His voice cracked the dome of the fabled Caveat and brought a spectral stampede to the floor. It ended with him reciting a poem in an ancient elven language that no one in Castleshire understood, including a Vermilion princess. First Keeper Makai was present and confirmed that his manifestations were of the Sight."

"Vermilion?" Obexx's eyes narrowed. "Now we have a visit from a Wing of the Vermilion led by a princess who doesn't understand her own language? Come now, Captain. You can spin a better tale than that."

"In her wisdom, the Great Keeper sent the Alaric boy home," Amoss countered. "In doing so, she saved his life. He was spared from the starfall."

Obexx shook his head, his face shining with disbelief. "And what will you do about that, *First Keeper*?" he asked, mocking the title with his tone.

Amoss looked around the room at his fellow Keepers, his mind whirling behind his eyes. "Perhaps if Daemus was brought back, the Erudian Sight would return to the cathedral. If he's the last Keeper with the Sight, the protectorate needs him to be here."

Radu didn't understand what Amoss was thinking, but the room of Keepers murmured softly in curious agreement.

Amoss turned to Hague. "I understand that Alaric is on his way to Abacus. Is that correct, Captain?"

"Aye," Hague replied. "Daemus left with some guardians to head to Abacus, where they felt his visions were leading him. He was being accompanied by Disciple Delling of the Watch. One of your own, High Watcher. He believes in Daemus, and in what he witnessed."

"Perhaps if we'd learned that the Sight was beginning to wane," Obexx growled, "we could have prevented this whole ordeal. Graytorris was right. Perhaps if he'd been the Great Keeper before his fall, none of this would have happened!"

The room fell aghast with more charges of insolence and sacrilege. One Keeper fell to the ground, fainting at the charge. A second rose to confront Obexx physically, but Radu stopped him in his tracks.

"How dare you?" Amoss raged. "He was blinded by the will of Erud! He was excommunicated in Erud's name!"

"Then why does he possess *The Tome of Enlightenment*?"

Obexx countered. "And why has Erud allowed him enough Sight to have his revenge?"

"Insolence!" Another Keeper cried. He stood, and this time he was joined by two other Keepers as the room exploded into chaos around Amoss.

"You should be excommunicated for such blasphemy!" one of the Keepers attending to his unconscious friend cried, her hand balling up into a waving fist. Radu felt the chaos before it fully erupted but was at a loss for what to do.

Hague drew his blade and headed for Obexx, who turned back toward the Hallow's double doors. The High Watcher flung them open and staggered into a crowd that had tripled in size since his admittance to the conclave.

Radu ran to the door, surprised to see some of Hague's Knights in the crowd, including his lieutenant, Rutger Lorraine.

"We don't seek blood!" Obexx called back. "Our hands are drenched in it from burying our friends and digging them from the rubble. The rubble of your mistakes!"

Radu felt the pain of Nasyr's loss welling deep inside him. He and Amoss were too old and spent too long to see the sects fight so. The animosity between them was an effect he'd not counted on when the Tome went missing. Their home and the seat of the Sight lay in ruins and inter-sect fighting had not been something he thought would occur.

"If not blood," he asked Obexx, desperate to quell the uproar, "then what do you seek?"

"It's time for the Keepers to step aside," Obexx cried from the safety of the mob. "Your order has failed us, old Precept. Now is the time of the Disciples of the Watch."

CHAPTER FIVE

*"To truly explore, one must possess the courage to go
too far, so that we may learn how far we can go."*
—Vorodin the Ageless

RETURNING TO THE TWERGISH stronghold of Rawcliffe
Forge in the subterrane, Solveig Jins made her way through
the old twergish warpaths, long forgotten to most. The
Forge, as the twergs of Clan Swifthammer called it, was an
underground city, founded on the mining of gold, silver,
and gems buried deep in the belly of the Dragon's Breath
Mountains. Many of the old warpaths were overgrown, but to
a trader and skilled mountaineer like Jins, the old trails saved
time and provided security from the treacherous trollborn
and rare cryptids that roamed the countryside.

She'd spent the greater part of the last month bartering for
her guild in the merchant city of Saracen and was returning to
the Forge laden with gold to prove it. She knew her Clanmaster,
Tancred Abeline, would approve. The trek home took nearly a
fortnight and she'd pined for the comfort of a warm twergish
stout and a hearty stew.

Solveig was a trollborn herself, half twerg and half human,
but she'd never met her human father. She'd been born at the
Forge and had grown up in the subterrane and the nearby
Thorncrest Hills. She'd realized at a young age that her size
made her the desire of many of the twergish bachelors and
bachelorettes. It was common for twergs to have an interest in
more than one sex until they chose a permanent mate.

Solveig stood half a foot taller than most twergish males,
possessing a thick braid of blond hair, yet her human blood left
her without a beard, which was uncommon amongst twergish

women. She had big brown eyes and a dimpled face, with the arms of a miner or a warrior. Her tail was shorter than full twergs, but she didn't mind, as it was spotted brown like her eyes, making it unique in the Forge.

In town, she usually wore the robes of a merchant, but for her trip home through dangerous terrain she'd adopted a form of red-white hide armor that she'd fashioned for herself from hoar fox pelts and ram skins. Like many twergs, she wore her battle-axe on her back. It was a family heirloom that her mother had passed on to her when she'd started at the merchant clan. The axe had been forged by the famous twergish smithies of the subterrane and had belonged to her grandfathers—or her *Opas*, as their kind referred to them.

"We're nearly home, girl," she said to her trusty pack mule, Phanna. Solveig's mother had kept and raised pack mules for decades, and this particular Phanna was the eighth of her generation. She didn't know why her mother kept using the same names for the mules, but she'd never bothered to ask.

As Solveig rounded a bend, she could see the entrance to her underground home rising before her. The subterrane was hidden from the surface world by a boulder lock system. To a human, it would simply be a door. To the twergs, it was much more than that. The door was massive, weighing countless tons, and its surface was designed to deceive unwary passersby, featuring worked stone that looked like the natural surface rock had been worn away over time. But when Solveig placed the forge-key in the void, the boulder lock groaned into life, activating complex mechanisms that lifted the gate far enough for her and Phanna to pass through.

"Ah, the smell of home," she said to Phanna, walking the long and lonely path to the Forge. Even from a distance, the distinct odor of mine dust and smoke from the heated forges welcomed her home.

They descended a modest slope for nearly a mile, but the last steps of her trek passed slowly. She could soon feel the warmth of the subterrane ovens on her face and she could see the dim lights ahead. Twergs could see in total darkness, much like elves, but they preferred the comfort of illumination for practical reasons. Rawcliffe Forge basked in the soft glow of the twergish furnaces as the subterrane opened in front of her. She looked out at the grand undercity of Clan Swifthammer. She'd made it.

"Ey, blondie," a deep voice called from behind her. "I'm glad to see yer back... and yer front."

She turned to see a familiar group of miners descending the flats into the mines below. They chortled at her expense, but Jins was having none of it.

"Aye, Remy Gurglestock," she fired back. "I'm guessin' you hafta look to others' fronts as you haven't been able to see yours over yer belly for a century, ya goat-bearded fool."

Gurglestock paused to let the friendly insult sink in as his crew laughed at the witty retort. A toothless grin appeared on his face as the miners took turns slapping him on the back.

"We missed ya, girl," Gurglestock waved at her. "Will we be seein' ya later for a stout?"

"If it's on yer silver, then yes," she replied as the men trailed off.

"When isn't it?" he cried back, sharing a distant laugh.

———✦———

SOLVEIG JINS NAVIGATED HER way through the perfectly-hewn underground corridors—a stamp of twergish craftsmanship—looking for her merchant guild and its clanmaster. When she arrived at her guild's doors, she found Tancred sitting atop his high stool, his legs folded beneath him and his tail dangling from the back of his chair. He scribbled away in a ledger, and she could barely see the twisting of his quill over the lip of his desk. He peered over his spectacles, which were low on his nose, as he stared intently into a ledger that weighed more than he did.

"I see some things never change." Solveig knocked on the door, smiling at him from by the archway.

Tancred looked up and returned the smile. "Welcome back, my girl!" he exclaimed, stepping down from the stool and grabbing at the hunch in his back.

"There's no need to stop." She raised her hands in a vain effort to halt him, but he approached anyway. "I see your back isn't any better."

"Ah," Tancred moaned. "I fear that centuries of leaning on that damned desk has made this a permanent condition. But never mind me, how profitable was the trip?"

They made their way over to an inspection table topped with a green cloth, where Solveig emptied her leather gem case. She said nothing but watched Tancred's aged eyes light up before he even reached for his magnifying lens.

"Very good." Tancred whispered as though he was trying to hide the treasure from prying eyes with his tone. "I've never seen diamonds like these coming from Saracen. And you received these for just the pelts and minerals?"

"Aye."

"Well done." He seemed to lose track of her as he appraised the gems with his spectacles.

"And my cut?"

He raised his head and grinned, satisfied with her work. He reached for an iron lock box under the table and signaled for her to turn around while he fumbled with the combination lock on its face. Once she heard it click, she knew it was safe to turn back.

Tancred worked quickly, counting out a stack of silver laurels and gold palmettes and then placed it in front of Jins.

The stack of laurels was to be expected, but the palmettes intrigued her.

"Are you testing my honesty?" Solveig asked. "The gold is too much for my share."

"Nay, girl." He shook his head. "I'm testing your resolve."

"Pardon?"

"I know the Saracen trip wasn't an easy one. And I'm afraid that I have to put you straight back on the road."

She rolled her eyes and groaned, but Tancred pushed through it.

"Shhh," he motioned, cupping his ear in jest. "Listen to the gold. Come closer."

She humored the old twerg merchant and bent lower to the table.

"Hear that? The gold's telling you that wealth and reward await you in Thronehelm."

"Thronehelm?" she gasped.

"Aye. The capital of Warminster awaits you, young Jins. Do you hear the gold telling you to go there?"

"Why Thronehelm?" she asked. "It's twice the distance and never as accommodating to trollborn like me."

"They're desperate," he replied. "Your friends in Saracen have cut off the king until he quells an uprising between their baronies and, as such, they'll pay more for less, especially as the seasons change."

"I was unaware of that." She raised her hand to her chin. "Very well. The gold has spoken."

Tancred raised a single digit and pointed to her. "There's one other thing."

"What's that?"

"I want you to take a new pass that the army has been carving. It's partly underground and surfaces around Foghaven

Vale, trailing off through Ravenwood to the town of Valkeneer."

"You mean the Bridge?" Jins questioned, recalling the town of Valkeneer's nickname.

"Yes, yes," Tancred assured. "That's the one. The new path is called the Garnet Pass. I have your wares for the trip in the shed, ready for you to depart today."

She frowned and said, "Tomorrow," beginning the opening salvo of a negotiation with her guildmaster.

"Aye," he conceded. "Tomorrow, Jins, but no later."

The room shook for a second and they both froze, contemplating the source of the disturbance. Then a more violent quake came and disturbed the dust and cobwebs on the rafters of the old shop.

"A cave in?" Tancred suggested, rushing to store the new gems in his lockbox. He ducked under the table and waved to Jins to join him.

"No…" She shook her head as she walked to the door. A shadow ran by the small alcove that served as a window for the shop, followed by a few more shadows. By the time she reached the door, the subterrane's alleys were full of curious eyes. She stepped out into the underground street and grabbed at a runner from the mines who was rushing by.

"What's happening?" she asked. "Gold?"

"No." His face flushed with fear, and he began to run away from her. "We don't know what it is."

Solveig looked back at Tancred and jogged before running toward the flats as a mob of twergs emerged from the mines, headed in the opposite direction.

"Careful, Jins!" Tancred yelled at her. "I don't want to lose my favorite trader to a collapsing mine or some toxic fumes!"

She flashed a dimpled smile over her shoulder to Tancred and descended the sloping corridors into the mines anyway.

She followed the rudimentary tracks of the gold carts and the steady flow of miners scrambling to the safety of the subterrane, and within minutes she found herself among the miners she'd been teasing moments earlier.

The group of twergs stood in near silence and stared at a roughly hewn wall. Judging from the taste of the air, the wall had just been carved out by their pickaxes.

Lantern light danced from the nervous hands of miners, held low to the floor. She saw the silhouette of a lone pick still digging at the cave, its distinctive grind turning rock to pebbles on the other side of the wall of miners. Solveig used her size and pushed her way to the front. The stunned twergs made a gap for her and when she reached the front, she stopped next to Gurglestock. A twerg was down on his knees and swinging his pick sideways, clearing a natural bubble in the rock wall.

"A pocket cave?" Jins asked.

"Aye," Gurglestock whispered. "But it's somethin'... somethin' else."

She dropped to her knees and braved the corner, looking out into the chamber. The miners had indeed found a pocket cave—a small, undiscovered chamber.

"Turn off the lanterns." Solveig waved to the group behind her.

"Why?" Gurglestock asked.

"Just do it," she said, winking at him.

Gurglestock gave the signal, and the miners killed their lantern light. As their eyes adjusted to the darkness, a soft glow of light, almost beyond perception, emanated from the chamber. She started to crawl into the void and the miners behind her gasped when Gurglestock grabbed at her.

"Don't," he warned, but she'd already crawled into the cave.

"Hand me your pick." She reached out to the twerg on the ground. He complied, and with a swing of her burly arms, she knocked a larger hole into the wall so they could all peer into the chamber. As the others approached, she spun the pick to its flat side and skimmed it gently over the glowing rocks, which broke loose and revealed the source of the glow. She cleared the rest of the debris from the rock wall until all that was left was blue script, radiating delicately in the blackness.

Solveig stood in silence as the miners viewed their discovery from outside the pocket cave. She handed the pick back to her new friend as she wiped her brow, stepping back to gain perspective.

"The runes aren't of a twergish language," Gurglestock remarked from the other chamber.

Solveig reached slowly to touch the runes with her extended finger, but Gurglestock grabbed her arm again. She shrugged him off, but could see the miners behind her shifting, their nerves piqued. She stepped to the wall and removed her glove, extending a finger to touch the glowing glyphs. She scratched the surface with a gentle stroke.

"It's not a powder," she told the assembled miners. "Nor is it a residue that I can remove, but it feels… cold. Unnaturally cold." She reached into her haversack and produced her merchant ledger.

"What are you doing?" Gurglestock asked.

"I'm scribing these symbols so that others can see what you've discovered."

"Enough of this." The gruff voice echoed into the chamber, and Solveig turned to find a brooding foreman in the opening. "This place isn't for you, Jins. You don't know what yer doin', and I won't have anyone hurt on me watch."

"I was just curious about what they found," she replied, quickly hiding the book with the markings.

"Git goin'." He thumbed her in the direction of the exit. "It's fer yer own good, lass."

SOLVEIG WAITED UNTIL SHE emerged from the flats to share her excitement. In the subterrane, she hustled across the courtyard to Tancred. She found him back on his usual perch, counting laurels and palmettes.

"Back so soon, Jins?"

She rushed over to his bench and placed her open ledger on top of his. "This is what the fuss was about."

Tancred cleaned his glasses first, as was his habit, before inspecting the markings.

"What's this?"

"Etchins, boss." Excitement buzzed from her words. "They discovered magic etchins. They opened a pocket cave and we discovered—"

"We?"

"Aye. The men were too afraid to enter, so I—"

"You're letting your human curiosity get the better of you," Tancred decreed, shaking his head. "The safest thing to do is to let the miners take care of it."

"But the inscription," Solveig insisted. "They were too timid to even look at what they'd found. If I hadn't been there, the foreman might have just collapsed the cave so that no one could have explored it."

Tancred shook his head again and tore her sketch from the ledger. She reached for it, but the old twerg silenced her with a "shhh."

"Enough of this, Jins." He held the page to the burning candle on his bench. "Listen to the gold calling. Don't you have somewhere to go?"

CHAPTER SIX

"A king is a king before he is a father."
—Saint Albion Cer, the Exalted Paladin
of Koss, the Ancient of War

THE SUN WAS JUST RISING as the *Sundowner* steered into the harbor, golden light spilling out over the horizon. Monty had come up to the deck to look out at the sea when he couldn't sleep. He and Joferian hadn't spoken more than a few words to each other in the final days of the journey. The time apart had cooled their tempers but had done little to heal the rift Monty felt between himself and his cousin. He missed Everett dearly, even more so as it sank in that he was home. He had left here without knowing it would be the last time he'd see his home with his brother at his shoulder, the last time he would ever envision Everett at his side when he eventually ascended to the throne. Instead, he wondered if their father's kingdom would crumble under the weight of war or some sorcerer's curse. The thought terrified him almost as much as the prospect of being forced to rule without Everett by his side.

Captain Halford was voicing orders to the crew, who carried them out in relative silence, only communicating in terse phrases and hushed tones. The atmosphere on the ship had soured a little after Monty's falling out with Joferian. Monty wasn't sure how to feel about that, aware that their status played a role in the crew's reticence but unable to summon the strength of will to care very much. As they approached the docks, the deck was silent, save for the creaking of the rigging and the lapping of the waves against the boards. No one on the *Sundowner* needed a reminder of the somber duty that they'd brought with them to the capital of Warminster.

"Boy," Halford yelled at length, addressing a young shoreman standing on the docks. "Fetch ye the harbormaster. We have royals that be need'n an escort to the castle."

"Straightaway, Cap'n." The youth saluted and trotted off.

"Are you certain that's necessary?" asked LaBrecque in an undertone.

Halford shrugged. "This errand is one of importance," he replied at the same volume. "Frankly, given how the prince and viscount have been acting, I don't think it's a sure thing that they would go to see the king by themselves."

"Dorian..." LaBrecque's tone was chastising, but Halford only made an equivocating noise and moved off.

Monty pretended he hadn't heard. He felt a numbness in his legs and a lump in his throat. He didn't want to get off the boat, knowing it would bring him closer to the moment at which he'd have to tell his parents of Everett's death. The *Sundowner* was a peaceful respite from that duty, but the floating sanctuary brought him home to a terrible task. He'd spent the last seven days trying to settle on an approach to it, but so far each had been as bad as the next. Conversations were starting to materialize in his head, different paths he might take, different ways he could tell the king what had happened. None of them felt right. Your son is dead. My brother perished in battle. Everett is gone. All of them stuck in his throat; he didn't think he could say any of them.

Joferian stepped out onto the deck next to him, silent but somehow not cold. Monty's anger at him faded a little. Pining after his five-minute fiancée only days after his own brother's death might still be impossible for Monty to understand, but his cousin's grief, the mirror image of his own, was still obvious enough.

"Prince," Halford interrupted his thoughts. "The harbormaster is on his way. We'll wait on deck until the castle guards arrive."

Montgomery nodded the barest of assents.

Halford produced a flask from his waistcoat and offered it to the prince, but Montgomery refused with a gentle shrug.

Joferian reached for the flask and before Monty realized it, the viscount gulped two big swigs before handing it back. "One for me, and one for Talath," he whispered.

"Wait." Montgomery intercepted the flask. "One for me, and one for Everett."

Montgomery drank, winced, but didn't lift his gaze to meet his cousin. He instead stared over the rail until the familiar face of Anson Valion, the captain of the royal Black Cuffs appeared on the dock, accompanied by a few members of the castle guard.

"Sires," he called, his face impassive. "Your return so soon is unexpected. Where is the *Wake*?"

When both Joferian and Monty failed to respond, LaBrecque shouted back, his tone forcefully cheery, "Out of commission for the moment," he replied. "She's being repaired in Castleshire." LaBrecque disembarked and approached Valion, and the two men had a quiet conversation.

Montgomery watched Valion's face pale with the news, the line of his mouth turning grim. For a moment, Valion and Montgomery locked gazes until Valion's trailed off, watching the crane as it slowly lowered Everett's casket onto the shore.

Joferian moved to follow LaBrecque, but Montgomery's feet wouldn't move. His eyes shifted to the rudimentary casket, unworthy as it was to hold the remains of his brother. He knew they'd arrive without fanfare this time. There'd be no parade, and no welcome wagons. There'd be nothing but silence.

"Come, Prince," Joferian called back to him.

Monty took a deep breath and steeled himself. Taking one step at a time, he descended the planks and mounted his horse. "I'll take the lead." Monty managed, and Valion waved to his soldiers to move out.

It was less than an hour before they arrived at the castle, the time passing in a blurry collection of images: eyes looking at them out of windows, Valion's back as he rode in front of them, Everett's casket being carted along behind them, Monty's own hand on the pommel of his sword. Being watched made him think of being ambushed or waiting for the assassin's return.

Valion exchanged a few words with Meeks, the castle steward, who met them at the portcullis. Meeks whispered into a servant's ear and watched the woman run off before leading them inside.

The group made a grim procession as they trudged through the castle to the main receiving room. Monty could see the news spreading among the servants, who knew better than to come out and gawk but couldn't help the rigid set of their shoulders and somber expressions as they hurried about their work. Many of them had known Monty and Everett since their boyhood, before they'd gone away to the academy.

At last, they reached their destination, where Monty's mother and father sat waiting along with a small host of others, among them his aunt, Cecily Maeglen. As if animated by magic, some force other than life that caused his heart to continue to beat despite its brokenness, Monty walked forward out of the escort. He heard Joferian following a couple of steps behind him.

The king was stone-faced, the queen's expression a mask of horror so painful to look at that Monty had to stare at her pearl-inlaid circlet instead of her eyes.

"You have returned, my son," King Godwin said at length, his lack of composure betrayed by the audible shake in his voice.

Monty couldn't look at him, or at his mother, or at the coffin. He couldn't speak; even breathing seemed only barely possible. Suddenly he wondered how he'd managed to get all this way from the ship, somehow riding and now placing one foot in front of the other without stopping. Faintly, he heard Joferian's mother choke on a sob.

"What happened?" His father's voice had increased in both anger and sorrow. "Speak!"

Monty flinched; his vision now so blurred with tears that he couldn't distinguish anything past his nose. What could he say? What was there to say?

"We were attacked," Joferian managed, ending the silence, sounding miraculously steady. Monty felt a rush of warmth and gratitude for his cousin, all his anger forgotten. "Everett died in combat, protecting the Vermilion princess from an assassin. Talath died when he was hoisted overboard before I... before I could save him." His eyes reached out for his mother.

"An assassin," commented the king. "You weren't able to identify them, by any chance?"

At last Monty found his tongue. "Yes," his voice sounding hoarser than Joferian's to his own ears. "It was the Bone elf who attacked and killed Dacre Elspeth at the masquerade. I kept this." He pulled the dagger that had killed his brother from his belt, showing its rose-stamped pommel to the king.

"You let him escape."

Monty wanted to vanish into the floor. Or perhaps to simply catch on fire and burn up, with nothing left but ash. "Yes." Or trade places with his brother, safe and blameless in his coffin. The bastard.

"What of the princess?" inquired the baroness, sounding

calm despite the tear tracks running down her face.

"She lives," her son answered. "Safely delivered to Castleshire, and she was able to address the Caveat and deliver her news... and ours."

"Well done," Cecily praised, her voice cracking. Monty glanced at Joferian, whose head was lowered, making his expression impossible to see. When he looked back at his aunt, her eyes were on him, and Monty blinked. "Both of you."

The king scoffed, his eyes flashing.

"We were attacked." LaBrecque stepped into the conversation, this time without his usual bluster. "Your son defended us in several battles, Baroness. He died a hero in the last, just before we reached Castleshire."

"Is this true?" she asked, grabbing Joferian's face and looking deep into his eyes.

"The admiral speaks the truth, Mother," Joferian replied. "I was trapped fighting three marauders, including their second-in-command. Talath came to my rescue. In doing so, he killed two of the attackers and saved me from the sword. I'm sorry, Mother," Joferian continued, fighting back tears. "This is all that's left of Talath."

Montgomery watched as Joferian presented Baroness Maeglen with Talath's sword. The Baroness took it from her son, who now knelt in front of her. She glanced at the sword and then bent to hug Joferian.

"Crowley," said Amice, speaking for the first time. "Please prepare my son for his funeral rites."

The servant nodded and began to slink away.

Godwin's countenance grew heavy again at the reminder, seeming to lose some of its fire but none of its steel. "Before you leave, Crowley, ensure Everett's armor is repaired and his sword cleaned. We'll display them forever in the Hall of

Fallen Heroes for generations to see. Have the historian draft a proper epitaph."

"Yes, sire," Crowley bent in reverence.

"Baroness," Godwin went on, "if you'd like Talath's sword to hang alongside Everett's, I'd be honored to make the arrangements. But if you'd prefer to take it back to Queen's Chapel, I'd understand. I'll leave that decision to you."

"Keep it here, my lord." She didn't hesitate. "They died together. So shall they remain together, in peace." She handed the sword to Crowley.

"Very well, my lady," the chamberlain pursed his lips and lifted the weapon from her hands.

"Now is not the time to grieve," Godwin turned back to Monty. "There will be plenty of time for that once Warminster has been restored. Tell me of Castleshire now."

Montgomery was struck by his father's coldness. He glanced to his mother and aunt and saw only pain. He struggled to believe his father could yet be thinking straight. "There was open dissention from Thessica Camber of Foghaven Vale," Monty began, his tone tinged in a mixture of emotions. "I swear, Father, only Addilyn Elspeth's quick wits stopped me from strangling her on the Caveat floor."

"Another ally of Von Lormarck stepping a toe out of line at a highly convenient moment," added Cray from behind the prince.

"That confirms to me Von Lormarck's involvement in this," Godwin sneered through his teeth.

"She wouldn't have spoken out without his permission," LaBrecque added.

Monty shuddered but kept quiet. Even in the face of mounting evidence, he still struggled to believe his own family would be responsible for this. His subconscious hand rubbed at the back of his neck.

"Gloucester seceded from Warminster and joined Foghaven Vale the day after your departure," the king informed them. "And we have Sasha Scarlett of Saracen and her merchant allies putting pressure on us with their combined embargo. Won't be a pretty winter here in Thronehelm, even if this conflict ends quickly. Warminster will run out of supplies and food. We're already deep within the Season of Colored Leaves."

"It won't end quickly, sire," muttered LaBrecque from somewhere in the back of the room. "Saracen isn't the only place we can source provisions. My fleet stands by and can import food by sea."

"From where?" Godwin growled.

"Castleshire perhaps?" Amice broke her silence again. "The Crown Isles? If Von Lormarck is behind this, he is landlocked and has no navy to stop seaborne goods."

"Sire," Makai rose to speak, his tone a bit hesitant. "I am First Keeper Aliferis Makai of Castleshire. The Caveat has sent me to first offer the city's condolences but more importantly to help you. The Regency remains on your side, as they demonstrated the night that your son spoke in front of them."

"And?" the king stared at the twergish Keeper.

"Perhaps... the Norsemen... can help?"

"The Vikings?" Monty blurted, his mind swirling in confusion. The suggestion was too much for him to grasp in this moment.

King Godwin stared first at his son, then turned back to the First Keeper, his eyes aflare at the suggestion but his tongue stilled by it. After a moment, his eyes narrowed as his hand flew to his chin.

"The Norsemen have long been our enemies." Godwin paused. "But they're no fools. Perhaps we can strike a deal. At the very least, we must try. With the encroaching Season of Long Nights, Thronehelm and the remaining five baronies of Warminster will soon need supplies."

"Father, no." Monty's face contorted, and his jaw dropped. "They are our sworn enemies." His thoughts jumbled in fear, hate, and suspicions. He doubted himself and couldn't fathom his father's contemplation of such a solution. Was the king so grief stricken that he would consider the Norsemen as an option?

Godwin paused again, his gaze stern, and he looked around the room for other suggestions but none came. His gaze landed back on the Master from Hunter's Manor. "Cray, I'm dispatching you to Saracen."

"Saracen, sire?" Cray's eyes widened, his face drawn up in confusion.

"You're to reproach Sasha Scarlett," Godwin commanded. "Let's put that silver tongue of yours to use for once. Convince her that she's made a mistake and that we need her to supply our people over the Season of Long Nights."

"And just how will I do that, sire?"

"Offer her what she wants most," Godwin explained. "I'll provide her with a bounty worthy of a king."

"Of course, sire."

Godwin turned back to the prince, his eyes settling on his son. He drew a breath and waited but Monty wasn't sure how to respond. "If that's all the news you have to share with us, my son, then it's time for you to be on your way." Godwin's eyes were hard.

"On my... On my way?" stammered Monty, feeling as though the wind had been knocked out of him. He glanced at his mother, then at Joferian, who looked as surprised and confused as he was. "On my way where?"

"The Viking capital of Hammerstead. We need to take action. And we are short of allies with the seeming Von Lormarck treachery. And the First Keeper is correct. You must travel north and try to treat with the Norsemen," his father stated. "I am sending you as my firstborn and only remaining son, as a sign of respect the Norsemen will appreciate. They have long been our enemies and as the foundation of Warminster crumbles beneath us, now is the time to assure a peace—and obtain their help."

"Father, you don't mean for me to leave now?" Monty tried to keep his voice level and failed, then ducked his head, realizing he was treading on dangerous ground.

"What if they take it as a sign of weakness and invade?" asked Cecily before Godwin could answer.

The king's eyes moved from his son to her.

"If they were going to take the opportunity to invade, they would have done it by now. They have deep ties to the Ancients, and it's a sure bet that they know about this coming war—probably knew it would happen before we did with the blindness of our Keepers. And for all their bloodthirstiness, they are straightforward. If we offer our hand in friendship and they take it, I know their king won't go back on his word."

"Sire," Monty tried in desperation, but didn't know what else to say.

His father looked at him again. "Yes, Montgomery, you will leave immediately."

"Godwin!" cried Amice.

At the same time LaBrecque uncomfortably interjected, "My king, I think that is unwise." The king's jaw clenched. "Perhaps just a day or two," LaBrecque went on, and in some distant corner of his mind, Monty was impressed with his bravery. LaBrecque was a friend of Godwin, but it still took an iron will to argue with the king in front of others. Even Cecily had remained silent, though her mouth had thinned into a distraught line.

"Just a little time for them to rest," implored the queen, staring miserably at Monty. "They have lost so much—we all have."

Not as much as this kingdom stands to lose if we wait," snapped Godwin at his wife, who flinched. "I have had enough of questions and arguments. They depart today."

Monty bowed, aware that he had used up his allotted latitude for imposing on the king's patience. A split second later, Joferian bowed alongside him.

"LaBrecque," Godwin said, turning on his friend, "perhaps you too need a reminder of where your duty lies. Captain Valion informed me you sailed here on a merchant vessel that flies our flag. You will take command of the *Sundowner* and accompany them."

"Take Halford's command from him?" LaBrecque sounded appalled. "But—"

"You," cut in Godwin before he could finish, "have no ship to your name at present, which means you have nothing to occupy your mind other than ensuring this mission's success. Besides, a merchant vessel sailing north will draw less attention than a warship. Do not question me again." The dangerous edge in his voice brooked no argument, and at last LaBrecque bowed. "Go with the Ancients."

"Sire, are you sure this is wise?" First Keeper Makai cringed as his king turned his thunderous visage on him.

"You forget, First Keeper, that this was your suggestion."

"It was, sire," Makai admitted. "But I thought that perhaps we could first mourn the loss of Prince Everett and Viscount Talath."

Their names rung like a bell in Monty's head. His brother lay dead in a coffin and his cousin lay dead in the sea. The image of the assassin's dagger reappeared, it's pommel fashioned in the form of a black rose, its blade stained in Everett's blood.

"The needs of Warminster must come first. A king must rule, even as he grieves."

The words jarred Monty from his thoughts. He looked to his father and tried to understand the lesson in his voice, but Everett...

"But father," Montgomery tried, "I—"

"Hold your tongue, Montgomery," Godwin interrupted. "It can only be you, son. *Only you.* Find their *konungr,* Atorm Stormmoeller. He's as close to a king as the Norsemen have. Present him with gifts and entreaties from Thronehelm. Don't show weakness but request their help in a potential alliance."

"Certainly, Father." Montgomery sounded sure of himself, but the color had now drained from his face.

"Atorm is an unpredictable ruler," Godwin continued, reaching for an axe that had hung on the study wall for as long as Montgomery could remember. "But he'll likely be intrigued by this. On top of the gold you'll carry, present him with this token of peace and forgiveness. It's his father's axe. It's adorned the halls of Thronehelm since I killed Wolfrick in battle, during the war between Warminster and Rijkstag. It's been a generation, but it may help in your negotiation."

"My king, are they the best legates you can send?" LaBrecque asked.

"No," Godwin replied. "But Atorm *will* respect a visit from the son of a king. Take bribes and buy their loyalty. It's necessary, now. I'm sure they'll ask for more, but we'll deal with that as it comes. In the meantime, we must do this now to secure their forces, and more importantly, their food in case Cray's effort in Saracen fails. I'll mobilize the forces of the baronies that remain loyal to Warminster, and I've already summoned the Faxerian, Lucien Blacwin, back from Halifax. He'll command my armies."

"I will happily go," Joferian added, a charged emotion in his voice. He nodded in approval.

Monty shot his cousin a look, but Joferian didn't return his gaze and instead turned to his mother, who remained speechless.

"Anson Valion," the king went on, "you'll be permanently installed as my new captain of the Black Cuffs following the death of Captain Shale."

"It's an honor, Your Majesty," Anson bowed and took a grateful knee.

Monty looked through stifled tears and stared at the man that was a king before a father. Self-doubt poked at his ribs and a lump rose in his throat. He knew he had much to learn, and little time to do so. Father, Monty wanted to say, even though he had nothing to say after it. Instead, he closed his mouth, saluted his weeping mother, and left. One foot in front of the other.

CHAPTER SEVEN

*"Always expect the unexpected but ensure
the unexpected never expects you."*
—Warminster the Mage

INCANUS DRU'WAITH STILL WORE his leather armor,
which was stained with dry sea salt when Thessica Camber,
the royal legate for Foghaven Vale, pulled open the door
to the embassy's cellar. Skullam, his imp companion, lay
unconscious on the cot beside him. The Bone elf's eyes didn't
move to meet Camber's, but instead stared into the distance.

Camber had helped Dru'Waith when he'd appeared several
nights before in her doorway, drenched in seawater and blood and
carrying Skullam. She'd hid the two in the cellar of the embassy.

"Replaying your stalemate?" Camber asked.

Incanus didn't answer her. He'd missed his opportunity to
kill a Vermilion princess, an invaluable prize, and he didn't
appreciate her reminder.

"Dru'Waith, I don't have all morning," Camber's voice was
forceful, and she found a barrel to sit on as she waited for him
to acknowledge her presence. "I need to know if you heard me
when I told you what happened on the Caveat floor."

The Bone elf didn't look at her, but he nodded ever so slightly.

"Good," she said. "There's more for me to tell. Your
anonymity is blown. No one knows you, but you're sure to be
the only Bone elf in the city. Castleshire's jailer is looking for
you, so I've arranged to smuggle you and your friend out of
here. You'll sail back to Thronehelm on a friendly ship of ours
this afternoon. I'll ride to Foghaven Vale, as I've been recalled
by King Dragich. But first, I'll accompany you to the docks to
make sure that you get off safely."

"King?" Incanus scowled, finally acknowledging her presence. "Dragich has won no battles. So how is he king?"

"That's where you come in," she answered, a stark tone in her voice. "You need to return to Thronehelm and finish the job that you failed to complete on the night of the masquerade. Kill Montgomery and Joferian. King Dragich wants Godwin for himself."

Incanus fell back into silence.

Camber reached for him, but his lightning reflexes caught her off guard as he grabbed her hand. She gasped, and Incanus considered punishing her for the offense, but he relented, letting her pull her hand back.

Camber paused for a moment and then continued. "I paid handsomely for some information from an Alaric servant that may interest you. And, of course, aid our efforts."

"What could that be?" Incanus asked, his tone harsh. "I have no interest in the young Keeper you told me about."

"The servant confided that she'd overheard a healer tell his parents of a message," Camber went on. "One she needed to send to her matron mother in the Silvercroft Mountains, the home of the Alarics. Apparently, Daemus confided in her about a vision he'd had about your benefactor, Graytorris. They say that whatever this message is, it could stop him from succeeding. The servant didn't know much more than that, but the Keeper and the Vermilion travel to Abacus today to stop Graytorris."

"What do you know of the fallen Keeper?" Incanus grunted. "Your 'king' has a loose tongue. He should not speak of our link."

"I know nothing of your relationship with Graytorris," she assured him. "And nor do I care to, but I do know that his alliance with King Dragich is important to all of our successes.

clean this up before you leave this afternoon. We need to stop this message from reaching its recipient."

Incanus nodded in silent agreement as Camber made a move to wake Skullam. He stopped her with an extended arm. "Leave him. I can handle one healer on my own."

THE TEMPLE OF SSOLANTRESS was peaceful after a long night, as Katja sat alone at a sunken pool encircled by a small bench made of simple stone. Vaulted ceilings and marbled halls didn't exist here. The stone manse was a simple, one-story structure, with the small pool in the center of the main floor. It looked more like a garden than a house of worship.

Katja didn't register the visitor's presence until he was a few yards in front of her. He lowered his cowl, and she took him in. He was tall for an elf, not much shorter than a human, with ashen skin. His almond-shaped eyes peered out from his long greyish-white hair.

"May I help you?" she asked.

The visitor leapt onto the bench, drawing his sword and holding it to Katja's throat.

Her eyes flicked but she didn't move. "What can I help you with?" she asked, noting the shock on the intruder's face at her question.

"Do you not fear death when it looks for you?" the elf asked, raising the tip of his sword.

The steel pinched at her neck, but she didn't flinch. "I don't." She paused and saw her attacker wore fresh bandages. "However, I do see your wounds now that you're closer. May I address them for you?"

The Bone elf glared at her. "I know you're helping the Alaric son. What message was sent through your visit?"

"I can't tell you what message was sent," Katja dared to say.

"That's not for you to know."

"I'll cut out your tongue," the elf snapped. Again, she offered no resistance.

"I would prefer that you didn't," she replied, her voice calm. "I won't resist. But I ask you not to. I'm a priestess of Ssolantress, and we're not afraid of death or injury. Nor do we discuss those under our care."

"You admit you cared for the Keeper?"

"Of course," she nodded. "I'll happily do the same for you if you lower your sword."

"In exchange for your life, of course," the intruder mocked.

"In exchange for nothing," Katja insisted. "You can kill me after if you must, but I don't judge my patients or ask how they came into my care. It is against the disciplines instilled by our goddess Ssolantress. I'd die before I told you about Daemus. Just as I'd die before I told him about you." She paused. "I can't give you the information you seek."

When the man hesitated, Katja continued, "Come, master elf. Sit next to the water and let me attend to your wounds." Her eyes guided his to the pool, but she dared not move.

The elf lowered his weapon.

At length, she stood and approached the shallow pool. He followed her and removed his cloak.

Katja gently unwrapped the wound on his forearm and pulled a cloth dressing from the folds of her robes. She leaned over the pool and whispered, "My Blue Lady of the healing waters, bless this chalice so that I may heal this man."

She dunked the dressing in the pool and then applied the wrap to the elf's wound. The intruder stiffened at her touch but relaxed a moment later under her hand.

"What's this?" he questioned, his face full of distrust.

"Ssolantress blesses you," Katja explained. "May I address

your other wounds?"

He paused as she worked, and his eyes met hers. "Yes."

Katja forced a half-smile and continued to work on his other injuries.

"What is your relationship to the Alarics?" the Bone elf said, shifting as she applied pressure. "Why did you care for the Keeper?"

"Why do I care for you?" Katja countered. "I am an acolyte of Ssolantress, and as such, every man, woman, child... or Bone elf... is in my charge."

The elf fell silent for a few moments. "You will come with me." His voice remained stern, but Katja could sense an easing in his inflection as she wrapped his other arm. "I have an injured friend who needs your help."

"Bring him here, and I will—"

The Bone elf shook his head. "He can't travel here." He looked to the confines of the holy ground, but Katja didn't quite understand.

"Am I to be your hostage then?" she asked.

The elf sneered and punched her in the face, knocking her unconscious.

KATJA WOKE UP IN a cellar of some kind. Her face had swelled with a raised welt. She moaned and lifted her hand to inspect a wound she couldn't see.

The room was cold and dark, and as her eyes adjusted, she noticed a single candelabrum in the far corner, illuminating the cellar. As she sat up, her head thumped with pain. She turned to look around and then jumped when she saw a small cot beside her with a bloody demon staring at her from it.

"Steady yourself," the Bone elf intoned. "He's just an imp. He won't hurt you unless I order him to."

Katja heard his voice, but she kept her eyes affixed on the grey creature in front of her.

"Give him a reason," the imp challenged her.

Katja scrambled away, despite her condition, and climbed to her feet. Her vision blurred, and her head spun, and the wooziness combined with the aches left her staggering. She reached out to balance herself on the cold wall.

"W-where am I?" she stuttered, struggling to hold her balance.

"You're in the embassy of the Kingdom of Foghaven Vale," someone replied from the other side of the room. "I'm Ambassador Thessica Camber, and you're my guest here."

Katja winced as she said, "I'm your *prisoner.*"

Camber emerged from the shadows but didn't answer the healer. A diplomatic smile crossed her face, and she hid her hands behind her back. "I'm sorry you were brought here," the ambassador confided. "I assure you that it wasn't my intention to receive visitors this morning, but my associate has made that choice for me." She turned and frowned at the Bone elf.

Katja gathered herself and looked at the hideous smirking creature in front of her. "Is this the friend you wished me to heal?"

"Yes." The Bone elf cocked his head in the direction of the imp.

"I can't."

"Can't? Or won't?" He took a step away from the wall and toward her, his hand resting on the pommel of his sword.

"My spells won't work on him," she tried to explain. "Creatures like this possess the dark trace. My spells might end up hurting him."

The creature scoffed, but the man held up a hand. "The dark trace?"

"The imp was conjured from... elsewhere." Katja tensed at the mere thought. "My prayers can't help him like they can help you and me. His body might look like flesh, but it's made of something that's not from this world. In fact, he leaves a trail of the dark trace behind him that certain sensitive people can detect."

"If you're lying..."

"Acolytes of Ssolantress don't lie."

"I wouldn't put it past her," the imp fumed. "Her kind don't sit right with me."

"Enough," Camber interrupted, taking a deep breath as she refocused the conversation. "I'm leaving this morning for Foghaven Vale, and I need to bring you with me, Priestess."

"What do you mean?" Katja's focus narrowed on the ambassador.

"Sit with me." Camber sat herself and patted at the open seat on the bench next to her.

Katja begrudgingly obliged.

"Unfortunately, your presence here was a mistake. My associate hoped you could help his imp, but he didn't want to take the damned thing into your holy temple in case it hurt him. That's why he brought you here."

Katja subconsciously raised her hand to the bruise on her face. Her eyes drifted to the Bone elf, who returned her stare. By his cold eyes alone, she knew she was only alive because she had information he needed.

"You see, my young friend, this puts me in a quandary." Camber reached gently for Katja's chin and turned her head back toward her. "Since I can't let you go and risk you sharing our secrets with the whole of Castleshire, I have had to find a different solution."

Katja took a deep breath and steeled herself. Her body tensed. "I am not afraid to die."

"No, no..." Camber's eyebrows raised, and her face curled into a half-smile. "You misunderstand me. My associate also wished to learn what help you provided to the Alaric son. Since you refused to tell him, I need to take more extreme measures. It's in our kingdom's best interests to stop the young Keeper from succeeding, you see. Therefore, I'm going to take you to meet with my king and sovereign."

"I shan't tell him, either."

"You might not fear death." Camber hesitated for a second, "But my lord has ways of persuading you to help. And since I can't risk the authorities finding you here, you must come as my guest to Foghaven Vale. We leave this morning. But first, let's clean you up. You will need to change into these clothes." She pointed to a gown that lay beside her. "They bear the Vale's insignia. I can't be seen carrying a soon-to-be missing healer out of town in my carriage. Wear your blue hair up and cover it with this cap."

"Anything else?" Katja asked, sarcasm dripping from her tongue.

"Yes," Camber said. "Say your goodbyes to Castleshire. You won't be coming back."

"YOU'VE KILLED THAT GIRL by bringing her here," Thessica whispered, once they were outside the chamber. "I gave you a simple task."

"I'm not your servant," Incanus reminded her. He had already gotten from her what he wanted. His only regret is that she couldn't hasten the healing of Skullam's wounds as she did for him.

Camber turned to Incanus. "I know who you are, and I'm ordering you to leave town as quickly as possible. I don't need any more trails of blood leading to our door. And before you leave, dispense with the cart you stole to bring her here. Can you handle that?"

The assassin said nothing.

"I can no longer risk accompanying you to the piers or being seen with you." She handed him a pouch with enough gold palmettes to pay for the journey to Thronehelm. "Take this and find Captain Lajos Kovi of a merchant ship called the *Bard*. He'll take you to your next destination."

Dru'Waith took the pouch and hid it in his armor.

"Oh," she added, pointing to Skullam, "and get that *thing* out of my fruit cellar."

ONCE OUTSIDE THE EMBASSY, Skullam turned to Incanus. The Bone elf had drawn his hood up and started to make his way toward the stables in the rear of the compound.

"What's next, my lord?" Skullam asked.

"I intend to miss the boat bound for Thronehelm," Incanus trudged away, not looking down at his companion.

"But my lord—"

"I'll take one of the horses from the stables and follow the Keeper and the Vermilion to Abacus. Can you fly?"

The imp flapped his wings and winced. "Yes."

"Excellent."

Skullam tugged at his master's cloak. "I'm sure I don't need to remind you that King Dragich won't be happy with this decision."

"Then don't." Incanus paused. "I've collected two skulls for the *new king* and only one for me, and the skull of a true Vermilion princess awaits. That means more to me than the skulls of a prince and a viscount."

Incanus knew he was wrong, but obsession pulled at his heart. It could be his last chance to claim her. She might never again come out from behind the walls of Eldwal.

Skullam stared at his master, seeming to ponder his decision.

"Besides," Incanus continued, "it's but a week to Thronehelm by boat, and there's no way for Kovi to signal Camber to tell her we didn't make it. By carriage, Camber won't reach Foghaven Vale for a fortnight. We have time."

Skullam smirked at the logic and the two left the embassy to steal a horse and ride for the grassy trail of Harbinger's Run.

CHAPTER EIGHT

"Never forget, the night belongs to the predator."
—Yaretzi the Haunted

"WHAT IS IT?" RITTER asked.

"Your hunting skills are uncanny." Marquiss shook his head as the two men field dressed a wild boar Silencer had dropped moments earlier. "Is it because of the falcon?"

"If I join with Storm, it shortens the hunt," Ritter replied. "But this time, it was just practiced skill."

The two prepared to load their dinner onto the back of Ritter's steed, but then Ritter noticed Marquiss slow and put down his end of the pig.

"I know Arjun's authority is final," Marquiss began, "but if I ride ahead, I can rally the Keldarin and members of the Emerald Shield to help. I know traveling through the forest will cost us some time, but it would be safer."

"The good captain doesn't seek safety," Ritter reminded him. "He seeks speed."

"I understand, but with a Vermilion princess, we're sure to be guarded, if not escorted by the Shield—and perhaps escorted by the Keldarin's Circle of Swords once we near Flowerdown Syphen."

"Syphen?"

"It's the Keldarin capital, to use your words," Marquiss explained. "Perhaps you've seen something similar in Ravenwood with your people."

Ritter shook his head. "Nay, Raven elves don't have settlements of any size. Attracts too many cryptids and trollborn from the Dragon's Breath Mountains. They're more nomadic. The largest settlement they have is Ravenshire, and that's nearly half human.

"The Syphen is a few days out of our way but is a safer trail. I fear we're making a mistake. I know the Keldarin coronel and his family from my time with them. I have no doubt that they'll help."

"Your time with them?" Ritter asked.

"Our father," Marquiss said, referring to both Faux and himself, "was a bit of a lothario. He had many children with women other than Faux's mother... and mine, for that matter."

"I see."

"I was never a child of Castleshire," Marquiss continued. "Our father had made me on one of his many travels to the Dalelands. I knew of Faux only after the fall of House Dauldon. Kester brought her to us for a time until bounty hunters came looking for her. It was somehow discovered that her father had close relations with the Keldarin, so the mercenaries sought her here. I fled with Arjun and Faux, as my bloodline may have proved fatal if I stayed."

"But you had nothing to do with—"

"I know, Ritter, but Castleshire's hunters didn't care. I have Dauldon blood in these trollborn veins. Arjun and I had to run with her. At that point, it was just Faux, Arjun, Burgess, and me. We stayed that way until we met Chernovog and Blue."

"Let me guess. In a tavern?"

Marquiss just smiled, affirming Ritter's intuition.

"I hear your concerns... and your idea has merit," Ritter said, returning to the original subject. "But we're already being followed by that beast, and maneuvering horses through a forest of thick trees would slow us down. He's faster than we are."

"You're a royal and so is the princess," Marquiss pointed out. "Is it time to pull rank on the captain?"

Ritter paused to consider the thought. It was a surprising question, but it was one that had value. Yet Ritter knew better than to cast the group into doubt. "Arjun knows this road and the way to Abacus better than any of us. I understand your concerns. Believe in the captain."

"I'll drop it under one condition," Marquiss smiled. "I need some help."

"With?"

"Jessamy," he started. "She's, uhh…"

Ritter's face lit up as he smiled. "You have an interest in the swordswoman?"

Marquiss shrugged.

"Do you and Blue have a few silver laurels on this?"

"I can't get a read on her," Marquiss continued, ignoring the question. "She turns me down and ignores my advances, but I still feel that she might be… open?"

"I'm not a good matchmaker." Ritter extended his hand to stop him from speaking any further. "I myself have trouble with matters of the heart."

"Perhaps you can ask the princess?" Marquiss interrupted, a coy smile appearing on his face. "I'm usually much better at these things. She just seems… well, you know."

"She's a Raven elf," Ritter stated. "I too have Raven blood in my veins, and I know our stubbornness can run deep."

"I'm not shy of a challenge. Will you help?"

"Marquiss, it isn't my—"

Marquiss cut him short. "Thanks, Valkeneer. I knew I could count on you. So, how about you and the princess?"

Ritter paused, not knowing how to respond, his face reddening. "It's forbidden."

"You're a hunter, Valkeneer," Marquiss admonished him. "Isn't the best hunt the hardest?"

SEVERAL DAYS PASSED AND the party traveled along Harbinger's Run for Abacus. The road was empty, which was unusual for the time of year, but that was a welcome surprise to the weary travelers. The fewer passersby, the sooner they'd reach their destination.

"What did Storm see?" Arjun asked as Ritter made his way back from patrol and into their makeshift camp. He and his falcon had been trailing the party, looking for signs of trouble.

"A few pilgrims on the road to Castleshire," Ritter replied. "But nothing in the grasslands. It seems we're safe tonight."

"Conney," Arjun said, "let Jericho guard the road and the rear tonight. Ritter, you and Storm should get some rest."

Blue nodded and sent the war dog off to attend to his evening duties.

Ritter meandered into camp and did his best not to complain. He'd taken the rear guard for the last four nights, without the benefits of warmth from the fire or the company of others, save for Storm. His mental link with Storm was draining when used often over a long period of time, and the last few nights had taken their toll. His head ached, his back was sore from the saddle and his heart longed to spend some time with Addilyn.

As he glanced around camp, he noticed her sitting alone and away from prying ears as she unraveled her bedroll for the night.

"Sir Ritter," Addilyn said, catching him before he could say anything. "I see you've returned."

"I have." He paused briefly before continuing. "May I sit with you for a moment?"

Addilyn slid over on her bedroll to give Ritter some room. He quickly sat down.

"No patrol for you and Storm tonight?"

"A needed rest." Ritter shrugged and pulled at a blade of grass. "Blue's dog is more than capable. His senses are as keen as Storm's and fatigue has dulled mine."

"Well then," Addilyn smiled, "enjoy your time around the fire."

"I've had a lot of time to myself while on watch these past few nights," he remarked. "One of the things that I've noticed, in a landscape filled with nothing but high grass, is a unique species that grows amongst it. Some might have to look for it, but it stood out to me."

"I didn't know you took notice of such things."

"I spend a lot of time in forests." Ritter gave a half-smile. "But this land is different from my home. I was unfamiliar with the grass, so I asked Marquiss about it. He said it's a plant called bluestem, although he calls it turkeyfoot."

Addilyn folded her arms over her knees and smiled again, waiting for him to continue.

"He said the name comes from this time of year." Ritter slid closer to Addilyn and peered around the camp to ensure that no curious eyes were upon them. "Bluestem blooms blue in the spring, turns golden in the summer, and sprouts red in the fall. Its flowers looking more like a turkey's foot than the grass around it."

"I haven't noticed."

"I found it to be a beautiful and interesting plant," Ritter continued. "So, I made you this during one of my nights alone under the stars."

He reached into his pouch and removed a small, circular wreath that he'd made from the golden reeds of the plains, the reddish blooms of the turkeyfoot woven within the circlet. Addilyn's face revealed her surprise as she took the token from him and looked closely at it.

"The blooms remind me of your hair in the moonlight," Ritter whispered. "The way you can still see the red, even against the darkness of night."

Addilyn's nose wrinkled, and she smiled with a tenderness that stole his breath. Their eyes met, and every instinct inside him told him to lean in and kiss her. Their passion was tangible, and he didn't care who else knew. But he knew that she did.

"Ritter, I…" Addilyn began, and then she stopped. He knew at that moment that he'd made her happy.

She smiled bashfully and lowered her eyes.

"My lady," he said with a bow, and then he left her before their closeness aroused suspicion.

THE ATMOSPHERE AMONG THE party had grown tense and ragged as the long days wore on. Although all of them had braved longer journeys, the lack of rest after the events of the previous weeks combined with the ever-present lurking danger of the Antlered Man was wearing their endurance thin. Delling and Arjun remained the calmest, trained officers that they were, but even they found it hard to keep up morale as the road wore on and on with the end never seeming any nearer.

Daemus, for his part, was the most on edge he'd been since the days of his endless recurring nightmares at the Cathedral. Visions seemed to flicker constantly at the edges of his vision, and he was unsure if they were dream-fragments, hallucinations from lack of sleep, or the Sight. He was starting to think that perhaps one day he would not be able to see what was in front of his face at all, that Erud might simply decide to only let him see the future until he was as blind as he had been at birth. There would be a kind of poetry to it, he recognized sickly. He had to rely on muttered conversations with Delling to be sure what was real and what wasn't, and the feeling of not being in control of his own hands or feet was even worse. Today there was a corpse flitting around in the corner of his eye, a man with a cutthroat who followed the movement of his gaze every time he tried to look away. Daemus was sweating, though the late afternoon air was chilly, and he could hardly bear the prospect of sleeping in his damp clothes. His hands shook slightly at his reins, which was making his horse irritable and tense. For a short time, Daemus considered how hard he would be able to throw himself from his horse, and if the resulting injury would be bad enough to allow the Antlered Man to catch up with him and tear him limb from limb.

"Let's break for camp," Arjun ordered. Nightfall was near and the group had found a small gulley that offered cover from the road, as well as any prying eyes that might pass while they slept. It was also home to a small stream that provided fresh water and a chance for them to clean themselves after a dusty day on the pass. "Marquiss, why don't you take first watch?"

"Certainly." He stepped away from the camp and began to sweep the area, looking for anything that could surprise them.

"So, now that we're close to Abacus, have you had any thoughts on what you're going to say to the Athabasica when you see her?" Daemus asked Arjun. He moved and sat on a stump near the captain.

"Of course," he replied, seeming caught off guard by the young man's frankness. "I… I've missed her. There's too much to say. I fear she'll refuse to see us because of my presence."

Daemus blinked, trying to remember if he'd been told that when he'd met Arjun. He didn't think so. "But you aren't from there?"

Arjun nodded slowly. "Not originally. I was a slave before I came to the city, sold off to a family in Queen's Prey to pay off a debt my father owed. Abacus though is a freeman's city, and is filled with scholars and merchants, many curious people, some of them with looser morals than others. One old man tried to trick me into entering his service as a poison-tester, and another man lied to me that the schools were full and there would be no place for me, and so I'd better take a position in his house and consent to be paid less than the value of the room and board I received as a slave."

"What did you do?" Daemus asked.

"Finally, though, I ended up being conscripted by the High Aldin... along with another former slave who became my good friend. We were both sent to the school, which did have a place for both of us, as it turned out."

Arjun's hand was worrying at a long scar on one of his arms, which made Daemus suppress a shiver. When he looked at Faux, her expression was stony.

"Willingly conscripted?" asked Daemus, sensing something odd. Arjun blinked.

"To a slave, there is hardly any such thing as will. Or if there is, it is twisted up with many other things. I was free, but in my mind, I was still a slave." He moved on, seeming unbothered by the question or his own simple but disturbing reply.

"I performed well in my training and caught the eye of an upper-level servant of House Dauldon who was visiting the city. He came to me and said that the Dauldons needed good men, and that if I agreed to serve them when my training was finished, I could remain a free man, with my own home and maybe my own family, and I would not have to stand around all day guarding the city or end up getting sent to the front lines of a war. I don't know if I believed him or not... but what he described sounded good.

"My friend and I, the other slave who was conscripted with me, we... we had fallen in love with each other. We both knew it could have no future; we were being trained for different things by the High Aldin, and she wanted to stay in Abacus, and I felt compelled to serve House Dauldon, which is why I chose to leave." Arjun's hand went to his chest, briefly gripping something that looked like a pendant. "Our parting was… not as amicable as it might have been. But I think she knew that I still loved her."

"After I left to serve House Dauldon, I found that I liked the family… I always knew that I could have left, could have returned to Abacus to be with… but as the years passed, I found more and more that I wanted to stay, that my will was to serve the family and to take care of the people who had changed my life and offered me the closest thing to true freedom I had ever known. I worked hard for them for many years, happily, until I was promoted to captain of the guard. And then, only a year later, the house was struck by misfortune." He glanced at Faux, who met his eyes flatly; Daemus saw him frown a little in response.

"Your fellow slave—former slave," Princess Addilyn corrected herself, "she is the Athabasica?"

Arjun offered a shallow nod. "She quickly rose to the top of our class. Her battle strategy even came in handy at Homm Hill, where she bribed Misael of Clan Blood Axe. Misael turned on the clan's then leader, Dragomir Jair, and Homm Hill was won."

"That is the part of the story you told me." Daemus poked at the fire, hoping for more.

Arjun ignored him, staring into the distance. "In truth, she's always been a better fighter than I, and a born leader."

"So, she's a master swordswoman, like you?"

Arjun paused for a moment to track a distant flock of birds as they took flight and flocked to the sky. "The two of us could outfight our entire class at times." He smiled at the memory. "Literally twenty against two. We'd stand back-to-back, our swords swinging in perfect harmony. It was as though we were in each other's heads."

"Like Ritter and Storm?" Daemus joked.

"Not exactly," the captain replied, still smiling. "I've done my fair share of spying on her. From a distance, that is."

"What do you mean?"

"I've learned of her ascension over the years," Arjun explained. "It came as no surprise to me that a former slave had risen to the office of Athabasica. She's clever and thoughtful. It's a role she was born to play. I've watched many of Castleshire's leaders blustering on, rising... and falling. She's smart enough to be practical and to hold her own among rulers, but she has the endearment of a poet, and aloof enough to run a city of freethinkers. She's... she's, well..."

"And the reason you never mentioned any of this to us?" Faux's voice was sharp, every line of her body tense with anger. "For all these years?"

Arjun looked at her again, seeming carefully blank. "It was a private matter, until now." He took a moment. "I wonder about her poetry." He looked to the ground and away from Faux. "It was her true passion. Each night, I wonder what she's written about. I ask myself whether the pain I felt when leaving her is reflected in her words. I never meant to hurt her, yet I knew we couldn't be together."

"As a woman, I assure you she would have felt your pain thrice over," Addilyn offered.

"Aye." Arjun nodded, knowingly. "And I assure you, her quill was always more powerful than her sword." He paused and appeared to consider his next words. "I wrote a poem for her. I promised myself that if I ever saw her again, I'd read it to her. I keep it close to my heart."

He pulled at the small pendant tucked under his armor

and gazed at it as though his greatest worldly treasure was held inside it.

"May I read it?" Daemus asked.

"Nay." Arjun's face contorted in mixed emotion. "It's for her only."

"I understand."

Faux made a face Daemus had never seen an adult make before, a face like a child being told she had to apologize. "You speak of her as if she's a goddess," Faux blurted. "Be careful not to stir the jealousy of Illustra, the Ancient of Love. She might curse you and turn you into a toad."

Addilyn cracked a weak smile at him. "I look forward to meeting her. You speak so highly of her it's a wonder you were able to leave her at all. Do you regret it?"

Arjun's face drew down into a serious stare, and Daemus could see the princess had struck a chord.

"I have a favor to ask." Arjun turned back to Faux, without answering Addilyn.

"What is it?" she asked, with a tone still in her voice.

"If I fall in battle before we reach her, would you give this to her?" Arjun lifted the pendant, and as Daemus looked closer, he realized it was a scroll necklace. The scroll inside had to be small, perhaps the size a pigeon could deliver.

The anger in Faux's face turned to confusion. She blinked.

Daemus shook his head. "Arjun, don't talk like that."

"Promise me," Arjun begged, not listening to Daemus and staring at Faux.

Faux sighed. "I promise. But in a few days, you can read it to her yourself."

"If we make it."

"*When* we make it," Daemus pressed.

"When we make it," Arjun repeated, "I won't need to read

it to her. I know the words by heart." He smiled and tucked the tiny scroll necklace back into his armor. "After I left, she never spoke to me again. No letters, no missives, and no contact. I know it broke her heart, but duty called. I promised to return when my service was up, and now I return having broken that promise, still in the service of the family I chose over her love."

"No woman will deny a man a chance to speak with a story like that." Faux's voice calmed. "You know of my love for Jaxtyn, as well as his love for me. Love can be eternal, even when people make choices that run counter to it. Remember, if it hadn't been for you and Kester, I'd be dead. Perhaps once Anoki knows the truth about what you've done and sacrificed for me, my family, and now Daemus and the realm, she'll understand. Once she sees Daemus and hears his story, she'll help. And she'll forgive."

"Midday tomorrow we should be seeing the Eternal Forest to the east," put in Marquiss, trying to lighten the tension a little. "Perhaps I should ride ahead, speak to the Keldarin."

"A detour into the forest would cost us time," Arjun replied as a statement of fact rather than a directive, but the undertone of command was clear, nonetheless.

The night continued in silence as the sky slowly began to darken. The blue color and Arjun's story of love suddenly made Daemus think of the young healer who had attended them at the inn, the priestess with the indigo hair. Katja.

Why he was thinking about her, he couldn't have said, other than that she'd been friendly and Daemus had had precious little of that for most of his life. As he considered it, the uncomfortable notion arose that the thought might have been put there by Erud. At that thought, Daemus put her out of his mind and prayed that he never saw her again. The more significant she was to his visions, the more likely it was that her life was in danger. Daemus knew it didn't make any sense to try and direct the future using his thoughts, but it hardly made any less sense than anything else he felt now. Trying to protect an innocent girl who had been kind to him was the least he could do.

Vaguely, he registered Blue and Marquiss chatting alone. "Have done with your gossip, man, the dog and I need to be back at the rear," Blue was saying with a laugh.

"Isn't gossip if it's true." Marquiss smirked and raised his eyebrows. "I've seen the two of 'em talking when they think no one else is awake."

"Maybe they're friends," Blue's face quirked, exasperated, but not enough for anger.

"Act like more than friends if you ask me. Like maybe something closer to Arjun and his, uh, friend." Marquiss waggled his eyebrows. "Perhaps the Vermilion will be looking at a new little prince come summer, after all this is done. Do you think?"

From near the woods, Daemus noticed Jessamy returning from a sweep and watched with alarm as she drew her sword and came very near to Marquiss.

"Hold your tongue," said the Raven elf in an icy tone, "you simpering little worm."

Marquiss sputtered. Daemus froze. He would never have thought Jessamy, little though he knew her, to be one for sudden outbursts of violence, but her demeanor radiated danger.

"It was a joke!" Marquiss was protesting, and Jessamy's blade lifted closer to his throat.

"I'll teach you to joke, dog!" The elf's eyes were wide with rage.

"Jessamy!" barked the princess, white-faced. "What do you think you're doing?"

Immediately, as if she were a puppet whose strings had

been cut, Jessamy's blade withdrew, and her arms fell to her sides. She sheathed her sword. "My lady."

"What are you doing?" Addilyn demanded again. Daemus had never seen the woman, almost always impeccably composed, in such a state of agitation.

"There's no time," cut in Ritter, looking from Addilyn to Jessamy and then at Daemus. "Storm caught sight of our pursuer—that beast. It's close—very close, maybe half a day away. We need to go."

"Looks like we'll be riding through the night, then." Arjun stood and grimaced, then turned to Delling. "You'll look after the boy?"

Delling nodded, shooting Daemus a reassuring glance.

"I'll cast an illusion," offered Addilyn, at last shifting her attention away from Jessamy. "Maybe that will confuse it. Buy us some time."

"Then you should cast it before we leave here," Ritter said, pointing in their new direction. "If this cryptid tracks like most predators, it will look for broken branches on our old path instead of following the seam of the road."

At Arjun's nod, she moved her horse a little way away and raised her hands.

"*Misser banaen ikke folger,*" she incanted, and then made a gesture as if she were twisting something apart. A soft hiss sounded in the air, and the trail left by the horses suddenly seemed to warp and turn off to the west in a hale of green magic. The terrain sweltered with an illusory spellcraft, painting the land that lay untouched by their horses.

Daemus's nose filled with the smell of resinous, woody pulp of pine needles, though they didn't grow anywhere near Harbinger's Run.

"And I thought Ritter was the one that had all the tricks," Daemus muttered in amazement with the spell's effects.

"It's meant to enchant the ground and confuse those that follow." Addilyn rode up beside Daemus. "Come now, Master Alaric," she said with a twinkle in her eye. "Ride by my side and I'll show you the ways of the Vermilion."

"On our way, now," said Arjun, his voice urgent. "There's no time to lose."

109

CHAPTER NINE

*"Casting lots to choose our Great Keeper, for this
seminal time, is an act of commitment to ourselves, one
keeper to another, and to the realm of W.arminster."*
—First Keeper Amoss D'brielle

RADU WATCHED THE YOUNG LOW KEEPER Caspar
Luthic as he and a few others herded the gryphs from one safe
spot to another. The stables had to be cleared, and moving the
animals, supplies, and other necessities had become common.
The boy had a way with the unpredictable gryphs, the likes
of which he had never seen. Gryphs possessed different
personalities, similar to horses—their half cousins—and it
took more than patience to win their trust.

A long night and an even longer day passed by for the
cathedral and all within its walls. The broken sacrament of
The Tome of Enlightenment, the blindness of the Keepers of
the Forbidden, and the unsettled relationships amongst the
sects of the Divine Protectorate of Erud had the campus on a
knife's edge. Soon, they would reconvene.

"Precept Radu," a familiar, though weary voice called from
a few yards back. Radu turned to find First Keeper Amoss
slowly making his way toward him.

Radu greeted him with as much strength as he could
muster. "You need sleep, Amoss."

The First Keeper shook his head. "I am here to ask a favor
and join in my vigil. I cannot sleep with so much at stake."

"Of course." Radu turned and walked abreast with Amoss
as they moved back toward Quehm's Hallow.

"It pains me to ask," Amoss went on, his eyes trained on
the rubble around them. "If…" He took a deep breath. "If

things should go in a certain direction—a direction against us—would you insert yourself into the company of the one that is chosen tonight by the conclave? The new Great Keeper?"

Radu stopped, his steps faltering. Never did he expect a man like Amoss to ask him to essentially spy.

"I know," Amoss sighed heavily, beckoning Radu to keep up with him. "You do not have to speak. You do not have to advise. And you don't have a vote as precept. Thus, beyond reproach."

"What about you?" Radu asked, concern lacing his tone. *Does Amoss think something more nefarious is afoot?*

"Just a precaution," Amoss said softly. "Like the others, the Sight has left me. I have been too dependent on it these past years. Now, we must rely on our own instincts for a time."

"And if you are nominated?" Radu asked.

Amoss smiled. "Then I will be glad to share your company."

RADU GLANCED AROUND THE chamber and saw that his brothers and sisters had gathered from all over Warminster. The Keepers of the Forbidden reconvened in their conclave, deep within the halls of Quehm's Hallow at the foot of the fallen Cathedral of the Watchful Eye. Here they would choose their new Great Keeper, and for the first time in their history, they'd do it without *The Tome of Enlightenment* and the wisdom of Erud. It was a grand sight to behold.

He noticed a new figure, Jhodever, the First Keeper of the newly formed Kingdom of Foghaven Vale. His eyes roamed slowly over the room, taking in the faces of many Keepers he hadn't seen in some time. Radu hadn't seen Jhodever in years, but the man was largely unchanged. Still tall and thin, yet his youthful glow had faded.

Amoss approached Jhodever, patting him on the back. "Glad to see you made it, old friend."

"I'm sorry it took me an extra day," Jhodever replied. "The roads to and from the Vale are harried these days. We took all the necessary precautions."

"Well, you're here now." Amoss smiled. "I didn't want to proceed without you. The responsibility of this choice hangs heavy around each of our necks."

"A burden but also a blessing," Jhodever countered, his tone light and hopeful. "Erud surely looks upon us this evening."

Amoss forced a half-smile onto his face, but Radu knew they shared the same thought within the solitary confines of their own mind: doubt.

"Forgive me, my friend." Amoss pointed to an empty chair. "But I must begin. Please, take a seat."

The two embraced for a moment and then Jhodever sat, disappearing into the crowd of robed figures that filled the hall. Amoss retreated to his seat and looked somberly at the First Keepers. He also caught a glance from High Watcher Obexx, who sat a few feet behind him alongside Captain Hague.

With a quick tap of his gavel, the room fell to near silence, a nervous energy filling the chamber.

"Fellow First Keepers," he began, "we're here this evening to choose a new Great Keeper from our ranks. We must do this without the guidance of Erud, something that's never before happened in the long history of the Keepers of the Forbidden. Worse, we must do this while coming to terms with tragedy beneath the shadow of the stars that fell. We must do this while grieving for the dead, including Nasyr."

A low murmuring of mixed prayers and hopeful well-wishes broke his stride. He raised his hand and quieted the Hallow in short order.

"To begin this process, we must hear from you, our First Keepers," Amoss advised. "I ask that you nominate a First

Keeper to assume the role of Great Keeper, one that will lead us in recovery. One that will lead us with hope."

Portia Brecken, the First Keeper of the Crown Islands, rose amidst a dull rapping of knuckles on the squared tables of the conclave. She lifted her hand to silence the applause.

"I rise this evening," she began, "with the distinct honor of nominating a longtime friend. I speak of one who's guided generations of our brothers and sisters toward the wisdom and knowledge of Erud. One who can recite the names of two generations of Keepers, from the lowest to the highest of our order, that he himself has helped to train and educate. One who's dedicated his life and soul to the study of our sect and to the sanctity it provides to all of Warminster. I rise tonight to nominate Amoss D'Brielle, the First Keeper of the Cathedral."

Amoss nodded his head appreciatively, then turned his gaze to the crowd as the throng of First Keepers rapped their knuckles on the table in approval of the nomination.

"First Keeper Amoss, do you accept our nomination?" Portia asked.

"Proudly," Amoss replied to more rapping of knuckles and a handful of claps. "Thank you, First Keeper Brecken. May I ask for any other nominees?"

A small mist of relief escaped Radu's lungs. Surely even Erud would have considered sanctioning Amoss. The man was a proud traditionalist, wise, well educated, and many in the cathedral admired him. Radu almost smiled. Amoss had nothing to worry about. He need not have asked Radu to be his eyes and ears should someone else take the position.

A measured silence fell about the hall for several seconds. Seeing no others rising, he reached for his gavel, hoping to call for a vote.

"Pardon me, First Keeper."

Amoss turned to see Obexx glaring, standing with a finger in the air. "I have a name."

"You're not a Keeper," Radu voiced, calmly. "You have no power to nominate a successor within the halls of the Hallow." He was waiting for this. He knew deep down Obexx would not forsake the chance to irritate Amoss, even if it only delayed the inevitable.

"I'm not nominating anyone," Obexx replied, refusing to take his seat. "I only want to say a few words." He cleared his throat and spoke a little louder. "There are matters happening around the realm of Warminster that many of you don't know of. You are not only blind to the Sight but sheltered here in these once hallowed halls."

"High Watcher..." Amoss murmured, an air of warning in his tone as he reigned in his rising aggravation.

"We all have our gifts," Obexx continued. "We all may see the will of Erud in our own ways. We need a wider vision."

The murmurs started afresh, quiet and soft, but rising. Radu squirmed in his seat, his blood beginning to boil.

"A Disciple cannot speak in this chamber," First Keeper Brecken warned.

"We must not fight amongst our sects," Jhodever pleaded from amidst their ranks. He stood and raised his hand for silence. "This is not the way." He glared at Obexx. "The High Watcher was merely making a point, I am sure. Yes, he is not a First Keeper, but that does not mean we should silence him."

All eyes fell on Jhodever and some even nodded in understanding.

"Thank you, brother," Amoss said with an exasperated sigh.

A few moments of silence followed as those who had risen took their seats again.

Obexx half-smirked but his eyes lit up with gratitude for Jhodever. "Thank you for hearing me, First Keeper, but I wish

I could have spoken sooner. For it is you I wish to nominate."

Jhodever looked to Obexx, an expression of surprise on his face. Another nervous silence fell over the Hallow. Radu's eyes sharpened, and his head cocked to the side. His mind began to race to catch up to Obexx's plan.

"High Watcher, I need you to sit and be silent as our order decides the fate of its leadership." Amoss's tone was polite this time. "I needn't remind you that you're here as a witness to these proceedings only. You are not a participant. I wouldn't presume to interfere with the elections of the Disciples, the Maelstrom Knights, or the Deacons. I ask for the same courtesy, nay, respect."

Obexx locked eyes with Amoss and slowly, almost mockingly, took his seat before folding his hands in his lap.

"Thank you," Amoss replied. "I ask again, are there any other nominations?"

Tarrant Cynric, the First Keeper of the Sea Kingdom, rose and paused for a moment. His eyes traced from Obexx to Jhodever. "After hearing the thoughts of the High Watcher yesterday," Cynric began, "I've spent much time in prayer and introspection. A great tragedy has befallen our order. It was a tragedy that could perhaps have been prevented. A tragedy that should have been seen by the Great Keeper and perhaps others in our sect, including myself."

The mood in the chamber changed, with many of the onlookers turning a serious look to Tarrant Cynric. Radu's eyes, however, never left Obexx.

"I'm sure many of you had similar thoughts overnight," Cynric continued. "The starfall and the disappearance of the Tome lead me to question if..." He took a deep breath, eyeing his audience. "If Obexx is correct. Maybe it's time to find a new perspective?"

The room broke out with banter and debate, but Amoss gaveled the crowd down and raised his voice. "First Keeper Cynric," Amoss said, "I return the floor to you. Do you have a nomination?"

"I do," Cynric replied. "My instinct was to nominate the First Keeper who first identified the boy, Daemus Alaric, and who brought him to us here in Solemnity as an initiate. He seems critical to our communication with Erud. But since First Keeper Aliferis Makai hasn't returned to the cathedral for this conclave, perhaps my instinct was incorrect."

"First Keeper Makai isn't absent by choice," Danton Hague offered. "I was in Castleshire when Lady Chessborough offered his services to the Kingdom of Warminster in an attempt to prevent civil war. He left to help Daemus and to replace the dead First Keeper Samuels. If First Keeper Cynric wishes to nominate him, I can take my gryph to the skies and have Makai back here in under a week with the right winds."

Radu appreciated the help Hague was offering to the tense gathering of Keepers. At least someone was trying to keep the peace.

"Thank you, Captain," Cynric said, "but I'm not going to nominate Makai. It seems he's made his own choice."

"Are you sure?" Hague pressed.

"Aye," Cynric replied, waving a gentle hand toward the captain.

Hague stepped back and took his seat.

"While Makai would be a fine candidate," Cynric suggested, "the Keepers of the Forbidden can't go another week, let alone another day, without resolving this matter. I believe it's time to choose a leader. As we've seen today, there is one among us who might be right to lead us in this time."

For the first time that day, a complete silence filled the chamber as they awaited the name. Radu's nervous fingers tapped the armchairs as he waited.

"And to that end, I nominate Jhodever of Foghaven Vale."

Jhodever looked up from where he had bowed his head onto his folded hands.

Again, a quiet susurrus seized the room, with murmurs between First Keepers rising from the crowd.

"He's been a loyal servant," Cynric continued, "and I've personally benefitted from our exchanges over the years. He's been kind and open to the people of the Sea Kingdom, and if he's also acceptable to the Disciples of the Watch, perhaps he's the correct choice. In this unprecedented time, we all need to trust in each other until the Great Book has been recovered. This is a compromise that, with the collected wisdom of this table, granted by the graces of Erud, everyone here can agree to."

The Hallow erupted with debate as Radu sat for a moment in his chair, exchanging glances with Amoss, First Keeper Brecken and then turning to glare at Obexx.

Obexx didn't reciprocate, instead nodding in approval to Cynric. The lines around his eyes tightened as if he fought to keep a smile off his face.

Amoss stood and gaveled the group down one last time. He returned their stares before looking at a tentative Jhodever, whose countenance remained calm but serious.

"First Keeper Jhodever," Amoss started. "You've been nominated for the post of Great Keeper. Are you willing to accept the nomination?"

Jhodever rose from his corner and appeared to ponder the thought. After a moment of silence, he said, "It's with a heavy heart that this comes to me. I personally don't want to run against my longtime friend and mentor, First Keeper Amoss. He's my former prefect and teacher, but I do agree with First Keeper Cynric. I see the wisdom in new leadership. Because of that, I humbly accept this nomination."

Amoss reached for the gavel and Radu too expected to hear the roar of the chamber, but the Hallow remained dead silent save for the crackling of the fire in the hearth. Amoss lowered the gavel and looked at Jhodever.

Jhodever matched his gaze but said nothing, allowing his remarks to settle.

"If there are no more nominations then it's time for us to cast our lots."

The gravity of Amoss's solemn words fell onto Radu ears. He could sense the room turning.

Hearing none, Amoss started around the table. Radu watched with pensive eyes as Amoss asked each First Keeper to rise and announce their vote. The ceremony had changed slightly. Typically, a First Keeper would rise, raise their hand, and cut their thumb. As the blood flowed—and just as Erud marked *The Tome of Enlightenment* with a never-diminishing thumbprint—the Keepers would bloody the first page of a new Great Keeper with their own thumbprints, casting their votes. Radu witnessed the ritual only a few times. Now, he suspected he'd never see it again. Things had changed and those like him could only stand by and watch. Each Keeper rose and announced their choice while Amoss kept tally. Each name felt like the ringing of a death knell.

"First Keeper Cynric," Amoss began.

"I vote Jhodever."

"Recorded," Amoss said.

He proceeded to take count of the votes of the Conclave. Every last Keeper stood, muttered or called out Jhodever's name, and sat back down. Amoss came to his friend, Portia Brecken. Radu caught Amoss looking across the table at her as she rose, and the pair exchanged glances. She hadn't even spoken the words before Amoss's shoulders fell. He nodded in defeat.

"Jhodever," Brecken announced, giving the First Keeper of Foghaven Vale enough votes to win.

Amoss finished recording the votes around the table, finally arriving at himself. From where he sat, Radu saw no other names on the parchment. Amoss's hand paused above it, not shaking but hesitating. The tally was unanimous for Jhodever.

Radu knew the historical gravity of breaking unanimity in times of strife, and he could see it pressing down on Amoss. But the First Keeper swallowed his pride for the sake of the order and rose.

"I vote for the next Great Keeper, Jhodever of Foghaven Vale." Amoss's voice was resolute, filled with strength, even if it meant he'd lost.

Instead of applause, the great conclave sat in silence, with hands covering mouths and faces that were bowed in shame. Radu turned to Hague to see the captain staring at his feet. His eyes sought Obexx next, and he found him sitting with a guilty smile, his countenance hidden in the obscurity of the shadows.

CHAPTER TEN

"Valor holds fast the shields of green
before the defenseless."
—Amira Killian, Lord Protector of Queen's Prey

DAEMUS WAS UNEASY. TWO days ago, his visions, which had become so frequent they seemed to be overtaking the reality before his eyes, had ceased. He had been staring at his horse's teardrop-shaped ears, trying to ignore the image of a pool surrounded by rocks that sat by the side of the road and followed the party as they traveled. When Delling caught his attention with something, he'd looked directly at it, only to find it had disappeared.

At first, he had been grateful for the reprieve, feeling that Erud must have realized he needed some rest from the constant, harrowing barrage of waking dreams. But even back when his gifts had been at their weakest and easiest to ignore, he'd still always had prophetic dreams while he slept, even if they turned out to be related only to trivial matters. The first night, saw blurry figures enacting nonsense rituals, so random and divorced from reality that he knew beyond a doubt it was no vision. Last night, he had not dreamed at all.

Despite his suffering during the first part of the journey, Daemus found that he liked the absence of communication even less. A creeping dread had begun to overtake him, combined with a prickle of anger that he could not remember feeling before. Had he somehow failed to act on his visions properly and caused the Ancient to give up on him? How could that be fair? He hadn't even been told what he needed to do! Here he was, acting on the single clear directive he'd been given, dragging his exhausted companions through an otherwise arbitrary journey, and still, it didn't seem to be enough.

In a fit of pique, he flicked at a fly crawling on his horse's neck, sending it spinning into the air.

Delling, riding near him, made a face.

"What?" snapped Daemus with a glare, then almost immediately looked down. None of this was Delling's fault; the man had been nothing but kind to him, even though Daemus felt he had offered little in return.

"Was it an omen?" asked Delling, his tone mild. "You have that look on your face again, like your soul is worn."

Daemus started to shake his head, then stopped. "Might as well be."

"Meaning?"

"My oneiromancy has... stopped." Daemus hadn't intended to tell anyone that, but Delling had a way of getting him to say things he didn't plan to. "Nothing at all for the past couple of days."

"I see."

Daemus glanced at Delling. His expression was interested and sympathetic, but decidedly neutral. At that Daemus felt better—even if only slightly so. Delling, at least, didn't appear to think it an emergency, which was better than Daemus's complete cluelessness at how to interpret Erud's unexplained silence.

"It's like I'm a toy," Daemus raged, the words spilling out of his throat almost before he had time to think them. "I never get a choice in anything. The Ancients treat us like we're—" His eyes burned; he took a different tack. "First, I have so many visions I can barely see outside of them. Then it's as though Erud thinks I would rather see nothing at all. As if I could ever be good for anything else."

Delling frowned at that, but Daemus looked away, embarrassed, and continued, "We have prayers and supplications to beg for blessings whenever they see fit. We're never asked what we want. And now Erud won't even speak to me at all!"

He swallowed, then said in a smaller voice, "I'm sorry."

"No need to apologize," Delling demurred.

Daemus checked his face, unsure, but the man looked as though he meant it.

"Life is something different for those touched by the Ancients," the Disciple went on. "I think the rest of us often don't understand what it's like. Erud has been with you for your whole life, both a blessing and perhaps a curse at times, but their presence has become a part of who you are. Of course you feel angry and betrayed when they suddenly seem to be gone. Doesn't that make sense?"

Daemus gripped his saddle horn. "But Erud isn't a person," he said. "Ancients don't behave like people."

Delling inclined his head, not disagreeing. "You're still a human. You think of these things like any other person would. Since the Ancients are inscrutable to us, all we can do is interpret and respond to what they do in whatever way we are able. You are not being blasphemous, Daemus, you are being honest."

"It doesn't feel right," muttered Daemus, his eyes still hot with tears. He blinked them back.

"Look over there." Delling pointed at two of their companions a little way up the road. Arjun and Faux rode side by side, talking, seeming more at ease than Daemus recalled seeing them since the start of their journey. Daemus paused to listen, and with a little focus was able to make out what they were saying.

"I'm sorry I did not tell you sooner," Arjun was saying in his grave way. "I've never told anyone by choice... I didn't know how to bring it up. I never wished to make you feel as though I don't trust you."

"No, I understand." Faux shook her head a little. "It was just never the right time."

"You see?" Daemus turned to Delling, who was looking at him expectantly, and frowned.

"I'm not sure." The young Keeper mumbled.

"Erud has not abandoned you, Daemus, not after being with you for your entire life, not after asking so much of you and giving so much to you. Our Ancient will speak to you again of the right things, in the right way, when it is the right time." Delling smiled, however slight. "Though I wouldn't bet on getting an apology."

Daemus snorted softly, then regarded Delling a moment. "Thank you," he said, with as much sincerity in his voice as he could muster.

The older man reached over to grip his shoulder." I'm going to go speak to Marquiss. He said we'll be reaching the Eternal Forest soon, and I wanted to know if there is anything particular about the Keldarin that we should know before talking to them. Don't want to offend."

"Let me know what he says."

The sound of a dog's howl startled them, and Daemus looked backward, heart pounding. His eyes scanned the horizon and he thought he could make out a spindly figure in the distance. It moved oddly, like a puppet with its strings cut. He knew it instantly.

"It's found us," he managed, his voice blank. "The Antlered Man is here."

He felt a bizarre rush of something like relief. After seeing it in his dreams, he'd known that one day it would catch up to him, and to finally see it before his eyes made him feel strangely reassured, like he was seeing the sun rise again after becoming unsure of its return sometime during the night.

But the relief was followed by terror. Delling ordered him off his horse and Daemus scrambled down to the ground. The nervous animal bolted the second his hands came off the reins. Shaking, Daemus fumbled for his mace. The group was shouting, but he couldn't make out what they were saying. After a few moments, several of his comrades stepped out in front of him. Ritter looked back and tried valiantly to shoot him a reassuring smile. He didn't quite succeed, but Daemus's spirit was bolstered when he saw Blue and Jericho bounding up the road, still alive.

"How did it find us?" muttered Marquiss.

"Creature of magic," Addilyn complained, her brow furrowing. "It can't be hunting us by normal means, or it would have been fooled by my spell."

"Maybe your spell didn't work at all?" Marquiss shot back, on edge.

The princess ignored him, her eyes intent on the beast in the distance.

A high-pitched, trilling whistle sounded in the air, lowering in pitch until it sounded like a chicken, then like an awful, deep, clicking drone that reminded Daemus of bones breaking. His entire body shuddered. Was Ritter's bow glowing?

"Princess." Arjun voice was calm but urgent. "Now, I think."

Addilyn nodded and launched into a series of fast, fluid arm movements. *"Retirada lentamente,"* she intoned in the conjurer's tongue.

A few interminable moments later, her hands flashed, and a ball of energy that seemed to bound like a rabbit hurtled at the creature.

As Daemus watched, it hit the Antlered Man, and the whining, clicking call came again.

"What was that?" Daemus asked in a whisper.

Addilyn was sweating now with concentration, her attention fixed on maintaining her spell, so Arjun answered, "It's too fast and too strong. We can't weaken it easily, so we thought to slow it down. Should last until the princess loses her focus, which she says will give us enough time to defeat it." His voice sounded steady, but his scarred face was pale.

Daemus looked at the Antlered Man again. It had slowed down, its unnatural movements labored now as if it was walking through honey.

With a soft command from Arjun, the party rushed forward to flank the creature while Addilyn, Daemus, and Delling remained where they were.

The attack looked well-coordinated. Ritter took a position a little way off, readying his shining bow, while Marquiss, Blue, Jessamy, Arjun, and Faux moved in on all sides.

"Maybe we made a mistake waiting this long," murmured Daemus. "We could have hunted it down ourselves, before now, and had the element of surprise." Delling only glanced at him, his eyes unreadable.

The assault began. The five warriors moved as a unit, unpolished but prepared, two of them at a time dancing in and out to chop at the creature's arms and legs. The Antlered Man clawked in a droning, languid call. It stumbled, swiping at them with its sharp claws, even kicking at Jessamy with its goat-like hind legs, but Addilyn's spell had worked. It was too slow to land a hit and could barely defend itself. Jessamy shouted something in Ravenish and leapt onto the creature's back, stabbing her blade into its shoulder, as Ritter fired off a shot. The arrow leapt from Silencer, imbued with the bow's peculiar glow, and buried itself into the Antlered Man's chest. The cryptid screamed, an ethereal wail that stopped the attackers and forced Daemus to cover his ears. The bow had an effect the blades hadn't.

But Daemus heard Addilyn's sharp cry to his right, her concentration on the spell broken from the shriek. The hale of the magic's effects dimmed.

A fire rose in the creature and the air of the battle changed. The Antlered Man ignored its closest assailants, instead focusing on moving closer to Ritter. Fumbling to ready another arrow, the ranger backed away.

"Ritter, run!" barked Arjun. "Turn and run!"

Clawking, as if pleased, the Antlered Man swept its arms in a semi-circle, once, twice, sending its assailants flying. Only Jessamy managed to hang on. When it reached to grab her, Jessamy leapt from his back and escaped, her sword falling to the ground. She landed and rolled, picking her blade from the grass, making the maneuver look effortless.

Ritter took the opportunity to scramble away and aimed with Silencer again. This time, Daemus could see the Longmarcher honed-in, and he loosed another shot. The ensorceled arrow streaked through the night sky, a greenish tail of white-hot light behind it. His shot hit its mark, and struck the Antlered Man in the eye. The vile beast screamed, its piercing cry stopping its assailants in their tracks again. Ritter winced, covered his ears, and dropped to his knees. Silencer fell harmlessly to the ground as he moaned in pain.

Daemus swallowed some vomit that managed to make its way up his throat.

It wasn't dead. How wasn't it dead? And the spell was broken.

The creature turned from the stunned Ritter and stared for a moment at Daemus, its lone eye meeting the Keeper's gaze. It would be on top of Ritter in seconds, and then with its greatest threat gone, the Antlered Man would pick them off one by one until it got to him.

Addilyn shook with exhaustion, her breath loud. Daemus knew she had maintained the spell for too long. He blinked as Delling ran forward, wondering what he could possibly do.

"Erud," called Delling, raising his voice and arms in prayer, "be with your servants now." The Disciple's eyes closed, and his hand reached for the Erudian signet that hung around his neck. When he grasped it, a pulsing white light began to emote from the holy symbol.

The Antlered Man paused, then stilled. A chill, mild but pronounced, fell over the valley.

"Help us face this beast, this abomination who was once one of your supplicants," Delling went on, his voice carrying over the battlefield. "Protect Daemus, whom you have seen fit to bless with your Sight, even as the rest of your Keepers have fallen from your favor."

Once one of your supplicants? Daemus wondered. His hands twisted uselessly at the handle of his mace.

"Go, Daemus," said Delling at a more ordinary volume, almost casual, his nerves calmed by the presence of his Ancient.

Daemus stared at him. "What?"

Delling's voice was quiet but serious. "You must go now. Go, into the forest. Run."

"What...? No!" Daemus bristled, finally understanding. "You can't ask me to do that!"

"He's right," Addilyn managed, her voice hoarse. "Daemus, let's retreat. We can't stop it."

"No," insisted the Keeper, his head shaking.

The Antlered Man turned to stare at him, sending a chill down his spine, then it looked at Delling, which was somehow worse.

127

"Be wise, Daemus," the princess's tone was sharp, nearly scolding him. "Go. Run!"

"Delling," Daemus tried to call, wanting to speak to him, to thank him or console him, but Delling only waved for him to go.

In the absence of his horse, Daemus turned in the direction of the woods and broke into a slow-footed run. He could hear Arjun shouting behind him, everyone moving. Faux said something; Marquiss gave a brief reply. Delling shouted in prayer again. Daemus kept running, his eyes on the forest ahead, his breath coming heavily and his throat dry. He could still feel that chill in the air, Erud's presence, the weight of it hovering over the whole valley.

Then, as sudden as it had come, the presence of his Ancient lifted.

Distraught, Daemus turned, just in time to see over the shoulders of his companions as the Antlered Man leapt out of its place and skewered Delling on one long claw in a single strike.

Faux, sprinting at Daemus, shoved him on the shoulder. "Go, you fool!" she snapped, and Daemus stumbled back into a run, trying to remember who he'd seen behind him. Faux. Jessamy. Marquiss. Blue, on Jericho. Ritter. Addilyn. Arjun? He glanced back. Yes, Arjun. Everyone was alive still, running. Except Delling.

Faux made a high-pitched whistle, which for a moment made Daemus seize in terror, thinking the creature had caught up to them, but she was only calling the horses.

"It'll keep chasing us," Daemus heaved to Marquiss, but the man shook his head.

"No! The Emerald Shield are coming, you see!" He waved in the general direction of a line of lights in the trees. Sure enough, within moments, Daemus was close enough to the tree line to discern a host of elven warriors, rushing to their defense.

The keldarin worked in symmetry, their camouflaged positions forfeited to help the fleeing party. As each stood, Daemus saw one pair of hands alight, then another and another, with the glow of silver magic. As he closed ranks with the unexpected force, he could feel the warmth of the combined spells and watch as the nearby woods illuminated in a light that rivaled the day.

"Hurry!" Faux yelled, and Daemus turned to see the creature on all fours, mowing down the high grass behind them.

It was gaining ground.

Daemus looked ahead. The trees were drawing closer together and he felt a twinge of hope igniting, but then he heard the powerful loping of the Antlered Man only yards behind him. He turned to see the creature racing through the trees on two legs, readying for a fight. He was within smelling distance. Daemus flinched and recited a fleeting prayer to Erud.

One man from the Emerald Shield screamed a command in a foreign tongue, launching their counterattack. In unison, the group of elven warriors lowered their hands to the ground, touching off their spellcasting. The light exploded and Daemus squinted to see, covering his eyes with a raised hand. Then he saw the branches of the trees in motion, animating like argent tentacles.

The Antlered Man charged into the trap and the tentacles whipped into a tornado of groping branches, entangling his legs and arms as he pressed on. The furious cryptid roared in protest, clawking against the enchanted forest, as it pulled him to the ground.

Daemus looked back at the beast, which had stumbled, now flailing, tearing through the web of magic that had ensnared him. The shrill clawking hit a higher octave, which Daemus hoped was a sign of desperation. He wanted to turn and avenge Delling, but he didn't know how.

"Keep going!" one of the soldiers yelled. "Don't stop until you can go no farther!"

He soon found himself dodging through the first quarter-mile of forest, weaving and bobbing through thickening trees. He listened to the man. *Face forward, keep going.*

"Daemus!" Arjun called. "This way! The horses!"

He turned to follow the captain and the group caught up with their frightened steeds. Before he knew it, he'd climbed onto his and the group continued with Marquiss in the lead. Daemus knew he was half human and half Keldarin, and so he trusted him to know where he was going. The thickness of the forest forced a slower pace, but they stayed at it for several hours with Marquiss leading them upstream and then down, around thickets and over dales that only a Keldarin could know. Before he realized it, they'd galloped and then cantered for several hours with no trace of either the Antlered Man or the Emerald Shield.

"Hold up," Arjun ordered.

The group gathered around in a small valley, not dissimilar to the gulley they'd just abandoned. Thoughts of Delling rushed back into Daemus's mind. His eyes welled with tears of anger, but he didn't cry. His eyesight, still empty of visions, thought back to the chill in the valley, how easily it had descended, and how rapidly it had lifted. Delling's body crumpling to the ground, lifeless.

The message was clear. Daemus wasn't sure if it came from him or from Erud, but it no longer seemed to matter.

I hate you.

CHAPTER ELEVEN

"Where the wolf's ears are, the wolf's teeth are near."
—Einar Skullgrimsson, Runecaster of Clan Hammerstead

THE SUNDOWNER SAILED INTO the port of Hammerstead, its flag of parlay flapping in the brisk sea wind. The sky was a mottled grey, matching the color of the North Sea's waves. Captain Halford had slowed the vessel, not daring to approach the Norsemen's cove without permission or greeting.

Montgomery looked out at Hammerstead from the deck, and Joferian and LaBrecque stood beside him. It was Monty's first trip to the foreign land, and the landscape was remarkably different. The horizon was dominated by the Dragon's Breath Mountains, their enigmatic peaks shrouded in perpetual mist. The city of Hammerstead sprawled in front of them. It featured hundreds of wooden buildings, many with thatched roofs and stovepipe chimneys, silhouetted against the late autumn sky. Yet no castles or walls guarded the city.

If Rijkstag had a capital, it would have been Hammerstead. Monty thought back to his classes at Halifax and the bedtime stories his father and mother had read to him when he was younger. Hammerstead was easily the largest Norseman settlement. He could already feel the icy touch of the winter wind, and he shuddered when he imagined how the rugged population would have to stave off the ravages of the Season of Long Nights every year.

"We should have sent word ahead," Monty breathed, his chest tightening in worry.

"We didn't have time," Joferian answered, his tone clipped.

"Hammerstead's history is one of glory and sorrow," Halford offered. "This place often bears the brunt of trollborn attacks, but it's stood the test of time. I don't know how they endure in the face of overwhelming odds against both the weather and the trollborn."

"They're our enemies," Monty countered. "This is wrong. They could take us now if they wanted. Look at their fleet."

Dozens of the Norsemen's long ships cluttered the cove in front of Hammerstead, and Monty wondered to himself how they maneuvered in such close ranks without toppling each other.

"I can't tell their fishing vessels from a common man-o'-war," he said.

"They look the same," Joferian agreed.

"Look at the shields." LaBrecque pointed to an approaching longship, which featured a shield wall on each side of the boat, protecting its rowers. "Fishermen don't need shields."

"Here they come!" Halford yelled from the helm.

The men watched a lone ship break from the chaos of the port and sail toward them. Its main sail had been lowered, and the grunting of the oarsmen rose as they approached the *Sundowner*.

"Is that a flag of surrender?" one of the bearded Norsemen called. He spoke common well enough, but Monty could tell it wasn't his native tongue.

"It's a flag of parlay," Halford shouted, cupping his hands to amplify his voice against the wind.

"Is there a difference?" The norsemen aboard the ship laughed to each other.

The visitors from Thronehelm shot sideways glances at each other, but none dared a response. Dread started to fill Monty's chest. The longship rowed to the bow of the *Sundowner*, and Montgomery looked down to greet the man who'd spoken. Their boat was long and sleek, fashioned with Nordic runes that were indiscernible to the prince. A map of battle scars crisscrossed on her prow.

Halford raised a salute. "Greetings, I'm Captain Dorian Halford."

Monty was glad the captain spoke when he did, saving him from stammering through a royal introduction.

"I'm Yngwie Cnute, son of Estridsson," the Norseman replied. "Why have you sailed into our harbor flying a flag of surrender? There hasn't been a battle... yet."

"As I explained, this is no surrender," Halford repeated. "I'm traveling with the crown prince of Thronehelm, Montgomery Thorhauer. He's seeking an audience with the *konungr*, Atorm Stormmoeller."

"Why would the crown prince sail in such a vessel?" Cnute asked, his eyes roving over the humble ship. "Surely a more regal ship would befit his rank?"

"I agree," Halford remarked, "but these are extraordinary times. The prince bears gifts for the *konungr*."

"You mean bribes?" Cnute responded. "We speak plainly in Hammerstead, Captain. I suggest that you do the same when addressing Atorm, our king."

"Then we shall," Monty said, joining the conversation. "I'm Montgomery Thorhauer, crown prince of Warminster, and I've come to offer gold in exchange for an alliance with your *konungr*."

Cnute smiled and put one hand on his waist while he peered up at the *Sundowner*.

"Well then," he said, tossing a rope to Halford so that they could connect their boats. "We'll rush you to your destination, Prince Montgomery of Thronehelm. Please climb aboard."

One at a time, Montgomery, Joferian, and LaBrecque descended onto the longship. Then, with help from Raynor and Hallowell, they lowered the chest of gold onto the foreign vessel.

"Captain?" Montgomery asked when Halford didn't board with them.

"He stays," Cnute replied. "The three of you can carry the bribe without him."

Monty glared at Cnute, who seemed to be enjoying the leverage he held.

"Signal our new friends' approach," Cnute commanded, and two of the Norsemen hoisted twisted horns and sounded a welcome to Hammerstead.

Finally, an entrance befitting a royal, Monty thought, as they slipped through the crowded port toward the city.

———✦———

THE MEN CLIMBED ONTO Hammerstead's docks amidst no fanfare. The three men were greeted by axe and spear wielding guards and escorted into the town, with Yngwie Cnute leading the way. The guards donned no family crests or flamboyant colors. Instead, they wore a mishmash of armor made from leather and hides. They weren't clean cut like the Black Cuffs of Thronehelm. Nearly every guard sported a beard and matted hair, some even wearing battle paint or brandishing facial tattoos of Norse runes.

The men followed their guards and didn't meander or stop on their trek. There were no greeting lines, but many of Hammerstead's inhabitants had wandered into the streets to see their Warminsterian visitors. All eyes were upon them, including that of a pack of wolves that freely wandered the city's streets.

Monty had learned of Norse cultures through the eyes of an enemy and from stories woven from a war that had been won before he could walk. He found none of the horror here.

As they made their way through the city, he started to appreciate how cleverly it had been designed. It housed about a dozen clans, each of them calling certain neighborhoods home and adorning long maypoles with their family symbols and totems. In total, he estimated that the population was close to fifteen thousand, half of Thronehelm.

Hammerstead had been the launching pad for Norse excursions into the seven baronies for centuries, including attacks on twergish settlements like Rawcliffe Forge. They terrorized the coasts and land alike, but he'd never wondered about their level of sophistication. Sure, they were unkept, but they seemed disciplined and organized. They weren't the barbarians he'd read about at Halifax.

"The trollborn," LaBrecque said, ending the silence between them. "Look at all the trollborn who live among them."

Monty and Joferian exchanged glances and nodded to LaBrecque in agreement.

Before long, their escorts brought them to the center of the city, where they found themselves standing in front of a wooden fortress that was walled and guarded. The structure towered over many of the other buildings in Hammerstead, and Monty was left to assume they'd been taken to some sort of barracks. He and Joferian lowered the clumsy chest they'd carried from the shore and looked to Cnute for instructions.

"Are we to stay in the barracks?" Joferian asked.

"Barracks?" Cnute replied.

"Yes," Joferian continued. "It's a word for military sleeping quarters."

Cnute bent backwards and let out a hearty laugh.

"This is no barracks," he said in his broken tongue. "This is the Great Hall of Ulthgar the Forger, our Ancient of security and protection. He guards our hall from the heavens above."

Cnute pushed the double doors open and passed by several guards, allowing Montgomery, Joferian, and LaBrecque to enter. Music and laughter spilled out as they stepped across the threshold of the hall. The stench of strong ale and sweat permeated the place, its walls bursting at the seams with Norsemen eating, drinking, and carousing. The trio looked to each other again for protocols, but none had an answer.

"I suppose if we'd have sent a letter ahead, we could have received a proper welcome," Monty whispered to Joferian.

His cousin grunted, adjusting the chest. "We should expect such disrespect from our enemies."

Monty shot a warning glance at his cousin, in spite of the fact he felt the same. They had to try to make peace, and not insulting them would be a first step. Yes, Monty felt embarrassed, but his mission was more important than pride. He couldn't join Joferian in his thoughts, but he could move them along.

"When will we be introduced?" Monty asked. "Where are your heralds?"

Cnute looked down his nose at the prince again and walked away from the group, disappearing into the throng of bodies and leaving the royals alone in the back of the hall. The men looked at one another again, but before they could speak, several thralls made their way over to them, offering horns full of a strange ale and plates full of half-cooked food.

"What's this?" Montgomery asked, but the thrall didn't respond, disappearing into the crowd a moment later.

Monty glanced around the room, hoping to find some order amongst the general chaos. He knew he must appear lost to them, if not even frightened. He stumbled, the strange culture taking him by surprise. The chamber was alive with the indiscernible tongue of the Norsemen, a language called Wartooth by those who didn't speak it.

"Well," LaBrecque said, "if they're going to ignore us, we might as well enjoy the food and drink." He found a half empty table near the door and sat down, taking a swig from his horn. Monty just looked at him, still frozen to his spot.

"They didn't ask us to forfeit our arms," Joferian pointed out.

"What could the three of us do?" Monty replied, eyeing the pack of warriors all around them.

"And the treasure?"

Monty shrugged, and the two moved the chest closer to LaBrecque before joining him.

"To our success," LaBrecque toasted, raising his horn to the prince and viscount. "May Nothos's dice roll our way."

The three lifted their horns and LaBrecque chugged what he had left. As LaBrecque emptied its contents, small twigs and pebbles tumbled out of his mouth from the tip of it. He sputtered and coughed, making Joferian smile weakly. Monty eyed the bottom of his horn, not wanting to suffer the same embarrassment. Not risking the last swallow, he set the horn down and let his eyes sweep the hall as anxiety still gripped at him.

Yngwie Cnute re-emerged from the depths of the hall and watched LaBrecque pick a pebble from his teeth.

"You're spitting out the best part," Cnute said.

"What is it?" Joferian asked.

"A powerful beer that dulls fears, incites rage before battle, and heals wounds, but only those caused in combat," Cnute replied. "It's called Heifenmager."

"Heifenmager?" Joferian asked. "What does it mean?"

"Salt of the mountains," he replied. "Many empty bottles have been found to contain gravel and twigs from the Dragon's Breath Mountains. It's the secret ingredient."

"In Queen's Chapel," Joferian began, "we make a wine known as the Queen's Nectar. The kingdom enjoys—"

But halfway through his explanation, Cnute rose, seeming to lose interest.

"When will we see the *konungr*?" Monty interrupted, trying to guide the conversation back to their reason for being there before the man might disappear again.

"It's up to him," Cnute replied, walking away from them.

LaBrecque and Joferian chuckled, while Monty shot them a disapproving scowl.

The men continued to wait, and after several more horns of Heifenmager, Monty began to forget what he was there to do. The music enchanted him, the women were attractive, and the food and drink were better than expected. In some respects, he was readier to meet the king than he'd ever been.

Then Cnute returned for them.

"Please follow me," the Norseman said. He pointed to the chest, and several of his thralls hoisted the treasure. The three rose without questions, LaBrecque clinging to his horn of Heifenmager like a protective mother. Cnute led them to the floor of the great hall, where the thralls placed the chest in front of Montgomery.

Montgomery found himself surrounded by a circle of brooding barbarians trying to take the measure of him. Each looked more ferocious than the next, and it was hard to tell them apart. The music stopped, and for a moment, the Heifenmager ceased to flow.

A herald of sorts stepped out from behind a faded and stained tapestry that was clearly the spoils of some conquest.

"Behold," the man said, in the common tongue, "Konungr Atorm Stormmoeller, son of Wolfrick, will take an audience with Prince Montgomery Thorhauer, son of Godwin."

Monty took a subtle breath and tried to clear his mind from the fog that had settled there thanks to the three horns of Heifenmager. He turned to the dais and waited for the tapestry to swirl once more, but it didn't. Then he felt a tap on his shoulder. He turned, expecting to see Joferian or LaBrecque, but instead found himself staring into the chest of a giant man looming beside him. He stood a full head taller than the prince, who himself was well over six feet. The crowd laughed at his expense, and Monty took a step backward to better look at the *konungr*. The man must have come from the crowd and not from some private chamber. To Monty, it appeared the king preferred to walk among his people.

"So, you're the next generation of our enemy, come on bended knee to ask for help from the people of Rijkstag?" Atorm asked for all to hear.

Caught off guard, Montgomery remained speechless for a second in embarrassment. He swallowed hard, trying to find his voice.

"Come, now," Atorm teased. "Has our Heifenmager stolen your tongue, Prince?"

Montgomery began to mutter something, but then Atorm ended his game and grabbed the prince around the shoulders, laughing boldly.

"I'm merely teasing, my puny friend," Atorm barked, breaking the tension. "Allow me to introduce my wife, Gullveig, and my two sons, Faxon the Red and Argantyr. And this, of course, is my daughter, Freya."

Montgomery tried to remember the names, but Atorm's staggering presence blotted almost everything else out. Gullveig was a striking Norsewoman who stood nearly as tall as Monty, and Faxon and Argantyr were almost their father's size. Freya was clearly in her teens but seemed fully a woman, taking after her mother in beauty, with long blond hair and captivating blue eyes. Montgomery wondered how a man of barely thirty years could have such a family.

"Thank you, Konungr," Monty replied. "This is Viscount

Joferian Maeglen and Admiral Valerick LaBrecque of the barony of Seabrooke."

"Tell me, Prince," Atorm began. "Why have you traveled to Hammerstead with a chest full of gold and no army to protect you?"

"Warminster needs your help," he said.

"I see that Yngwie, son of Estridsson, has taught you to be direct in his short time with you."

"He has," Monty confirmed, feeling the tiniest bit of courage returning to him.

"Then what help do you seek?"

"Warminster is preparing for conflict against a number of enemies," Montgomery admitted. "Many of them are unknown and faceless. My uncle, Baron Dragich Von Lormarck, has ceded from the united baronies of Warminster. And a Vermilion ambassador has been slain, as were my brother Everett and Joferian's brother Talath."

Atorm raised his ale horn high in the air. "I'm glad to hear your brothers died in combat. They now sit at Koss's table in the Hall of the Ancients. I hope you're fortunate enough to join them soon!"

A great cheer arose in the hall, and Monty realized that the words weren't meant as an insult but that they'd instead been said in reverence. The king raised his horn and took two swigs, calling out Everett's name with the first and Talath's name with the second. The whole hall followed suit.

"I remember stories of Von Lormarck from my father's war with Thronehelm," Atorm recalled. "He's a formidable opponent. Is he behind your woes?"

"We have suspicions." Monty's eyes narrowed. "There have been historic tensions between my family and his. The barony of Gloucester has left with him, which is why I'm here."

"Why don't you just conquer them?" he asked. "Why do you need Rijkstag?"

"The barony of Gloucester feeds our seven baronies," Montgomery explained. "And the merchant city of Saracen has ceased trade with Warminster due to caravans that were lost to brigand assaults and civil unrest. It seems that we're to starve this winter."

"You know who your enemies are, then," Atorm said. "I ask again, why are you here on bended knee?"

"We're not the only victims of this treachery," Montgomery answered. "Rijkstag is as well."

The great *konungr* laughed. "How so? All of this has passed far to the south."

Monty blanched at being the centerpiece of their laughter, but the effects of the Heifenmager pushed him through it. "The same brigands that attacked the caravans have also struck to the north," Montgomery reminded him. "They've raided the Rijkstag settlements of Ralsweik and Vendal. Fortunately, we were able to stop them and to kill Veldrin Nightcloak, their leader."

"Are these the same brigands?" Atorm asked, his mood seeming to change as he made the connection.

"Yes." Montgomery nodded. "When we vanquished the Nightcloak, we came across the assassin who killed the Vermilion ambassador and then attacked us on our way to Castleshire." Slowly and without threat, he removed the assassin's dagger from his belt and handed it to Atorm. "The assassin used this weapon to kill my brother. Everett's blood still stains its blade. You'll see a black rose design on the pommel. He also fashions the same black roses on his arrows."

"Do you know the man?"

"Nay." Montgomery shook his head. "But I've seen him in combat twice, once in our castle and once on our ship. I swear to the Ancients that I'll one day return his dagger. My brother's blood will mix with his."

"You mentioned Saracen, Prince Montgomery?" Atorm asked. "Their greedy guilds have become a thorn in our side."

"How so?"

"Saracen has dipped into Rijkstag's trade of slate iron."

"Slate iron?" Montgomery asked.

"Rijkstag is blessed by one of our Ancients, Ulthgar the Forger," Atorm explained. "Before Ulthgar left for the Halls of the Ancients long ago, he cast shavings from his great anvil into the Dragon's Breath Mountains, gifting our people with a special ore that we call slate iron. The ore was meant for us, the people of Rijkstag, and not the thieving merchants of Saracen. They even founded a small city to the east of our territory and named it Vallance. At first, it was just a trading post, but it's grown six-fold over the last generation. They must be stopped."

"Then Saracen is a common problem," Monty observed.

"Aye."

Monty looked back at Joferian and LaBrecque. Joferian's brow dipped low, and his subtle head turn told Monty he didn't agree with the prince's tactics thus far. But he held his tongue. Saracen's food was important to Warminster, and Montgomery knew that Master Cray had been sent to secure a deal. Joferian's eyes warned that he was walking a thin line with the half-truth.

"We brought more than just gold." Monty decided it was time to sweeten the negotiation. He reached deep into the chest, rifling through the trove of coins and gems until he found the handle of the prized treasure. He flicked his wrist and gold and garnets spilled out from the chest as Monty raised Wolfrick's axe. Coins rolled in circles around the great hall, but all the Norse eyes were looking at the weapon. The room fell into silence.

Monty knelt in front of Atorm.

"We present to you your father's axe." Montgomery lowered his eyes in false reverence, playing his hand as best he could. "It's the one that my father won from him in single combat, ending the war between our two peoples fifteen years ago. It's been displayed with honor in our Hall of Heroes, deep within Castle Thronehelm, ever since that day. My father offers it to you as a token of enduring peace and fellowship."

Atorm stared at the axe.

"Such a gift," he muttered, his voice broken. The crowd sighed.

"This isn't honorable," a voice rang out. Someone rose from the crowded ranks.

Montgomery turned, fear striking through him, as one of the Norse *jarls* made his way to the fore, pushing through the gawkers.

"You can't be gifted such a weapon," the man barked. "Nor should we accept their desperate gold."

"Explain yourself, Henrik Hjordis, son of Henrik the Keen-Eyed," Atorm replied, his gaze not leaving the axe.

"It's a matter of honor, Konungr," Hjordis pleaded. "We have an unfinished blood feud with Warminster and the Thorhauers. I lost many ancestors in that battle, including my cousin, your father. If we accept that axe, the Ancients will see it as a symbol of defeat and weakness. It needs to be won back with blood." Several other *jarls* and their *hersars* joined with Henrik, the crowd parting even further.

Atorm lifted his gaze from Wolfrick's axe and turned to Hjordis, his voice laced with protest as he spoke in the Norse Wartooth. Monty glanced back at Joferian and LaBrecque, who both shrugged. The argument continued for a minute and then Atorm hoisted his legendary warhammer, Urnst Jamner, from his belt. The crowd oohed at the gesture while Atorm waved to his two sons along with the group of protestors. They marched through the parting crowd and out into the open streets of Hammerstead.

"What's going on, Cnute?" Joferian whispered.

"They're going to settle the dispute outside," Cnute replied. "Come and watch."

CHAPTER TWELVE

*"There's a peace that can only be found
on the other side of war."*
—King Dragich Von Lormarck

IT WAS MIDDAY IN Krahe, and King Dragich Von Lormarck sat atop his perch on Dragon Ridge, observing the bustling town below. The bracing, late autumn wind caught his attention when he stepped out onto the balcony to glance at his visitors as they arrived inside the walls of the Ridge, but he didn't react to it. His mind was far away, fighting battles that had yet to come.

He watched Ambassador Thessica Camber, his royal legate in Castleshire, climb out of her carriage. She quickly fixed her dress and then looked to him on the balcony, giving a respectful curtsy from the courtyard below. They exchanged knowing glances from afar, and Dragich pondered what news had dragged her all the way to Krahe from Castleshire. It had to be news she wouldn't trust to be delivered by messenger or magic.

The familiar voice of Kail Ilidari interrupted his thoughts. "Your Majesty, your war council has gathered inside and awaits your presence."

"Thank you, Ilidari." He turned back into the castle and emerged into the square chamber. The war council had been seated around the center table, where the relief map of all Warminster lay.

The Thessaly family from Gloucester sat to his left. His first wife, Loralei, had died in childbirth while giving life to Donnar and Emmerich, Dragich's twins. Baron Kellan Thessaly, Loralei's younger brother, was present alongside his own two sons, Darrick and Jareth. They'd sided with the Vale in the secession from Thronehelm, and Dragich now represented both baronies.

To his right sat his twins and their half-brother and half-sister, Aarav and Ember Fleury. They were without Lady Isabeau Fleury, Dragich's longtime mistress and Aarav and Ember's mother. She'd long since forsaken Foghaven Vale for the more hospitable climes of Deadwaters Fork, her ancestral home.

Rounding out the square sat two of Von Lormarck's most trusted generals, Ralnor Edda and Vestri the Eldest. Ralnor commanded his forces against the twergs of Rawcliffe Forge, and the Eldest was a mercenary trollborn general that commanded a hodgepodge group of trollborn tribes in the Dragon's Breath Mountains and sell-swords from the Killean Desolates.

Vestri had raised three sons, and all of them had perished in Von Lormarck's war for twergish gold. Their own lust for treasure had driven them into an ambush that the clever twergs had set for them near one of their troves. None had returned from the collapsed twergish mines, but Vestri had honored his dead by doubling down on his commitment to recruit and wage war with his trollborn thugs.

Dragich sat in his newly minted throne on a side of the table that belonged only to him, listening sporadically to the droning of his brother-in-law, Kellan Thessaly, about certain matters of their nascent state.

"In conclusion," Thessaly said, bringing Dragich's wandering mind back to matters at hand, "I shall leave this afternoon to ensure that the grain stores have all been harvested as you asked, my king. Not a kernel of corn nor a shaft of wheat shall find its way to Thronehelm this Season of the Long Nights."

Dragich gave an approving glance and waved a dismissive hand at Thessaly. The baron returned to his seat among his sons.

"What of my orders to stand up your army?" Dragich asked. "Five thousand men are marching here, with another two thousand due by the end of the Season of Colored Leaves. Many are farmers and are finishing their responsibilities at home."

"And you, my generals?"

"Sire, we're fully engaged with the twergs in the north," Ralnor Edda offered. "The struggle continues, but we've been able to raid several of their troves. The gold and gems will arrive at Dragon Ridge any day."

"And you, Eldest?"

"Sire, we've recruited well. Our gathering forces in the north will be ready by the end of the fortnight. The forces from the Desolates have left Spine Castle and are on the march as we speak. Some have gathered already in your courtyard below."

"Well done," the king half-smiled, before Ilidari re-entered the room and interrupted. The king waved at him, and he announced the arrival of Ghyrr Rugalis.

"Ah, Rugalis." The king motioned for him to approach. "What word from the negotiations with Saracen?"

"My liege." Rugalis bowed. "Saracen is in receipt of the first delivery of golden palmettes as you asked.

"And?"

"It's as you expected sire. The guildmistress demanded more. We settled on a second train of gold, as you'd previously agreed."

"You have my thanks, Rugalis, for a job well done."

"Sire." Rugalis took another respectful bow.

"It's time for you to finalize our arrangement with them. Leave for Saracen once the next shipment of gold arrives from General Edda's efforts. Let's ensure that Saracen's food doesn't find Thronehelm and that their mercenary forces will join us on the battlefield. The truth has always been a casualty with Sasha Scarlett, so we must ensure her loyalty at all costs. Invite her to return with you so that we may discuss next steps."

"As you command, my liege." Rugalis stepped away and returned to the shadows of Dragon Ridge's corridors, where he belonged.

Kellan Thessaly rose again. "Sire, speaking of embargoes and food from Saracen—"

"Enough of food." The king grimaced and covered his eyes with his hands. He'd had enough of a quartermaster's duties. He was king now.

"But how do we stop the free flow of food from reaching Thronehelm by sea?" Thessaly pressed. "We are, after all, a landlocked nation."

"Let me worry about that, Baron," Dragich scowled with an unsettling glance. "Ilidari, bring me Thessica Camber."

EMBER FLEURY HAD SAT next to her brother during the war council's proceedings, dreaming of home. The weather was only going to get colder and even though she'd been in Foghaven Vale for several years, she was still unaccustomed to the snow and ice that was soon to follow.

She perked up at the announcement of Camber's arrival. Camber was the first woman to attend and speak at the council meeting, and Ember had held onto King Godwin's words from her betrothal ceremony. Camber wasn't Queen Amice, Baroness Maeglen, or Lady Isabeau, but she *was* an accomplished legate in Castleshire. If she hoped to become a baroness herself one day, she needed to learn lessons from a woman like Thessica Camber.

Those thoughts also brought her back to her quick dalliance with marriage to Joferian of House Maeglen, and how in a brief few hours, that arrangement had been destroyed. Was it ever true? Or was it just for show, to hide her father's insurrection?

Camber entered the war room in the shadow of the monstrous Ilidari and again curtsied to Von Lormarck on his throne. "My king."

"Cousin," the king glanced at her through narrowed eyes. "What urgency has brought you here today and pulled you from your important responsibilities in Castleshire?"

"I come bearing news from the Caveat."

The king leaned forward. "Continue."

Over the next few minutes, Camber flooded the chamber with an account of the dramatic events in the Caveat, describing in great detail the spectacle brought on by Daemus Alaric, the Low Keeper who'd risen to prominence during the proceedings. The king sat silent and absorbed the information.

"Also, my liege," Camber continued, seeming shaken by the king's silence, "the Cathedral of the Watchful Eye has fallen. The Keepers are blind, but this Daemus Alaric still possesses the Sight. It was confirmed by the First Keeper of Castleshire himself. It's clear that Alaric remains untrained, however, and that may play to our advantage."

"The Keepers are just blind to their old ways," the king asserted. "Jhodever traveled to Solemnity a few days ago and we hope to have a new Great Keeper presently. One who can see in the *new ways.*"

Ember wasn't sure what the king meant and continued to feign disinterest in the conversation, but it was obvious to her that Camber was confused as well.

"Also," Camber continued, "First Keeper Aliferis Makai has left Castleshire at the direction of the council to join Thronehelm."

"How so?" the king lamented, sitting forward in his throne. "Has the Caveat ignored your lead?"

"They still recognize Warminster as a whole, my king." She

cringed as the words left her mouth. "As of yet, they've failed to recognize Foghaven Vale and Gloucester's sovereignty."

"I blame you for this failure." The king's voice dripped with dissatisfaction and his brow furrowed. "But it matters little, as the wheels of war are hard to slow once they move. They'll only be stalled by blood."

"Apologies, my sovereign," Camber offered. "Please forgive me."

The new king sneered and waved his hand, absolving her of her transgressions.

"What else do you bring that could not have been sent by messenger?"

"The young Keeper and his troop have departed for Abacus in search of answers to the visions he had on the floor of the Caveat. He travels with the Vermilion princess and several others, under the protection of the Longmarcher from Valkeneer."

"The Vermilion?" Dragich asked. "This must mean that Morley failed."

"In part."

"Go on, Ambassador." Dragich cocked his head, waiting for more.

"The *Phantom* found *Doom's Wake* in Castleshire's harbor. A great naval battle ensued, and Morley was slain by Valerick LaBrecque."

"Damnable man," Von Lormarck muttered.

"However, a prince and a Maeglen were killed as well."

Ember couldn't help but jump to attention with the news of a fallen Maeglen. She looked to Aarav, who'd noticed her expression, but the king's eyes were still on Thessica Camber. She wanted to blurt out Joferian's name, but her head caught up to her heart and her tongue held fast.

"Which?" the king asked.

"Talath of House Maeglen and Everett of House Thorhauer."

"This is wonderful news, cousin." Von Lormarck smiled. "The war has claimed its first royal blood. What of Incanus Dru'Waith?"

"He was to take a boat north in pursuit of Montgomery and Joferian. They departed Castleshire the morning after the battle. It was his blade that killed the second son of Godwin. I haven't received word from him since."

"He should have already arrived in Thronehelm, then." The king rubbed his chin and his eyes narrowed. "Let him finish the job there, where it should have been done the first time."

Ember felt lightheaded. The news that Joferian lived trumped the deaths of the other royals, but she hated herself for thinking that way. Her only pure thoughts were for his safety. Her mind raced to find a way to extricate herself from the morass her father had drowned her in, but nothing came to her. She glanced sideways at Aarav, as he stared silent daggers at her. Her feelings were too evident, and she couldn't tell if he was upset with her or trying to quietly implore her to watch her body language so that the room wouldn't notice.

"Was Dru'Waith discovered?" the king asked.

"Nay," Camber confided. "It was revealed in front of the regency that a Bone elf assassin had been dispatched to kill the royals, but none were aware of who retained his services."

Von Lormarck chuckled to himself and shook his head.

"The realm of Warminster will not have to wait much longer to see the full story. I have an assignment for you, Camber. One you're uniquely qualified for. And since you're so far north already, your assistance with this will be greatly appreciated."

"Of course, sire. What is it?"

"The baronies of Foghaven Vale and Gloucester are presenting our arrows of war to the Thorhauers and I need you, Thessica

Camber, to deliver them to Godwin himself. Before you do, ask first for his abdication. If he doesn't concede, then deliver the arrows and in doing so, declare open war as our combined response. It's time for the Von Lormarck reign to begin."

"My liege," Camber begged, shaking her head. "I'm not the right person to—"

"Of course you are," Von Lormarck interrupted. "You're an elegant orator and a cousin to the false king. He'll treat you with respect."

"Please, sire, I beg of you. Should you not, as an honorable man, deliver these arrows yourself?"

"Enough, cousin." The king rolled his eyes. "I would, if I didn't need to be at the head of my army, which will already be on the move by the time the arrows are delivered."

The table fell silent with the gravity of his statement. Ember's eyes widened and her heart sunk even farther. *What deceit? Where was her father's honor?* The wrapping of knuckles on the table by her father's war council snapped her back to the present.

"Sublimely clever plan, sire," Baron Thessaly confessed.

"Don't fret, good cousin," the king smirked at Camber. "I'll send my sons to Thronehelm alongside you. They'll represent the Von Lormarck dynasty well. A historic moment, no doubt."

Dragich waved to Ilidari, who presented the legate with a finely crafted but ancient box. He opened the lid, revealing two war arrows—one from the Vale, and the other from the barony of Gloucester. She looked at them with dismay.

"And cousin," the king added while wagging his finger, "while you're there, make contact with Dru'Waith. Assure him that he'll have his personal war with the Vermilion if he continues to collect royal skulls for Foghaven Vale."

"Of course, my liege," Camber bowed, her face reddened.

"And find our spy, Meeks Crowley. Tell him that I said it

was time. He'll know what to do."

"It will be done." Camber motioned to someone in the hall. "I have one last gift for you, sire."

"A gift?"

Thessica motioned to an unseen figure in the hall, and a woman appeared, bound and gagged. Ember sat up and stared at the poor woman, as did the rest of the eyes in the chamber.

"What's this?" The king nearly laughed at the restrained woman.

"The girl is a friend of Daemus Alaric," Camber explained. "Perhaps her capture gives us an unexpected advantage. A pawn to play at a later date?"

"Ah, Thessica," the king grinned. "A reference to chess. My favorite game."

They both exchanged smiles while Ember's heart went out to the helpless woman. She looked to the girl and found her unique. Her hair was blue, as were her eyes and lips. She looked to have been magically altered in some way, but the girl didn't fight her bonds. Perhaps her magics were muted.

"One of my spies caught her trying to deliver a message to her Matron Mother in the Silvercroft Mountains. This may run afoul of whatever Graytorris has planned, sire. If I may, Your Majesty, the girl would make an excellent trap for Daemus Alaric. If the Keeper discovered her capture, he'd want to rescue her."

Von Lormarck shot Camber an opportunistic look. "Perhaps you're right."

The king rose from his throne. He walked to a raised desk where a black book lay closed beside an inkwell and a pointed quill.

"What is it?" Camber asked.

"It was a gift from our ally, Graytorris," Dragich announced, loud enough for the whole room to hear. "It was presented by Ghyrr Rugalis on his way back from the Killean Desolates.

Perhaps it's time to try its magic."

He invited Camber, his sons, and his only daughter to approach him. Ember stood and followed her brothers to the pedestal, keeping to the rear but staying close enough to witness the magical powers of the king's new gift.

The king slowly opened the book, revealing a blank page. In one quick motion, he dipped the quill into the ink and scribbled a missive in the ledger. Ember couldn't see the entire message, but from what she saw, it dealt with the fate of the captive in front of them. As he finished writing, the ink slowly disappeared from the page.

The small group waited in silence, wanting to see what would happen next. Soon, a new message appeared on the page with two simple words.

"Send her."

As Ember read the message, they too disappeared, leaving no trace of the communication.

"It appears that your supposition was correct, cousin." The king turned to Camber. "Our new guest would make a nice prize for our ally, the fallen Keeper. We'll send her to him." Von Lormarck waved to Ilidari, who handed the young girl over to his guards. "Remove her. Congratulations, Thessica. Your trip here proved very useful. Now, don't fail me in Thronehelm."

The legate stepped back from her new king and curtsied, leaving the room in a hurry.

Ember's mind raced in a strange mixture of disappointment, embarrassment, and treasonous thoughts. She disagreed with the king's sentiments, and her hope to learn from Camber had been dashed. This wasn't honorable, and nor was it necessary. *Ransoming a young woman who wasn't much older than she was? Another pawn on Von Lormarck's chessboard?* She herself had been called a pawn. She couldn't let this happen. She had to find a way to help her.

Von Lormarck waved for his twins to approach. "Go with the Ambassador to Thronehelm. I want you to help her as she may have little will to do this chore. If she fails, present the arrows to your uncle. I want his remaining allies to see that the Von Lormarck family is still intact and in control."

"With pleasure," his sons said, nearly in unison.

As the war council adjourned, Ember sat alone in her chair, contemplating the events that had just unfolded. She had to help the girl, but how? She was a victim of circumstance, in the same way that Ember herself was. She had to act.

CHAPTER THIRTEEN

*"The Eternal Forest is a pageant of green
too rich for one to ponder."*
—Melexis, the Ancient of the Elves

THE WEATHER HAD SLOWED Incanus and Skullam down during the first few days of their voyage, with rainstorms forcing a slower pace as they trudged through the mud and muck just east of Castleshire. The inclement weather had discouraged passersby from stopping and asking questions, and they'd mostly traveled off-road to the south to avoid gazing eyes.

But the two companions had soon caught better weather, reaching the Turn a full day ago. They were a long way behind, but they pressed on undaunted.

As night began to fall, Skullam returned from his scouting mission with news.

"My liege," he said. "There seems to have been a skirmish just a few miles from here."

"A skirmish?"

"I don't share your nose for tracking," the imp replied. "Follow me and I'll lead you there."

Within the hour, the pair had reached a gulley tucked away from the Run, one that allowed them some cover and the ability to monitor any travelers below. As they descended into the depths, Incanus could smell the odious leftovers of the battle.

Incanus looked at his imp, as his horse plodded down the crooked path. "Death awaits us."

When he arrived at the scene, he found the remnants of a battle. Not fully understanding what they were riding into, he waved for Skullam to circle the area and make sure they weren't walking into an ambush.

As the imp flew into the nearby woods, Incanus jumped down from his horse and inspected the remains of a ruined campsite. The battle scene was only a few days old according to his trained eyes, and there was evidence of a great struggle.

Incanus walked around the battlefield, replaying the melee in his head. A group of a half dozen or more booted swordsmen had fought a giant bear of some kind, leaving one of the swordsmen dead. Scavenger birds had left a pile of unrecognizable carrion behind, and some smaller animals had feasted on the corpse as well. There was precious little for him to go on, but he did notice something familiar.

He bent over the corpse and saw the remains of an Erudian robe. Looking closer still, he saw that the dead man's hand was clutched around a holy symbol. Something had nearly beaten him to his prey, but as the Fates would have it, it seemed as though his Vermilion target survived.

Incanus stood and walked the remaining part of the battlefield. His tracker's instinct showed him the route carved into the tall grass where his targets had fled in a hasty retreat. Whatever the creature that had encountered them was, it had stalked them in the same direction.

He heard the familiar flapping of Skullam's wings and turned to look at his companion.

"What have you found?" the Bone elf asked.

"It appears that there was a second battle, a mile or so from here."

"Take me there," Dru'Waith ordered, and after a few minutes' ride, they were at the second site.

"What do you see, my liege?" Skullam asked.

"It appears that a large creature of some kind chased the

Vermilion from her camp to here." Incanus pointed at the signs on the ground. "Then they joined a different set of foes. Perhaps a dozen Keldarin from the Emerald Dales."

"I can sense that this ground has been tainted," Skullam confided. "The hale of druidic magic persists, but I also feel a dark trace. Perhaps from the creature that was in pursuit? Something of my kin. It was no giant bear."

"There's some blood here," Incanus indicated, pulling at some broken reeds of grass where the incident had taken place.

"Is it Vermilion?"

"Nay," Incanus said with a shake of his head. "It's human and Dale elf. I also see a white substance. It feels like sap to the touch. It might be the creature's blood. But no trace of Vermilion."

"What do we do next, my liege?"

"Our prey must be off the trail," Incanus said, with the certainty of a man who could read the dirt. "They fled from the Run into the safety of the Dalelands. The creature is still in pursuit of them, but it was delayed by the Keldarin. This is the break we were looking for. We should be able to catch them now if we make haste to Abacus."

"As you say, my lord," Skullam replied, taking a deep bow.

"Use your powers of concealment and fly to Abacus to seek out Helenius. If we find him, the Vermilion princess will come to us. I'll ride there and join you as soon as I can."

"How will I find a man I don't know in a city like Abacus?"

"Make contact with some old friends of mine," Incanus sneered through a rare smile. "They own a brothel called the Twin Snakes. They're known as the Ophidian, and they may know where to find him. Helenius is a peacock, and it wouldn't surprise me if he'd visited their brothel. They themselves are local legends, and I think Helenius may find them… *interesting* to say the least."

Skullam looked strangely at Incanus.

"They're a unique trollborn," Dru'Waith explained. "I think Helenius would enjoy... *meeting* them."

"As you say, my liege."

Skullam leapt into the air and disappeared. Incanus took one last look at the remains of the battle and climbed back onto his horse. The Bone elf wasn't religious, but for once, the Ancients seemed to have been on his side.

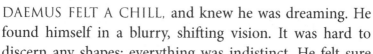

DAEMUS FELT A CHILL, and knew he was dreaming. He found himself in a blurry, shifting vision. It was hard to discern any shapes; everything was indistinct. He felt sure that this was not the Sight visiting him, and after a moment he realized it was because he felt safe. The light was a powder blue color, flashing whitish at times. As the spectral light grew closer, Daemus felt no heat emanating from it.

A few of the shivering forms around him coalesced into something bright and spectral, almost person shaped. As Daemus watched, he became able to discern the image of a man, wild-eyed and long-haired. Unlike the moment the specter appeared, it seemed as though the details were pre-formed, and were only revealing themselves to his eyes.

The apparition, noticing his attention, created an impression that Daemus could only describe as a wary smile, although its face did not change.

"Am I dead?" he wondered aloud to the ghost floating in front of him. "Are you here to guide me to the Hall of the Ancients?"

The spirit smiled, its eyes never blinking, and shook its head, pointing a finger behind Daemus where a second light grew.

He turned to find that the Eternal Forest had vanished, replaced by a ghostly road matching the powdery blue of the specter that created it. The road ran into an ethereal town, surrounded by illusory buildings Daemus didn't recognize. The open portal seemed like the canvass of a watercolor, blending away at the edges into celestial immaterialism.

Daemus floated toward the portal, following the bodiless ghost into it. He felt no hale of magic as they passed through the entrance, and he progressed without effort, floating through the phantom town, taking stock in the wonderful yet intangible structures as he wafted by. A gentle tugging in his stomach pulled him to the center of the town, soon becoming more forceful, and he realized he couldn't stop himself.

The figure leading him continued to smile. Daemus felt no fear.

A massive tree appeared in front of him, forming out of the ether just as the man had. He thought at first that it must be part of the Eternal Forest, but as he looked closer, he could see it was surrounded by buildings, as if it was in the center of a city.

Daemus glanced back at his guide, whose nodding encouragement turned him back to the tree. He focused his gaze on the trunk, into which was carved a grand door. He observed the details of the door for a few moments before realizing it was not as far away as he had thought. He reached out to touch the handle.

Withering, biting cold met what he thought was his hand, and he was yanked forcefully away from the door so strongly he saw his guide fly past him as he was pulled away. The man's face, expressionless though it was, did not seem shocked—only a little chagrined.

After an indeterminate time, his flying had not ceased, and was beginning to feel more like falling.

Daemus's bleary eyes refocused, and the contents of the vision fogging his mind slowly dissipated as he realized he'd fallen asleep on his horse. The beast was plodding along, following its fellows. The mare like him was exhausted but needed no direction from him to keep going. Daemus imagined they must be deep into the woods by now, having only taken an hour or so to rest after they had gotten far enough to feel a little safer, but all the trees looked the same to him. It was impossible to say how long it might be before they stopped to rest.

His thoughts were still sluggish, moving slowly between confused impressions of the bizarre vision and his sore and exhausted muscles. He'd never stayed on a horse for this long before and felt with resigned certainty that he would not be able to walk easily for a couple of days after this at least. What had the vision meant? Some kind of tree? Thinking of the specter that had accompanied him through it, he suddenly remembered—it wasn't the Sight sent by Erud.

Erud. Delling.

Daemus's eyebrows snapped down, and he felt his expression settle into a scowl. Of course, it hadn't been a vision from Erud.

Though I wouldn't bet on getting an apology, Delling had said in his wry way. The memory made Daemus grip his reins so tightly his nails dug into his palms. The idea of Erud apologizing was laughable, but the idea of Daemus continuing to serve his Ancient without one was even more so.

I am not your toy, he thought. I am not your tool. If my only choice is to serve a careless master who rewards their servants with death, I'd sooner—part of him cowered at the ensuing thought, but he pushed forward to finish it anyway—I'd sooner choose my own end. At least that way Erud's will couldn't be done. Daemus cared little that destroying himself to spite Erud was exactly what Graytorris would have wanted. For the moment, he savored entertaining the idea.

Delling would have balked at him, he felt sure, would have been shocked at the level of vitriol with which Daemus wanted to denounce their Ancient, would have tried to remind him that the place of the god-touched was to serve. Or would have reminded him, in his always neutral tone, that he really had no choice. Perhaps the older man would have told him he was behaving and thinking like a child. None of it seemed to matter. Daemus did not have it in him to tolerate any more.

"Daemus," came a soft voice at his shoulder, and he flinched. It was Faux. "How are you doing? We're nearly there, I think."

"Fell asleep." He bit off the words, not bothering to soften his tone. "Just after watching my friend die. Was so dull I nodded off."

Faux recoiled, staring at him, her eyes filled with concern.

"No shame in it," said Arjun from behind him. His tone was exhausted but collected and calm. "Men react differently to seeing death."

"Tell me another," snapped Daemus. Faux inhaled sharply at that and shot him a look, offended on her friend's behalf.

Daemus could feel himself doing something wrong, taking out his anger at Erud on people who were only trying to help him. He met the observation in Delling's stoic way, unable to feel anything about it one way or the other. Arjun and Faux both fell silent, apparently realizing that he needed to be left alone.

Daemus pulled the cowl of his cloak up higher, hiding his white eyes in shame. A signal from Ritter at the front of the procession halted them. It turned out Faux had been right. The surrounding trees turned into what were elven dwellings of sorts, with curious locals peering out at them from the windows. The party came to a halt outside of a very large pair of trees that had been shaped to grow in an intertwined and beautiful pattern. Neither was as large as the one Daemus had seen in his dream, but each was still bigger than any tree he'd seen with waking eyes.

Within moments, two figures emerged, one of them a finely dressed woman whom Daemus identified as a royal from her elaborate, amber-adorned circlet, the other a tall, loping man. The woman signaled something with her hands, and seemingly from nowhere a herd of servants came forward to take the reins of their mounts.

With most every motion causing him some degree of pain, Daemus dismounted and let a round-faced youth take charge of his horse. Jericho whined when the servants moved to take him away from Blue, but the springheel spoke to him for a moment and patted his head, and the beast went quietly.

"Greetings," said the royal girl with a wide smile, revealing small, pearly teeth. "Welcome to Flowerdown Syphen. I am Liesel Briar, child of the coronel. We are delighted to receive you, travelers and friends."

"Hello," said Ritter, then smiled as an afterthought, presumably not wishing to appear rude.

Princess Addilyn fidgeted slightly. Daemus felt sure their general lack of decorum was making her cringe.

The other elven princess seemed unbothered, however. "Before we get you settled, travelers, I will take you to meet my father." Her chipper tone suggested this was an honor extended only to the very welcome.

"Um—" Ritter, ashen-faced and looking dead on his feet, seemed about to protest, but at a glance from Addilyn he closed his mouth. Daemus, anger still prickling under his skin, fought the urge to roll his eyes.

"Follow me," said the princess, and she turned without

another word. Slowly, they all obeyed.

Daemus noticed that the princess and Marquiss exchanged glances and seemed familiar, perhaps even casual acquaintances. Perhaps it was outside of their custom to greet one another before meeting the coronel. More protocol...

The party was led inside the tree, where their surroundings turned out to be humbler than Daemus had expected. The coronel's receiving room, at the end of a short hallway, was simple and homey. Its only adornments were a tall-backed wooden chair in the center of the room—not thronelike at all, Daemus thought—and the intricate carvings on the walls.

They stood alone for five minutes, accompanied only by the princess, until a shuffling, plain-clothed figure stepped into the room after them. He was so quiet Daemus almost didn't notice his presence and would have assumed he was a servant if not for the intricate gold earring dangling from one ear.

"Greetings," said the man with a small, awkward smile. "I bid you welcome, travelers. We are very happy you're here." He looked at Addilyn, his eyes bright. "Especially you, Princess, if I may say so. Have you visited the home of Melexis before?"

Addilyn, caught in the middle of an elaborate bow, wobbled, and blinked at him uncertainly before recovering. "No, Coronel, I have been deprived of the joy. It is my honor to be in your presence, and may your reign continue until the stars fall from the sky." The last part was rote, but she said it with grace enough that it sounded halfway sincere.

"We were all grieved to hear of your father's passing," the coronel replied, his face somber.

Daemus, his eyes burning with exhaustion and suppressed anger still tightening his throat, tuned out the conversation. The coronel spoke with Ritter, then with Faux and Arjun, and exchanged briefer pleasantries with Blue and Marquiss. He was polite but all but ignored Jessamy, seeming to have understood that she did not wish to make small talk. In Daemus's case, however, the elf became suddenly oblivious.

"And you, young one."

Daemus twitched.

"You are Erud's chosen," the coronel burbled on, his tone warm, even bordering on reverent. "I know your mission is one of great importance—my people have been waiting years, preserving our knowledge, in the hopes it might one day be useful. You must let me know if there is anything I can do to assist you while you are here."

"You can shut up."

A dead silence fell, and everyone stared at Daemus. Faux, Blue, and Marquiss wore expressions of open shock. Ritter cringed. Arjun and Jessamy glared. Addilyn's face remained a composed mask, only her widened eyes betraying any emotion. The coronel himself looked briefly surprised, then blank. Daemus couldn't tell if the king had taken offense, but it was obvious he realized that Daemus hadn't meant to say it out loud.

After a very long pause, the coronel pursed his lips and then said, "It appears I have been over-eager in my haste to speak with you."

Silence. Daemus could hear his heartbeat pounding in his ears.

"Perhaps this meeting would be better left until the morning."

And then he left.

The void of the silence yawned wider. With a curt gesture, the princess directed a servant to bring them to their lodgings, her former cheery demeanor replaced with careful blandness. Just as quiet, the eight of them left the coronel's tree and trudged along behind him for another quarter of a mile. Soon, they reached a meadow bathed in the light of the setting sun.

Typical of an elf to expect guests to sleep outside, Daemus thought, and told himself he didn't care that that thought sounded like something his father would say.

Moments after the servant had left them there and vanished into the trees, Addilyn rounded on Daemus, and the silence snapped.

"What were you thinking?" she demanded. Her voice was much less controlled than usual, betraying her exhaustion—or perhaps just how much Daemus had offended them all. "The coronel is our host! That aside, he does not bear responsibility for the cause of your anger. What possessed you to show such total, foolish disregard for decorum and diplomacy? We are all fortunate he did not choose to refuse our passage through the forest then and there!"

Daemus looked at her, a bit puzzled, and to his shock she actually rolled her eyes.

"You are a political figure now, Daemus," her sharp words pointed out. "Do you not see that your conduct reflects not only on your people but on all of us? Your actions have consequences!"

As if any of his actions were even his at all. "You're a hypocrite," Daemus barked without thinking. He looked at her surprised, frozen face, and realized that he believed it.

"Mind your tongue," Jessamy warned. Her eyes were hard, despite her visible exhaustion, but Daemus ignored her.

"It's true. You don't care about decorum at all, Addilyn, unless it's convenient to you. All of us can tell you're breaking your own rules by being so close with him." He jerked his head at Ritter. "I don't know why it's such a problem, but it's obvious you can't decide between being with him and obeying your people. Which also makes you a coward." The words were tumbling out of his mouth now, unfettered, and a sick feeling was bubbling up in his stomach.

"That's not fair," Ritter said in a low voice.

Jessamy had taken her hand off her sword and was watching, her eyes moving between Daemus and Addilyn.

"Daemus," Faux cut in, "stop. You're tired. We're all tired. There's no need to be talking about any of this now."

Daemus's head swiveled and his mouth opened, and he found himself talking again, the sick feeling intensifying. "Oh, then you take the god's touch. You be born into a noble house only to be known as the family shame who can never inherit, treated like a pariah among all your fellows. You have nightmares every night, and then live through them again when they all come true, all with nobody there to explain what's going on. You be cast out from the only place you've ever belonged, and hunted by an implacable madman, and watch your only true family in the world die while you can do nothing. And you realize one day that your Ancient cares nothing for you, and nothing is all any of it is, or ever was, forever. And then, Faux—" He met her eyes and spoke, his lips downturned—"then you can tell me we are all tired."

His friend's eyes were wide with rage. In the back of his mind Daemus realized he had just dismissed the entirety of her life, her suffering at the hands of the state, growing up a fugitive and criminal after losing her entire family. The sick feeling intensified until he almost couldn't stand it.

A heavy hand fell on his shoulder: Arjun. "Time to sleep now, lad."

Daemus felt a sudden pain on the side of his head and heard his companions beginning to shout at each other before everything went dark.

CHAPTER FOURTEEN

*"Fate is what happens to us when
we're making other plans."*
—Warminsterian Proverb

THE NEXT MORNING, SOLVEIG departed the subterrane with Phanna, following the new warpath as Tancred had instructed. Not knowing the route, she hoped that the Garnet Pass would save her time and offer some protection. The war with Foghaven Vale still raged to the south and traveling the same road as twergish soldiers seemed like a good idea.

She was also aware that once she reached the surface, other terrors might await her. Although the recent brigand strikes in Queen's Chapel and the Bridge hadn't plagued the twergs yet, she was keenly aware of them. And, of course, taking paths through Ravenwood invited encounters with wandering trollborn.

A week passed, and Tancred's advice proved wise. The new pass wasn't just safer, it was also much quicker. She found herself ascending from the underground portion of the Garnet Pass into a secluded grove in Ravenwood. The rocks and boulders that camouflaged the entrance had been cleverly placed by the twergish miners who built it, making it appear as an old and dangerous rockslide from the foothills.

She rarely traveled to Thronehelm, knowing the trading towns of Saracen and Connor Bray much more intimately. Thronehelm was Warminster's largest city and to Solveig, it was intimidating.

She and Phanna entered through the front gates, and she followed the other merchant caravans up the steep slope to the castle. She'd been to outdoor markets inside the castle's walls before, but it had been many years. As she passed through the gates and under the raised portcullis, she was thrilled by the wonder of the daily bazaar. Hundreds of merchants had opened their carts to display their wares. She thought she'd have the advantage of being one of the first, but it appeared she was one of the last.

Thronehelm's bazaar was assembled and torn down again every day, welcoming merchants from all four corners of the realm. It was said that outside of Saracen, it was the best place to search for the rarest of the rare and the most exotic of goods. The courtyard was covered with tents and carts of all shapes and sizes, flying banners from as far east as Queen's Prey and as far north as the Silvercroft Mountains. It appeared every speck of green grass was occupied by the guilds, which fought for corner spots at turns or for locations closer to the castle gates where the royals might descend to peruse their merchandise.

"You, girl," a gruff voice called. Solveig spun and saw a man wearing a purple tunic, the color of the Thorhauers, the royal family of Thronehelm. His cape was of gold and white, and muddied from the splashing of passing horses and carriages.

"Yes, you," the man pointed. "You look lost."

"I'm here from the Forge to sell my—"

"Twenty laurels." The man held out his gloved hand.

"Twenty laurels!" she exclaimed.

"Aye, twenty," he confirmed, "but for an extra five I can situate you nearer to the castle gates."

"Twenty-five seems steep for a twerg with a pack mule," she bartered. "I don't need much room."

"Twenty-five." His voice was resolute. "Or you can have this spot in the corner." The man pointed to a patch of muddy ground tucked near the front gates, which meant it was farthest from the royal procession. It also smelled as if the area was used by merchants and animals alike to relieve themselves.

"Twenty-five it is." She frowned and handed the man the silver coins.

The spot the organizer had found for her was better than Solveig had expected. It was as near to the gate as he'd said but offered her some cover from the elements. It was against the west wall of the courtyard and a catwalk above provided shade and protection from the rain if the Klyme, the Ancient of Storms didn't cooperate.

She didn't need much room, just a space for Phanna to rest and for her pop-up cart to open. She quickly set up her wares and then waited for customers. As she settled in, Solveig couldn't help noticing the many guards that stood just outside the castle gates. At first, she thought it was her proximity to the royals, but after some time it became clear that the castle was on high alert.

The morning progressed, and she overheard stories from passersby of the tragedies that had befallen the Thorhauers, proving her instincts correct. Until then, she'd been unaware of the news, and she was almost sure that no one in the Forge knew either. It was information that she could take home with her.

The hustle and bustle of the bazaar continued to grow as the morning wore on, but Solveig was having little luck, even with such a prime spot. At this rate, she'd be there for a month, and Tancred Abeline wouldn't be pleased with her extended absence. She stepped back from her table and went to grab one of the waterskins hanging from Phanna's back. As she fumbled around in her saddle bags, she noticed two figures approaching the front of her tent. *A sale*, she thought. She heard a lilted whisper from one of the figures, as if to softly silence the other. Perhaps they saw something they liked and didn't want to squabble over price before asking to inspect an item or two.

"Welcome to my tent!" Solveig announced, stepping out from behind Phanna. "What's caught your eye?"

It was only then that she noticed the two visitors—a middle-aged man of thin build and a striking young woman dressed in the black and orange of Foghaven Vale—had been unaware of her presence. Solveig knew she'd interrupted a conversation between two royals, and it hadn't been about her jewelry. To make matters worse, she was a trollborn twerg, and so she waited for the woman of Foghaven Vale to accuse her of more than just selling gems.

"Apologies, my lady, my lord," Solveig offered, hoping her trollborn frame would buy her some clemency from the obvious awkwardness. "I was thinkin' you were talkin' about me wares."

She didn't need to speak with the accent, but sometimes it helped her to extricate herself from predicaments like this. Royals often took kindly to foreigners if they showed a modicum of respect.

The man sneered down his pointy nose at her as if she'd interrupted him not once but twice, but the comely woman offered a smile, breaking the tension.

"Again, a thousand pardons." Solveig bowed. "I... I'll leave ye two a few moments to finish up."

She turned in haste to walk back to Phanna, but the woman stopped her. Solveig grimaced and slowly spun to face her, hoping for a tinge of mercy.

"No need for that, Guildmistress." The woman forced a smile onto her face. "We'll continue our walk. We thought no one was here."

"What did you hear?" the sniveling man asked, scratching at a spot behind his left ear.

"Nothing," the woman answered for Solveig. "Correct?"

"Yes, ma'am," Solveig nodded. "Just the growlin' of my pack

mule's empty gullet. Was lookin' fer her feed pack is all."

The man looked unconvinced, but the woman grabbed him by the arm and smiled politely before turning them to walk away.

"You sure yer not needin' a new necklace for that lovely outfit?" Solveig called out, but the lady ignored it, escorting the man away and disappearing into the thick of the crowd.

THE MORNING SOON RAN into early afternoon, and Solveig was still struggling to sell her stock. She moved a few baubles here and there, but all in all, it was a tough first day in Thronehelm. She leaned on her table and daydreamed, looking up at the castle, wondering when the next customer would come by.

"Come all the way from the Forge, did ya?" a twergish voice said, awakening her from her state of solitude. She looked over and an old twerg pushed his way through the crowd, wearing white robes with a brooch affixed to his chest. The brooch was of Clan Swifthammer, featuring a pair of crossed hammers— one for war and one for the forge—encircled in platinum. He wore a holy symbol she didn't recognize around his neck. He looked brawny and stout, as a twerg should be, but his hair was full and flaxen in color, despite his obvious age.

"Aye," she replied with a polite smile. "Guessin' yer not interested in any necklaces, friar?"

"I'm no friar," he chuckled in the twergish tongue. "And you're correct, I'm not interested. But my travel companion may be."

A woman leading a horse emerged from the crowd. Her strides were purposeful and confident, and her chin was fixed parallel to the ground. Her riding cloak was pulled up and cast shadows on her face, but Solveig could tell the woman had the kind of beauty and poise unique to the upper echelon of society.

"Good day," the woman said as she reached Solveig's table, a polite smile on her lips.

"My lady," Solveig said once she'd found her voice. Her knees suddenly felt like jam. She always felt awkward around human royalty as she didn't understand their protocols well, but she knew the woman could afford her stock.

"So, are you going to show off the wonderfully crafted jewelry I see there?" the noblewoman asked, taking the initiative.

"Of… of course," Solveig mumbled, trying to recover. She backed up from her table to let the sun sparkle on her gems.

"Twergs make the finest jewelers, don't you agree?" the woman addressed her twergish companion while inspecting the wares. "I'm always on the lookout for quality. Such as this piece, here. It's stunning."

Solveig lifted the necklace and handed it to the woman.

"Who forged this beautiful necklace?" the woman asked.

"Clan Swifthammer, ma'am."

"Isn't that your clan, First Keeper Makai?"

Solveig had heard of both the Keepers and Aliferis Makai, though she'd never met either. It was said that Makai had left the Forge hundreds of years earlier to join the sect, and he was a cleric of repute, even back at the Forge.

"It is," Makai replied.

"It seems that by the good fortunes of Nothos, you've been given a taste of home of sorts with…?"

"Uh, Solveig Jins, ma'am."

"Aren't your people at war with Foghaven Vale? What are you doing so far away from home?"

"Business, ma'am. And I'm no soldier. I am a trader. The invaders have raided many of our troves. Wars cost lives and treasure."

"Well, good fortunes fall to each of us, then. I'm happy

you're safe and that the Fates have placed you in my path today. Nothos himself had to have led me to such a beautiful ornament." She held it to her neck and looked at Jins for an opinion.

"Lovely, ma'am, just as you say."

The woman held the necklace and quickly reviewed the rest of the goods. "I'll take the lot," she waved her hand over the table and cast a warm smile at Jins.

Solveig stood for a moment, not understanding what the woman had said. "The lot, ma'am?"

"Aye," her customer replied. "I'm buying you out of stock. I'll be the envy of everyone with these new trinkets."

"It seems that Nothos has blessed you, too, as the lady suggests," Makai added.

"Thank you, ma'am!" Solveig exclaimed, bursting with excitement. "Please, allow me a brief moment while I total the lot."

Solveig set to work, barely registering the hushed conversation happening in front of her.

"We should return, my lady," Makai murmured in a hushed tone. "We must prepare for—"

"Yes, I know, First Keeper. This has been a lovely distraction, but it is time to return to less appealing matters."

Solveig arrived at a number and then rounded it down for the noble. "The total for the lot, ma'am, is three thousand laurels." She looked at her feet, hoping that the number didn't scare her customer.

"Four thousand laurels, you say? What an agreeable price."

Solveig was taken aback. "Ma'am, that's more than what I was seeking."

"Manners, young Jins." The woman smiled. "Four thousand it is."

Solveig didn't dare open the bag passed to her, but by its size and weight, she could tell she'd been well compensated for her travels.

"I don't suppose you could meet me back here tomorrow morning, right by these gates?"

At Solveig's hesitation, the woman elaborated. "I have one more commission for you. I promise it will be worth your while."

After a moment more of consideration, Solveig nodded. "Tomorrow morning it is."

SOLVEIG ARRIVED AT THE castle gates as the sun was peaking over the castle spires. Various merchants were only just starting to set up their tents and lay out their wares. Solveig didn't have to wait long before the clang of iron sounded, and Makai approached her from behind. He'd clearly come from inside the gates. They still hung open as Solveig turned.

"Where is your companion, First Keeper? I thought she would be meeting me here."

Makai gestured to a group of royal guards behind him. They surrounded a regal, human woman who was wearing a crown. It had to be the Queen, Amice.

"My lady," Solveig bowed, dropping to one knee.

"Enough of that." The queen motioned for her to rise. "You'll only dirty yourself in the mud."

"Yes, ma'am." Solveig stood, but her nerves had taken over and derailed her train of thought.

"I am sorry to have deceived you yesterday, but sometimes it's unavoidable."

Solveig nodded. The queen had a talent for rendering her speechless.

"I'd like to offer you a position as my personal jeweler, Jins," Queen Amice continued. "We can discuss it inside if you'd like."

"Inside the *castle*?"

"Come," the queen beckoned with a regal wave of her hand.

SOLVEIG LED PHANNA UP the long, sloped walkway toward the gates of Castle Thronehelm. Her eyes wandered from parapet to parapet and from tower to tower. She'd never been in a castle. In fact, she'd never even been this close to one. It was a wonder to her, a structure that even the most skilled twergish artisans would struggle to match.

As they reached the top of the hill, the queen signaled for Solveig to walk beside her as they entered the castle. Solveig jumped at the opportunity and politely handed the Phanna's reins over to a stableman at the top of the runway.

She stumbled around, her head high, looking at the size of the portcullis at the main gate, the vaulted spires of the twin towers guarding the entrance and the view from atop the great hill. Her feet spun with her head in all directions as she tried to absorb the skyline.

As they walked through the keep's entrance, Solveig recognized the man and woman who'd accidentally visited her booth yesterday. The woman noticed her and then nodded to the man, who turned his head to meet Solveig's wide eyes. Neither approached, but as they walked by, Solveig felt imaginary daggers at her back.

"Do you know those two?" the queen asked, noticing that Solveig had latched onto them.

"I met them briefly, ma'am. In the market."

"The woman in black and orange is your enemy. She represents the barony of Foghaven Vale, which has just left the unity of Warminster."

"I know, ma'am," Solveig replied, with an air of disappointment in her voice. "Though she was kind to me in the market. The man, however, was quite rude. I thought perhaps I was safe here, on neutral ground of sorts."

"You *are* safe, Solveig." The queen chuckled. "The man is our servant, Meeks Crowley. He's harmless. But the woman is Lady Thessica Camber of Foghaven Vale. She's a cousin to your enemy, and therefore not friendly to you. She herself is a diplomat, which is why I assume she left without incident."

The procession led Solveig to a private chamber and the queen signaled for one of her servants to fetch wine for their guest. When the servant returned, she had a bottle in her hands.

"Now, please," the queen said, "have a glass of wine."

"Of course."

"How's the war going?" the queen asked, with Makai hovering near her.

"Not well, ma'am," Solveig replied. "The jackals of the Vale have conscripted trollborn tribes from the mountains and the Killean Desolates to help them. Some are scouts, some are mercenaries. But the Forge is strong. We'll outlast their advances."

"And your reserves?" the queen pressed. "You said they've stolen much."

"Aye. Several of our troves and mines have been raided. At great cost to them, as well as Clan Swifthammer."

The queen took a sip of her wine. "You say you're a trader. Do you often make it to Saracen?"

"Aye, ma'am. I just came back from a trip there before coming here."

"Successful, I assume?" the queen said, leaning closer to the half-twerg.

"Uh, yes," she replied. "It... was... successful."

"So, tell me of Saracen," the queen went on. "What have you heard of our plight with them?"

It became obvious to Solveig that her encounter with the queen and invitation to the castle was no stroke of luck from Nothos. The extra thousand silver Queen Amice had given her the day before wasn't for the jewelry.

"Now," the queen said, "tell me about the forces your warriors have been fighting from the Vale."

AFTER SPENDING NEARLY AN hour talking about the war with the queen, the subject turned back to Saracen. The queen mentioned Thronehelm's desire to reopen trade with the five guilds, but that Sasha Scarlett had been reticent to do so.

"As I mentioned before," Solveig said, dispensing with the pleasantries after a bottle of wine had been opened and finished, "I've just returned from Saracen. I know the Guild of the Copper Wing well, and they seem comfortable in their new alliance with Foghaven Vale."

"Alliance?" the queen asked.

"Aye," she replied. "Seems as if they've cut some sort of deal and will be supplying items to the Vale. I understand that Saracen might have shut its gates to Thronehelm, which is why my guildmaster sent me here. He thought that Thronehelm would need products, so I left for your city. I'm not sure how gems and jewelry can help a war effort, but—"

"You already have," the queen interrupted, with a wry smile. "Sometimes conversations are more valuable than transactions."

The two women clinked their glasses, as both had found value in their dealings.

Solveig turned to her fellow twerg and changed the subject. "Keeper Makai, I have a question for you."

Until then, the twergish Keeper had stood silently by, listening to Solveig's information. "If I can answer, I will."

"Clan Swifthammer has uncovered magical runes graven in a pocket cave during a dig. The site has become a great mystery in the subterrane. May I show you something in the hopes that your years and wisdom could shed some light?" Before the Keeper could agree, Solveig had already removed her ledger and opened the cover.

The old twerg leaned in.

"Here," she said. "Our miners discovered these glyphs. They glowed a cold blue and seemed to have been there forever. The clan warned no one to touch them, but I was able to copy them down before my guildmaster burned the page. Luckily, I traced over the missing page with some charcoal to expose the markings of my quill on the next sheet of vellum. This is what we found."

Makai inspected the runes and raised an eyebrow while rubbing his bearded chin. "These symbols appear to be ancient. They're beyond any written tongue known to the twergs of the Forge or the Keepers of the Forbidden. They might even be from the time before the Ancients left Warminster for their place in the heavens. I've seen nothing like them. It's an extraordinary find."

"How do we learn more about them?" she asked.

"Well," he began, "you'll need to find someone considerably older than me, if you can believe that. Seek out Yenroar Silentall upon your return to the subterrane. Yenroar is a friend of mine and a twergish magus. In the meantime, tell the twergs not to mine into it or through it. Do nothing until Yen sees it."

Solveig could see the concern on Makai's face and knew that what they'd found was more important than a vein of gold. "I'll pass your sentiments along."

"Enough of that," the queen broke in. "May I convince you to stay as our guest at court for the remainder of the day? I've never met a half-twerg before, and neither has my husband."

"You mean that I'll meet the king?" Solveig's eyes widened in anticipation.

The queen laughed and called for her servant. The two turned to see Meeks Crowley entering the room.

"Your Majesty." The servant bowed and shot a sideways glance at Jins.

"Crowley, I want you to meet my new personal jeweler, Mistress Solveig Jins."

"We've met, my queen." Crowley bowed again while scratching behind his left ear. "Brief though it was."

"I understood as much," the queen replied. "And I believe you owe our guest an apology for your behavior. I'm willing to forgive this transgression as I'm sure you didn't know at the time that she was here at my request."

"Of course, Your Grace." Crowley bowed deeply and swung one arm in front of him in a gesture Solveig had never seen. It seemed almost like an actor performing on a stage. "And I ask for your forgiveness, Mistress Jins."

Solveig took a sip of her wine and let the offer to make amends dangle for a moment or two.

"I accept your apology," she said, and they both shared a false smile.

"Now, Crowley—" the queen motioned with a hand—"fetch the royal tailor immediately. Mistress Jins will be joining us in court today and we need to make her more... presentable."

"At once," Crowley replied before disappearing to retrieve the tailor. The two women shared a smile at the butler's expense.

"So, young Solveig." The queen raised her glass. "What else does your guild have coming from its mines?"

CHAPTER FIFTEEN

"As I live under the runes of Koss and Ulthgar, as I march under the raven tapestry of the great hall, and as I obey the ways of the north. By the ancients, I have so sworn."
—Norseman Blood Oath

MONTGOMERY FOLLOWED THEIR BARBARIAN guide to a window of the great hall. Outside, Henrik Hjordis and his supporters and sons encircled Atorm and his two sons, Faxon the Red and Argantyr. One other man, a warrior the group hadn't been introduced to, joined Atorm. He was nearly as big as Atorm and stood bare chested, wearing only leather leggings and boots made of bear fur.

"This will end swiftly and against us," LaBrecque moaned. Joferian agreed.

"Should we help the *konungr?*" Monty asked Cnute, confused and concerned their negotiations would end before they began.

"That would be dishonorable," the Norseman replied. "This is not your fight, little prince."

"But they're outnumbered three to one," he pressed. "How is this honorable?"

Cnute nodded, with a knowing sneer. "Henrik Hjordis is at a disadvantage."

"*Dis*advantage?" Monty exclaimed.

"Henrik is fortunate that he has more warriors than Atorm. He'll need them."

Monty gave Joferian a worried glance while LaBrecque took a deep swig of his Heifenmager, eyes glued to the spectacle.

"If he loses, we run," Joferian murmured, half in jest and half in honesty.

Monty sniffed and shook his head, his hand shifting to the pommel of his sword. If Atorm fell, it might be wise to run, but he couldn't. Duty to country was far more important despite the risk.

He needed to make ties with Hammerstead.

After a brief exchange of raised voices, the two sides drew their weapons. The first to move was Henrik Hjordis, who grunted in indiscernible Wartooth and crossed behind two of his jarls, darting for Atorm's right side. The other two feinted to the left, then attacked the *konungr* head on.

Atorm reacted with a speed Montgomery didn't expect from such a large man, using the flat of Urnst Jamner to pummel his first assailant in the face. The iron caught the man just under the nose guard of his helmet, sending him to the ground, either dead or unconscious.

As the second jarl turned to his fallen ally, Atorm spun and dropped the head of his hammer into his opponent's leg. An audible snap of bone was followed by a cry of pain and the second barbarian fell, clutching at a protruding femur. His blood stained the matted snow pink, and he raised a hand to stave off the lunging *konungr*. The gesture was met with a boot to his face as Atorm knocked him prone and stepped by him into the next wave of assailants.

Atorm's sons rushed into Hjordis's lines, brandishing their round shields like battering rams and punching a hole in their ranks. Howling like two silver bears, both sons started swinging their axes, one unrelenting cut after another, tearing through leather armor and barbarian flesh.

Monty watched as Henrik Hjordis, surprised at the brazen assault, was left behind by the three advancing Stormmoellers and forced to stare down at the clenched fists of the bare-chested ally of the *konungr*. The half-naked man wielded two matching warhammers fashioned with a hammerhead on one side and a pickaxe on the other.

The man clinked the heads of the warhammers together and flashed a smile at the outflanked Hjordis. In a swift and violent whirl, he spun one warhammer to reveal the tip of the pickaxe, which he used to catch the top of Hjordis's shield. The maneuver wasn't meant to injure, but its intent was deadly enough. The warhammer's curved beak snuck over the top of Hjordis's shield, splintering it as it lodged itself in the wood.

Before Hjordis could react, the man violently ripped the hooked hammer down, tearing the shield from in front of him and exposing Hjordis to further attack. Then he swung his other warhammer, slamming the head of the weapon into Hjordis's chest. The blow was partially absorbed by his thick hide armor, but Hjordis buckled to one knee nonetheless from the power of the blow.

Atorm used the moment of respite provided by his two attacking sons to launch Urnst Jamner at an approaching enemy. The big hammer flew through the air and found its mark, slamming into the man and knocking him to the snow. As he fell, he flung his hand axe.

Atorm grabbed it in the air and, in one motion, spun and threw it at another enemy. The axe barely cleared the tip of the charging man's shield and embedded itself in his shoulder.

The wounded Norseman cried out in pain, spinning away from the charge. His futile attempts to remove the axe only led to more bleeding and he slumped to the ground in agony.

Monty afforded himself a brief smile, knowing Atorm and his allies had killed or incapacitated five of their attackers within seconds. But there were still twice as many enemies to face down.

Atorm grabbed for the fallen man's shield and tugged it from his failing hand. He raised it just in time to absorb the swing of a sword from one of Hjordis's sons. The weapon, made of their favored slate iron, slid easily through the wooden shield and sliced through the iron bands of its brace. The blade stopped inches from Atorm's burly forearm.

Instinctively, the *konungr* spun the shield, using it to twist the embedded sword out of the hands of the inexperienced barbarian. His attacker screamed in protest, but the weapon slipped from his hand and was flung harmlessly into the snow. Hjordis's son looked into the eyes of his king one last time before Atorm's free fist punched him square in the jaw. The jawbone shifted from the force of the blow and the young Norseman's face contorted in agony.

Monty winced as if the *konungr*'s fist had hit him instead of the enemy. He saw Atorm's attacker's eyes roll into the back of his head and his body fall limp.

"Ouch," LaBrecque said, taking another swig from his ale horn.

Cnute chuckled at the admiral's commentary, but Monty turned his attention back to the melee. The battle was far from won.

A roar of defiance erupted from the rear of Hjordis's supporters, and three of the attackers abandoned the fight with Atorm's sons and ran to the defense of their leader.

The half-naked barbarian growled at the approaching group and dropped to one knee, using the other leg to kick the stunned Henrik Hjordis flat in the snow. As the hapless challenger fell, the man lifted his spinning warhammers in defense and was back on his feet before the men reached him. In a blur, the warhammers danced in a circled wall of steel in front of him, swinging in short bursts, forcing the other Norsemen to stop before attacking.

Monty's eyes never left the outnumbered champion of Atorm. The three assailants fanned out around the lone barbarian, who stood his ground, trapped in a triangle of swords. They began to attack, each testing and probing for weaknesses in his defense, but each lunge or slice was parried or blocked by whirring warhammers.

One of the men barked an order at the other two, and the pair attacked from each side at the same time. Their hulking target ducked to one side, charging low at one of them, his impressive frame slamming him into the man's legs.

The man groaned. his feet leaving him and toppling over the barbarian. Before he could regain his footing, the pointed end of one Warhammer came crashing down, impaling the man's skull through his helmet. The weapon lodged so deeply that when the barbarian tried to recover it, the piked end of the hammer remained stuck in a twist of metal and bone. He let go of the handle and spun, just in time to block the blade of the second Norseman.

The two met, sword landing on hammer, and for the first time in the battle, Monty saw the larger of the two men retreat. He stepped back, nearly losing purchase in the snow. The remaining man charged in, perhaps sensing an advantage had been gained, and the three met in tangle of blood and steel.

A flash of a blade drew a thin line of blood across Atorm's champion's chest. Monty half-expected the burly barbarian to falter, but instead his eyes flared and, in a rage, he screamed something indiscernible to Monty's ears in Wartooth. The two men seized for just a second in fear and uncertainty, which is all the barbarian needed to regain the advantage.

With an effortless flick of his wrist, his remaining warhammer leapt from this hand, spun in the air, and crashed into one of the swordsmen. Monty heard the thud, followed by the crackle of bone popping, and the man fell to the ground, grabbing at his chest. For a second, he struggled to breathe, writhing around before the barbarian finished him with a boot to the face.

The remaining warrior lunged in, sending his steel sailing past the great Norseman, and found himself exposed in the maneuver. The beastly man huffed and grabbed the warrior around the neck. In one swift move, Atorm's champion wrenched back, snapping the man's neck and ending the fight.

As Monty's attention turned back to the rest of the battle, Atorm and his two sons had made quick work of the remaining Hjordis supporters. Monty found Atorm, Urnst Jamner back in his hands, standing above the recovering Henrik Hjordis.

Cnute chortled at the sight. "I told you Hjordis was at a disadvantage."

Monty could only agree.

"Yield," Joferian mumbled as if he were talking to Hjordis.

"There will be no yielding," Cnute snapped at the viscount. "There is no honor in surrender."

Moments later, Atorm re-entered the great hall with his two sons and bloodied champion to the cheers from the onlookers. He made his way back to Montgomery.

Monty couldn't help staring at Urnst Jamner, which he still held in his mighty hand. The spike was matted with clumped hair and remnants of the bloody skull that had once belonged to Henrik Hjordis.

"The blood feud is now over," Atorm bellowed, his mighty voice rising above the crowd's cheers and toasts. "Come," he said, throwing his hulking arm around the prince. "Let's continue our negotiations. I have an idea."

"RIJKSTAG THANKS WARMINSTER FOR such wonderful gifts," Atorm said to Prince Montgomery.

"You're welcome, *Konungr*," Monty replied.

The *konungr* reached for the axe, which Monty readily parted with. Atorm turned to his firstborn son, Faxon the Red, and motioned for him to take it. Faxon stared reverently at the weapon and then lifted it slowly from his father's outstretched hands. The crowd cheered at the return of such a relic. It seemed more important to the throng of Norsemen than the treasure at their feet.

"What did you think of the battle?" Atorm asked Monty, sitting next to him.

Shaken by the direct question, he replied, "At first, I thought you were outmatched. I see now I was wrong."

Atorm smiled and poured him more Heifenmager, letting him continue. Joferian didn't sit with them, content to stand, arms crossed, by the window. LaBrecque sat near Monty, across from the *konungr*, sipping from the horn that was again filled to the brim.

"The way in which your men battle shows they know each other's strengths well," Monty went on. "But…" His voice drifted away as he thought carefully about his next words.

"Go on, Prince," the *konungr* encouraged him, taking a big drink and signaling for food to be brought.

Monty didn't want to offend the mighty man, but he'd be a fool to try to backtrack in his statement. "You put your life in danger. For what?" He gauged the big man's reaction. Seeing him take no offense, he went on. "As a king, is it your duty to—"

"As a king," Atorm interrupted, "it is my duty to fight when the Ancients will it. To defend my honor and the honor of my people. It is part of the ritual of the role of being king. I am Konungr. I am not always Atorm."

The Norseman's words struck Monty deep in the heart.

"But I am also mighty!" Atorm roared, baiting the gathering. The crowd cheered and raised their drinking horns high. He took another swig, washing down a bite of meat. "Will you be a mighty king, little prince?"

He hoped to be. But now he wasn't even sure what that meant. "There is much beyond my reach." Monty's voice was steady. He caught Joferian's furrowed gaze. "I hope to surround myself with good council and wise leaders."

Atorm nodded, thinking. With a quick wave of his hand, he signaled for someone to approach. The crowd parted again, revealing a lanky man leaning on a walking staff festooned with Norse runes. His hood hid his face, but his free hand pointed a crooked finger at Montgomery.

"What of the boy with the white eyes?" the man asked, his voice cracking. "Does he fight with you?"

Montgomery didn't respond at first, wondering instead how the man knew about Daemus.

"Your Keepers may be blind, but our Ancients aren't." The man waggled his bony finger in Montgomery's face.

"You mean Daemus Alaric?" Monty asked.

The room quieted except for the crackling embers of the hearth in the center of the chamber, as though he'd just said a word he shouldn't have.

"Yes. Daemus White-Eyes."

"We fight alongside his cause, but he's traveled south with—"

He was interrupted again, but this time the hooded man was speaking in Wartooth and only to Atorm. The audience of half-drunk citizens of Hammerstead began to murmur to themselves.

"What are they saying?" Joferian whispered, finally joining the prince at the table.

"He's our runecaster," Cnute replied, sitting next to him. "A wizard, to use your words."

The runecaster finished his discussion and then turned

back to Montgomery.

"The Ancients have warned us of this Daemus White-Eyes," Atorm remarked. "Einar Skullgrimsson, show him."

The runecaster tapped Montgomery, Joferian and LaBrecque with his staff and urged them to follow him to the hearth. The men complied and sat on half-circular benches as they watched the runecaster drop to his knees and thrust his staff into the flames. The stick didn't ignite, and the flames didn't seem to char it in any way. They looked at each other in amazement.

"*Etor est gamugli,*" Einar chanted. "*Gehufnis lochte throh.*"

A few seconds passed, and then he reached into the flames with his bare hand and pulled a heated ember from it. Monty doubted what he was seeing for a moment, thinking the ale had clouded his senses, but as Einar turned to him, he flames encircled the man's hand.

Einar reached toward Montgomery, with the flame in his hand. Monty tried to remain still, though every instinct was screaming for him to bat the runecaster's hand away. The man extended his crooked finger and touched the prince on the forehead. Monty winced. He felt no heat. Just cold skin and a broken fingernail. He exhaled in relief.

The runecaster kept his eyes locked with Montgomery's and used his finger to draw a Norse rune over his skin. The prince heard Einar's voice in his head, repeating the magical words in Wartooth. Monty didn't dare to break Einar's gaze in case the cold turned back to fire.

"He's ready," Einar declared aloud, as the fire dissipated from his hand.

Montgomery looked to Joferian, whose face was racked with confusion over what he'd just witnessed. Monty knew he'd get nothing from him, so he turned to LaBrecque, whose expression mirrored Joferian's.

"You're ready," Atorm nodded in assent, recapturing Monty's attention.

"I am," he replied, an odd feeling of assurance gripping at him.

"Good," the burly king smiled. "Then take your gold and my father's axe back with you."

"What?" Monty asked. "I thought I was being tested. I'm ready."

"You have much to learn of our customs," Atorm replied. "We thank you for your offer of gold, but in our culture, gold is earned and not given. Keep your chest until we've earned it."

Monty glanced to Joferian, who shook his head just enough for Monty to see. But Monty's feelings went against his cousin's advice.

"Very well." Monty's words were unsure, but he knew he had no choice.

"Also, you must keep my father's axe," Atorm continued. "Henrik Hjordis was right. It hasn't been earned with blood." He waved subtly to Faxon the Red, who handed it back to Montgomery.

"But your fight with Hjordis…" Monty's brow furrowed. "If not for the axe, what was the battle for?"

"Honor."

Monty paused. The differences in their cultures were even more pronounced than he'd expected.

"And our alliance?" Monty pressed, cautious to keep the reason for his visit at the forefront.

"Einar said you're ready. But instead of gold and an axe, I require a different payment. I have two requests for you in exchange for this alliance you seek."

"Of course," Monty replied. "If I can grant them, they are yours."

Atorm's voice intensified, "First, Koss, the Ancient of War, has told us it's time for the poachers of our slate iron to fall. Together, Rijkstag and Warminster must sack the town of Vallance, and then our two great armies will move on to Saracen!"

Cheers from the Hammerstead drunks filled the hall.

Monty tried to stay poised, but the offer made no sense. He knew Warminster had no claim to Vallance or Saracen, and the wolves were already at the door in Thronehelm. He also knew his father had sent his cousin, Zendel Cray, to negotiate with Saracen. Any attack on Vallance or Saracen would end all that.

"So, you want us to divide our forces?" the prince asked, struggling to hide the confusion on his face.

"One warrior of Rijkstag is worth ten of Saracen's mercenaries," Atorm replied.

Monty couldn't argue. And he was too close to an agreement. If Vallance needed to fall, so be it. Rash as it may be, he knew he had no choice.

"And the other request?" Monty asked, still unhappy about the first one.

Atorm waved at his young daughter, Freya. She stepped away from her family to stand next to Montgomery and Atorm.

"You must take my daughter as your wife, forever linking Rijkstag and Warminster in blood," Atorm announced to another roar of the Viking crowd.

Lightning struck through Monty, sticking him to the floor. No words came to his open lips.

"Your father—" Joferian took an aggressive step forward.

"Your father wants this alliance, no?" Atorm growled, interrupting the viscount.

Monty nodded. How many more surprises could he endure before he cracked?

"My daughter will make our alliance permanent." Atorm's stare was cold. "With Rijkstag and Warminster standing side by side, our enemies will tremble in fear."

"That's it?" Monty asked, his mouth dry.

Atorm's lips curled only slightly. Of course, there was more. "If you agree, you must prove your worth. As Einar boasted, the Ancients have declared you worthy."

"Worthy? How can I prove my worth?" Monty asked. His hands began to shake where they hung at his side.

"By participating in *Bardagi*," Atorm replied, as a matter of fact.

At the mere word, the crowd started to chant, at first in a slow cadence, "*Bardagi, Bardagi, Bardagi.*"

Monty's face quirked and he looked at the king as the chants grew in force. "What is *Bardagi*?"

"A battle to the death, young prince."

Monty couldn't stop his mouth from falling agape nor the look of cautious fear that widened his eyes. The blood, still wet on the head of Urnst Jamner, was enough to make his heart pound.

"As the gods intended," Atorm went on, noting Monty's apprehension. "I see you understand. You will fight with your bare hands, in single combat with Freya's betrothed. After all, I can't very well end their betrothal without great dishonor to Ulf Skuli, son of Metter Fetterhand.

He'll need to defend his honor. And if he defeats you, who better to marry the *konungr*'s only daughter than the man who redeemed Rijkstag's blood feud with Warminster by killing the king's first son? His only remaining son."

He paused, allowing the gravity of the moment to sink in. Monty turned to Joferian who had a look other than disdain on his face. His eyes thinned but he offered no counsel.

"It's the right thing to do," Atorm placed his sizeable hand on Monty's shoulder. "I can't allow my daughter to marry a man when I haven't seen him fight. If you defeat Ulf, Rijkstag would be honored to form an unbreakable alliance with you and your kin."

Monty looked to Freya, who, like her father, appeared unfazed by the moment. Then he turned to Joferian, whose head was already shaking, followed by LaBrecque, who averted his eyes and took another sip from his horn. The crowd's fervor continued to grow and the chants of *"Bardagi"* echoed throughout the hall.

Ulf Skuli, son of Metter Fetterhand, stepped from the crowd and stared at Montgomery, waiting for an answer. Monty had just watched the barrel-chested barbarian fight against Henrik Hjordis outside. He was as formidable a warrior as Atorm and killed at least three men.

Monty steeled himself, his heart hammering against the inside of his chest. He forced himself to glower in bravery, and he held his head high. The words of his father rang in his head. What did it mean to be king? Was it just doing his duty for his country? Or did it mean something greater? Did it mean what was necessary and courageous in the face of fear, putting himself aside? To his surprise, his hands stopped shaking.

"I accept," said the prince.

CHAPTER SIXTEEN

*"Some snakes kill by squeezing very slowly. Others kill
quick with venom. The Ophidian kills by means of both."*
—Incanus Dru'Waith

THE CITY OF ABACUS lay nestled against the western
coastline of the Great Sea, just south of the Emerald Dales.
Incanus Dru'Waith was familiar with the city, as he'd done
business there before. Incanus didn't know all, but he knew
enough about Abacus to feel safe. The city was unique, and
the Abacunian culture was lenient enough for a Bone elf to
not have to hide in the shadows to survive.

Abacus took its name from the unorthodox wizard-
inventor who'd founded the unusual town. In his time, Abacus
Athobasca had been a renowned inventor, using his wizardry
to enhance his peculiar devices and inventions. After adopting
basic models of scientific thought and augmenting them
through his mastery of magic, Abacus Athobasca attracted
like-minded inventors, wizards, clerics, and academicians to
his new town, where unconventional thought was embraced.
Unfortunately, Athabasica's penchant for discovery and
invention finally caught up to him, and one of his many
dangerous experiments exploded, costing the dear sage his life.

The Bone elf rode in on horseback and wasn't harassed
by the Castellan, the town guards of Abacus. It wasn't their
place. The Castellan consisted of trained soldiers from the
High Aldin, who guarded the port and policed the town, but
they didn't stop the free flow of people to their city. All were
welcomed. They donned distinctive royal blue surcoats, each
featuring a golden mace in the center of their chests, encircled
in a wreath of peace. The mace was known as "Peacemaker,"

and it was wielded by the Knight Castellan, the leader of the High Aldin. Peacemaker appeared to be made of solid gold and was enchanted with a powerful magic that attacked its opponent's will, forcing them to submit to the commands of the wielder. Incanus had witnessed its power several times when it had been used to break up simple bar fights or to control greater uprisings. He feared its grip—and more to the point, he feared the head of the mace.

Incanus skulked through the streets, his hood covering his face. He was to meet Skullam in the Penny Quarter, the seediest part of town. He found his way into a local watering hole and waited for Skullam to find him. It didn't take long. The imp appeared from nowhere, and in any other city, the mere sight of him would have made a scene. Not in Abacus, though.

Incanus took a sip of his ale and watched the imp climb onto the chair beside him.

"I see your talon has grown back." Incanus remarked at the imp's powers of regeneration. Sir Ritter of Valkeneer had claimed the talon in their battle in Castleshire, and it had taken Skullam a month to heal.

"It has, my liege," the imp replied. "The Longmarcher will rue the day he cut it from me."

"Have you found Anselm Helenius?"

"No, but the Ophidian tells me they know where he is. They wouldn't share his location until you visited them first."

"I owe them." Incanus shook his head in acknowledgement. "They're a last resort, but it seems we're out of options. Follow me to the Twin Snakes."

———✦———

FOR INCANUS, THE WALK through the Penny Quarter was like a walk back through time. The cobbled streets and lantern posts hadn't changed in the decade since his last visit here.

His horse carried them along, winding their way through the crooked corners and sagging eaves of the buildings, looking suspiciously for troublemakers as they passed. Abacus was unlike many cities, and Incanus didn't need to be on guard. But old habits die hard.

He stopped and tied his horse in front of a three-story house that featured balconies on the second and third levels, where the prostitutes of the Twin Snakes bordello could advertise their wares to passersby.

The Bone elf entered the lobby and was approached by one of the female workers who seemed to be drunk, or worse.

"What can I do for you?" she asked with a lustful smile.

"The real question is, 'Who can you find for me?'" he replied. "I'm looking for the Ophidian. I have some gold for them."

The woman shot a look of disappointment at him but sauntered off to fulfill his request.

A few moments passed, and Incanus heard the wheels of a wagon turning from deep within the bordello. A pair of double doors across from him soon opened and a wagon entered the chamber, being pulled by two nearly naked men, fitted as though they were horses. A makeshift throne sat atop the wagon, occupied by the Ophidian.

Incanus hadn't seen the girls for some time, but he knew they wouldn't have forgotten his debt. The Ophidian had the body of single human woman from the waist down but was a conjoined twin of two middle-aged women from the waist up. The sisters shared a partial torso at the pelvis but had separate chests and four arms.

"It's nice to see you again, Ophidian." Incanus bowed to the sisters.

"Incanus." Their voices greeted him in unison. "You still owe us from your last visit. Are you here to pay?" The two-headed creature shared a knowing glance with themself, and then both faces turned back to the assassin.

"The only currency I work in is death," the Bone elf threatened.

After a moment of awkward silence, Incanus let up and tossed a sack of coins to them. The two women fought, their four arms flailing at the gold, as the heavy purse fell into their cart.

"I put something extra in there for you. For the time it took me to return. Your information was, shall we say, helpful in securing my prey."

"It's about time," the Ophidian blurted in a dual voice, speaking over themself.

"Who's your little pet?" the head on the left asked, leaning down from the throne to get a better look at Skullam. The imp retreated and stood at Incanus's knee.

"His name is Skullam."

"We could use the services of such a creature," the sister on the right said. "Perhaps we can put him to work for our guests with more… discriminating tastes."

"He would make a great server," the left sister replied.

"Enough." Incanus was growing impatient.

"What brings you to the Twin Snakes today?"

"More business." The assassin began rifling through the bar and helped himself to a bottle. "We're looking for a man who visits your brothel. He's one of the guests with the tastes you describe."

"We know," the Ophidian remarked in chorus. "Your imp tells us you seek Anselm Helenius."

Incanus nodded. "He's someone who I believe would enjoy your… *unique company.*"

The Ophidian giggled and their heads turned to one another. "Of course, we know Anselm. He's one of our loyal customers. He has an interest in women like us." They both began to giggle again.

"Are you a cryptid?" Skullam asked.

Incanus slapped him for interrupting. The imp had a limited social understanding, and he didn't want him costing them more money by insulting the Ophidian.

"I didn't know whether you provided *services* to him." Incanus took another swig. "Do you know where he is?"

The sisters turned to one another and began to whisper. Incanus waited and the two quickly turned back to him. "And our fee? This time, we demand you pay up front."

Incanus removed the silver holy symbol that he'd pilfered from the dead man's body on Harbinger's Run. He knew silver would open their mouths. It always did.

He tossed it to the Ophidian, and the four arms swatted together again, trying to grab it from the air. The left sister retrieved and inspected it, then handed it to her twin. "Silver from Solemnity?" the right sister asked.

"There's still blood on it." The twin on the left rubbed at the stain.

"Killing priests, these days?" they asked in unison.

Incanus said nothing.

"Helenius is one of our best customers when he comes to town." The right twin shared. "Telling you his whereabouts will cost us many future visits."

The Bone elf's patience wore thin. "Where is he?"

"He stays with a man here in town who owns an apothecary and alchemy shop. It's called the Boiling Beaker. You should be able to find him there."

Incanus looked to Skullam and they both turned to leave, satisfied that their deal was complete.

"However," the Ophidian called in one voice, "we expect

to see Helenius this evening."

"He hasn't visited us yet this week," the head on the left remarked, pouting like a child who'd waited too long for a gift.

"If you like," the other sister motioned with her arms, "you can stay here and finish your job. But it will cost you extra."

Incanus turned back to the Ophidian. "How much?"

The Ophidian giggled to themselves again. In unison, they said, "Welcome back to the Twin Snakes."

CHAPTER SEVENTEEN

"When the voices of the ancients speak to
you, their words come with courage."
—Warminster, the Mage

DAEMUS WOKE FROM SOMETHING more like a dark fog than a dream. His head throbbed where Arjun had hit him, a thought that brought him some annoyance until he recalled how shamefully he'd acted. Sitting near him on the ground were Princess Addilyn, straight-backed and composed as usual, and Faux, hunched over a knife she was sharpening as if her life depended on it. Both were silent.

Addilyn noticed him first, glancing over with a dispassionate expression. "Good morning, Daemus."

"Where are the others?" he asked, rubbing the delirium from his eyes.

"Eating." Unlike Addilyn's clipped politeness, Faux's tone was a little cold. Not that he could blame her, he thought with a rush of shame. "We came back early." She tossed something at him, which he fumbled and nearly dropped; it was a breakfast roll.

"I need to apologize." Daemus stood, his head pounding, and he found his dizziness getting no better. "To both of you."

"Yes, you do." Faux's voice didn't hide her anger. Addilyn kept her eyes lowered and made no reply.

Daemus flushed and pressed on, forcing the words out. "I'm so sorry I said all of that. To both of you. I was angry... at... I was angry, and I took it out on you. I didn't mean any of it, and it was unfair. You didn't deserve to be treated that way."

Addilyn tilted her head. "For my part, your apology is accepted," she managed with her usual grace. "Not all the things you said about me were entirely false."

Faux toyed with her knife, then put it away. "I can't forgive you yet," she admitted, her words forceful and blunt, but her tone was a little less cold than before. "I need some more time to think about it."

Daemus nodded. "Of course. I understand."

"However." Addilyn stood and stared at Daemus. "We must think of how you will apologize to the coronel. If you had been anyone else, your offense would have been very grievous. I think the safest way would be for you to perform a ritual apology." She folded her hands together. "I know of one that is shorter than five minutes. I can easily teach it to you."

"All right," Daemus almost whispered after a long pause, unsure what else to say.

"He's not an elf, Addilyn," Faux protested, looking as confused. "Traditional apologies would have no meaning coming from him. He should speak in his own words, shouldn't he?"

Addilyn glanced at her. "You assume his own words are to be trusted. At least if he used a rote apology, the coronel would be sure to understand his intent."

Faux still didn't like it, but Daemus was willing to learn the apology, which consisted of a bow in which one's head needed to touch the ground and about ten lines of poetic groveling. Addilyn made him aware of the fact that unlike many ritual apologies from her culture, this one contained no pretense of saving face and was instead a simple, severely worded acceptance of guilt.

The three of them left the grove, Daemus inhaling his breakfast roll as they went, repeating the words of the apology to himself and feeling sure he would get something wrong. His trepidation grew as they approached the coronel's tree, where he could see their other companions waiting outside for them. Daemus prepared himself to tell them good morning, but the chilly, awkward atmosphere as he reached the group kept his mouth closed. He missed Delling.

"Sorry for that," muttered Arjun, gesturing at his head, though the look on his face was too neutral to discern if he really was. Daemus jerked his head in silent acquiescence.

The group proceeded into the tree's throne room, such as it was. This time the coronel was already seated in the tall-backed chair, with two figures standing at his shoulders: his daughter Liesel, wearing an expression of combined wariness and restrained curiosity, and a human man that Daemus didn't recognize. Seeing the coronel in his place now and not hunching into the room as if uninvited, it was much more obvious that Daemus was looking at a king. His countenance was mild, and a little expectant. Something in his eyes made it clear that Daemus would have to make the proper amends if he wanted forgiveness for his insults.

He dropped to the ground and touched his forehead to the dirt in something more like a collapse than a bow. "Coronel," he began, his voice unsteady, "my shame overwhelms my sight so that I cannot see you. Uhh—" The next words came to him. "The Ancients have thrown me aside like the clothes of one dead from plague and burned me with remorse to cleanse my wretchedness. To you, may I be only a crawling thing to be stepped upon. I—" He realized he was shaking and searched his mind for the next words, repeated to himself over and over on the walk from the meadow, but they didn't come. Tension built in the room as the silence stretched out.

"I'm so sorry," he blurted out instead of continuing. "Not only did I speak in a manner not befitting your honored station, but I was also cruel and petty toward my friends, who have loyally stayed with me and protected me throughout our journey, and who deserve only thanks. I don't know why I did that. But to you especially, I most humbly apologize. After you graciously accepted us into your domain and even came to see us in person, I responded with such disrespect." He fell silent, feeling that he ought to go on, but not sure what else to say. He heard Addilyn exhale quietly behind him and wasn't sure if it was a sigh of relief or exasperation or worse, resignation.

"I know why you did it." Coronel Briar stood, his face stoic but his tone serious. "You were exhausted and overwhelmed after a night of horrors. And for all the gravity of your station, you are still only a young man. Look up at me."

Daemus did and was relieved to see that his expression had lost its dangerous edge, though he still spoke with an air of grave warning.

"I accept your apology. See that you take care in the future not to repeat such foolish missteps, because not everyone possesses my forgiving disposition."

With a respectful timbre, Daemus nodded. "Thank you, Coronel."

The king smiled at him then, and the atmosphere in the room immediately lightened. "Get up." The coronel waved, and Daemus stood, taking a half-step back to be closer to his companions. With a glance around the room, he saw that their faces had all eased. A hand gripped his shoulder: Arjun's.

"May I now introduce you to Lachlan Barrett, a druid of the Emerald Dales, as you call our Eternal Forest." The coronel motioned to the man, his voice now cheerier. "He met your uncle, I think, Daemus."

"Thank you, Adulth." Lachlan stepped forward and inclined his head at the king before turning to address the group. "Only briefly. I advised him and, uh—" His eyes flickered toward Arjun in obvious recognition.

"Arjun," the soldier supplied, then added, "He told us of

the threat posed by Clan Blood Axe."

Lachlan's eyes fell on Daemus. "It is a pleasure to meet you, Daemus," he stated, although his tone was serious. "I had hoped my warning would protect you, and I am glad to see that your uncle heeded me wisely enough that you stand before me now."

Daemus stared at him, holding onto his hopeful but blank expression with all his might. He could think of nothing to say. After a short pause, Lachlan spared him further awkwardness and stepped back to his place at the coronel's shoulder.

"You were pursued," began the coronel, speaking with more gravity now, "when you arrived at our forest, by a fell beast more dangerous than any natural animal that walks this forest. My soldiers, the mighty warriors of the Emerald Shield, were with much difficulty able to repel it. But it pursues you still, and it will be back in search of your blood. You know this already, I see. It is implacable." He scrutinized their faces. "But despite its terrible strength, it is not invincible."

"Do you know how to defeat it?" Ritter asked, his tone colored by urgency rather than anger.

The coronel looked over at him, then raised a long-fingered hand to point. "On your back, Valkeneer," he gestured. He was met with stunned silence as everyone turned to look. "Do you know the story behind your weapon?"

Ritter's lips moved soundlessly for a moment. "Yes and no," he spoke at last. "It has been passed down through my family line, and so I know its relationship to our familial history. But I've always sensed there's more to the story."

The coronel nodded. "Your bow is hewn from special wood, taken from the forest where that creature was born. Long ago, a necromancer killed his enemies by stealing the life from the forest around them. It is dark, ugly magic, the kind of spell that is almost impossible to survive casting. I could not say whether the Ancients were at hand, shielding his life..." He trailed off, looking pained. "It is a question that has troubled me. But this spell created the monster that pursues you and petrified your Ashen Hollows. My people keep its memory because we are bonded to the trees and the spirit of the forest, you see."

"It was a terrible loss," put in Liesel with a bare whisper, her face pulled into an expression of deep discomfort. "Even at our distance, three of our great sages perished from the shock."

"Yes," the coronel confirmed with a glance at his daughter, bearing the same look on his face. "We have no name for the event. Words cannot encompass its meaning to our people. But it has been given the name of Ghostwood among your people, as I'm sure you can attest."

"Yes." Ritter's face became sullen, his eyes meeting the coronel's.

Daemus looked away from his friend and turned his thoughts inward. He felt a horrible foreboding, and he was chilled to the bone as the coronel spoke his next words.

"The necromancer at the center of all this was a former Keeper. He is now known by some as Graytorris the Mad."

"So, the creature is seeking Daemus for the purposes of its master," Blue concluded, a grimness to his tone.

"And those 'purposes' can't be good," put in Marquiss.

Despite himself, Daemus exhaled through his nose in a silent laugh at the extreme understatement.

"Indeed not." The coronel's eyes crinkled slightly before his face regained its somber cast.

"If Ritter's bow can defeat the Antlered Man," Faux began, her voice hesitant, "can it also kill Graytorris?"

"I cannot tell you that. I know it can kill the beast because they came from the same unholy source—that is, the same spell. As for the effects on the caster, I cannot say. Magics such as this are not well documented because they are so rarely found." The king steepled his fingers. "What I have told you is all the Keldarin know of the matter. I hope this knowledge proves useful to you."

There was a pause, like an exhale of combined relief and resignation. They knew more, but it was still not enough.

"Coronel." Daemus steeled his nerves. "I have one more question. I had a vision, shortly after we arrived in the forest, of a great tree. It was huge, just like this one, but it was in a city, not a forest. Do you know anything about that?"

The coronel's brows rose. "If it looked like this one, there is only one place you could have seen. This tree and that one are said to be twin saplings from the Faye Tree, vanished into myth. Both were gifts of Melexis, in her mercy. One is here, to serve as the Keldarin pathway to the Hall of the Ancients and a testament to Melexis's love of our people. The other was turned into a great library by a powerful and wise sage known as Vorodin. The city of Abacus was built around it. And it is known there as Vorodin's Lair."

Shortly afterward the party departed, saying their goodbyes to the coronel, the princess, and the druid. Everything seemed to be fitting, but in a way Daemus didn't know if he liked. It was as though he could see all the pieces of a vast puzzle coming together cleanly, but he suspected the completed picture would only bring him grief.

As they were leaving the tree, he opened his mouth. Faux, who was walking with him, turned to listen.

"It's my fault," Daemus blurted in a rush before he could explain what he meant. "As much as it is Erud's, it's also mine. They both died protecting me. And I failed to save them. I didn't even really try." He felt cold. "Erud didn't... make me do that. It was me."

Faux was staring at him.

"It was me," he repeated desperately, trying to make her understand.

"Daemus," his friend murmured in protest, her face pained.

Without another word, she pulled him into a hug.

Daemus closed his eyes against the tears.

CHAPTER EIGHTEEN

"To truly understand your enemy, you
must first become them."
—Annals of Halifax Military Academy

"MY BEAUTIFUL LADY FLEURY," Kail Ilidari said as he took a deep bow while opening the door to her carriage. "It's a pleasure to host you again. I've missed you these many moons."

"Ah, my lovely guardian," Isabeau reached for the trollborn chamberlain to help her from the coach. "It warms my heart to find you well." Isabeau had made the long and arduous journey from Deadwaters Fork to Foghaven Vale. The trip had dragged on for nearly two months, delayed by weather and her own brand of wanderlust. She hadn't dared to pass a foreign land without stopping for food, drink, or the warmth of a man in her bed—or in her carriage for that matter.

She lovingly stroked Ilidari's rough cheeks and then kissed him on the forehead. Their friendship was one-sided; Kail held a soft spot for Lady Fleury, and she played to it when she could. In truth, she felt badly for the trollborn, who'd suffered first under Dragich's father's reign and now under his.

"I'll take you to the king." Ilidari lifted his elbow for her to take.

"The king?" she jerked her head, surprised with the title. "Why, my good man, I didn't come all this way to see him. I came for you."

Ilidari might have blushed, but if he did then it was unnoticeable, hidden within the blotches of his trollborn skin. He led her through the castle and ushered her into the war room, where Isabeau had always found her former lover.

"The Lady Isabeau Fleury," Ilidari announced, as he

escorted her into the chamber. As she entered, she noticed the fire had been stoked in the large hearth at the far side of the room. *The Ancients do provide small mercies,* she thought, making her way to warm herself by the flames.

To her surprise, Aarav and Ember were both there, and they greeted her with the love of a child to its mother while Von Lormarck sat on his new throne, reading from a ledger. He didn't look pleased.

"Mother, I'm so glad you came here for my wedding." Ember hugged her tight again. She sensed both happiness and a trembling in Ember, something she'd later address in private.

"Of course, my dear," she replied. She kissed Ember on the forehead. "I wouldn't have missed the union for the world."

"I fear, however, that you've traveled for a wedding that won't happen." Dragich's voice rose, his eyes still buried in his readings. "Haven't you heard? We're on the brink of war with the very family she was betrothed to. A pity."

"I've heard," Isabeau admitted, "but I haven't come empty-handed."

Dragich closed the ledger, his eyes impatient. "This isn't the time for a visit." His tone was abrupt. "The fate of our people could hang in the balance."

She curtsied, with a mockingly low bow.

"I fear I've disturbed the new king," Isabeau turned to Ember and Aarav. "Come, my children, let's go and talk. It's been far too long since I've seen you. I can catch up with the king when he's... ready. I'm here to help."

"Aarav is fighting a war to the north against the twergs," Dragich growled and lifted his gaze to Isabeau. "He must leave *immediately* to attend to his responsibilities. Correct, son?"

Aarav stared at his father and shot a sideways glance at his mother. "Mother, I do apologize, but duty calls."

Isabeau blinked but expected nothing more from her son. "And what of Ember?" she asked. "Is she to disappear to practice her singing or to tune her harp?"

"I could have saved you the long trip." Dragich stood and walked to her. "Which is why a royal invitation was never sent to you."

"Finish your planning and then come to me when you're free, *my king*. I'll keep our daughter out of your hair for the time being. But just so you know, there are ripples of war as far south as Deadwaters Fork. The waters there tremble with the echoes of horses heading off to the fight. I needed no invitation. I felt it from as far away as home."

Dragich glared at her. "How did you learn of this?"

"There are many ways to see things from afar."

"What? Your superstitious witches? Soothsayers?" He shrugged in disbelief.

"They're called the Pilque," she reminded him. "I know you have some *societies* around here that practice the same magics, don't you, Dragich? How are your relations with the Moor Bog, these days?"

Dragich looked at Ember and then back to Isabeau. "Societies? Dammit! Enough with the superstitious lunacy. It's the reason you no longer share my bed. Now, if you'll excuse me…"

"I know I've interrupted you. I'll take my leave of you, but find me when you take supper. We have much to discuss."

Dragich groaned and waved to Ilidari to escort the two women from the war room.

"You're the real reason why I came north," Isabeau whispered to Ember as they stepped into the corridor. "Now, let's have some wine and talk. Kail, may I ask you for a few moments of privacy? My daughter and I should spend some time together."

"Of course, my lady." Ilidari stepped back to his chamberlain duties and the two ladies began a slow stroll around the castle, keeping only each other's company. When they reached Ember's room, they sat and locked the door.

"Mother," Ember began, as her mother poured out the wine, "I fear for my life, and for Aarav."

Isabeau smiled disarmingly and took a minute to respond. "I, too, am concerned for you. There's no place for you here. Your father has lost his way. I, and the people of the Fork, won't let our legacies die because of one man's megalomania."

"What are we to do?" Ember whispered, placing the untouched glass of wine on the table.

"You don't drink?" Isabeau asked.

"When I do, bad things happen."

Isabeau grinned and placed her wine glass aside. "I want to bring you home, to the Fork."

"I fear Father will never allow it." Ember looked down, her hands folded in her lap.

"What's happened already?" Isabeau asked. "Spare no details."

Ember spent several minutes replaying the events of the past several months through teary eyes and a crackling voice, including the assassination, the conspiracy with the Thessalys, and the marriage betrothal to Joferian Maeglan.

"Do you want this marriage?" Isabeau asked. She could see that her daughter was conflicted.

"Joferian is a gallant and good man. He risked his life to stop Father's brigands and fought to save my life from the assassins at the masquerade. We only spent a day together, but we stayed up all night and…"

"And?"

"And I know we began to have feelings for each other. It's not a fairy tale, Mother, but he seemed so… right."

"Did you sleep with him?" Isabeau asked.

"Mother!" Ember protested. "Of course not. Though we kissed at the end of the night."

"It was one night, child. The Fork is your home. Your people are there. We'll find you another match. One that won't be heading off to war."

"There's more," Ember said. "I met a Vermilion princess at court. She's seen a two-horned tetrine."

Isabeau sat to attention and leaned in, a disbelieving frown on her face. "Ember, don't lie about such things. The tetrine are sacred to the Fork."

"It's true. She and a group of champions left for Castleshire to learn more. That's when Joferian's brother was killed."

Isabeau's mind raced with possibilities. The fabled horses of Deadwaters Fork had shown themselves to a Vermilion? And a special tetrine had led the harass?

"Tell me more."

"Her name is Addilyn Elspeth. She rode with her father to warn the Thorhauers of trouble. Now that I've seen behind the curtain of Dragon Ridge, I know father and his dealings are the cause of it."

"Where did she see the two-horned horse?"

"In the Dragon's Breath Mountains, not far from Warminster," Ember said.

"This far north?" Isabeau blurted, unintentionally doubting her daughter.

"Yes. I made friends with the Vermilion princess, but it was her father who was assassinated at the masquerade. They'd ridden out from behind the walls of Eldwal to warn us."

Isabeau sat in silence, contemplating the meaning of the sighting. She drifted into her own thoughts, wondering what it could mean. Isabeau was the lady of Deadwaters Fork and the tetrine were indigenous to their ranges. The people of the Fork often worshipped or looked to the tetrine as divine, taking care not to share their secrets with outsiders who might abuse or even hunt the sacred horses.

"Mother?" Ember said, stirring her from her thoughts. "You know more about the tetrine than anyone. Can you help her?"

Isabeau reached out to hold her daughter's hand, only to find Ember trembling.

"I won't let any evil befall you, my daughter," she reassured. Deep down, Isabeau knew that the tetrine's appearance and Dragich's lust for power could have been linked, and she knew that the gamble she was about to take could cost them both.

"Maybe I will have a sip or two of the wine," Ember said, trying to break the tension with a teary voice and false smile. The two women shared a soft laugh and sipped from their glasses.

"One other thing. Father has taken a girl prisoner. She's my age, and she's being held in the dungeon below."

"For what purpose?" Isabeau asked. "That's low, even for Dragich."

"I don't know," Ember replied. "As far I could tell, the poor girl was just trying to protect a friend. He bartered her off to a mage that's helping him with his war. She's to be sent to him as he's an enemy of her friend. She's to be a hostage, and we can't let that happen. What can we do?"

"Let me see what I can learn from your father over supper. I know you, Ember. Don't do anything stupid in the interim. Now, what of Aarav?"

"Aarav isn't the same boy you knew. He's Dragich's favorite, even above his own sons. He doesn't say it, but he trusts Aarav with the twergish war and other tasks that he doesn't give to his twins."

"We'll see about that," Isabeau said. "He's a bastard with the last name of Fleury, not Von Lormarck."

"WELL, MASTER HELENIUS, IT'S been some time." A comely worker at the front of the establishment beckoned to him. "What's your pleasure this evening?"

Helenius looked at her, flashing some leg in a high cut dress, her hair still matted from her last encounter.

"My dear, I'd like to see the Ophidian," he replied, tipping the girl for her efforts regardless.

"Wait here." The girl shot him a disappointed glare, taking his copper sheaves regardless.

Helenius waited in the darkened lobby, listening to the women on the balconies out front as they catcalled to potential customers as they strolled by. He smiled and took a seat on a comfortable couch. He soon heard the familiar grinding of the Ophidian's cart's wheels as it neared the lobby. The double doors swung open, and the Ophidian emerged in all their glory, riding in the back of her male-drawn carriage. They were dually dressed to entertain their favorite customer.

"Come now," the left sister said to Helenius. "We heard you were in town."

"We were wondering when you were going to visit us," the other said, as they both tantalized him with their soft hand gestures and provocative outfits.

To Helenius, the great cryptid hunter, the Ophidian was his perfect woman—or, more accurately, *his* perfect *women*. Their physical beauty was barely enough to intrigue him, but their unique form spoke to the essence of a man who hunted the rarest of the rare. He was afraid to ask them where they came from, and part of him didn't want or need to know. There was no one else in all of Warminster like the Ophidian, and the joys of being entangled in their arms surpassed any sensual experience he'd ever had. They were worth their weight in gold. Helenius climbed onto the back of their wagon and dangled a sack of gold in front of the twins. They both smiled and their four arms interwove around his torso and legs, pulling him, and his gold, to his seat. The two men pulled the throne cart slowly back to the Ophidian's personal chambers.

The doors flung open to the smell of incense and alcohol. The two men assisted the sisters from their throne to a large set of bed pillows strewn on the floor. The two drivers took their leave, closed the door behind them, and Helenius was alone with his Ophidian.

"The gold palmettes are compliments of a wealthy Vermilion I was helping in Castleshire," he bragged, hoping to impress them.

They both giggled.

"Should we bother to count it?" one said to the other.

"He's always paid upfront... and tipped well," the other replied. "I think we can trust him."

Helenius smiled and jumped into the bed of pillows, twisting as he did to lie on his back. He slowly removed his tunic as the Ophidian crawled on top of him, one sister under each arm, their legs wrapping around his. He lit his pipe and took a deep puff as they began to swallow him in their warm embrace. Four hands and twenty fingers massaged him as he looked to the mirrored ceiling, enjoying his tobacco. He exhaled.

The Ophidian looked at each other and laughed at the man, then crawled up next to his head. He waited anxiously to see what new tricks they had in store for him.

Then their singular body pinned his legs to the bed, each of their heads taking turns smoking his pipe for him. He smiled as the sisters wrapped their two arms around each of his. They whispered something in each ear, but he didn't understand what they said and nor did he care. Then they used a silk rope to tie his arms to a pillar of the bed behind him.

"Interesting," he whispered to himself, allowing them to proceed. He relaxed his neck, nearly disappearing between the pillows and closing his eyes for a second. Then he felt the sisters tighten their grips on both of his arms.

"Is this a new pleasure?" he asked.

"No," a male voice said, forcing Helenius to open his eyes in surprise.

A Bone elf stood at the edge of the bed, holding a sword in one hand as he sniffed a black rose in the other.

Helenius tried to move, but the Ophidian's torso had him pinned. Then he heard a hiss behind him and tilted his head back to see a small, grey creature surface from under the stack of pillows.

"What's the meaning of this?" he exclaimed. "I didn't pay good money for—"

The creature behind him interrupted his tirade and lunged forward. His taloned hand covered Helenius's mouth and his wicked tail wrapped around his neck, squeezing just enough to stop him from yelling again. Helenius, a master of the rare, recognized the imp for what he was, and he knew this wasn't a roleplay gone wrong.

"What do you want?" his muffled voice muttered, hoping more gold would buy his freedom. "I'm a rich man. There's more where that came from."

The Bone elf slowly raised his blade, sliding it up the man's leg to his torso. Helenius struggled against the touch of the cold steel, but the imp's grip tightened, as did the Ophidian's. He relaxed, knowing he couldn't fight this off.

"Please, what do you want?"

"The Vermilion," the Bone elf whispered. "Why are they giving you gold?"

Helenius stopped struggling and saw an opening. Perhaps this wasn't about him.

"By the Ancients, man." The cryptid hunter breathed a sigh of relief. "Is that all? You needed only to ask. They paid me to find information about a creature that doesn't exist. I used their money to pay for my travel to Abacus."

"What creature?" the Bone elf replied.

"A tetrine," Helenius managed, grimacing against the tightening of the tail. He could tell the assassin didn't know what that meant. "It's a black unicorn. A rare beast indeed."

"Helenius, here, once rode a tetrine," one of the twins mentioned, running a teasing finger down his face.

"Or so he claims," the other retorted.

In synchrony, the Ophidian started singing the bardic tale about Anselm Helenius. "So whips the Tetrine's mane, as the rider grips with no reins," the twins sang. "A lone horn from its head appears, as the rider smiles, with no fears."

Helenius couldn't help tasting the irony. He struggled while listening to his tune, hoping the Bone elf would see value in his information and spare him.

But the Bone elf just tilted his head and looked into his desperate eyes. Then he heard the imp hiss, exposing his sharp teeth.

The elf's eyes narrowed. "A song about a man who rides a beast that doesn't exist?"

"Yes. I did ride one... once. When I had the pleasure of visiting the Vermilion city of Eldwal."

The Bone elf's blade slid all the way to Anselm's neck, drawing uncomfortably close to cutting him.

"You saw Eldwal?"

"Only once. They required my assistance."

"It seems like you're an ally and friend to the Vermilion."

"Yes, I'd like to believe it so," Helenius replied. "And you're a sworn enemy?"

"But of course, cryptid hunter," the elf sneered. He turned the tip of his blade.

"What is it that you want of me?" Helenius asked.

The Bone elf thought for a second. "I want the princess. Where were you to meet her?"

"Castleshire, in two weeks."

"Then why does she travel here in haste to seek you out?" the elf asked.

Helenius was genuinely confused. "I don't—"

The Bone elf interrupted him by forcing the point of his blade deeper, nicking him in the neck.

"I don't know." Helenius struggled against the blade. "But I've found a clue to the answer she seeks."

The Bone elf let up on the sword while the imp loosened his grip slightly.

"She seeks to know about a sighting of a tetrine with two horns. That's the beast that doesn't exist."

"Do the Moor Bog seek to capture the two-horned tetrine as well?" the Bone elf asked, after contemplating what the hunter had confided.

"The Moor who?"

The blade again cut into Helenius, punishing him for the lie.

"I'm supposed to believe that the great cryptid hunter, Anselm Helenius, doesn't know about a cult of cryptid worshippers in the Dragon's Breath Mountains? Ones that I'm sure would know of your tetrine?"

"You're correct," Helenius said, conceding his falsehood. The elf knew more than he'd hoped. "I thought the cult had vanished. No one has seen them in years."

"I have," the elf replied. "Do they seek the two-horned horse?"

Helenius could read the pieces of the puzzle coming together on the Bone elf's strained face. "If they do, that may make sense, my elven friend."

"I'm not your friend," his attacker muttered, quickly opening a fresh wound on Helenius's face with a twist of his wrist.

The Ophidian twins giggled sadistically in his ears as he squirmed.

"Then what will it take to buy my freedom?"

The Bone elf didn't reply.

"The Vermilion princess told me she saw a two-horned tetrine in the Dragon's Breaths. I didn't believe her at first, but there's more to her story. After all, from what I know of them, the Vermilion don't lie."

"You know much of the Vermilion." The Bone elf's tone had turned clipped. "I wish we had more time. I'm sure you could teach me much about them."

"Of course," Helenius managed. "I'd be happy to. No cost to a friend."

"Like I said," the elf replied. "I'm not your friend."

Helenius watched the Bone elf drop the black rose he was holding onto his chest, but before he could look back to the man, he felt the sharp incision of the blade across his exposed throat.

As he gargled in his own blood, he heard the Ophidian twins teasing, singing his ballad to him one last time.

CHAPTER NINETEEN

*"It's better to stand and fight. If you
run, you'll only die tired."*
—Koss, the Ancient of War

MONTY TOOK A DEEP BREATH as the floor of the
great hall cleared in moments. The Stormmoeller family,
including Freya, moved to the rear of the chamber to give the
combatants some room, leaving him to stand alone. Horns
blared outside, signaling that Bardagi was about to begin.
Outside, the incoming horde clamored to watch the noble
foreigner battle their champion, likely to be crushed to death
on their stone floor.

"This is ridiculous and barbaric," Joferian growled
approaching Monty as he prepared for the combat.

Monty had already started to unstrap his armor, and
Joferian aided, all the while shaking his head.

"LaBrecque?" Joferian shot a glance to the admiral when
the prince refused to acknowledge him.

Montgomery didn't mean to ignore his cousin, but his
mind spun in his skull. His face went slack, and he wondered
if he looked braver than he felt. LaBrecque didn't answer and
Monty didn't turn to see what most likely was a disapproving
countenance. "This is something I have to do." Monty was
shocked to hear his own voice sound so strong. Was he wrong,
or did he hear dissent in Joferian's tone again? Why his cousin
was upset of eluded him. Was it because of the fight on the
Sundowner? That scuffle seemed an age ago.

"Think of Warminster," Joferian pleaded, switching tactics.
"If you die, your father and mother will be heirless. This isn't
the way to win an alliance."

"I *am* thinking of Warminster," Montgomery snorted, noting the change in Joferian's tone. "And Everett... and Talath. But it's the only way. We tried gold. They want blood. And I fear that if I don't do this, they might join the fight against us in some twisted code of honor. Or are you willing fight in my stead? Be my second?" He regretted the last words, afraid Joferian just might.

"They want the prince." Joferian backed away and looked at his cousin.

Montgomery looked at him. "If I die, tell my father that I died doing everything I could to ensure an alliance."

Joferian only nodded and hugged his cousin.

Monty turned to face Ulf Skuli, who stood ten feet away, both stripped of weapons and armor and wearing only leather leggings to ensure a fair fight. Monty had been trained in hand-to-hand combat at Halifax, but this was different. He knew Ulf was probably stronger than he was, and he was likely to have fought like this many times before. He knew he was the underdog and that the *konungr* had entrapped him, but he had to force everything out of his head except for Ulf Skuli. Ulf had fought well outside and had no wounds, and so Montgomery had to hope he could outsmart the Norseman.

Atorm rose and held Urnst Jamner high, looking to both men to see if they were ready. They nodded their assent, and the *konungr* dropped the massive warhammer to the floor, signaling the start of the fight. Monty raised his hands in a pugilistic defense, but Ulf wasted no time in charging the length of the clearing in a bull rush, tackling Monty to the floor. The crowd cheered as the action started and Monty felt the weight of the barbarian on top of him. The charge knocked some breath from him, but he used the momentum of the man against him, spinning to one side and punching the Norseman on the back of the head.

The two scrambled to regain their composure, but Monty wouldn't let Ulf stand. Instead, he kicked at the back of his legs, knocking him to the floor. Ulf reached out and grabbed the prince around the throat, pulling him to the ground with him. The two rolled awkwardly over each other several times until Monty felt the back of a table against his side. Ulf leaned in, his hand still choking the prince.

Monty switched tactics and grabbed the barbarian's arm with his right hand and smashed the back of the Norseman's elbow with his left. Ulf growled in pain as Monty bent his elbow the wrong way. He was free for a moment and had control of Ulf's arm. Monty stretched to his feet, but the Norseman's free arm swung around and clipped Montgomery in the face. He felt his lip split and tasted his own blood. The move had stunned him, allowing Ulf to set his feet again.

Ulf charged, grabbing the prince in a bear hug, and slammed him into a wooden pillar in the center of the hall. The crowd started chanting Skuli's name as he lifted knee after knee into the prince's side.

Monty knew he was pinned but used his opponent's frame to place one foot on Ulf's leg, pulling himself above the Norseman. He reached for a hanging lantern on the pillar and smashed it into Skuli's face.

Ulf moaned in pain as the metal container broke, sending shards of glass into him and the prince alike. Monty didn't care. It bought him freedom from the brooding man's bear hug. The two men separated for a moment before Ulf tackled Montgomery over a bench, the rickety wooden frame collapsing under their weight.

Splinters cut into Monty's back, and he growled in pain. Slipping his arm around the big man's neck, he squeezed tightly and heard Ulf choke for air. With a snarl, Ulf opened his mouth and bit down hard on Monty's bare arm.

The prince screamed and let the Norseman go.

"Skuli! Skuli!" the crowd continued to chant.

The Norseman's face was bloodied, but so was Monty's. The initial rush of adrenaline now gone, Monty found himself outclassed by the brawler. He gasped for air. Then, an idea struck him. The man liked to charge, so he'd let him.

Ulf growled and took two strides, moving to tackle Monty again. This time, Monty was ready. The prince leapt to the side, dodging the attempted tackle. Ulf's huge wingspan still caught Monty, spinning the prince sideways on impact.

Monty spun but then grabbed the man around the neck. His bloody forearm snaked under his chin while his second arm caught him around the head. Monty could feel his neck compressing and the barbarian's hands reached to break the hold, but Montgomery clung on like a vice grip. Ulf struggled to breathe and backed the prince up against the center pillar. With a grunt, he smashed Monty into the pillar once, and then again.

The wood crushed his chest with both desperate throws, but more importantly, he felt Ulf's strength diminish with each thrust. He just needed to hold on.

The barbarian finally staggered but had one last breath in him. Ulf reached back to scrape at Monty's face, but Monty tossed his head back, away from the clawing hands. The man fell to one knee and then two, and Monty squeezed and groaned until his opponent fell flat to the floor, unconscious.

The room went silent for a moment. Gasping, Montgomery disentangled himself from his foe. His hands shook from exhaustion and he and wiped the blood out of his eyes to take in the room.

The horde jeered, egging him on. "Bardagi! Bardagi! Bardagi!"

"To the death, Prince!" Atorm shouted from somewhere behind him.

Monty turned to find the *konungr*. "Mercy, good king," he begged more than asked. "This wasn't his choice."

Atorm laughed. In the back of his mind Monty heard his father Godwin telling him not to show weakness. Atorm saw mercy as weakness. But mercy wasn't weakness to the prince.

"You have honored me with your tradition," Montgomery began, forcing himself to stare into the *konungr's* eyes. "I understand that and have partaken in your ways. I will continue to do so." He glanced at Freya.

The Norse princess narrowed her eyes at him. Not in judgement, he thought, but in comprehension and curiosity. Her lips parted as if she was going to speak, and he wondered if she understood.

When she raised her head and smiled just enough for him to see, he continued, "To me, mercy is not weakness. I won't do it. I won't kill the innocent."

"And if it costs you your alliance?" Atorm asked, his voice low and steady.

To his right, Joferian turned, face buried in his hands.

"That," Monty said, fully gaining his composure, "is up to you, great *Konungr.*"

The crowd turned to their king, waiting on his word. Montgomery watched the king rise from his seat and walk toward him, holding Urnst Jamner in his hand. For a second, he thought Atorm was coming to kill him, as he must have violated the protocols of their culture. Instead, he lifted the warhammer to rest on his own shoulder and chuckled heartily.

"You have much to learn of Rijkstag," the smiling *konungr* conceded, "especially if you're to be the husband of a

Stormmoeller woman. I'll grant you the mercy you seek for Ulf Skuli, but he's been dishonored. I must strip him of his family titles. He'll be your thrall, Thorhauer. His shame no longer has a place in Rijkstag. If he has any honor that you haven't stripped him of, he'll take his own life when he recovers."

"Thrall?" Monty asked, wondering if it meant what he suspected.

"Your slave," Atorm supplied in a deep, meaningful growl. "Or does that offend you?"

Realizing he'd pushed the luck Nothos had granted him, Monty accepted the terms. Atorm motioned for Ulf's unconscious body to be removed and helped the prince back to the fire, where Einar Skullgrimsson awaited.

"A blood oath," Einar announced solemnly, handing both Atorm and Montgomery a dagger. Monty watched as Atorm cut his palm with the dagger and waited for Montgomery to do the same. Monty thought about the strange ceremony and paused, but only for a second. Then he sliced his hand with the runecaster's dagger. Einar encouraged the two to shake bloody hands, consummating the blood oath between Thorhauer and Stormmoeller.

"The alliance is sealed." Atorm motioned to the approving crowd, a half-smile on his face.

Einar raised his crooked finger and waggled it in the prince's face. "Blood oaths are forever, Prince. Let your scarred flesh serve as a daily reminder of this vow."

Monty looked at the dagger, the blood on his palm, and then to Atorm, who embraced him as a son. Over Atorm's shoulder, Monty caught sight of Freya. Her secret smile had grown into a full smirk. She nodded once to acknowledge his gaze.

"This moment calls for a great feast!" the *konungr* decreed to the crowd's delight, spinning Monty back to face the crowd.

"The party never really ended," Joferian murmured to Montgomery, helping the prince to a nearby bench.

"My tent," was all Montgomery could muster in reply. His adrenaline had burned off.

Joferian and LaBrecque lifted him under each arm and assisted the prince out of the hall and back to his tent. As they neared the door, Cnute cut them off.

"Where are you headed?" he asked.

"To rest and recover," Monty replied.

"Not without real Norse women to help tend your wounds."

"I thought the Heifenmager dulled the pain." Monty grimaced.

"It will," Cnute replied, sending the trio out the door accompanied by wenches from the crowd with arms filled with flagons of ale. "Compliments of Atorm."

"Well, if the king insists," LaBrecque smiled, wasting no time in accepting Cnute's offer.

"And you?" Cnute looked to the viscount, with two women draped over his arms, waiting for the word from Joferian.

Joferian shook his head. "No, thank you."

Monty helped himself into his own tent and laid down, watching the exchange from inside.

"If you prefer men, I can arrange that," Cnute suggested.

"I'm betrothed," Joferian replied curtly.

Cnute spit out some of his beer, surprised at the notion, but patted him on the shoulder. "I'll never understand Warminsterians. More for me, I guess."

The two men clinked ale horns and Cnute departed with one of Joferian's women under each arm.

"You must really love her." Montgomery was now flat on his back as Joferian ducked into the tent. He poked at his bruises, instantly regretting it.

"I do." Joferian crossed his arms and glared down at his cousin.

Confused and in pain—the Heifenmager hadn't dulled it yet—he looked up at Joferian. "What? You still disapprove of what I've done? I did it for all of us. No one died and we have won our necessary alliance."

"Remember our trip back from Castleshire?" Joferian snapped, his hands gripping his crossed arms so tight his knuckles were white. "Our dead brothers? Our oath to protect one another in their absence? Their bodies lay not more than a few years from us, and you would not allow me to speak of Ember Fleury?"

Even more confused than before, Monty nodded. "I'm sorry that I struck you—"

Punching the air, Joferian shouted, "That's not what I mean." He gripped his hair and paced. "You take risks such as this with your life, speak without forethought of what is good for Warminster and now take a *Viking wife* and I am not allowed to speak of Ember?"

Monty gripped his aching sides. "It's not for glory. I do this for us. Ancients damn the accolades, I don't care. I just needed to win the alliance." Something in his chest popped and pain overcame him from shouting at his cousin. He doubled over where he sat, clutching himself.

Joferian reached out, the slightest tinge of remorse on his face. "Are you all right?"

Just then, a shadow appeared in the tent's door. Monty lifted his head to see Freya, his newly betrothed, standing in the doorway. He exchanged glances with Joferian. Sighing in frustration, Joferian nodded and bowed out of the tent, leaving them alone.

Freya raised her brows, eyes to the floor, as Joferian brushed past her. Her icy orbs then shot up to meet Monty's gaze.

"I assume you're here to protest my victory over your beloved?" he asked. "Understand that I had no choice."

"No," she said in Warminsterian. Her accent rolled over her next words, making them foreign and enthralling at once. "I'm here to help you recover from your wounds."

"Thank you for coming, my lady, but I need to rest." He looked away from her, signaling he was finished.

Freya turned her back to him only to close the flaps of the tent. Monty looked up. His inexperience of such situations made his heart leap into his chest. Would she not leave?

"My lady, this is unbecoming of—"

She faced him, dropping her outer dress. The thin chamise she wore under clung to her form from damp sweat. The skirt opened all the way up to her hips, exposing her thighs. She stepped out of the fallen gown, revealing her long, lithe legs even more.

"Please, you don't—" Monty began.

But it was too late, and the half-naked Freya leapt onto him, pinning him to the bed. He groaned in pain under her weight, his wounds still too fresh for her aggressiveness.

"That's the sound babies make," she smirked in her broken common, slapping him playfully in the face.

Monty grabbed her arms and sat up quickly with another moan. "You don't have to do this. I don't expect it."

Freya looked at him, blue eyes wide. "Are you not to be my husband? I'm Freya Stormmoeller, daughter of Atorm. Do you not desire me?" This time, she punched him in the chest. "That's for insulting me!"

Monty flinched from the punch but knew better than to groan again. "Yes, you and I are to be married, but—"

Freya interrupted him, kissing him softly on the lips. He stopped moaning and she pulled away, glancing lustfully at him. She placed her hands on his chest. He leaned back on his elbows and looked back at her.

"This is unnecessary," he said. "I don't want to make you do anything you don't—"

She stopped his words again with her lips. "In my country, this means be quiet," she whispered into his mouth.

She pulled his arms out from under him, making him flop down. She held him there, smiling down, showing all her teeth. When she saw he didn't move, Freya grabbed him by the throat and hiked up her skirt, her other hand going for his belt.

CHAPTER TWENTY

"Sometimes, the traveler chooses the journey.
Other times, the journey chooses the traveler."
—Quehm, the Great Keeper

THAT NIGHT, DAEMUS FOUND himself looking down at his own sleeping body. The same strange dream from a few nights before returned. He sat away from his body, a spectral image of himself, and watched as the ghostly lights returned to him.

They appeared as multiple flickers at first, seemingly swirling free in the night sky. But then they collected in a rush, forming the apparition of the man who'd visited him in his dreams in Flowerdown Syphen.

Again, he felt no fear. The presence of this ghost brought him strange comfort, not the dread that his oneiromancy typically bestowed. And just like their last encounter, it was less a dream and more an out-of-body experience.

The free-formed half-ghost wafted whimsically above his friends, apparently unaware that Daemus had taken a similar form. The ghost was more defined than last time, though still missing his bottom half, and appeared to Daemus as an extended bust of an illusory sculpture from his parents' gallery.

This time, Daemus felt more comfortable in the unfamiliar dreamwalk state and tried to speak to the man, but realized his voice was muted in this form. Even the chirping of the forest had disappeared.

Daemus concentrated and began to float toward the man.

The ghost turned, his spectral eyes startled at Daemus's presence. Then a smile flashed on the apparition's face. He floated closer to Daemus, stopping only when he levitated inches from him. The man bowed theatrically, one arm wrapping around his torso and the other waving in the air like a servant signaling he was ready to receive orders. His wild hair flipped and flopped as he bowed, waving through Daemus's incorporeal form.

Through some distant instinct, Daemus knew the ghost's pantomimes were friendly. Daemus mimed his own response, pointing to a tree and then back to the ghost.

The specter nodded, and Daemus presumed he understood his meaning. Then it spun like a whirling dervish before suddenly stopping and pointing behind Daemus. The mysterious portal that had opened in his dreams a few days earlier appeared behind him, spinning at first like a child's colorful pinwheel before silently tearing a hole in the night sky.

The two hovered for a moment in front of it, and then the irresistible tug returned to Daemus's stomach. They drifted at first, gliding through the portal until the wrenching in his torso pulled them in a flash, stopping abruptly in front of the gargantuan tree again. Daemus took a moment to recover from the unfamiliar movement.

His ghost friend feigned a chuckle at Daemus's expense and then drew upon the tree with magical fingers. Daemus thought that they'd merely pass through it, but the man conjured a light at the tip of his finger and sketched a keyhole on the bark. He then tapped on the hallucinatory door, and it opened into a large building filled with books.

This has to be Vorodin's Lair, Daemus thought, the fabled twin tree that Coronel Briar had mentioned back in Flowerdown Syphen.

When the ghost floated through his own ethereal creation Daemus followed at a tentative pace, watching the man entering a long hallway that seemed to have no end. Then the specter rushed down the hall, leaving Daemus alone among a stack of illusory tomes.

Daemus tried to follow, but as he entered the hall, he saw that the corridor wasn't as straight as he'd thought. Ghostly turns and secret tunnels revealed themselves as he floated by, and he soon found himself lost within the stacks. He spun around, realizing he wasn't sure which hall was the one he'd entered by.

The specter returned, startling Daemus as he emerged from one of the side corridors. His face was stern, the smile gone. He stared at the Low Keeper and pointed two fingers to his own eyes, demanding that he look into them.

Daemus conceded.

They locked gazes and he felt the tugging again in his gut. But this time was different. He watched, his own floating image shrinking in size, while his spectral essence drew into the man's eyes, like a ship caught in a whirlpool. He swirled, slowly at first, until he began to slide inward, closer and closer to the eye of the whirlpool. His speed hastened, and delirium seized him. He closed his eyes, his blind hands flailing to grab onto something—anything. Instead, he slipped through the eye and began to freefall, tumbling over and over. He tried to cry out, but his voice still hadn't returned to him.

With a sudden tug, the motion stopped. He dared to open his eyes. Darkness filled the void he'd fallen into but soon his dizziness left him, and his sight returned. The man appeared from the blackened edges of his vision, floating in front him. Behind the ghost, an archway made of stacked books materialized from the darkness, revealing a mysterious alcove to nowhere.

Daemus's spectral friend floated away from him. This time, the ghost changed directions, hovering horizontally under the books. To the young Keeper, it appeared to be lying on his back, or at least the part of a back that he had and dangled in mid-air. He tried to replicate the man's position, struggling at first, but then he realized that in his form, there was no true up or down. As he spun, so did his point of view.

The man's face fell stern again, and the pair bobbed weightlessly, side by side and upside down. Daemus turned to the ghost, watching his gaze. The man's spectral eyes traced along the inscriptions of the spines of the books in the magical archway.

Daemus inched closer, but the man spun away, catching Daemus in the spectral turbulence of his whirl. After a few seconds, they both returned to their original orientation, or so Daemus thought, but the books and the mystical archway melted away, slipping back into the darkness.

The man raised one finger to his shushed lips, and Daemus somehow understood his meaning. This was one secret that he needed to keep to himself. What it meant still escaped him, but in this rare occurrence, his oneiromancy didn't scare him.

With a wink, Daemus watched the world around him dematerialize and the figure of the man burst into the familiar flickers, returning in a rising spiral to the stars.

The dream slowed and started to fade as a hand shook Daemus awake. The chirping of the night bugs returned as the last of the vision dissipated. He turned over to find Liesel, weapon in hand and face warped with worry.

He began to panic, reaching for his mace, forgetting where he was. "What's going on?"

"I bear important news," the Keldarin princess said. "The Emerald Shield stood vigilant guard along Harbinger's Run to ensure that the Antlered Man couldn't pursue you any farther. During a night's watch a few days past, they spotted a Bone elf traveling by horse, heading south along the run before he left the view of the Eternal Forest. They didn't pursue him."

Ritter's voice interrupted the pair. "It must be the same

assassin. He must have survived the battle in Castleshire."

Daemus turned to see Ritter awake and in his gear. Did the Longmarcher ever sleep?

Ritter continued, his voice serious, "Was there an imp traveling with him?"

"The Emerald Shield didn't see anyone or anything else." Liesel hauled Daemus to his feet and began to hand him his things. "We can take you as far as the end of the forest. You'll be safe with us and our scouts until then, but we must hurry."

DAEMUS NORMALLY COULDN'T STAY silent about his oracular experiences. Most of the time, he'd wake from night terrors, or in some cases, they'd wrack his body and leave him drained and in need of help. This time was different. He felt in control.

As the party left for Abacus, Liesel led them to the far reaches of the Eternal Forest. They emerged on a sloping hill, overlooking the distant scholar city below. The warmth of the southern weather lifted their spirits, a big difference from the waning days of autumn in Castleshire.

"There it is." Liesel pointed from the head of the group. "Abacus lies a half day's travel below."

"It looks a lot closer," Daemus remarked.

"The way the crow flies." Liesel turned to the young Keeper. "But the hill and the path wind down through the peninsula and will take you longer than you think."

"I can't thank you and the coronel enough." Marquiss rode alongside Liesel, and he made a gesture with his hand that Daemus had seen several times while in the Syphen. It must have been a Keldarin expression for gratitude.

"Be careful, Dauldon," she said with a smile. "I've had to protect you too many times. I grow weary of carrying you."

Marquiss smiled back but made no promises.

"Your people have been a great help," Addilyn added. "Bards will one day sing the song of the Emerald Shield from the alabaster walls of Eldwal."

"You're too kind, my princess. We hope to learn of your great victory soon. May Melexis watch over you from the Hall of the Ancients."

Daemus watched the members of the Keldarin's Emerald Shield as they descended. Arjun led the party down the hill, and he knew they had many hours on horseback in front of them, meandering back and forth through the broken ground. His eyes caught hold of Lachlan Barrett, who waved at their departure. He'd only spoken briefly to Lachlan. Words were hard to come by. To Daemus, if Lachlan hadn't convinced Kester to head away without him, Clan Blood Axe would have caught them all on the open road. He knew the man had saved his life, as well as the lives of his friends.

In that moment, he realized he had no one to say goodbye to. The control he felt in the dream didn't carry over into his waking life. His thoughts drifted to his uncle.

Kester.

He wondered if Kester would have been proud of him. He had flashbacks of the rickety cart with the troublesome wagon wheel. How far had he come since then? He wished his uncle was there—in Abacus—to help them. He longed to hear just one more of Kester's traveling tales or to hear his voice calming him after a nightmare, reassuring him that all will be well. Clenching his eyes tightly, he reflected on his conversation with Faux from the night before. And he reminded himself to keep his darker thoughts at bay.

"THERE SHE IS," ARJUN said, stirring Daemus from his daydreams.

The group had traversed the steep grade and arrived at the flatlands in front of the gates of Abacus. Daemus couldn't hide his amazement at what welcomed them—a main gate that rose several stories high, encircling the city in a wreath of golden bricks that gleamed in the sun.

Arjun interrupted Daemus's wonderment with the simple phrase, "They're not real.

"Some wizards colored them this way long ago," Arjun continued. "No one knows how or why, and no one moved to change it. They're stone, I assure you."

"It's unforgettable," the young Keeper managed, mesmerized by the glimmering stones.

"You can find it on the coat of arms for the city," Arjun replied. "A golden wreath and a mace of peace, similar to the mighty weapon that felled Sinnistyr of Clan Blood Axe."

Daemus chuckled and glanced at the mace by his side.

Arjun smiled. "Nothing like yours."

Abacus rose in front of them, a tiered city of walled neighborhoods sprawling as far as the eye could see. The buildings inside were like no others. Some towered into the sky, and some leaned like the crooked works of a novice sculptor. A harbor lay to the east, the maritime entrance to the city where boats of all sizes entered. Two waterfalls cascaded from one of the tiers into the ocean, creating a sight unseen anywhere else in the realm.

"Are they real?" Daemus asked Arjun. "The waterfalls?"

"They're dams," the captain explained.

"A dam?" Blue Conney's face twisted. "Like a Costere beaver?"

"Aye," Arjun replied, "but they don't block water as much as they move it. They vent the water into the ocean for show, and spin a contraption like a grist wheel, but underground."

"To grind grist?" Ritter asked.

"To make things work." Arjun made a circular motion with his hands. "It moves the great gears of the Abacunian Clock in the center of town, among other things. It's connected throughout the city."

The group made their way through several city blocks, their heads cocked in every direction.

"How do they keep the streets so clean?" Ritter wondered aloud.

"Magic." Arjun made a pantomime of a wizard casting a spell. "The trainees at the Horn of Ramincere are tasked with using minor magics to sweep the streets clean."

Addilyn's eyes widened and she leaned forward in her saddle. "The Horn of Ramincere?"

"They're the war wizards of Abacus," Arjun explained. "They're trained to fight at the High Aldin. You should see them in the field. It's a spectacle to behold."

"There are no beggars on the streets," Jessamy observed. "And there are no merchants throwing goods in our faces."

"It seems that everyone has a task or a chore to get to," Addilyn noted.

"A group bearing arms such as ours might not have been allowed into other cities," Ritter observed. "But no one here seems to notice."

"They're steering clear because of Blue," Marquiss quipped.

"Let's keep our wits about us," Arjun warned. "The Bone elf is afoot."

For first time visitors, the wonders of the city were an easy distraction. But Daemus's white eyes drifted toward the captain. Even though Arjun answered the group's questions, Daemus sensed his preoccupation with the coming task.

"Nervous?" he asked Arjun, when the group was distracted by the appearance of a bubbling fountain in a town square. It, too, was powered by the dams in the harbor.

Arjun didn't answer, but his countenance told the story. He looked back and thanked him without words.

"She'll see us." Daemus feigned a reassuring smile, but his voice wasn't as convincing.

"So where do we find the Athabasica?" Ritter asked.

Arjun pointed in the general direction. "The Gatehouse."

"Then lead us." In truth, Daemus was just grateful to finally be inside the city and reaching their next goal. He stole a moment of personal introspection, his thoughts drifting back to Disciple Delling and the long and arduous trek here.

"We're here for two reasons," Addilyn reminded the group. "I need to find Anselm Helenius."

"Aye," Arjun nodded in agreement. "Perhaps I should go to visit the Athabasica while you search for the cryptid hunter?"

"Faux." Addilyn turned in her saddle. "Why don't you and Marquiss escort the good captain to the Gatehouse with Daemus, while we look for the man named Jeric Tuttle. Helenius told me about him in Castleshire. He's a local alchemist of some repute, so I'm sure we can ask around and find him."

"Agreed." Faux urged her horse forward, Marquiss following closely behind.

"May Nothos follow you to the doors of the Gatehouse." Ritter nodded to both Arjun and Daemus before turning to leave.

ADDILYN RODE ALONG THE streets of the scholar city, heeding Arjun's advice. She trusted Jessamy and Ritter to be on guard, and Blue seemed to listen to her more than usual as they passed through the town. Normally, a Vermilion, a springheel, and two Raven elves traveling together would catch everyone's attention, but the unique was common in Abacus, and no one in the streets seemed to notice them. They'd asked a few passersby about Jeric Tuttle but had discovered few clues to his whereabouts. The same was true for Helenius.

As they wandered the brick roads, Addilyn noticed the massive clocktowers that Arjun had described. She didn't know how to read the clocks, but she admired the way they were of all shapes and sizes. Some seemed to tell time by the movement of celestial bodies, and others by a series of mechanical arrows and human numbers.

It was all curiously intriguing to the Vermilion, as magic was being displayed in the open and there were several stores that featured a mixture of spellcraft and invention in their windows. In one corner, there was even an experiment of some sort being conducted in the street.

"Kind sir." Addilyn leaned down, interrupting a man who was involved in the display. He was a human of middle age, with a frothy white beard and a bald head. He stood next to a lardal of a peculiar kind that she didn't recognize but which possessed a full mane of orange hair that was parted down the middle of his skull, as well as rustic red skin that matched a winter sunset. The pair seemed to be stumped and involved in an argument about their failed invention. They'd placed a little black box, similar to a small chest, flat on the street but at a distance from themselves.

"Not now, lass," the bald man remarked, turning his back to Addilyn. "You tinker lardals just keep tinkering till you can't tinker no more! It was fine where you had it."

His lardal partner looked up and rattled off a sentence or two in a language Addilyn didn't understand, but the man seemed offended.

"I'm not gonna tell you again, you orange-haired meatball,"

the man barked in Warminsterian. "Get your grubby little fingers outta the gear box."

"Thank you anyway," she began to say, until Blue rode up on Jericho.

"The lady's talkin', gents," Blue said, with his usual ruffian style. "It pays to listen when a Vermilion speaks."

Jericho growled, breaking them from their personal feud. The two shot uncomfortable glances at one another and the bald man wiped his appreciable brow.

"Uh…" he stammered, looking at the dog. "No offense, ma'am. My associate and I were just tryin' to get our little experiment to work when you, uh…"

"Please ignore my springheel friend," Addilyn smiled, trying to diffuse the situation. "He does the barking."

"Who does the biting?"

Addilyn's eyes guided the man's stare to the snarling war dog.

"Then my meatball of a friend and I are honored to help and, uh, what did he call you?"

"A Vermilion."

"Of course, of course." The man wiped his face again, while his arms swung nervously. "What is it that you seek?

"We're looking for a man known as Jeric Tuttle."

The orange lardal rattled through a sentence or two in gibberish as if Addilyn understood him, but then the man calmed his smaller friend. "I know, I know. I'll tell her."

"Tuttle owns an apothecary and alchemical shop called the Boiling Beaker." He turned and pointed in a direction of winding streets. "You'll find it on Mephisto Quad, in the Mistchapel Quarter."

"And which way is Mistchapel?" Addilyn asked.

"Keep going straight." The man pointed again. "You'll see the signs for Mistchapel. Nearly ten blocks."

"Thank you." Addilyn bent at the waist from her saddle. "And sorry to interrupt you."

"Just tell Tuttle to give us a discount for sending him some business."

"And who shall I say sent us?"

"Oskar Lefardeux," the man replied, before turning back to his experiment.

———✦———

ADDILYN TOOK THE LEAD, guiding the group through the streets of Abacus until she found the door of the Boiling Beaker, just as Lefardeux had described. The old apothecary was a three-story establishment tucked into the middle of Mephisto Quad, its blue doors and trim standing in stark contrast to the rest of the houses around it. Even its windows had a blue tint to them. The sign above the door depicted a cockeyed glass beaker that bubbled with a blue liquid.

The group tied their horses off outside and Addilyn led them into the establishment. The shop opened in front of them into a two-level vaulted ceiling, its walls lined with various custom shelves, brimming with innumerable bottles, jars, and flasks of all shapes and sizes. A ladder led to a second floor of the alchemical treasure trove with a small catwalk that ran along the four corners of the store, just large enough for a human to stand on and inspect the bottles. The window's blue tint gave the room a mystical, azure glow.

A small tinker lardal sat at a counter in front of Addilyn. The man's hair was as orange as the lardal she'd greeted minutes earlier, but the blues made his hair appear to be a deep tan. His spectacles clung to the end of his bulbous nose and his eyes rose above them to meet Addilyn's.

"Welcome to the Boiling Beaker," the lardal said in Warminsterian. "I'm Uriah Loring, the shopkeeper. What are you looking for today?"

"Hello," Addilyn bowed, as the man jumped down from his tall stool and waddled over to her. He was only half her height, but likely the same weight. "We're looking for Jeric Tuttle. Anselm Helenius sent us to find him."

At first, the tinker lardal ignored her, approaching Blue Conney instead, who was looking carelessly through the bottles.

"Now, now, don't drink any of that," he said, snatching a bottle back from Blue. "That's for healing, not for drinking."

Ritter shot the springheel an agitated look and Blue shrugged.

"Master Loring," Addilyn tried again, "we're—"

"What manner of creature are you?" the lardal interrupted. "I've never seen your like, and that's saying something, living in this city all my life."

Without asking for permission, Uriah withdrew a magnifying glass from his waistcoat and started looking more closely at Addilyn, who backed away.

"I'm Vermilion," she replied.

"Never heard of yer kind," the lardal's fuzzy eyebrows rose. "I see your ears are elven, but the skin is different. How do you not burn in the sun?"

"I… I don't know." Addilyn took another step back.

"Hmm," he grunted to himself, reaching for a jar from a nearby shelf. "Use this. It will help with your lack of pigmentation."

"My what?" she asked, feeling somehow insulted.

"Uriah." Ritter stepped in. "We don't need any of your wares. We seek—"

"Jeric Tuttle," Uriah interrupted again. "I might not be able to see well, but this old lardal can still hear."

"Is he here?" Jessamy asked.

"He's not." Uriah climbed back onto his stool. Addilyn waited for him to offer more, but when he picked up his quill and started writing in the ledger, it was obvious he was done talking.

"Uriah?" she managed with a tentative voice.

"If you aren't going to buy anything, I'm sorry but our dealings have concluded. Good day to you."

The group shared awkward glances until Blue's temper spoke for them. "I didn't come here to be stonewalled by an old tinker lardal short on patience. This is a matter of life or death. Now, tell me when Tuttle will return so that we can speak to 'em. Otherwise, I'll sick me war dog on ya. He likes the taste of lardal meat in the mornin.'"

"War dog?" Uriah replied, looking down at the springheel. "You have a war dog? May I see it?" His mood swung and his eyes rose above his glasses again. "Is it for sale? I'd like to add it to our menagerie."

"He's not fer sale," Blue growled.

"Well, I'd have to inspect him before I made an offer." Uriah ignored Bllue's denial.

"Menagerie?" Ritter asked.

"You asked me about Jeric Tuttle," Uriah began. "He, along with Anselm Helenius, have done their best to save the realm's rarest animals. They've created a sanctuary here in Abacus for our scholars to study... and save them."

"I thought Helenius was a great hunter," Ritter added.

"He was." Uriah's eyes widened and his nose hairs stood on end.

"Was?" Addilyn caught the inference.

"He hunted some of the most dangerous cryptids in the realm. But in recent years, he's started to help them. Not the cryptids, mind you, but other rare species he's been asked to hunt or trap. He's brought injured animals here and Master

Tuttle has healed them. With his potions and unguents, you understand. But in many cases, they can't rejoin the wild, so Master Tuttle keeps them in his zoo. He calls it the Marvelria Sanctorium."

"You referenced Helenius." Addilyn stepped in between Blue and Uriah, bringing the conversation back on track. "We're not actually interested in Jeric Tuttle, but in his friend."

"Then I have some grave news for you I'm afraid." Uriah's voice turned sullen. "Helenius was slain but two days ago. His body was returned to our shop the night of the killing and left outside our door in a wagon."

Addilyn's stomach turned and she blinked in disbelief. "How?"

"A blade across the throat." Uriah motioned, slashing a thumb across his neck. "The body and wound were still fresh when we discovered him, but none of us were sure why the killer bothered to bring him back to the shop. It was no ordinary mugging. However, the knight castellan did find something peculiar on his body. Someone had placed a single black rose atop his corpse. Whoever did it must have known that Helenius was staying at the Boiling Beaker."

Pangs of guilt and anger ravaged through Addilyn. Her usual collected demeanor melted, and she grabbed onto the lardal's pedestal for balance. She could hear the voices of Ritter and the others behind her, but the words no longer translated. Memories of her first meeting with Helenius back in Castleshire flooded into her mind's eye. She remembered their dinner, his flamboyant and late arrival, and her father's annoyance with the man.

Her father.

Her eyes fixated on Uriah, who seemingly realized too late that his words and manner were too plain. He stepped back, pocketed his magnifying glass and lowered his gaze. "I'm sorry."

Addilyn stared past him, watching the imaginary visages of Helenius and Dacre disappearing before her. Her gaze dropped to the floor, and she felt Ritter's presence at her side. She now was the only one left from their first meeting. One her father set with Helenius to learn how to protect her.

"Jeric is safe." The lardal dared to touch her hand, jarring her from her state. "But he's under the protection of the Athabasica and the knight castellan in case the murderer is interested in him, too. I'm minding the store in his absence."

"We came here to meet Helenius," Ritter said for Addilyn, anger oozing from his tongue. "He was to help us with the sighting of a cryptid she encountered. He was under retainer to her father, who was also killed by the assassin who left the black rose."

"Again, I'm sorry to be the one to tell you." Uriah wrung his hands and turned to the others. "Is this man after Jeric too?"

Addilyn took a deep breath. "This assassin is after me, and if he thinks Jeric is here to help, then I believe the answer is yes."

"We must get word to the knight castellan, and of course the Athabasica then." The lardal rubbed his considerable moustache. "I hope Master Tuttle is all right..."

A moment of silence gripped the apothecary, long enough for Addilyn to catch her breath. She looked at Ritter, who returned her gaze with his own worried countenance. She straightened, attempting to regain her composure. Killing Helenius made no sense. He was no Vermilion, so why kill him? If the assassin knew they were coming to meet him, why not wait in the shadows for their arrival? Perhaps there was more than obsession to this killer.

"You know much about cryptids and rare beasts?" Jessamy,

of all people, broke the muted awkwardness. "Have you ever had a tetrine in your Sanctorium?"

"A tetrine, you say?" Uriah almost laughed, his visage going blank with the ridiculous question. "Nay… but I know Helenius was familiar with their kind, or at least as familiar as any. I heard him mention to Jeric that he was sent here from Castleshire by a wizard friend. He was seeking information on a special tetrine."

Addilyn leaned on the desk, eye-to-eye now with the lardal. "Did he find anything?"

"I think he did."

The barest of smiles crept onto Addilyn's face. "Did he leave anything here? Books, notes?" Her voice held none of her usual calculated tone.

Uriah leaned away and shook his head. "If he did, the knight castellan likely took them with him. Evidence, you see."

"You need to leave," Blue said to Uriah. "The assassin could be watching you and the shop as we speak."

"Nonsense," Uriah scoffed. "The Boiling Beaker is protected by our magics. No one can enter undetected. Nor can they enter *unharmed*, if we chose it."

"Where can we find the knight castellan?" Addilyn knew they had little time. Blue was correct. The assassin could be lingering in the alleys near the Boiling Beaker. Or perhaps its rooftops. If the lardal was confident about the Beaker's magic protections, at least, she thought, the imp couldn't be skulking around inside the apothecary listening to them.

"His name is Millen Bane." Uriah gestured to a city map hanging on the far wall and led the party to it. "Millen and Jeric are friends, and Jeric sometimes teaches at the High Aldin. Alchemy and such. When we discovered the body, we sounded the alarm and Millen came to investigate. He can either be found at the Athabasica's gatehouse or within the walls of the High Aldin itself." He pointed to two buildings on the map and then traced his fingers to a neighborhood labeled at Mistchapel. "We are here. They are not far."

"If this place is protected as you say," Ritter added, "may we see Helenius's old room? He may have left clues and it may be a safe place for us to hide the princess."

"I won't be a willing prisoner!" Addilyn blurted, the words escaping her mouth before she considered them. Ritter was merely trying to protect her, but his suggestion, however wise, insulted her.

"My lady—" Jessamy tried, but Addilyn interrupted her.

"I didn't travel from Eldwal to hide like a cowering child." Her eyes locked on Ritter, who shifted on his feet as if he were being dressed down by a superior officer. "This must end. We must stop him, and me hiding in an attic doesn't help anyone."

"You may stay here, of course," the lardal offered. "Regardless of your decision. I think Master Tuttle would appreciate that. But I warn you, the knight castellan and his constabulary removed all of Helenius's effects. I am sure they too are at the Gatehouse, or the High Aldin."

"Thank you." Addilyn's voice had calmed, but she shared a determined glance with both the Longmarcher and her champion.

"Now, Master Springheel." Uriah tried to relieve the tension. "Bring that dog of yours inside and let me have a look."

CHAPTER TWENTY-ONE

"In war, there's no substitute for victory."
—Annals of Halifax Military Academy

"MY LORD, MY LADY," Meeks Crowley announced. "Your royal guests are arriving."

"Thank you, Meeks." Godwin rose, as one of his servants struggled to ready the king's purple robe.

"Sire, there's an urgent request from the delegation from the barony of Foghaven Vale. They ask that you attend to them first."

"Ah, an apology from my cousin Dragich. Is he here already?"

"No, sire, it's Ambassador Thessica Camber and the baron's two sons, Donnar and Emmerich."

Solveig Jins knew nothing of the politics of the human court, but she was shrewd enough to see confusion and anger on the faces of both Queen Amice and King Godwin.

Solveig had stood by the queen at her request and was party to Meeks's announcement. She wore a quickly tailored dress so that she could attend court as the queen's guest. First Keeper Makai sat in the corner, stroking his beard and enjoying a last swig of stout, seemingly bored out of his mind.

"My dear Solveig," Amice turned to her, "feel free to mingle in court and to help yourself to the food and drink. First Keeper, would you be so good as to accompany our guest, so she feels at home?"

"With pleasure," Makai nodded, guiding Solveig out of a side door and into the main drawing room of Castle Thronehelm. They emerged at the rear of the room.

Solveig never imagined herself as the guest of a royal court, let alone in Thronehelm. The room was nearly filled with anxious nobles, and a pleasant susurrus descended in the chamber as they awaited the arrival of the king and queen.

Makai guided her over to the banquet tables and helped himself to another mug of ale.

"It's free, lass," he whispered to Solveig in the twergish tongue so as not to embarrass her. "Don't be shy. Help yourself."

Not wanting to make a spectacle, Solveig fixed herself a small plate of delicacies, trying to gather foods that she'd never tasted before. Then she left Makai to his own devices and slipped her way along the corner wall so that she could have a view of the thrones. Being the size of a pre-pubescent human didn't help her line of sight.

Then a trumpet blared, announcing the arrival of the king and queen. Solveig took a bite of some meaty legbone and watched happily from afar. The meat was tender and spiced, unlike the goat meat or ram stew she ate along the Garnet Pass. This was a lifestyle she could become accustomed to.

Godwin and Amice took to their thrones on the raised dais. Solveig watched Godwin scanning the audience and then pulled the ever-present Meeks aside. After a shared whisper between the two, the chamberlain nodded and slunk away. It was obvious to Solveig as the royal couple began to see visitors that Thessica Camber was likely to be last. The king, of course, would have his way. She couldn't help but chuckle at her enemy's family.

As the afternoon progressed, Makai caught up with her and they found their way back to the banquet tables for another round, but this time Solveig tried the Nectar of the Queen. She'd heard a lot about it and couldn't wait to make Tancred jealous with stories of it when she got back to the subterrane.

Then she spotted Thessica Camber through the crowd, impatiently standing with two human twins that wore the livery of Foghaven Vale. She subtly made her way closer but was careful not to get too close. She could tell that the men were anxious, and Camber was outright nervous.

As the last order of business was conducted, the king stood. "Are there any others present who wish to speak with me or my queen?" he asked, looking deep into the crowd.

Thessica Camber raised her hand. "Aye, my lord."

"You may approach." Godwin waved her forward. "So, the traitors have come to see me. Have you traveled all the way from Foghaven Vale to speak on behalf of my treasonous cousin? Where is he? He should be here to plead for his own clemency."

The three made their way to the front of the dais, the crowd parting to allow them to move to the fore. Solveig looked at Camber, whose hands were visibly shaking. She knew the woman was fighting to maintain her composure. The two men stood silently behind her with a small chest.

"My lord—" Thessica started.

"Your Majesty," Queen Amice corrected her in a helpful tone.

"Your Majesty," she repeated with a curtsy.

"Let me guess." Godwin stroked his beard and paused for effect. "Dragich has finally come to his senses?" The king's face drew up and he snorted.

"Your Majesty, I'm the bearer of grave news." Camber's voice wavered, and her eyes stared at the floor. "It's with a heavy heart—"

"Spare us the theatrics and false diplomacy," Godwin grumbled. "Spit it out, cousin."

Camber turned and stepped away, allowing Donnar and Emmerich to lift the box and approach them. Captain Anson Valion stopped them from getting any closer, raising a hand.

"They're unarmed," Camber pleaded. She was addressing Valion, but the Black Cuffs surrounded the trio regardless.

The king nodded to Anson, and the captain reached for the chest. He opened it and immediately stepped back, his face telling a disappointing tale.

"What is it?" the king asked.

"We're here to present the arrows of war," Camber announced, inducing a low groan and some cries from the attendees. "One from the barony of Gloucester and one from the Kingdom of Foghaven Vale. We're here on behalf of the Kingdom of Foghaven Vale, to present these arrows of war to Thronehelm, unless you surrender unconditionally and peacefully abdicate the throne."

Godwin leapt from his throne to the edge of the dais while Amice grabbed at her heart, recoiling from the open chest in front of them.

"I now see Von Lormarck's deceit for what it is," the king raged. "I've lost a son, Cecily Maeglen has lost a son, and now your false king brings us to war?"

Camber looked to her feet, peering sideways at Donnar and Emmerich, who stood stoically by.

"If that bloody maniac wants war, he'll have it."

Again, groans and shouts for Von Lormarck's head rose from the surprised court. Amice stood and wrapped an arm around her husband. Solveig lowered her ale mug and shared a silent grimace with Makai.

"How much of this treachery is already of his doing?" Godwin demanded.

The sons looked at Thessica to answer, but the ambassador froze. One of the sons stepped to Camber and addressed the king. Solveig didn't know if it was Donnar or Emmerich, but whoever it was stood at Godwin's feet, looking up at him.

"I'm sorry, Uncle, but your family has brought Warminster to this. We're at war unless you concede to the demands of King Von Lormarck."

"And you, Thessica Camber?" Godwin growled. "Where does the Camber family's loyalty lie? Are the Cambers with Thronehelm or against us?"

At length, she answered. "Against you," She peered sheepishly from behind the dark curtain of her hair.

Godwin reached for Anson, who handed him the two arrows, signifying the declaration of war. For a second, Solveig thought the king was asking for a sword. In the subterrane, no declaration of war would have been done through ill-prepared proxies like this.

"I, Godwin, King of *all* Warminster, accept these arrows of war." The king raised each arrow, one at time, high above his head in a near ceremonial ritual for all to see. When he was done, he handed the arrows to Meeks Crowley. "Master Crowley, please hang these arrows above the throne until this war is at an end. They will serve as a constant reminder to the throne and all of its visitors who the true enemies of Warminster are."

Meeks bowed and tried to scamper away with the arrows, but Godwin stopped him.

"And Meeks, bring me the arrows of war for the five remaining baronies of Warminster. I wish to present them to Ambassador Camber so that she may return them to my traitorous cousin."

Meeks hustled off without protest to retrieve the rarely used artifacts.

"Ambassador," Amice said, her voice stern and her eyes steely, "is there no other way to resolve this without spilling the blood of Warminsterians? Nephews, I beg of you. Please speak to your father."

"It's too late," Godwin growled before either the Von Lormarck sons or Camber could reply. "Nephews, let this be the start of a lesson. One you'll learn through your own eyes and hands. Many of your friends and family will die to sate your father's taste for power. Look around you at the faces in this room. The next time you see them, they'll be looking at you from the other side of the battlefield."

Solveig watched in horror. This wasn't what she'd been expecting, but she'd never forget it.

"Meeks!" Godwin screamed for his butler, only to see the gangly man stumbling back to the dais with the five arrows. He handed them to Godwin and the king placed them back in the same box the Thessaly and Von Lormarck arrows had come from. He closed it with a resounding bang. "Crowley, call for my war council and send a messenger to Halifax Military Academy to return the Faxerian, Lucien Blacwin, to Thronehelm. He'll lead my armies."

The king jumped down from the dais to stand next to his nephews. Neither of the twins backed away.

"All remaining members of the Thessaly, Camber, and Von Lormarck families must leave Thronehelm," the king ordered. He then turned from his nephews back to Camber. "Ambassador, you and any members of the Von Lormarck and Thessaly families have until the great hourglass completes four turns to leave Thronehelm or be arrested as prisoners of war."

Amice stepped down and took her husband's arm. She leaned in and whispered something in his ear. Godwin turned and his steely eyes caught Solveig's as he waved for her to approach. Solveig nearly choked on her wine and walked tentatively to the fore.

"I understand you're here representing the twergs of Clan Swifthammer and Clan Battleforge?" the king said.

Solveig flushed in embarrassment, but before she could respond, the king spoke again.

"Good! Tell your chieftains that the enemy of my enemy is my friend. We're now allies, Solveig Jins, and we'll share the same fate on the battlefield against my treasonous cousins."

Solveig turned to the Von Lormarcks and Camber, all of whom stared back at her like cryptids stalking their prey.

Godwin motioned to her. "Approach, good legate of Swifthammer. We must speak privately."

Solveig walked tentatively toward the dais, each step its own act of bravery until she reached Amice and Godwin. Without another word, the king and queen turned away from the Von Lormarcks. As Solveig looked back, she watched Anson Valion and his Black Cuff guards lead Donnar, Emmerich, and Thessica from the drawing room.

"I'll be looking for you on the battlefield," she heard Valion say to the sons, yet the boys looked undeterred.

SOLVEIG DUCKED THROUGH THE thick curtains that partitioned the drawing room from the royals' personal quarters. Her face ran red with embarrassment; her nerves ran rampant with fear. She looked to Makai with no words as he joined her alongside the king and queen and, of course, the stalking Meeks Crowley. Her hands trembled and she struggled to find her breath.

"Your Majesty," Solveig blurted in a breach of courtly protocol. "I'm not who you think I am. I… I'm just a humble merchant that found the fortune of our Ancient, Renshaw, at your door."

"Not anymore," the king barked, barely looking at her.

"Please, Renshaw, Ancient of the Rockfolk, protect your servant," Solveig mumbled in prayer.

"Renshaw?" the king asked.

"Renshaw Battleforge," Meeks explained. "He's the twergish Ancient of—"

"I damned well know who he is," the king spat.

"Godwin," Amice said, in a voice that was made to capture the attention of a poorly behaved child. "This is no time to lose your composure."

"I'm not!" Godwin stammered, then caught himself. "Damn it!"

The queen took him by the arm. "One breath, then another."

"What am I to do?" Solveig asked, as though she'd missed the interlude between the royals. Makai threw his arm around the startled twerg and led her to a seat.

"You're half human, aren't you?" the king asked, grabbing the armrests of Solveig's chair and staring her in the eyes.

"Y-yes." She leaned away from the imposing man, but the back of the chair left her nowhere to go.

"Good," he grumbled. "And that half belongs to the Kingdom of Warminster, of that I'm certain, which makes *you* my subject. You're now in the service of Thronehelm."

Solveig gasped, but Amice was already ahead of her.

"Godwin!" Amice yelled. "She's far from your subject. You're scaring the poor girl."

Godwin stood up straight and looked to his wife. Her stare could have cut diamonds. He took a deep breath and looked to Solveig, who was on the verge of tears.

"Meeks." The king's voice calmed. "Wine."

"Of course, my lord."

"Jins," he bellowed as Meeks poured a generous portion for the king. "You?"

Solveig didn't have an answer, but Meeks had a glass in her hand in seconds and she took a few hearty sips to calm her nerves.

"It was a show, Jins." The king's voice tempered now, after his nerves had calmed. "Just as they did for us. Political theater, nothing more."

"But now they think we're allies and that I'm someone I'm not."

"We *are* allies," Godwin replied. "We need Clan Swifthammer as much as you need us. You need to return to the Forge and tell them exactly what transpired here today."

Solveig nodded, swallowing hard.

"Crowley, fetch me a scribe," the king waved. Within moments, Forwin, Castle Thronehelm's historian, had followed Meeks back into the antechamber, dragging his scrolls and quills.

"Take this down." Godwin took a deep swig from his goblet as Forwin fumbled with his spectacles. "Address this to your king. What's his name?"

"*Her* name is Yrsa Dagny," Solveig replied. "And address her as *Krol*, which is the closest term we have for king in twergish, whether male or female."

"Very well." Godwin began an eloquent rant that lasted several minutes, dictating a message as Forwin scribed a note to Dagny, offering an alliance between the Forge and Thronehelm. When the ink was dry, he sealed the missive and handed it to Solveig.

"I'll send you home with an armed escort of ten of my best guards, the Black Cuffs, and provide you with a horse."

"I have a mule, Your Majesty."

"Very well," Godwin replied.

Makai stepped closer to the king. "Sire, I'm your First Keeper, but I'm also a twerg, originally from Clan Swifthammer. I'm without the Sight and little use in my role here. Perhaps I can help young Jins. I know one of Clan Swifthammer's warlocks, a magus as we call them. His name is Yenroar Silentall, and he's a wizard of some repute. Last I heard, he was in good standing with Jins's *krol*. If he's still there, perhaps he can vouch for me and I can play the part of a diplomat, which our dear merchant friend isn't."

Godwin looked to Amice for a second, who nodded at the thought. "Excellent idea, Makai. You shall accompany young Jins home."

Solveig's moment of comfort faded as Meeks Crowley's presence overwhelmed her once more. He watched her from the shadows, and Solveig shivered.

———✦———

AMBASSADOR THESSICA CAMBER HURRIED to pack her belongings. She traveled light, expecting the outcome she'd received from the king and queen, but the recent event played over in her mind. Never in her life did she expect to see, let alone participate, in a revolution. She loved the Thorhauers as much as the Von Lormarcks, and now she twisted against their coming war. She yearned for Castleshire's peace and the predictability of the Caveat.

Two Black Cuffs stood in her doorway while a lieutenant supervised, loitering in the hall. She heard a woman's voice coming closer and turned to see who had arrived. A friend perhaps coming to see her off, or perhaps a courtier digging for gossip before she was banished from the capital.

"Who are you?" one of the guards asked the woman at the door.

"I'm Ambassador Camber's right hand." Camber didn't recognize her, and the poor woman appeared stressed but wore the black and burnt orange of the Jackals. "And if you'll excuse me, I'm here to help her pack."

The guard spun to his lieutenant, who looked at the servant

decked in black and orange in the doorway. With a tilt of his head, he permitted the servant to enter.

"My lady, I came as quick as I heard." The woman curtsied in perfect form. "But I was detained *elsewhere*." She shot an annoyed glance at the Black Cuffs.

"I understand." Camber played along, not sure where this was leading.

"Now let me pack, my Lady. And you sit. I am certain you have more important things to do."

Camber let the woman approach and then whispered, "Who are you?"

"Meeks Crowley," the servant murmured, low enough not to arouse suspicion.

Camber knew Meeks spied for Von Lormarck and had magics at his disposal. Her sovereign had apprised her of that before her trip to Thronehelm. But she had no idea this was his talent. She wasn't sure how to feel about it. This was an advantage she wished she'd known sooner.

"What are you doing here?"

Her back to the door, Meeks slipped from her robe a scroll and placed it in the wardrobe, hiding it among Camber's clothes. Her gaze shifted to the ambassador for a moment and then she winked.

"My lady, please deliver this to Aarav Fleury for me."

Camber's face showed her confusion, but she held steady. "What's the nature of it?" she whispered.

"It contains orders for him." Meeks closed the trunk. "The half-twerg the king introduced you to as an ambassador from Rawcliffe Forge is false. She's merely a merchant of some kind. As we saw in the market."

Camber paused. The ruse was a clever one. She knew she'd met the woman in the market but had nearly forgotten the chance meeting through her jumbled nerves and botched declaration of war. She'd appreciated the political theater performed by the king, even more as she had fallen victim to it.

"However," Meeks continued, "the king has sent First Keeper Makai and ten men with her to the subterrane to offer an alliance to the krol. They must never reach the Forge."

"How can Aarav stop that?"

"He's now charged with dealing with the Moor Bog for our sovereign. Since the killing of the Nightcloak and the disappearance of the Black Rose, that duty now falls to Aarav Fleury."

"So Dru'Waith hasn't been in contact with you?" Camber asked. "He left Castleshire before I did. I was to meet him here, but he's nowhere to be found."

"I don't think he ever arrived here." Meeks's face turned down. "He would have sought me for help."

Camber grimaced. She knew in her heart the Bone elf couldn't be trusted. She doubted he ever boarded the *Bard*.

"My Lady," the lieutenant called from the hallway. "Your time is short."

"Coming, Lieutenant," Camber said. She turned back to Meeks. "What will you do?"

"Disappear." Meeks's face twisted and bubbled under the skin. "And then reappear somewhere else. I believe it may be time to pay the queen a visit."

Camber fought the urge to react to the revelation of Meek's powers. She caught a slight glimpse of what Von Lormarck described as magic, but this was something far more sinister. Her face paled.

"We're ready." The ambassador straightened, struggling to keep her poise. She drew a deep breath and closed her eyes for a moment. Turning, she approached the Black Cuffs. Looking over her shoulder at Meeks she said, "Please bring my things, Lynor," and pointed to her effects.

"As you command, my Lady," Meeks Crowley bowed and followed Camber to her carriage.

WITHIN ONE TURN OF the great hourglass that hung inside Castle Thronehelm, Valion had appointed an armed entourage, ready to escort Solveig and Makai back to the Forge. Makai had brought some traveling items and they met Solveig just outside the marketplace where she'd entered.

The king didn't come to see them off, but Queen Amice did.

"This is a day that you won't soon forget," the queen said as she fiddled with her hair and scratched behind her ear.

Solveig found the gesture oddly familiar, and the queen's smile just a tad too tight. "Thank you for all that you've done for me," the half-twerg acknowledged. "The day ended differently to how it began for us both, my lady."

"They often do," the wise queen replied, smiling even tighter.

Solveig brushed off the chill down her spine. "I'll guide them to the Garnet Pass," Solveig assured. "It's a new path that our army has just constructed. It will save us a week."

"May Nothos watch over your travels, and may your Ancients go with you."

Solveig smiled and turned, mounting Phanna. She waved back as she and the company of warriors descended the high road into the city proper.

Makai turned to her and in a low voice said, "Thronehelm is in for a long winter."

CHAPTER TWENTY-TWO

"Darkness can only be scattered by light. Ignorance
can only be overcome by knowledge."
—Great Keeper Quehm of the Keepers of the Forbidden

THE KEEPERS OF THE FORBIDDEN had gathered outside
Quehm's Hallow. The entirety of the remaining Divine
Protectorate of Erud waited with bated breath to hear the
name of the new Great Keeper. There was no ceremony, no
fanfare, and no dignitaries from around the realm had come
to Solemnity to celebrate the ascension.

Instead, the weary protectorate stood scattered among the
rubble of the Cathedral of the Watchful Eye as the leaders of their
sect emerged, one at a time. First Keeper Amoss came to the front
of the assembled masses and raised his hand for silence.

"Brothers and sisters of our order, the Keepers of the
Forbidden have chosen a new leader," he said, turning to
the gaggle of Keepers behind him. "First Keeper Jhodever of
Foghaven Vale, please step forward."

Murmured voices rose from the crowd, and Radu felt
the doubts of the protectorate emanating from the gathered
masses. He tried to ignore the instinctive urge to agree with
them, choosing instead to tend to his duty and stand by the
new Great Keeper, to support him in his decisions, offer
counsel and continue to offer the counsel of Erud to the greater
world. He watched as Jhodever reached the First Keeper of the
Cathedral and stood by his side.

"Kneel," Amoss asked.

Jhodever dropped to his knees and leaned on a knighting
stool made of ancient wood and worn leather. The stool had
been used during ascension ceremonies for as long as anyone

could remember. Radu noted the serious lines in Jhodever's face and appreciated his solemnity.

Amoss lowered his head in prayer to Erud and extended a blessing hand, touching Jhodever's forehead.

"As the ordained witness for Erud, the Keeper of all knowledge, the all-seeing, the sexless and the raceless Ancient of eternal wisdom, I grant you, Jhodever Nellivar, the humbling mantle of Great Keeper of our holiest of orders. May you wear your white cloak of wisdom with faith and possess the one true Sight."

He turned to First Keeper Portia Brecken, who handed him Jhodever's new robes. Jhodever removed his old cassock and Amoss helped him into his new one.

"Arise, Great Keeper." Amoss raised his hands and gently slid his thumbs across Jhodever's closed eyes, sealing the ceremony with one final blessing. "May the Sight of Erud shine through you and upon us all."

Jhodever stood and raised his arms wide. The joined masses of the Divine Protectorate of Erud all knelt and bowed to their new leader.

"The oath of fealty," the new Great Keeper called, "as one."

In unison, the combined orders took a knee, bowed their heads in respect, and began to recite the oath.

"On my faith to the Ancient Erud," Radu chanted with them, "I swear unwavering allegiance to our sect and my Great Keeper. Never shall I cause him harm. I shall pay homage to our faith completely, and without deceit."

"Rise, my flock," the Great Keeper ordered.

Radu looked to his friends Amoss and Portia as the Great Keeper moved to walk among his people. Amoss himself appeared defeated, and both his friends followed in somber silence.

"My first order of business as your Great Keeper," Jhodever said, now standing amidst the collective near Radu, "is to appoint *no* First Keeper of the Cathedral of the Watchful Eye."

The stunned crowd groaned in protest.

"It's unprecedented," he explained, trying to bring the restless crowd back to a simmer, "but these are unprecedented times. There's a need for a new direction, and many changes to our order. High Watcher Volcifar Obexx, please step forward."

The disciple stepped through the crowd to greet his new master, pushing past Radu.

"In honor of your great deeds and dedication to your order, I'm retaining you as High Watcher of the Disciples of the Watch."

"Thank you, Great Keeper," Obexx replied, taking his place to Jhodever's left.

"Captain Danton Hague, please step forward," Jhodever continued.

Hague emerged from the crowd to stand in front of the Great Keeper.

"Captain, you too shall retain your post," Jhodever announced to all.

"Thank you, Great Keeper." Hague took a respectful bow and moved to Jhodever's right.

Radu noted the relief that floated with Hague's words. Despite the normal appointments, something still felt wrong to Radu. Events were swirling around him, and he could not stop or even slow them. *Is Amoss right to be wary?*

"But," Jhodever continued, "I'm placing the Knights of the Maelstrom under the command and authority of the Disciples of the Watch. Your order shall henceforth report directly to High Watcher Obexx."

Another groan of confusion came from the crowd, and

some voices from the ranks of the Knights raised in protest. But the Great Keeper pressed on.

Hague's subtle turn toward Amoss was not noticed by the crowd but Radu saw it. The pair shared a silent, unspoken conversation.

Radu stepped in to quell any further dissent. "Enough," he called to the crowd. "The Great Keeper has spoken." But something still felt wrong.

"We're but simple soldiers of our faith," Hague agreed, nodding to Radu, then to his troops. "We follow the orders of the Great Keeper and the Ancient Erud."

"What position shall I take?" Amoss asked, interrupting Jhodever's moment. "Now that mine has been eliminated?"

"Ah, Amoss," Jhodever replied. "I've dedicated a great amount of prayer to this. The people of Foghaven Vale balance themselves on a knife's edge, nearing the brink of civil war. I've seen it firsthand. If we're to stave this off and help them to establish themselves as a new nation, the fledgling kingdom will need someone with your wisdom and experience. You'll serve and advise King Dragich Von Lormarck. Erud commands that you go there."

The shock of this rattled Radu. Amoss was to leave the cathedral? The old Keeper fought his ill temper, clenching his fists behind him. Radu understood; this was surely just a way for Jhodever to remove his greatest rival from Solemnity, dispatching him to the faraway Vale. Amoss had been correct. Nothing had been by chance: not Jhodever's late arrival, not Obexx's interference, and not Cynric's nomination of Jhodever. The urge to protest rose in his throat. The others of the faith watched their reactions with held breath.

No, this isn't the time nor place to voice unfounded suspicions.

He forced himself to remain calm, clasped his hands behind his back, and nodded to Amoss.

"Oh, and First Keeper Amoss," the Great Keeper added, "the post needs to be filled quickly. You'll depart this afternoon. I'll have some of my Disciples and Knights escort you and protect you, as the road to Foghaven Vale is both long and dangerous. I've traveled it many times. May Erud grant you wisdom on your journey."

Radu knew that Jhodever's travels were by way of his mastery of catoptromancy, and not by horses. He saw the future through the use of magical mirrors and could use his expertise to travel through them. One such mirror called Dromofangare still hung in the inner sanctum of the cathedral. Its twin, Traumefang, hung in the halls of Dragon Ridge and could be used as the other end of the portal. If the Great Keeper wanted him to appear in Foghaven Vale without the rigors of a month's trip by carriage, he could easily light up the mirror and send him through. He could even send him with a hippogryph to cut the travel to days and not a month. But that clearly wasn't his plan.

"Lieutenant Lorraine," the Great Keeper called, "will you please escort First Keeper Amoss to his quarters so he can pack and depart?"

Lorraine stepped from the mass and walked toward Amoss, his hand resting subtly on the pommel of his sword.

"One more thing, Amoss," Jhodever added. "A Keeper must wear the robes of his station."

Amoss looked to the approaching Volcifar Obexx, who handed him his new First Keeper robes, adorned with a black and burnt orange brooch of a jackal's head. He took the robes and started walking toward his cloister when Jhodever stopped him.

"A Keeper must wear the robes of his station," the Great Keeper repeated, more sternly this time.

Amoss looked to Jhodever and then shared glances with

Radu and Hague. The old man slipped from his cathedral robes in front of the staring and silent crowd and donned his new garb.

———✦———

RADU WAITED OUTSIDE THE cloister with Captain Hague for Amoss to reemerge. Not long after his public embarrassment, Amoss trudged back to the campus courtyard, looking for his escort to Foghaven Vale. Seeing the two friendly faces waiting for him, his steps did not falter.

You stand apart from the protectorate to see me off?" Amoss asked. "I'd call it brave but displacing yourself from the rest might not be a wise choice."

"Nonsense," Radu replied. "Just an old friend wishing another well."

"You are too bold," he said through a pained smile. "I'm shocked you've stayed silent this long. But thank you for coming."

Radu wiped a tear from his eye and struggled to speak again.

Amoss turned to the captain. "Hague, take care of the gryphs and watch over Precept Radu. I fear his mouth will land him in trouble here if I'm not present to keep him in check."

Radu managed a weary smile.

"As you command, *Great Keeper*," Hague whispered, quiet enough so only the three of them could hear

"Danton, don't," Amoss begged. "This is a time when the protectorate needs us the most. Let's show them humility in our service to Erud."

Hague's lips pursed and he looked away from Amoss.

Unconvinced that he'd stopped the man from pursuing a rash course of action, Amoss hugged his friend. Then, looking back at Radu, whispered into his ear, "There may be a time when Erud calls upon us, but it's not now. Find Daemus Alaric and restore the Sight to our cathedral."

Radu hugged him one last time. "Be careful."

"First Keeper?" a voice called from his carriage. He looked to see Rutger Lorraine standing amongst a group of ten Knights and two Disciples of the Watch. "Your escort awaits you."

"Coming, Lieutenant," he replied, taking one last look at his friends. He climbed into the carriage and Lorraine shut the door, waving to the driver to depart.

"May Erud grant you wisdom in your journeys," Amoss called to them as the carriage began to roll.

Radu stood in the rubble of his former home and watched more than his old friend fade off in the distance.

CHAPTER TWENTY-THREE

*"Hammerstead doesn't want words. Hammerstead wants
the groan of a horn that sends her to battle—to destiny."*
—the Saga of Qvinne Linnea, Daughter of Lykke

THE MORNING CAME, BRINGING with it an early frost.
Montgomery peeled himself from the bearskin blankets and
looked for his betrothed, but Freya was nowhere to be found.
He dragged himself to his feet and opened the tent flaps,
letting the mountain air rush in. For a second, he wore the
chill like an unexpected kiss from winter. His eyes widened
and his breath escaped him.

As he regathered his senses from the night before, he
realized that Yngwie Cnute was right. He wasn't sore from his
wounds, but he knew they were still there. *The rumors about
Heifenmager might be true after all*, he thought.

He ventured a few more steps outside his tent in no more
than his leggings and wolfskin blanket, then looked around.
He heard LaBrecque's distinctive voice yelping from behind
his own tent, like a dog in pain.

"That's the sound babies make," Monty called in jest,
conjuring up Freya's words from last night.

"My piss!" LaBrecque lamented, trying to shake off its
effects both literally and figuratively. He urinated at the back of
his tent. "They said the beer helped with healing and brawling.
They didn't tell us it would hurt to piss!"

Monty laughed. "When you're done whining, we should
check in on the viscount."

Just as he spoke, the viscount opened the flap of his tent
and squinted against the glare of the frozen dew. "My head…"
Joferian managed, one hand cradling his face. "Did it snow?"

Monty laughed as LaBrecque mumbled something about "just wait till you piss." His mood far lighter, Monty felt bold. He jokingly pulled Joferian's hands from his face. The viscount winced and lowered his eyes from the unfriendly sun, moaning. He shoved Monty away, cursing.

"Prince Montgomery!" Cnute's voice sounded, interrupting the men in their hungover morning revelry. Montgomery looked over to see Cnute walking up to them with Ulf Skuli in tow.

"What's the meaning of this?" Montgomery asked.

"He's your thrall. He's yours to command," Cnute reminded Montgomery.

"What exactly does that mean for him?" Montgomery asked.

"He's your slave," Cnute said. "Until death."

"I don't want—" Monty began again.

"It's not about what you want," Cnute interrupted. "For him to live, he must serve you." He reached behind and grabbed Ulf by his massive shoulder, hauling him forward toward Monty.

The enslaved man did not pout, but his eyes looked firmly at the ground.

"If you refuse," Cnute went on, "you will break tradition... again. And you will put your new alliance in jeopardy."

Feeling trapped, knowing he could deal with it later, Monty nodded.

"It's time for you and your men to meet with the *konungr* and discuss strategy on our shared campaigns," Cnute said. He and the others await you." He extended a leading hand, gesturing for them to follow him.

"Clothes first," Monty said, disappearing into his tent to ready himself.

Ulf followed him and stood, eyes trained on the ground as Monty dressed.

Finding the silence awkward, Monty said, "I need you

to translate for me. Their Wartooth is too quick for me to understand. I need your help navigating the customs and ways of this place."

Ulf swallowed but did not answer.

"You understand me, right?" Monty asked, looking around for wherever Freya had tossed his belt the night before.

Ulf nodded and spoke a single word in Warminsterian: "Aye."

"Good." He found it under a wad of discarded blankets. "Tell me what to do and I'm sure everything will be fine."

"I dare not," Ulf murmured in his deep voice. "It's no longer my place."

This was becoming more and more frustrating. Monty gritted his teeth. He'd have to find a way around his new thrall's stonewall beliefs.

"Ulf, look at me." The man raised his eyes. "I am commanding you, as my thrall, to translate the discussion and inform me of your customs and ways. To avoid looking like an ass," he added with a small smile. "Understood?"

The huge man's shoulders slackened a little. "Aye, I do."

―――

PRINCE MONTGOMERY ENTERED THE great hall with Joferian and LaBrecque. Ulf Skuli was in tow, but stayed far to the rear, near the giant doors of the hall. Overnight, the great hall had been transformed into a war room. Tables had been moved and Atorm, Einar, and a group of men Montgomery didn't recognize stood in the center of the hall near the hearth. They spoke in Wartooth.

Monty turned to the three men following him and signaled Ulf to step forward, replacing Joferian on his right side.

Joferian opened his mouth to protest at being replaced by the thrall, but Monty hissed at him to be quiet and stand down. He whispered to Ulf to interpret for the trio so as not to offend the great *konungr* with his presence.

"The gathering is known as a *Hammelgung*," Ulf explained, his voice low. "In your tongue, it's a war council."

Monty nodded.

"Atorm wants to summon allies from the nearby colony of Hrolt," Ulf continued. "It should double our numbers. He also wants to send word to the Lothian Flock."

"What's the Lothian Flock?" Joferian asked.

"They're a separate clan of Norsemen that live outside of civilized culture."

"Outside 'civilized' culture?" Montgomery repeated, before he caught himself. To him, Hammerstead was already outside of civilized culture. *How chaotic must this Lothian Flock be?*

"They're, uh…" Ulf stuttered for a moment and Monty guessed he was struggling with the right translation. "Berserkers. Atorm wants to see if they wish to participate in our war."

"Don't they answer to Atorm?" LaBrecque asked.

"No," Ulf whispered. "They've always been outside his influence, as with the kings before him. The Flock's numbers are small, but they can account for the strength of three or four warriors in a battle. They wish to die and go to the Hall of the Ancients, so they fear no battle."

The discussion in Wartooth continued outside of Montgomery's understanding for a few more minutes, then he saw Einar walk away from the table.

Monty tried to pay attention to the conversation and to appear engaged, but his curiosity drew his eyes to the enigmatic runecaster he'd met the night before. Einar boiled something in a cauldron in the wide hearth, adding a powder of some kind that made the mixture smoke terribly. He inhaled deeply, breathing in the boiling fumes. His head started to bob and roll, and he appeared to fall into a trance, mumbling incoherently.

"What's he saying?" Monty asked.

"I don't know," Ulf replied. "It's not Wartooth."

The prince continued to watch Einar, who lowered himself slowly to the ground. He sat, legs crossed, and his head swiveled uncontrollably. Then the runecaster drew an axe hammer from his belt and cut his hand on the blade. His spindly fingers were soon covered in his own blood, and he spoke louder. Leaning forward, he drew crimson runes on the floor. He finished with a howl and a swoop of his bloody hand in an arc above the runes. As he finished, a searing bolt of lightning crashed through the roof of the great hall, etching the ground at his feet.

The trio lurched away to protect themselves from the flash of heat. In that moment, Montgomery recalled the thunderclap that had cracked the dome of the Caveat weeks earlier. Again, there were no rainclouds and there was no storm.

Then came a second bolt, followed by a third, all arcing through the same hole in the great hall's ceiling. The air grew thick with static energy, but the hall didn't burn.

"No thunder," Monty noted, sharing sideways glances with the viscount and admiral.

Once it seemed safe, the three rose to their feet. Monty looked where the lightning had struck and saw scorch marks on the floor. But the marks weren't blackened scars, instead forming unique runes at Einar's feet.

Einar began to drift back to coherency, and the room of Norsemen formed a circle around the dazed runecaster. When he came to, his eyes had changed.

"Einar..." Atorm leaned in to check on him, but the runecaster didn't respond.

"He's caught the spirit," Ulf said to Monty, who frowned in confusion.

"The war god Koss possesses him," the Norseman went on. "Look closely. Those are the eyes of an Ancient, now. They no longer belong to Einar."

At length, Einar spoke in a voice that wasn't his own. It was deeper and it echoed, as if two people were speaking at the same time.

"What's he saying?" Joferian asked.

"I'm not sure." Ulf's face scrunched in confusion. "He's speaking in an ancient version of Wartooth, but it seems that both Koss and Ulthgar the Forger are pleased with our alliance and will bless this blood oath."

Then Einar made his way up to the men and stopped to look into Joferian's eyes. At first, Montgomery thought it was Joferian's whispers that had brought him, but he soon understood that Einar—in his possessed state—didn't care.

Einar grabbed Joferian around the collar and dragged him to the first rune, pointing at the symbol. Joferian, after righting himself, stood on the markings. Einar called the names of other men, who soon joined him.

"Argantyr, son of Atorm," he said, "Bjorkmar, son of Insulgil. Strunk, son of Helmgard Forkbeard."

Einar turned to one last man and added, "Yngwie Cnute, son of no name, you shall earn your family a name in the war to come."

All four Norsemen left Atorm's Hammelgung's circle and joined Joferian on the lightning rune. As they did, Einar's spirit eyes faded, and he slowly returned to his forceful self.

"The Ancients have spoken," the runecaster announced. "You shall ride first to Hrolt, to combine forces with Jarl Four Fingers, and then on to the cursed city of Vallance. That's where the pilferers of our slate iron have stolen our precious ore from the womb of the Dragon Breath's. They huddle in their warm beds. The Ancients want us to take back what's rightfully ours."

The Norsemen, hearing this and led by Atorm, cheered, chanting the names of Koss and Ulthgar over and over. Joferian looked at Montgomery, a helpless look upon his countenance. But the prince knew he was powerless to change the minds of their allies. Their Ancients had decreed it.

Then Einar came for Monty and LaBrecque, pulling them to stand upon the second rune.

"Atorm, son of Wolfrick," Einar called, and the *konungr* joined Montgomery. "Raevil, son of Roevil. Drott, son of Gunnar the Whelp. Magnus Bearslayer, Faxon the Red. Haeming, son of Brutus. Kjar, son of Wilkegard."

They all joined the prince and the admiral on the runes.

"We'll sail south into the port of Thronehelm to join with King Godwin," Einar called, placing himself on the same rune. "We'll face the Jackal and his armies."

The group cheered and yelped various war cries in Wartooth again, but this was different. Montgomery caught the term "jackal" and understood the reference too well.

Had Einar, through the eyes of his Ancients, discovered the truth?

Finally, Einar looked at the shieldmaidens—who'd been left standing alone—and asked them to take their place on the third mark. He walked more respectfully toward Gullveig, Atorm's wife, and peered deeply into her eyes.

"Gullveig, Qvinne of Atorm Stormmoeller and all of Hammerstead," he said. "You'll travel to the Lothian Flock. They won't listen to Atorm, but they'll listen to a shieldmaiden of Koss."

Gullveig and her shieldmaidens tapped their weapons softly but rhythmically against their shields, growing in volume until the echoes filled the halls. They stepped to the third rune and cried out in unison, their tongue foreign to Montgomery's ears. He understood the passion, though.

As the sudden ritual concluded, Einar began to lose control of himself and stumbled a few feet before passing out on the floor. The Norsemen ignored the fatigued man, sounding off with more war cries and songs to Koss and Rijkstag. Then the Norsemen left the hall to begin their preparations for war.

MONTGOMERY AND HIS FRIENDS left the great hall to follow Atorm. "Good king," Montgomery said, rushing to catch the man. "May we have a word?"

"Walk with me," Atorm replied, his sons Faxon the Red and Argantyr in tow.

"I heard what Einar said," Monty began, before being politely interrupted by Atorm.

"What the Ancients have demanded, you mean."

Monty chose his next words carefully, so that he wouldn't upset his ally and future father-in-law.

"Yes, what the Ancients have demanded, but the Ancients don't have to feed an army, especially one that's foraging for food. It will become harder and harder as winter closes in. it's unsustainable. We'll starve."

Atorm continued to walk toward a large barn in the center of town. Neither he nor his sons responded.

"Also," Monty went on, "we may be outnumbered. Our enemy, if Einar is correct, is Baron Dragich Von Lormarck. He's known for employing trollborn troops as mercenaries. Combined with the forces of Foghaven Vale and Gloucester, we're likely to be outmatched. If so, are we wise to split our forces by sending some to Vallance?"

Atorm belly laughed and opened the doors to the barn.

Inside, a gallery of finely crafted weapons, all glowing in the silver blue of slate iron, hung in the darkness. The prince looked on in awe and exchanged glances with Joferian and LaBrecque.

Atorm plucked up a random blade of slate iron and swung it against a suit of armor. The blade sliced through it with little resistance. Montgomery, Joferian, and LaBrecque shared a wide smile.

"No longer concerned?" Atorm asked.

"Not for the weapons," Monty answered. "But what of the food?"

"We have to go and get the food," Atorm replied.

"But from where?

The hulking Atorm threw his arm around his daughter's betrothed and looked him in the eyes.

"Our food awaits us in Vallance and Saracen."

This time, the men didn't smile. Joferian stammered.

"Don't worry, young prince," Atorm said meaningfully. "Joferian, son of Queen's Chapel, will bring it to us when he conquers the cities. Otherwise, we'll starve!"

AS THE DAY WORE on, the Norsemen split into three groups. Joferian waited to command the troops heading to Hrolt and then Vallance. Gullveig had departed with the shieldmaidens, looking for the nomadic Lothian Flock.

Montgomery waited with LaBrecque for Atorm and his sons to return from offering prayers and sacrifices to Koss and Ulthgar. They were sitting around the tables in the great hall when they heard the footfalls of their new allies. Atorm approached Montgomery and took a seat beside him, offering him and the admiral a horn of Heifenmager.

"Drink it," Atorm said. "It was blessed today at the totem of Kaelic, the Ancient of the Seas. It will bring our sails strong winds during our voyage to Thronehelm."

"*I... have... much... to... learn... of... your... ways,*" Montgomery replied with some difficulty in Wartooth, appearing to surprise the *konungr*. Monty had Ulf Skuli to thank for teaching him the single sentence while they waited.

As the men finished their drinks, Atorm took Montgomery's horn from him and held it up for him to take a closer look.

"I've tricked you, Thorhauer," Atorm said with a grin. "I made you drink from the Horn of Hammerstead."

"What does that mean?"

"It means that it's yours now." The konungr forced it back into the prince's hand.

"I don't understand."

"The Horn of Hammerstead is an ancient relic, taken from the crown of a magical ram that our people hunted many years ago. It's been carefully preserved and kept for times like these."

Monty held the horn out to inspect it. It was bigger than the typical horns they'd been drinking from, nearly making a complete curl. It was a dull grey in color and had runic carvings adorning its spiral.

"It possesses its own particular beauty." Atorm looked appraisingly at the relic. "And now it's yours." Atorm slapped Monty on the back. "The man or woman who carries the Horn of Hammerstead is the leader of our army."

"Then this belongs to you." Monty forced the horn into the *konungr's* breast.

Atorm resisted. "This is *your* struggle. And this war is for your people. This horn was last blown in a battle against your father. It's right that it finds its way into your hands."

"I'm not ready to carry such an artifact," Montgomery insisted.

Atorm turned, putting one leg on either side of the bench to face the prince. "You sailed north as a beggar and leave Hammerstead with an alliance, an army, the Horn of Hammerstead, the *konungr's* daughter, and the blessing of our Ancients. You *are* ready."

Monty looked to the horn and then back to Atorm. The two embraced.

"Use it *only* to signal the start of the battle," Atorm warned. "Any Norseman worth his salt will find his or her warrior spirit when they hear its bellow."

Monty nodded, gripping it. Soon, two thousand Norsemen would march to the docks of Hammerstead to board their vessels. He'd stand on the deck of the *Sundowner*, at the head the largest fleet he'd ever seen. They'd they set sail south to Thronehelm to deliver the terms of their alliance to King Godwin.

FIRST KEEPER AMOSS JOSTLED back and forth and from side to side as he sat silently in his horse-drawn carriage, only a few days into his long journey to Foghaven Vale. His escorts had removed him from the Cathedral of the Watchful Eye and, since then, few words had been shared with him. He rode with a retinue of ten Knights and two Disciples, one of which accompanied him at all times.

The confined carriage was comfortable enough, but his old bones told him he was in for a long ride. They rode in the glow of midmorning, but he kept his weary eyes with him in the cart, one watching the disciple who escorted him and the other staring at the ring First Keeper Portia Brecken had given to him before his reassignment. He knew the Disciple, a man named Borheigh Szalla was more of a guard than an escort, and he wondered if "guard" was too kind a title for the man.

His mind was kept busy with thoughts of lost opportunities and a lifetime of work ripped away from him. He twisted the ring subconsciously around his finger, but his mind was in the courtyard, watching the falling stars as they destroyed the campus. He could hear the ghostly cries of the dead and dying haunting his ears as if they were still burning in front of him. He stared ahead, the silver of the ring capturing his thoughts and reminding him to run for cover as he saw the Cathedral ignite in a fiery ball of black wind.

"The ring," Szalla said sternly, ripping him from his thoughts. "Why are you wearing it?"

"It was a gift from Nasyr," Amoss lied. "I wear it to honor her memory."

"May I see it?" Szalla asked.

Amoss carefully removed the ring and handed it to him.

Szalla looked at the bauble for a second or two and then tossed it from the carriage window. "We'll have no reminders of our failed past."

"Does that include me, Disciple?" Amoss asked, shifting in his seat.

"I am afraid it does, First Keeper. I'm to return to the cathedral and tell of a trollborn ambush as we swept by the borders of the Killean Desolates. The desperate trollborn will have attacked the carriage first, you see, assuming it contained gold or a person worth a ransom. We'll have fought them off, but not before you were torn away, a victim of their raid."

Amoss sat in silence. It was the moment he'd been dreading since they'd left. He'd been wondering how long they'd wait before killing him.

It appeared the answer was two days.

Szalla knocked on the carriage roof to order it to stop and Amoss heard the driver obey. The Disciple produced a venomous dagger from the folds of his robe, slick with a poison Amoss could smell from across the carriage. The blade was stained inky black, and its acrid odor reminded Amoss of the festering boils of the plague victims he'd treated as a Low Keeper.

He sat there, helpless.

"It's the Venom of the Abyss," Szalla remarked. "It will be quick, but painful. Just like the Great Keeper wanted."

Amoss tried to remain courageous in the face of the Ancient of Death. "Jhodever is not the Great Keeper, Disciple."

Szalla just smiled and leaned toward him, ready to make a move.

Then the whistling of arrows filled the air. Amoss heard screaming outside and armor clanging to the ground. Horses neighed and a stray arrow pierced the door, sticking between the two men. Amoss wasn't sure why he noticed, but the arrow's shaft was white and adorned with crimson feathers.

Szalla looked anxiously out of the window and Amoss wasted no time. He jumped at the man, his sizeable body giving him an advantage. The two tugged at each other, but Amoss's size won over and they both tumbled to the floor. Amoss's clenched hand struggled against the youthful strength of his opponent's wrist as he forced the dagger away from him. Szalla dropped his arm to gain some leverage, but Amoss bit at his hand. The Disciple growled in pain, the dagger slipping from his grasp and falling harmlessly to the carriage's floor.

The two began to wrestle, Szalla's bleeding hand finding Amoss's exposed throat. The First Keeper tugged at the Disciple's wrist, but the man crawled on top him, his free hand reaching for the loose weapon.

Amoss grunted and released all of his strength, desperately fighting for his life. He pulled Szalla's stranglehold off with his right hand and grabbed him by the scruff of the cloak with his other, pulling him down. He rolled over with the man's free hand pushing at Amoss's jaw. Amoss's elbow glanced across his face, stunning him for a second, which was long enough for Amoss to recover the lost dagger.

The carriage ground to a sudden halt and the two combatants rolled over, exchanging positions yet again. Amoss grunted and rolled back, forcing Szalla flat and holding the blade to his face. The Disciple's eyes widened and Amoss could feel his hurried breathing as he sat on his chest. Szalla winced, awaiting the final blow.

Then the carriage door swung open behind him. Amoss didn't bother to turn and look, assuming his escort had come to finish the job. But at least he'd take one with him to the Hall of the Ancients.

"Stop, First Keeper," a man said in broken common tongue. "The battle is won."

Amoss stopped, still holding the blade to his opponent. He turned for a second to see an unexpected figure in the doorway, a Vermilion soldier with his arrow nocked and pointed at the downed Disciple. He wore stark white armor and his crimson eyes stared calmly at the trapped Disciple, begging him to move. Szalla stopped struggling and lifted his hands from Amoss.

Vexed by the appearance of his savior, Amoss stabbed the poisonous dagger through the carriage floor and screamed, venting his rage. He felt Szalla relaxing beneath him. He looked down at the frightened man to find him looking up at him. Amoss balled his fist and punched the Disciple unconscious.

THE VERMILION OFFICER HELD Amoss's wrist. "Steady..."

With a single, swift motion, the elven warrior popped Amoss's dislocated finger back into place. Amoss felt the quick jolt of pain and winced. He looked down at his injured hand, marveling at his new ally's work. It was a procedure Amoss had done for others, but he'd never had to do it for himself.

"Thank you." Amoss rubbed the jarring pain in his hand away.

"First time in battle?"

"Aye, and hopefully the last."

"I doubt that, First Keeper." The Vermilion shook his head. "There's no peace in the direction that we ride."

Amoss nodded and looked around. A wing of the Vermilion had ambushed his troupe and either killed or captured the Knights. One Disciple was dead with an arrow through his neck, while the other sat on the ground, his arms tied and a look of defeat across his bruised face. In all, the Vermilion had killed seven Knights and one Disciple, leaving four prisoners to attend to.

Amoss slumped to the ground and buried his face in his shaking hands. He knew it was over, but it didn't feel that way to him. One Vermilion stood out and appeared to be their leader. He was wearing matte black leather armor and ordering the others around in a language that Amoss didn't understand, his men scrambling at every point of his sword. Then the man approached him.

"Thank you, my lord," Amoss managed through labored breathing. "Forgive me if my legs don't allow me to rise to greet my savior. I fear they're feeble from battle."

"Take your time," the elven commander managed in broken Warminsterian. "You're the First Keeper of the Cathedral of the Watchful Eye, are you not?"

"I was, yes."

"Coronelle Fia Elspeth, our queen, has sent us to find you."

"And not a moment too soon, I might add." Amoss, finally calm enough, rose to his feet. "I was once the First Keeper, but the cathedral has fallen into insurrection. The Keepers are no more."

"We're here to change that." The commander removed his helmet so that Amoss could get a good look at him. The man was tall and athletically thin, with the sharp features common to elves. His eyes were a dark crimson, nearly blood colored, and his hair was a tinge darker than the rest of his troops.

"Who are you, sir?" Amoss asked.

"My name is Evchen Vischer of Eldwal. In your society, I believe you'd refer to me as a noble."

The two men shook hands briefly and Vischer led him back to the empty cart.

"Come now, First Keeper," Vischer said, his voice brimming with confidence. "We ride for Thronehelm, where your services are desperately needed."

"What of the insurrection?" Amoss asked. "And what of my sect?"

"Someone else is coming for them," Vischer replied.

"Thronehelm is a long ride. May I take a minute?"

"We're not riding there." Vischer laughed. "Come, First Keeper, and learn how the Vermilion travel."

CHAPTER TWENTY-FOUR

"Denying what you feel won't make it go away."
—Illustra, the Ancient of Love

ARJUN STARED AT THE ENTRANCE to the Gatehouse. He'd stood guard at the mansion many times before, never believing he'd stare into it from the other side of the threshold. He'd keep the unwanted out by word or sword, and now it was his turn to petition for an audience with the Athabasica.

The Gatehouse stood only five stories high, but from the street, it appeared taller to Arjun than ever before. The white building was square and walled with a one-story walkway, allowing the castellan to guard the only government building in Abacus. Long windows, arched at the top, adorned the outside of the building, and the roof featured an outdoor area for gatherings and occasional pronouncements from the Athabasica. Crowds would congregate in the round promenade in front of the Gatehouse to hear from their leader, who would address them from above.

In typical Abacunian fashion, a mechanical walkway could be extended over the crowd by means of a set of contraptions, allowing the Athabasica to walk out and above the crowd, suspended on the temporary bridge. The promenade was empty, the walkway had been retracted, and Arjun was staring at two guards who flanked the entrance to the Gatehouse.

"Ready?" Faux asked Arjun, who'd stalled yards from the front door.

Arjun fidgeted in his armor but turned away from Faux to look at Daemus instead. "Any signs from the Ancients?" He hoped his futile question would meet with direction from the gods, however slight the chance may be.

Daemus shook his head.

"Why is it that when you need them, they're never around?" The captain forced a nervous smile.

"You can do this." Faux's gentle hand turned his face back to her.

Arjun harnessed his courage and walked forward with Faux, Daemus and Marquiss in tow. The guards were wearing all-too familiar uniforms, emblazoned with the Abacunian coat of arms, the Peacemaker mace in the center of a gold sheath. Before they could address him, Arjun began. "My name is Arjun Ezekyle, former sergeant of the High Aldin and friend of the Athabasica. I'm here to see her as a messenger from Castleshire. I have words of great importance."

One of the guards began to shake his head, but before he could speak, Arjun flashed the tattoo on his left arm, which could only be earned at the High Aldin. He also removed his sheathed katana and laid it at their feet as further proof of his tale. Arjun could tell his effort to prove himself had won some favor from the guards, but both had motioned for him to come no closer.

"I'm sorry, sir," one of the guards said. "We must deny entrance to everyone today. Orders from the Athabasica herself."

"I can't leave without delivering my message." Arjun tried to remain calm, although he felt anything but. "What do you suggest? I'm under orders from the Regent of Castleshire herself."

The two men looked at each other for a moment. "Come with us."

They led the group inside the wall of the Gatehouse, but not to the mansion itself. The Castellan soldiers escorted them to a small guard station sparsely decorated with a few uncomfortable chairs and a rusty spittoon in one corner. The room smelled of pipe smoke, and a single window looked back into the promenade.

"We can't take you to the Athabasica, but I can fetch an aide," the soldier offered. "For an old sergeant of the High Aldin, of course."

The group waited anxiously for a few minutes, and Arjun realized they'd found themselves sitting behind a locked door. He didn't know if they'd posted guards outside, but his nerves hadn't settled.

"This reminds me of House Alaric." Arjun jiggled the doorknob. "Are we prisoners here, too?"

Faux shook her head. "They have no reason to arrest us here."

Footfalls approached and the door unlocked. A man walked into the room in the blue and gold robes of Abacus. The guard that had accompanied him stood inside and closed the door.

"Good morning." The man made a perfunctory but polite bow. He was obviously of trollborn descent, possessing the size of a human but with an unnaturally large head and hands. His skin color was a dull blue, nearly matching the color of his robes. "My name is Dashiel, and I am a steward of Athabasica the Poet. Now, how may I help you?"

The man was polite enough, but Arjun struggled to suppress his true feelings about being presented with an underling. "My name is Arjun Ezekyle—"

"I know very well who you are," the man interrupted. "The guards informed me. You're a messenger from the Regent of Castleshire."

"Correct, and I must deliver my message to Anoki."

"You mean the Athabasica?"

"Yes, I am sorry." Arjun looked to the floor, a bit embarrassed to fumble through his opening remarks. His hand rubbed at the back of his neck, and he felt his face flush. "The Athabasica, I meant to say."

"Unfortunately, she's not receiving guests today." Dashiel sat back in a chair, appearing bored and looking at his manicured fingernails. "I'm her attendant and would be happy to deliver your message to her."

"That, sir, is unacceptable," Faux interjected. Arjun shot her a look, but the words had already been said.

"Well, then, enjoy your stay in Abacus." Dashiel forced a half-smile and stood to leave.

"Sir, please." Arjun reached across the table but held fast when the guard stepped toward him. Dashiel froze and his gaze returned to Arjun, his smile gone. "Understand that we've traveled for nearly a month and lost one of our companions to an attack on Harbinger's Run. We need to speak with her."

The man turned and looked at the group. He seemed to be scanning Arjun's eyes for signs of deceit. "Very well," Dashiel exhaled, impatiently. "What brings you here?"

"The last Keeper of the Forbidden needs her help." Arjun motioned to Daemus, who moved closer to Dashiel.

"The *last* Keeper?" Dashiel repeated in a deliberate and perhaps doubting tone, his eyes squinting at Daemus. "But I've seen your kind here recently."

"Another Keeper?" Daemus leaned in, his eyes intent.

"I believe they belonged to a sect within the cathedral. Disciples, I think they said."

"I'm of another order," Daemus replied. "The order that leads our protectorate through visions and prophecy."

Dashiel's voice was metered, emphasizing each word. "These men were no prophets." He paused, his head turning to look Daemus up and down. "They sought a boy with white eyes. Someone like you, in fact. They said he'd been expelled for not following their edicts and that they were supposed to retrieve him. Are you that boy?"

"I'm no boy."

"Perhaps the Disciples were looking to help," Faux suggested, a gravity in her words.

Dashiel's half-smile returned, and one eyebrow rose. "No, they weren't. They tried to threaten the Athabasica. She explained that you weren't here, but they were sure that you were. One of their own had told them as much, though I don't know whom. Their empty threats were embarrassing. I had to escort them from town, with the help of the knight castellan, of course. They said they'd return with orders from the Great Keeper himself."

"*Himself?*" Daemus's head cocked. "Did they say who *he* was?"

"We didn't ask," Dashiel shook his head and he smirked. "The Athabasica had already asked them to leave. The first time was with kind words. The second was at the point of her katana."

"That's why we must speak with the Athabasica," Arjun broke in. "The fate of Warminster hangs in the balance."

The trollborn aide laughed and slumped back in his chair. "A bit dramatic, no?"

Arjun stood and the guards leaned in, but he raised his hands in peace and took a deep breath. "The Cathedral of the Watchful Eye is no more. The Kingdom of Warminster is on the brink of civil war. And a Vermilion is traveling with us after seeing a two-horned tetrine."

Dashiel paused, and seemed to let the information settled in. "And how does this affect Abacus?" He folded his hands on his lap and tilted his head.

Incredulous, Faux's face contorted, and her jaw dropped. "How doesn't it? We're here to warn you and to find answers."

"If there's a problem due to my past with the Athabasica—" Arjun began, but Dashiel didn't let him finish.

"There isn't, I assure you." He turned his attention back to the captain. "She's busy with her work."

Arjun took the measure of the man and knew he was lying, and not trying very hard to cover it up. "It's not about the two of us. It's about Daemus. We believe he's being chased by those who destroyed the cathedral. On our way here, we were hunted by a cryptid that killed a Disciple of the Watch who sacrificed his own life to save Daemus. As a Keeper, he has visions. One of them led us on this perilous journey to the Athabasica. He saw her in his dreams. She's a part of this, somehow."

Dashiel feigned disinterest in his story, but Arjun could tell the man was interested in Daemus. "The city is full of places where you could find information without disturbing the Athabasica," he suggested. "Search for a mage that can help you. There are plenty of Abacunians who'll find your tale intriguing."

"I had a dream prophecy at Flowerdown Syphen," Daemus said. "A specter of a half-man who guided me to a library of sorts."

"A half-man?"

"He led me to a giant tree that acted as a library. I think he was telling me that I could find answers to our questions there. I'm told there such a place here."

Dashiel looked at Daemus and then scanned the group, "It sounds as if you seek Vorodin's Lair."

"We do," Daemus nodded.

"You can find your answers there. You don't need the Athabasica after all." Dashiel rose and the guards turned to open the door.

"Wait," Arjun demanded and took a step forward. "We *do* need to see her. She was in Daemus's vision."

"Can Vorodin help us?" Daemus asked.

"Don't get your hopes up, Keeper," Dash warned. "Vorodin is mysterious and absent. Few see him or can even find him in the lair. The library is free to all, but to access the lair, the Athabasica must grant entrance. But as I've said—"

"Yes, we heard you," Faux grumbled. "The Athabasica isn't receiving guests today."

"It sounds as if I've been abundantly clear."

"I beg of you," Arjun pleaded, his hand trembling in a mix of anger and disappointment. "She must acknowledge the validity of the Keeper's dream. She must help."

"If you have the vision of a Keeper, I'm sure your Ancient is leading you in the right direction. You have no need of the Poet. Good day." Dashiel bowed, then turned to leave.

Arjun's anger was too pronounced to hide. He stepped to stop Dashiel, but Faux's calming hand grabbed his arm, pulling him back. He looked down at her and her eyes tracked to the scroll necklace around his neck. Arjun stopped her from taking it, but then he relented when he saw that it was their only chance.

"Dashiel, thank you for your time." Arjun voice startled the departing attendant. He stopped before exiting and looked back at Arjun. "I have one final message for her." Arjun removed the chain from around his neck and handed Dash the scroll necklace. "Tell her that this poem was written for her over twelve years ago. She may want to read it. That's all I ask."

Dashiel drew a deep breath and looked into Arjun's eyes. Then he held out his hand, snapped his fingers twice, and took the scroll necklace from him.

"I'll deliver it." His voice was reluctant. "Wait here."

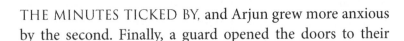

THE MINUTES TICKED BY, and Arjun grew more anxious by the second. Finally, a guard opened the doors to their room. His expectant eyes rose, hoping to see Anoki's face, but instead a guard appeared in the doorway.

"Princess Addilyn Elspeth." the man announced.

Arjun leaned forward and watched as Addilyn, Ritter, Jessamy, Marquiss and Blue were escorted into the small chamber. Before the door was closed, Addilyn's face drooped, and Arjun could tell bad news was coming.

"Helenius was slain." Her eyes turned down and away, her usual composure absent.

"What?" Daemus questioned from the rear of the room, and Marquiss stood, exhaled, and put his hands behind his head.

"How?" Arjun's mind raced to the answer before Ritter said it.

"The Black Rose." The Longmarcher's shoulders slumped. "Left his body in front of Tuttle's place for him to find in the morning. The assassin is here."

"And Tuttle?" Faux approached Addilyn, but the Vermilion waved a diplomatic hand at her, stopping her advance.

"I'm all right," the princess managed, but looked anything but, to Arjun. She went on, recalling the scene at the Boiling Beaker and their chance meeting with Uriah Loring.

"So Tuttle may be here?" Faux's eyes were hopeful.

Ritter nodded and pursed his lips. "We believe so."

"Anoki?" Blue looked at Arjun, who only shook his head.

"Well," Addilyn said, a new air of confidence in her voice. "She may deny you, Captain, but I doubt she can say no to a visit of a Vermilion princess."

Arjun snorted a laugh and his eyebrows rose. There was a knock at the door, and the group turned to see the appearance of a heavily armored man, his blue armor adorned with a gold cloak and a golden mace on his side.

"Knight Castellan," Arjun blurted, and snapped to attention. He felt silly once he had done it, knowing he'd been far removed from his days at the High Aldin. But it was an ingrained reflex and one that hadn't left him. The rest of the party turned to face Abacus's military leader and head of its constabulary.

"My name is Millen Bane," the man announced, "and I'm the Knight Castellan of Abacus. I'm here to escort Princess Addilyn Elspeth and a man named Daemus Alaric to the fifth floor. The Athabasica wishes to welcome you to the city."

"Thank you, Knight Castellan." Addilyn saluted Bane with an exaggerated bow. "I look forward to meeting her."

"I knew your poem would work," Faux whispered to Arjun as she approached the captain.

Arjun felt a flutter in his stomach and his heart filled with hope.

"We'll escort you and your associates. Please, follow me." Bane stepped from the room and stopped in the hallway, extending his arm in the direction of the corridor.

"Thank you." Addilyn followed and turned to look Arjun's way.

"Perhaps it's best if I wait here," the captain said to her.

"Nonsense," Addilyn grabbed him by the arm and walked him into the hall with her.

Arjun bowed and looked to Faux, who seemed to agree with the Vermilion princess.

ARJUN HAD NEVER BEEN to the top floor of the Gatehouse. He'd spent time guarding its entrance, but he'd only ever dreamed of visiting the fifth floor. Faux held his hand at the back of the group as they climbed the stairs, saying nothing. Arjun needed her more than ever before. His courage had deserted him, and Faux's touch brought him a steadiness he wouldn't have possessed without it.

Here he stood, a captain of warriors, fearing an apology more than any enemy he'd ever faced in battle.

The Gatehouse itself was unremarkable in such an unusual town. It was a basic square with a center courtyard and a rooftop balcony that could extend over the palisade. It was designed to be practical, sparing the extravagant expenses that had plagued many other capital buildings. It was Abacus's equivalent of a palace, and yet it looked more like an old school building.

The knight castellan led them to a set of double doors that opened into a large room. The chamber was mostly empty, save for a large stone table surrounded by matching chairs. A pair of glass doors led out onto the famous balcony, from which three figures emerged.

The first was Dashiel, who hastily entered the room and headed for Arjun's group. A man with a slender build, disheveled brown hair, and an unmanicured beard and moustache followed closely behind him. As he walked in, he was cleaning his Abacunian spectacles on his tunic.

But Arjun had waited a decade to see the final figure. Anoki was wearing a light blue dress that fitted her slender form and brushed the floor as she glided gracefully into the room. Her hair was long and free, just as Arjun remembered it, as the wind had caught it on the balcony. A golden wreath crowned her black hair, the mark of the Athabasica.

Arjun felt Faux's hand leave his, and his eyes searched to meet Anoki's gaze, but she was looking at the Vermilion.

"You're the princess, I presume?" Dashiel asked. "Allow me to introduce you to the Poet, Athabasica of Abacus."

"Thank you Athabasica for seeing us." Addilyn bowed in respect. "I know that you don't often see guests, so we're honored."

"Welcome to the city of Abacus, Princess." The Athabasica

returned her gesture with a slight nod. "And please, call me Anoki."

"As long as you call me Addilyn." The two exchanged a pleasant smile.

"I understand that you've had a long and arduous journey." Anoki waved to a table that had been arranged close to the balcony. "Please sit and take some refreshments."

Dashiel turned and clapped, and several servants entered the chambers bringing delicacies from the south along with wine and water. As everyone took their seats, Bane stood guard at the door and Dashiel sat next to Anoki.

Arjun sat at the end of the table, concerned that his presence would ruin their visit. He could feel his heart beating in his chest, and an unfamiliar lump in his throat.

"Try the crabapple verjuice." Anoki offered a decanter to the princess. "It's squeezed every morning and our chefs spice it with saffron. It's a signature of Abacunian culture."

Addilyn tasted her glass while other dishes, including another Abacunian specialty—a marzipan cake—was plated for them.

"I have someone I'd like you to meet," Anoki turned to the spectacled man who sat at her side. "This is Jeric Tuttle, the owner of the Boiling Beaker. I understand you were looking for his associate, Anselm Helenius. Helenius, as I am told you have learned, was unfortunately murdered before you arrived. Master Tuttle has been staying in the Gatehouse with me ever since to ensure his safety. When you asked for an audience, looking for the cryptid hunter, I thought Jeric might be able to help you. He knows what Anselm was doing here."

"We're relieved to see that you're safe, Master Tuttle." Addilyn pursed her lips and spoke with sincerity. "Your associate, Uriah Loring, told us of the tragedy. We're sorry for the loss of your friend."

"Thank you, Princess," Tuttle managed, choking back unspoken feelings. "I've known Anselm for much of my life. His passing came as a shock to me. He had enemies, but his death seemed senseless. And his killer delivered him to me, which confused us all. He only stayed with me from time to time as he passed through, but the killer must have been following him to know of the Boling Beaker."

"He likely was," Addilyn agreed. "And he likely knows where you are now. You won't truly be safe until we're gone. He's chasing me. He also killed my father, who retained Anselm back in Castleshire."

"I'll send word through the Castellan to look for a Bone elf and an imp," Bane remarked from the Athabasica from the doorway. "We have certain magics and other ways to find them. They won't get away." He turned to pass along orders to some of the constables in the hall.

"Helenius arrived in the city over two weeks ago." Tuttle paused and gathered his thoughts. "He told me that he'd been retained by a Vermilion to research something. I barely believed him. He's as great a storyteller as he is a hunter, so you never know with Anselm."

"Did he tell you about the tetrine?" Addilyn asked. "Our reason for coming here?"

"He'd said he'd found the answer to your problem, but didn't tell me much more. I'm sorry."

The table sighed at the news. Addilyn took a deep breath and adjusted herself in her chair.

"But he did leave this parchment," Tuttle added. "He asked me to keep it at the Boiling Beaker, where Uriah's magics could protect it. I didn't understand why at the time, but then when his body was returned, I didn't want it to leave my possession."

Tuttle reached into his waistcoat pocket and produced a small piece of parchment, which he slid across to Addilyn. "It looks as if it's written in Melexian of some kind. Can you read it?"

Addilyn looked at the ancient Melexian script with Jessamy rising from her seat to look over her shoulder. "I—I can't," she admitted.

Daemus, who had been sitting next to Addilyn, looked at the writing and his head bobbed a little.

Arjun turned to the Keeper. He'd seen Daemus manifest the Sight several times and recognized the presence of his Ancient had entered him. He reached for his friend. "Daemus? Are you all right?"

Daemus's head rolled, and his white eyes lit up with the Sight.

Arjun braced the young Keeper's back, knowing that sometimes his companion's body seized when the mystical possession took hold.

Daemus's held tilted forward, and his hand reached for the parchment in front of Addilyn. As his eyes met the scroll, the markings began to glow white.

Tuttle rose from his chair and looked to Anoki, who appeared to Arjun as equally stunned. Bane entered the room and headed for Daemus, but Anoki halted him with a look.

Daemus's head rolled back again, his eyes now staring blankly at the ceiling. His voice left him, replaced by one that wasn't his own. He began to recite the words from the parchment, in a deep, ominous tone.

Ihm throlla mochal lemm.
kastus whyrren zzaknolen.
Viram kondast, regar vonnpast.
Puna toonch paprashash.
Florescu solamash.

Ihm throlla zzaknolen.

"It's the same words from his vision at the Caveat." Ritter turned to Addilyn and they both looked to the ceiling.

Arjun glanced back at Daemus and noticed his eyes losing their glow. Then the Keeper's voice returned to him and he began to mumble. His head dropped, bobbing uncontrollably for a few moments more. "A hallowed ground," he said. "A tree of books. A broken poem."

Arjun stared at Daemus until the glow in his eyes disappeared. As he recovered, Arjun let go and sat back. The room fell into silence.

"Daemus, are you back with us?" Faux moved to attend to him. He appeared groggy to Arjun, but to his surprise, Daemus seemed to fight through the malaise that often followed his reveries.

Faux wiped the Keeper's face with a napkin from the table. "We thought the poem might have been yours, Athabasica. Which is why we rode here. Daemus has the power to—"

"To see things like this?" Anoki replied sternly, shooting a glance at Faux. Then she turned away, looking to Dashiel. "Who's this woman that speaks without my permission?"

"I'm Faux Dauldon."

"And this is the woman you left me to protect?" Anoki asked, speaking to Arjun but still looking at the red-haired rogue.

Arjun swallowed hard. At least she had acknowledged him. He thought long and hard before answering, "I left to serve her family. And now I protect her."

"A corrupt family." The Athabasica turned back to Faux. "One that no longer exists. Where's the honor in that?"

Arjun paused before answering. Her usual vim was absent, shamed into silence by the Athabasica. He knew he had to choose his next words carefully, not wanting to risk Anoki denying them entrance to Vorodin's Lair. "She wasn't part of the treachery. Her death would have served no one." He paused. "You would have done the same."

"I wouldn't have left—" Anoki began, avoiding Arjun's gaze. Arjun knew that she was about to scold him, but she caught herself mid-sentence. "I wouldn't have left Abacus for such unnecessary duties. But that's not why you're here. Proceed, Princess."

Addilyn let the moment of tension pass before restarting. "Daemus had a vision on the floor of the Caveat in Castleshire. We heard horse hooves, which we interpreted as a portent of the tetrine. That's why we sought the help of Helenius."

Anoki nodded in silence.

"The poem, however, led to you." Addilyn's voice was steady and purposeful. "And with the ancient Melexian language? Well, it was unclear. Our hope was that Anselm would find something in his research, which it appears he did. This scroll seems to match Daemus's vision. Do you know what it means?"

"The words aren't a poem." Anoki cleared her throat of emotion. "Although they sound like one. They're a Melexian dialect that no longer exists. That language only lives in the Faye Tree."

Daemus's eyes narrowed. "You mean Vorodin's Lair?"

"There's a sacred chamber in the center of the lair that's perhaps as old as Vorodin himself," Anoki began. "It is said that Vorodin hides himself there, and those seeking his assistance often go to the tree and ask for his help. Few requests are answered."

"But it seems that we need him." Addilyn left no question to her intentions. "We need to find Vorodin. For the realm's sake."

"This might get his attention." Anoki's interest seemed

piqued. "Especially if Daemus recites it as he did just now." The Athabasica gestured to Dashiel, who produced a tattered book from the folds of his robes.

Arjun leaned closer but couldn't glean much from his exile at the table's edge.

"I'll grant you permission to enter Vorodin's Lair," Anoki said to Addilyn. "This book is the key that will take you from the library to the hidden lair. As the Athabasica of Abacus, it's my duty to hold this key and offer it to those worthy to visit Vorodin. You must discover how to unlock the entrance to the Faye Tree on your own. Even I have no such knowledge. I'll offer you this key under one condition."

"Anything," Addilyn said.

"I ask that Captain Ezekyle stays here with me." Anoki finally looked at Arjun, whose eyes met hers. "We have much to discuss."

The group turned to Arjun. He felt his face flush and his arms went numb. His voice choked and his eye fluttered. "I'd love to stay."

The Athabasica slid the book to Addilyn, who took it and leaned forward in her seat in gratitude. "Thank you, Athabasica."

But Anoki's eyes didn't leave Arjun's.

"May I join you, Princess?" Tuttle asked, adjusting his spectacles on his nose. "I'd like to help, if it makes some meaning of Anselm's death. I know the lair well. Well, at least the library."

"It would be an honor to have you."

AFTER THE GROUP HAD departed, Anoki led Arjun away from the large hall and into her private quarters. They were alone, without Dashiel's patient hand guiding her and without the knight castellan standing guard. Arjun couldn't stop looking at her, fighting tears that he knew would come. He struggled to maintain his composure, but with every step, he knew the fight was a lost cause.

The room was as square as the rest of the building, but Anoki had made the room her own. Silk tapestries hung on the walls, and the floors were covered in soft pillows, the center one posing as a bed. Her writing lectern stood prominently against the far wall near a private balcony that overlooked the center courtyard. Various well maintained and preserved musical instruments sat upon a small escritoire near the desk.

Arjun picked up a violin and picked at the strings, finding them perfectly tuned. He smiled. "The Dauldons bought my freedom," he began, breaking the silence. It was all he could think to say, as his mind was occupied with the fragrance of her hair and the way it softly bounced between her shoulder blades. "I owed it to them. My service wasn't required, but it was noble, principled… virtuous."

"Fighting as a rogue was noble?" Anoki turned to him, her eyes also filled with tears. "Didn't you overstay your service by two years?"

"Those two years brought me back to you." He took a few steps toward her, closing a decade of distance between them and gently put his hands on her face as she stared up at him.

She smiled through her tears. "We've already lost so much time."

"Did you read it?" His voice broke and tears welled in his eyes. It was all he could muster.

Anoki opened her hand, revealing the unrolled parchment, hidden in his scroll necklace for a decade. Staring only into his eyes, she recited the words from memory in a soft whisper.

Oh, how I yearn to curl you up in my arms,
and peer into the delicate face I know so well.

Now, only familiar in my dreams.
I ache to find the etchings of each word we wrote,
with loving hands, our souls graven in our notes.
If I could only catch a glimpse of us,
bound and brave together, tucked in a message scroll,
hanging from the neck of our love.
Bring me everything that tells you to play your music,
And all that's driven you to stand against me.
And when you hand your pain over to me,
I'll gladly accept the aching, sorrowful parts for you.
I'll wear their scars and steal the ghosts of sadness from you.
Because if I have caused these curses, my beloved Anoki,
then they are mine to heal.
Our bond snapped like your violin strings,
and I know if I climbed into the breach of your heart,
I would feel the fire of your soul and find joy in the sea of
your melodic notes.

Oh, if I could only bear the sadness that makes your
music cry,

I'd hold fast against their tattered waves and let their weeping
wash over me.

Once, I stood a simple soldier with a life-debt to pay.

Now, I stand a free man with apologies on my lips, with no
idea how to say it.

With nervous voice and shaky scrawl, a soldier's heart calls.

My shining North Star.

My courage.

My beloved Anoki.

Can you ever forgive me?

Arjun looked down at her hands. She was cupping his poem, lightly holding it like a feather as a tear ran down her cheek.

He said nothing but wiped the tear from her face, as his own streamed from his eyes. She put her arms around his neck, and he leaned in to kiss her. As their lips met, Anoki gently dropped the scroll, and it was swept up by the Abacunian winds in her balcony, tumbling away as if it had never been there.

CHAPTER TWENTY-FIVE

*"A leader often chooses between the lesser
of two evils, with an invisible sword dangling
by a thin string above his head."*
—King Dragich Von Lormarck

"FATHER," AARAV KNELT IN front of Von Lormarck.

"Go on." The king of Foghaven Vale bit his tongue. He loved his half son as his own, but he felt unwelcomed news coming. A few days had passed since the unexpected arrival of Lady Isabeau at Dragon Ridge, and now his bastard returned early from the twergish front with news. But the Fates showed mercy this time. They were alone.

"I regret to report that the war is starting to take its toll. We've lost many warriors that were loyal to the Vale. And I fear that the secession from Warminster will leave us fighting on two fronts. I see no end to the conflict with Clan Swifthammer."

"What else?" Von Lormarck replied, making sure to appear nonplussed.

"We've discovered that the twergs are carving a new war path from the mountains into Foghaven Vale. We have intelligence from a spy, deep in the Forge, that suggests as much. The Clan, however, doesn't know that we know, yet."

"And?"

"And our troops can't reach it to stop its completion. What they've built is partially underground and the surface portions pass through treacherous terrain near Ravenwood."

Von Lormarck took a sip of his wine, leaned back, and frowned. He didn't respond.

"Father, if they're successful, their warpaths will be able to reach into the Vale, both on the surface and underground. That could compromise our fortifications, including Dragon Ridge."

"Dragon Ridge is impenetrable," Von Lormarck decreed, his eyes rolling in his head. "It lies atop ancient stones too thick for the twergish picks to threaten."

"As you say," Aarav replied.

"However, if they do try, we should be ready for them."

He walked with Aarav to the balcony that overlooked the courtyard below. The gates had been opened, and Dragich revealed to his bastard the mighty forces of a thousand trollborn henchmen marching their way slowly up the road and gathering in platoons below.

"We've culled the trollborn from the Killean Desolates," the king beamed.

Aarav's eyes opened in amazement. "Reinforcements," he murmured to himself.

"With more to come," the king assured him. "The fallen Keeper and Vestri the Eldest have done well for us."

"How can we afford such an army?" Aarav asked. "Promises of land and treasure? Why should we risk an alliance with such an unpredictable lot?"

"Most of them will die in battle." Von Lormarck put his arm around his son. "Which you, my son, will assure. Thus, we won't need to make payments or fulfill promises. We'll accommodate those who survive. We'll always have need of such forces."

Aarav nodded, approving of the stratagem.

Von Lormarck turned to stare at Aarav, eye to eye. "Show the twergs no mercy. Drench the stones of the Forge in twergish blood. These new troops will be under your command."

Aarav looked to his father's pointing finger and identified a half-giant of some kind standing amongst his soldiers. It stood nearly nine feet tall.

"That creature is your new captain. His name is Zendzack Jahdiel. Find the warpath and collapse it. That will buy us time to face our real enemy."

"I won't fail you, Father."

"Take your new troops north. If the Moor Bog know of the trail, they can lead your men to it. They have cryptids that can find it and help root them out. The twergs won't know what hit them."

Again, Aarav nodded in agreement.

"Ilidari," the king called. The trollborn chamberlain entered with a bow. There was a man beside him in a dark cape. It was adorned with small bones, colored black and cut from the skin of some mysterious animal. "Aarav, this is Amaranth, an acolyte of the Moor Bog."

Aarav reached for the man's hand, but Amaranth's eyes told him that a handshake was neither necessary nor welcome.

"I sent for Amaranth's help. He'll take you to the Moor Bog in the Dragon's Breaths."

"Of course, Father."

"Now, go and meet Jahdiel. I'm sure he's anxious to spill twergish blood."

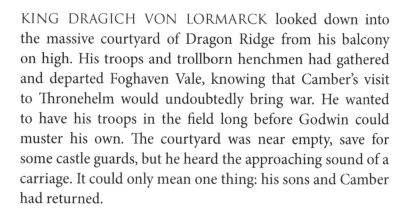

KING DRAGICH VON LORMARCK looked down into the massive courtyard of Dragon Ridge from his balcony on high. His troops and trollborn henchmen had gathered and departed Foghaven Vale, knowing that Camber's visit to Thronehelm would undoubtedly bring war. He wanted to have his troops in the field long before Godwin could muster his own. The courtyard was near empty, save for some castle guards, but he heard the approaching sound of a carriage. It could only mean one thing: his sons and Camber had returned.

He watched the portcullis rise and their carriage arrive. Thessica Camber and the twins emerged and looked at him. He motioned for them to join him immediately and then re-entered the war room to warm himself by the fire. Moments later, Donnar, Emmerich and Camber were escorted in by Ilidari.

Dragich said nothing, waiting for a report.

"Father," Donnar began with a greedy smile, "war with Thronehelm has been declared."

Donnar motioned to Emmerich, who carried the chest containing five war arrows from what remained of Warminster.

"Hand them to Ilidari," Dragich said to Emmerich. "Place them above the throne, as is tradition."

"Of course, sire," the trollborn chamberlain replied before slinking back into the shadows.

"You should have seen it, Father—" Emmerich started, but he was stopped mid-sentence by the king.

"I'm less interested in your tales, son, and more interested in what the good ambassador has to say. Her opinions won't be tainted with bloodlust or youth."

Emmerich stopped and looked to Camber, who had barely entered the room.

"Come closer," Dragich commanded, his voice kind.

"My king." Camber curtsied and approached the throne.

"Congratulations on starting your first war, cousin. What have you to say about your encounter?"

"King Godwin was enraged at your treachery and believes you're responsible for his son's death, as well as the assassination of the Vermilion ambassador."

"Perceptive of him." Dragich drew his brow up and smiled, expecting such an answer.

"Emmerich is right," she confided. "He made a spectacle of

us. For a moment, I thought he'd have us arrested, or worse."

"Not King Godwin," Dragich mocked. "He'd never dare to break protocols or tradition. Tell me, what of our spy?"

"Meeks told me that he's… *changing*." Camber shivered, seeming bothered with the thought. "I was able to have a scroll with that message delivered to Aarav before I left. I understand he's with our troops, far to the north. Meeks asked me to make him aware of that so that he can tell the Moor Bog."

"Is that all?"

"No. Godwin has sent word to the Krol of the Twergs hoping to strike an alliance. Aarav was to stop them from getting word back to Rawcliffe Forge. He sent the twergish First Keeper to lead those discussions."

"Well done."

"Sire…" Camber paused, then said, "I know it's not my place, but are we dealing with the Moor Bog? They're nothing but a cult of cryptid-loving lunatics."

"We are," Dragich confirmed. "We need their help to win control of this kingdom."

"At what price?" she asked, impertinently.

"They don't seek payment," he replied.

"Then what?" she asked. Dragich noticed she'd taken a step backward with the thought. "If this news reaches Castleshire…"

"But it won't," Dragich reassured. "You'll make sure of that. Now, what of the Black Rose?"

"Unfortunately, I've lost track of him. He was to sail to Thronehelm, but Meeks Crowley told me he never arrived. And from what I'm told, Montgomery sailed north with LaBrecque to seek an alliance with the Norsemen."

Dragich laughed aloud. "Those barbarians hate Godwin more than I do. A fool's errand indeed. Godwin must be desperate."

Ghyrr Rugalis appeared at the door then, and the king motioned him inside. Sasha Scarlett followed the messenger, and Dragich brightened at her appearance. "Guildmistress Scarlett, thank you for accepting my invitation."

Sasha bowed. "Of course, Your Majesty."

The king gestured to his left. "Please, have a seat, and let us discuss Thronehelm and this embargo."

———✦———

EMBER CREPT FROM HER room, intent on helping the unfortunate healer that her father had taken prisoner. Her mother's plan was simple. She'd distract Kail Ilidari, who'd been stalking her since her mother's arrival. Both she and Isabeau suspected that Ilidari was tailing them on the orders of the king.

Isabeau had arranged for Ilidari to bring her some wine and then had offered to share the bottle with her old guardian, under the auspices of a long overdue reunion. She'd known the trollborn would fall for the trap, and that they'd talk and enjoy each other's company, sharing tales of the Fork and the Vale. Ember hoped it would buy enough time for her to make her way to the dungeons below.

She'd never been to the cells of Dragon Ridge and braced herself for what she might find. Ember wasn't afraid of the guards, who could be bribed or frightened by her presence, but she *was* afraid of Ilidari. He was fierce and loyal servant to her father and if she was caught, there'd be no bribe big enough to keep him from turning her in.

As she approached the doors to the dungeon, a young guard stopped her.

"What are you doin' down here, my lady?" the guard asked. "I've never seen your likes in this part of the castle."

"I have business with a prisoner." Ember feigned a smile.

"Now, let me pass. I'll only be a moment."

"I… I can't, ma'am." The man stiffened, seemingly concerned for Ember's well-being. "If I do, it'll cost me my head. It's no place for you."

"Let me pass." She appeared indignant, but the guard moved to the front of the door.

"My lady, please," the youthful man urged.

"I'm the princess of this castle and I'll go where I want. If you don't believe me, I can guarantee you an audience with my father and you can explain it to him."

The man's eyes rolled as he considered her threats. "Very well. But under the condition that I accompany you. It's dangerous down here, even when you're on the outside of the cages."

Ember resisted a triumphant smile. "Agreed but keep your distance. My business is of the state and not for your ears."

He acknowledged her order with a short bow and fumbled with his key to open the outer door. As they entered, a stench washed over Ember. The odor was a mix of bile and rot, and she raised her draped arm to protect her from the smell. The dungeon descended only fifteen feet, but each step down the spiraled stonework gave more life to the foulness in her nostrils. It was all she could do not to gag.

Her chaperone stepped from the last stair and picked up a candelabrum that held a single candle, its pitiful flame casting a dim light in the long hall.

"Where's the woman that was recently brought here?" Ember asked. "The one with blue hair?"

"Last cell, ma'am." The guard pointed into the darkness.

"The key?" she asked.

"I… I can't." He shook his head. "There's a food hole on the floor. You can speak through that."

"I'm not crawling through this filth," she frowned, with an air of false incredulity. "You'll let me in. You may stand in the hallway, but as I said, my business is my own."

The man cowed to her, hastening their walk down the hall. As they proceeded, Ember heard feeble voices calling out from behind wooden cell doors bound with iron straps to strengthen their hold on the unfortunates inside.

"Help," a meek voice whispered from one. A second voice added, "Kill me, please."

She covered her ears and quickened her pace, nearly running into the back of the guard in front of her.

They came to the end of the long hall and he placed the candle on a shelf before producing a key from a ring on his waist. As he opened the door, Ember saw the young healer, illuminated by the soft touch of the candlelight. She'd only been there for several days, but it looked like she'd been wearing her soiled garments for years. The young woman looked up and shaded her eyes from the dim light.

"That will be enough," Ember said with authority.

"What if she attacks you?" the man asked.

"She won't." Ember frowned. "She's a priestess of Ssolantress."

The man's face held doubt, but he did as the princess asked and moved back toward the stairwell.

Ember stepped into the cell and bent to help the woman up. The priestess was still in good health, albeit dirty and unkempt. She rose to stand and squinted at Ember.

"I'm here to help you," Ember whispered. "I was present when the ambassador brought you in as a prisoner."

The woman squinted through the dim light. "I remember you." She paused then continued after seeming to contemplate her situation. "The Goddess Ssolantress has a plan for me, as with all of her followers. This must be my trial, and no matter how hard it is, I'll walk this path."

Ember leaned back, shocked at the healer's poise. They were nearly the same age, and if the roles had been reversed, she would have broken by now. The young woman's faith in her Ancient appeared unwavering. Ember produced a small roll of bread and a skin of water that she'd tucked away. The woman gladly accepted it, opening the waterskin and drinking as if she'd been without water for some time.

The woman started in on the bread. Ember wondered if she'd been fed since she arrived.

"What's your name?" Ember asked.

The woman paused her chewing. "I'm Katja Seitenwind of the Temple of Ssolantress in Castleshire."

"How did you end up as a prisoner?"

"I was aiding a man when he took me prisoner. He wanted me to assist his companion, but I couldn't."

"Was the companion too far gone?"

"No," Katja mumbled over a piece of crust. "He wasn't of this realm. My powers would have harmed him, not healed him."

"Not of this realm?" Ember felt an uneasiness in the thought. "The man didn't let you go after you nursed him back to health?"

"He took me to your father's embassy and held me captive."

"Who was this man?" Ember asked in disbelief, her voice trembling. She knew in her heart who it was before Katja muttered the name.

"He was a Bone elf," Katja replied. "I believe his associate called him Dru'Waith."

Ember felt the horror of the masquerade rush back with the simple name. Katja melted away as visions of Dru'Waith and his deeds filled her eyes. The blood, the death. Her future.

"Are you okay?" Katja eyed Ember. "Please sit on my cot."

The healer moved, revealing a stained shelf on the wall that contained a woolen blanket that was scarred from years of use in the dungeons of Dragon Ridge.

"I know the man," Ember admitted. "My father employs him."

It was Katja's turn to be surprised. The young healer lowered her crystal eyes and she appeared to wander away from Ember in thought.

"The man killed a Vermilion ambassador, along with many others. I saw his creature when he argued with my father outside Castle Thronehelm. But I have little time. My mother, the Lady Isabeau Fleury, and I will get you out of here. We won't let the king send an innocent servant of Ssolantress off to that man my father has aligned with. I need a little time to make arrangements for you. I'll ask my mother what to do."

Then the dimness of the lone candle behind her diminished, replaced by the imposing shadow of Kail Ilidari in the doorway.

"MY KING." ILIDARI RELEASED the struggling Ember from his vice-like grip. "I caught the princess in the dungeons."

Ember staggered forward, reeling from the trollborn's strength. Her dress had been torn in her useless struggle against him, and her hair hung in her face.

"What was she doing there?" the king asked, paying no attention to his guilty daughter until he caught a whiff of the odor she'd brought with her and shielded his nose.

Ember fixed her dress and turned an evil glare to Ilidari, who seemed dispassionate about his role in dragging her here. She took notice, however, that the king was not alone. Sitting beside him was Guildmistress Sasha Scarlett, a woman she'd met once at the masquerade back in Thronehelm. Her eyes shifted between them as Scarlett watched the scene with bemusement over her wine goblet.

"She was speaking to the healer," the chamberlain replied. "I overheard her discussing a plot to help her escape."

"The girl?" Von Lormarck asked of Ember, his face doing little to hide his anger and disappointment. "What's your interest in her?"

"I felt pity for her, Father," Ember admitted. Tears began to well in her eyes in fear for what was to come. "I only took her food and water. She's my age, and when I saw her, I felt her pain."

"Foolish girl." Von Lormarck sneered. "She's more than a prisoner."

"Why must she be kept a prisoner at all?"

The king scowled. "She could be a key ransom for our ally. Do you remember our discussion when we last left Thronehelm? Do you remember that long carriage ride back to the Vale?"

"Yes!" she blurted. "You called me a pawn! I'll never forgive you for such an embarrassing and terrible moment."

"There are many pieces on this chessboard," he growled. "And your healer friend is but one of them. This is none of your concern."

"What's the meaning of this?" Isabeau asked as she entered the room, appearing to time her arrival to perfection.

Von Lormarck ignored her and turned back to Ilidari. "Make sure that the healer leaves immediately for the Cathedral of the Watchful Eye. Have her sent on one of Jhodever's hippogryphs. She's no longer safe here."

"As you command." The trollborn bowed, turning to leave.

"Father, no," Ember pleaded. "I beg of you."

"Dragich, take a moment," Isabeau interjected. "The guards

told me what happened."

"She's your daughter," he said, shrugging. "If you'd reared her well, she'd know better."

Isabeau eschewed the insult. "Dragich, have some wine." She poured him a glass which he accepted and then returned to his throne.

"I'm sorry," he murmured, a stillness settling in before taking a sip.

"Nonsense." Isabeau smiled and turned to her daughter. "The child is unruly. And you have your mind set on greater matters." Her gaze lifted to the arrows of war, which hung on the wall behind him.

"Father," Ember tried.

"Enough!" he barked.

"If she's a continuing distraction, allow me to take her home to Deadwaters Fork," Isabeau implored, her voice tinged with the slightest of desperation. "At least until you've won this war."

"I have a better idea." The king's eyes narrowed, and his stare returned to Ember.

"What could be better and safer than her returning to the south?" Isabeau asked.

"Sasha needs a royal match. We've been negotiating for some time," Von Lormarck said, but his eyes remained on his daughter.

"One of your sons I assume?" Isabeau's eyes rolled, and her hands rested on her hips. "In exchange for what?"

"Five thousand Sentinels of Saracen." Sasha sat back. She looked Ember up and down, then took a sip of her goblet.

Isabeau straightened and her face lightened. "This sounds like a fair agreement, even if Sasha is a commoner."

"Good," Dragich commented and began to pace. "I am

glad you approve."

"Which son?" Isabeau asked?

"None." The king's face straightened, and he put his hands on his belt.

Ember's face contorted in confusion. Dragich walked to her and touched her gently under her chin.

"I had promised our *princess* a marriage to the Maeglen bastard, but we are now at war with his family," the king reminded the room. "Sasha, I wonder if you may indulge me in considering an unbreakable alliance by marrying my only daughter, Ember?"

For a moment, Ember thought she'd misheard him. Then she looked to her mother, whose countenance was equally confused.

"Father!" Ember cried the same moment Isabeau said, "Dragich!"

"Our kingdom will be strengthened by this bond." His voice was both calm and resolute. "And I'll keep my promise to you, dear daughter. You'll be married—if the good lady agrees and lends her five thousand mercenaries to the war. I believe that is a fair deal. She will of course be entitled to a dowry as any male suitor would—in addition to a knighthood."

"No, Father." Ember nearly lost her voice and her face reddened. "Please."

The king turned his attention to Sasha, who hesitated, blinked, and finally, nodded. "It is an unconventional proposal, but an ingenious one at that. I do prefer the princess to your other bastard. She is much more pleasing to the eye."

Ember squirmed under Sasha's wolfish gaze.

"I am inclined to accept, my king," Sasha added before finishing her wine.

The king unbuckled his sword and unsheathed the blade

known as Malice.

"Father, you can't be serious!" Ember appealed. "This is a jest, correct? A lesson for me to learn after what I've done today?" Her thoughts still hadn't caught up to what the king had just commanded.

"Dragich, this can't be." Isabeau approached but the king's eyes stopped her in her tracks. "The girl has suffered enough for one day."

The king ignored them and motioned for Scarlett to kneel before him. He lifted Malice and began an impromptu knighting ceremony for the Guildmistress. "I, King Dragich Von Lormarck, of the Kingdom of Foghaven Vale—"

"Think, Dragich," Isabeau begged. "Your only daughter prefers the company of men. For there to be an heir, your daughter will be forced to take another man. Such a public shame will cast a shadow upon your new throne!"

"And?" Dragich's eyebrows raised, waiting for an answer that never came. "She's a bastardess anyway. Does it matter if she also plays the whore?"

The two women cried in protest, but the king waved for his soldiers. "Guards," he called, "please remove the Lady Isabeau and Princess Ember. Hold them in the princess's chambers until I order otherwise."

The guards converged on the two women, and when their cold, gauntleted hands grabbed Ember by the arms, she swooned.

———✦———

"MOTHER, WHAT AM I to do? How can Father do this to me? It can't be possible!" In her chambers, the princess sobbed, inconsolable despite her mother's attempts. An hour ago, she'd been betrothed to a Maeglen son and now, her path was skewed in an entirely different direction.

Isabeau embraced her daughter in a bone-crushing hug. "My dear, sweet, daughter, your father is not thinking clearly. His temper has blinded him to reason, but he will soon calm. I've seen it happen many times. You'll see. He won't go through with this."

Ember blinked up at her mother, hardly seeing her through tears. "And if he doesn't calm? What then?"

Isabeau hugged the princess even tighter. "I will get you out of this nonsensical marriage. I promise you, my darling."

"YOU SUMMONED ME, DRAGICH?" Isabeau's rage was barely contained.

"I did."

"You coward," Isabeau growled. "You've sold your blood for the sake of an ally."

"Steady yourself," the king warned, his patience wearing thin. "It was a matter of time. The Maeglen bastard—or the Lady of Saracen. It makes no difference."

"You could have sent her home with me," Isabeau yelled, her arms splayed in desperation. "I could have protected her and waited for a safer match. If she's just a distraction, a nuisance for you, then I will take her. She'll be out of your hair until the war is over. Or keep the engagement to Joferian Maeglen. If he doesn't die in the war, you can use it as an olive branch to join the families and the important territory of Queen's Chapel."

"What's done is done." Von Lormarck took a sip from his chalice, calming himself.

"Let me buy her freedom from you," Isabeau begged. "Stop this before it's too late."

"Buy?" Von Lormarck chortled. "I'm getting five thousand soldiers in return. What can you possibly offer?"

"Mercenaries from Saracen that will run at the start of battle?" Isabeau stepped closer to the king and her voice leveled. "I can offer you one thousand tridents from the Fork. Experienced men who won't turn in the face of adversity."

Von Lormarck scoffed at the idea. "You'll offer me your Tritons? The famed cavalry of the Fork? It will take a month to mobilize them and get them here. It will be too late."

"I told you before, Dragich. I didn't come here empty-handed." Isabeau pointed to the far balcony, which overlooked the town of Krahe below. Von Lormarck stood and walked to the window to see a long line of cavalry in the distance, approaching peacefully and flying the flags of the Fork, their silver trident sigil shimmering in the morning sun.

He took a moment to gather himself.

"This was your plan all along?" He half-smirked. "To offer the Tritons for the safe return of our daughter?"

"Yes," she admitted, squaring her shoulders proudly. "One thousand cavalrymen for one teenage girl."

"Clever," the king acknowledged. "What of our bastard son? I assume you want him too?"

"I think you know that he's no longer a son of mine." Isabeau joined him at the window. "All I want to do is save her from this fate."

A moment of tension passed and the two shared a smile, something they hadn't done in many years.

The king nodded. "I'll send word to Ghyrr Rugalis to stop her departure."

"Thank you, Great King." Isabeau kissed him on the cheek. "I'll depart for the Fork when Ember returns." She tidied herself up and began a dignified walk from the room.

"You'll leave today," the king ordered, "once you relinquish command of your troops to me. I don't want you in my castle any longer."

Isabeau bowed in mock respect and took her leave. Once she was out of earshot, he called for his chamberlain.

"Yes, my lord?" Ilidari stepped in from the hall.

"Prepare the Lady of the Fork for her departure home and send a welcome party to invite her soldiers to join our ranks."

"Yes, sire."

"Oh, and Kail," the king added. "Make sure you kill her after she's seen leaving Dragon Ridge. Perhaps one of your newly arrived trollborn thugs can raid her carriage on the way out of Foghaven Vale."

Ilidari looked at his sovereign, offering no response. Dragich turned to his trollborn guardian and noticed his giant hands had balled into fists.

"Is that in defense of the lady, Kail?" the king asked. "Was my order not clear enough?"

"It will be done, Your Majesty," Ilidari replied with a respectful bow.

"Good," the king hissed.

Then he turned back to counting his newly arriving troops. He had no intention of sending for his daughter. And for the price of one bastardess and an old mistress, he'd greatly improved his prospects in the war for Warminster.

EMBER SAT ACROSS FROM Sasha Scarlett in the new Lady of Saracen's carriage as the horses pulled it away from the castle. From the window, she could see two knights carrying the young healer away on the back of a hippogryph. Ember fought back tears. She would *not* cry.

"You'll love Saracen, Princess. It is beautiful, with spacious grounds and gardens for long walks." Sasha moved to touch Ember's hand, but she pulled it back with a glare. Who was this woman to barter with her future? Because of her, she would no longer marry Joferian.

"I hope you said goodbye to your brother," Sasha continued.

"I'll see him shortly, as my mother is bound to talk sense into the king and have this whole spectacle left in the past."

Sasha paused. "You have much faith in Aarav's combat skills against the twergs, then?"

Ember's head shot up. "He's leaving again?"

"Yes. My apologies. I thought you knew. Your father sent him to ambush the twergs at some new warpath near the Bridge in Valkeneer."

Ember turned back to the castle as it grew smaller in the window of the carriage, knowing Aarav wasn't there, but still hoping. Her eyes looked one last time at the castle she grew up in, committing her home to memory as the two women traveled away from the kingdom of Foghaven Vale.

CHAPTER TWENTY-SIX

"I've walked the fires of hell and i've suffered
the ridicule of men, yet I shall return."
—Graytorris, the Mad

THE DAYS AT THE CATHEDRAL of the Watchful Eye
passed as they had since the Tome vanished, but now Radu
had other duties to attend do. As he started across campus, two
shadows passed over him, drawing his eyes up. Two gryphs
circled, coming in to land. They were heavily burdened with
riders. He lifted one hand to shade his eyes from the late day
sun and when they got closer, he noticed the riders wore the
livery of Foghaven Vale, not the Knights of the Maelstrom.

Radu hastened his pace. He wanted to find his old
apprentice. When he reached the Hallow, he found the great
double doors closed and locked. He could hear the nearing of
booted footfalls from inside before the doors unlocked

"What's the meaning of this?" Volcifar Obexx stood in the
door, his eyes narrowed. "We gave orders not to be disturbed."

"Messengers from Foghaven Vale," Radu pointed to the
gryphs over his shoulder. "I am certain they are here for the
Great Keeper."

He noticed Jhodever standing behind Obexx near the
center of the Hallow. The man had only been Great Keeper
for a few days, but by the clouds over his brow and the tension
in his shoulders revealed some hidden burden already weighed
heavily upon him.

Jhodever approached and gazed out into the courtyard.
Radu turned and watched as the two men on hippogryphs
slipped from their mounts and walked toward them. Jhodever
pushed by Radu and trudged out to meet them, with Obexx

trailing at his side.

"These men aren't Knights of the Maelstrom." Obexx's heated voice held no diplomacy. "They can't ride our gryphs. It's a sacred—"

"Enough," the Great Keeper interrupted. "These are my men. I have much business to finish in Foghaven Vale."

Obexx shifted his booted feet and shot a sideways glance at Radu, who maintained his silence. The old precept understood the High Watcher's meaning, but times were changing in front of them and what once was sacred may no longer be.

Wasn't that what Obexx declared in the midst of the conclave?

Perhaps the High Watcher was finding it more difficult to adhere to the new way of life at the cathedral.

"We cannot hold every tradition," Radu replied, earning him a raised eyebrow from Jhodever.

"Welcome, friends," Jhodever held out open arms and greeted the Knights like old friends.

Both men bowed to the Great Keeper. "I bring tidings of war from Foghaven Vale," one of them said, his voice just loud enough for Radu to hear. "And a present for you, from the king."

The man pointed to the second gryph, where a woman was tied to its saddle. Her clothes were tattered, but she herself seemed no worse for wear. The two riders chuckled at her, but the gagged woman kept her poise.

"A priestess of Ssolantress as a prisoner?" Obexx recognized the marks of the Blue Lady. "There's no humor in this. Let her down. She's no threat to us."

"We were ordered to bring her here intact," the second messenger said. "And so we have." He cut the woman loose from the back of the saddle and pushed her to the ground. She fell, landing on her side in an awkward heap.

"Brutes." Obexx moved to the woman's aid and helped her to stand. He removed the ties from around her wrists and lowered her gag, but the woman said nothing.

"Thank you for the 'present.'" Jhodever looked back to the first Knight. "Pray tell, what of the war?"

"Von Lormarck's armies left Dragon Ridge the day we departed for Solemnity. He's marching to Thronehelm with an army of ten thousand. Soldiers from Gloucester are already on the move from the south and will arrive at his flank within the fortnight."

"What of Thronehelm?" the Great Keeper asked. "And the embargo?"

"Our spies report that Ambassador Camber and the two princes delivered the arrows of war," the Knight continued. "Saracen has held its word. The only way that supplies can reach Thronehelm is by sea, where they still have the advantage."

"Thank you." The Great Keeper couldn't hide a half-smile. "You may return to Foghaven Vale."

The two men climbed onto their gryphs and were in the sky before Jhodever turned to Obexx, who was still standing silently beside their prisoner.

"We must starve their armies." Jhodever said as he cut between the two men and approached the priestess of Ssolantress.

"We?" Obexx asked. "What have we to do with their conflict?"

"It's time to tell First Keeper Tarrant Cynric to call upon his Sea Kingdom for help." Jhodever turned from Radu and Obexx to their new arrival. "I see that you're not shaken." He shot a false smile at the healer. "I'm surprised by your resiliency."

The woman looked around at the carnage of the once proud campus. "Is anyone hurt?" she asked. "I may be able to help."

The offer of aid, despite her brutish escort, warmed Radu's heart. Yes, the priestesses of Ssolantress were healers by faith and trade, but this young woman appeared to be more.

Jhodever smiled but dismissed her question. "My king tells me that you know Daemus Alaric and that you've spoken to him," Jhodever prodded.

The woman offered nothing.

"Our Disciples tell us he still has the Sight," Jhodever continued. "Is this true?"

Radu held his breath, listening to Jhodever speak in such an open manner. The woman gave no reply. Jhodever leaned in close to her and Radu braced himself.

"We have someone we'd like you to meet." The Great Keeper turned to the High Watcher. "Obexx, order Lieutenant Lorraine to escort our guest to the holding cells... for now."

"But Great Keeper, I must protest," Obexx replied. "A healer of Ssolantress poses no—"

Jhodever's tone changed. "Now."

"Of course." Obexx bowed and left to find Lorraine.

"What's your name?" Jhodever looked at the healer.

"Katja Seitenwind," she replied.

"The holding cells are nothing more than secure rooms here. Our brothers and sisters rarely need locking down. I feel you'll find them palatial compared to your stay in Dragon Ridge."

RADU WAITED OUTSIDE QUEHM'S Hallow for Obexx, who'd accompanied Katja Seitenwind to the holding cells as ordered, when he spotted First Keeper Cynric stumbling out of a side door near the base of the cathedral ruins. Radu scanned the cathedral, all the way to the top then back down to Cynric.

Radu met Cynric and laid a concerned hand on the First Keeper's shoulder. He looked pale and shaken.

"I thought you'd left," Radu said.

"Precept." Cynric shook his head, his voice hoarse and a little unsteady. "I was summoned to speak with the new Great Keeper as he was using Dromfangare—the fabled mirror—in the inner sanctum."

Radu nodded. He knew how his old student used the mirrors to scry. "We each use the Sight in our own way," Radu confirmed. "Jhodever uses the mirrors. One, Dromfangare, that once belonged to Graytorris, hangs here. The other hangs on the walls of Dragon Ridge in Foghaven Vale. I am certain he is happy to know it wasn't destroyed in the starfall."

"No longer," Cynric sighed, his eyes quickly darting up to the top of the tower.

"What do you mean?" Radu asked, sensing the First Keeper's urgency.

Cynric gripped Radu's shoulder and pulled him away from where reconstruction was being done. He hissed, "He said it's time."

The ominous phrase hung between them before Cynric went on.

"He said it was time for me to call upon the Sea Kingdom. To prepare for war. For a great war that will divide Warminster."

"Are you certain?" Radu asked. *Had Amoss been right in his paranoia? Was Jhodever planning something sinister?*

Cynric nodded. "He told me his Sight had returned and Erud told him that he was not to be the Great Keeper."

Radu held his breath, frowning in thought while he tried to follow the shaken Keeper's story.

"Even Obexx was concerned."

The longer Cynric spoke, the more anxious Radu became and the more his brow furrowed.

"He said Dromofangare helped him understand what Erud wanted. He had a great vision of Dragon Ridge. He said Erud calls for reform. Erud calls for a new Great Keeper."

"Why didn't he tell the other Keepers during the conclave?" Radu pressed.

Cynric swallowed hard. "He couldn't. Erud told him to hold his Sight until he wore the robes of the Great Keeper. Radu... it's because the Sight showed him that Erud had forgiven..." He gasped. "Erud has forgiven Graytorris and that tonight, he will walk through the mirror, returning to don the robes of the Great Keeper."

With his breath stolen in shock, Radu couldn't reply. His eyes bored into the First Keeper's. "Are you certain?"

The First Keeper nodded. "I must get back to the Sea Kingdom. Great Keeper Jhodever will remain First Keeper of the Cathedral and I am to rally the armada of the Sea Kingdom against Thronehelm."

"Thronehelm?" Radu echoed in horror.

"It is a mere test of faith, I was told," Cynric assured him, seeming surer of his position now that he had spoken about the meeting out loud. "Jhodever sees the assistance of the Sea Kingdom's navy in this war as imperative. We will be guided by the Disciples of the Watch. He told me I will see a vision as well: a great naval victory in the harbors of Thronehelm!"

"Have you had this vision?" But Radu already knew the answer.

"Not yet," Cynric sighed. He dropped his hands from Radu's shoulders. "Not yet."

RADU AVOIDED THE HIGH Watcher and the new Great Keeper until later that night. He kept them under his gaze but waited for them to move. Jhodever and Obexx returned to the top of the Cathedral of the Watchful Eye, the inner sanctum exposed to the elements by the damaging starfall. The builders had been dismissed, and the two believed they were alone in each other's company. Radu followed at a distance, hiding in the shadows of the rubble, the broken halls, and gave thanks to Erud for the many hiding places.

"Do you remember Graytorris?" Jhodever asked Obexx as they approached Dromofangare, whose surface had been repolished and hung back on the ruined walls.

"I was a younger man when Graytorris fell," Obexx said flatly. Radu heard the hesitation, the uncertainty in Obexx's tone. Cynric hadn't mentioned how Obexx had responded to the brazen proclamation of Graytorris's return, but even from his silhouette Radu saw Obexx felt uneasy about being excluded from the plan.

"It is time for the fallen Keeper to return." Jhodever stood before the magical mirror. "*Kalla um framkalla, vekja foram,*" Jhodever whispered in front of Dromfangare. The conjurer's tongue brought the magical mirror to life. Dromfangare flared in a magical hue of greens and blues.

Radu chanced a glance around the shattered corner he hid behind. The reflections of the two men disappeared, replaced by an amethyst mist. Obexx's eyes grew wide, mesmerized by the spectacle. For a brief second, he turned to see Jhodever staring at him.

"Don't move from the frame of the mirror, High Watcher," Jhodever warned him. Then he turned back to the mirror to begin a second incantation.

"*Aduceti un tunel la,*" Jhodever continued. "*Done sitte*

tunel du."

The purplish haze in the mirror began to swirl into puffs of boiling clouds, rolling in and out as if something was about to form from the chaos. Then Jhodever produced a small bowl and began to burn harsh incense, lighting it with the candle from their lantern.

Obexx didn't dare to move. After a few more minutes of Jhodever's incantations, the mist took form. Its color dissipated into grey before an image appeared of a crooked tower, leaning on an eroded foundation. Radu had never seen Spine Castle, but he recognized the image from his readings. As the mist cleared, the unmistakable environs of the Killean Desolates provided an outline.

A slight breeze emanated from the mirror, then the smell of the acrid odor of the Desolates wafted into the inner sanctum. Obexx covered his nose, but he didn't avert his gaze from the mirror.

Jhodever stepped toward Dromofangare and called into the magical portal in a language Radu didn't understand. It was neither Warminsterian nor the conjurer's tongue. A figure appeared from the other side of the mirror and lurched toward the opening. The two mirrors, Traumefang and Dromfangare, had become one. Radu's heart raced.

No, it can't be!

The hooded frame of the man Radu remembered as Graytorris staggered his way through the portal. His eyeless face, still covered with its bloody blindfold, tilted itself as he stepped slowly through the mirrors.

Radu's mind raced back to the battle of Ghostwood. He ran from this man many years ago in fear and irredeemable guilt. It was an old wound reopened, as he saved himself then and abandoned his friends, consigning them to a horrible death at the hands of the fallen Keeper.

Jhodever dropped to one knee, genuflecting in reverence. He tugged on Obexx's cloak, and the High Watcher joined him.

Radu froze. *Would the fallen Keeper feel his mere presence? No,* Radu chided himself. *He's a man. Not an Ancient.*

A second figure arose from behind Graytorris. She was a beautiful woman wrapped in a dark cloak with black hair and eyes.

"My Great Keeper, we are honored in your return," Jhodever dared to speak, his head still bowed.

"Where's Daemus Alaric?" Graytorris growled, ignoring the platitude.

Radu wanted to sneak away, but his legs wouldn't respond. His heart raced and his limbs were numb. He peered out from his hiding place. Obexx looked to Jhodever, a wellspring of fear rising in his eyes.

So, the High Watcher had his reservations too, Radu thought. His eyes moved to Graytorris and the woman standing beside him. *Why is the curse still upon him if Erud has forgiven him?* But he knew the answer. Jhodever was Graytorris's tool, needed only for Graytorris to make his triumphant return.

"The Low Keeper has made his way to Abacus." Jhodever stood from his crouch. "Captain Hague informed us of his trek from Castleshire."

"I have dispatched Rrhon Talamare to pursue," Graytorris cackled. "He won't get far."

Rrhon Talamare? Radu wondered. *Hadn't Graytorris killed him long ago?* He'd seen Talamare's demise firsthand at the battle of Ghostwood.

Obexx stood at length, and the betrayal carved into his face told the story of his heart. He was ignored by everyone, save for Radu. Radu squinted and stared at Obexx. He knew the High Watcher now understood: Graytorris hadn't been restored in the slightest by Erud. He returned to usurp the mantle of the Great Keeper.

"But remind me, Jhodever—" Graytorris stopped and turned to his servant—"of the revenge we must take on the Emerald Shield and the Keldarin. They aided the Alaric son, an act our order shan't forget." The fallen Keeper moved slowly around the chamber, sniffing like an animal in the air and gently running his pale fingers over items as he passed. He took in the room as best as a blind man could. "And the Keepers that remain here?"

"The Keepers shall be no more," Jhodever reported, filling the empty air. "I'll order the sect to disband tomorrow and send the blinded seers back to their homes."

"They live?" Graytorris tilted his head and stopped his pace. "So long as they draw breath, they'll always be a threat to us. Dispatch them while they're all still here."

Obexx looked at them both, his jaw agape as Jhodever's face paled. Radu's eyes filled with sudden tears.

"That will shortly be remedied," Jhodever's voice wavered.

"What of the rest of the protectorate?" Graytorris asked.

"The Disciples of the Watch control the campus with the Knights of the Maelstrom," Obexx offered, feigning a brave tone when Graytorris turned his eyeless gaze to him. "Most of the protectorate has fallen into line. There are some traditionalists left, but we've silenced many of the traitors by throwing them in the jails or sending them into exile."

"They live as well?" Graytorris grumbled, his voice laced in disappointment and anger.

"Not for long, Great Keeper." Jhodever chose his words with caution. When a silence fell, he tried to end it. "When do we announce your triumphant return, Great Keeper?"

"After your purge. Root out and kill those who oppose us. In their cells, on their roads home and in what remains of my cathedral."

Obexx gripped his sword but didn't move. "Are you certain, Great Keeper, that this is what Erud has shown you? A revolution was necessary. But to slay the traditionalists? They've already acquiesced to the reform. We won their hearts at the conclave."

"Do you question my divine authority, High Watcher?" Graytorris spun and pointed the tip of his obsidian staff at Obexx. "I sense hesitancy in you."

Obexx's eyes widened, and he removed his hand from his pommel. "The will of Erud will be done, Great Keeper." The High Watcher turned and marched toward Radu's hiding place.

Radu pressed himself into the fissure of the wall to hide in the shadows as Obexx's booted footfalls rushed past him. He fought against the urge to reach out to his Erudian brother. He clamped his hand over his mouth and willed himself to not make a sound no matter the urgent agony that rose in a sob in his throat. If he moved now, they'd see him. He couldn't rush down the tower, trying save his brothers and sisters just to be slaughtered among them. His mind raced as the three inside continued to move. He needed to get word out to someone. Anyone. But how? He couldn't again succumb to his fears and not fight this man. He wouldn't be damned to repeat the same mistake he made in Ghostwood.

The woman stepped away from Jhodever and Graytorris and approached the divine tree pedestal that had survived the starfall. She produced *The Tome of Enlightenment* from underneath her cloak and laid it upon its surface, keeping it closed. Radu choked upon seeing it.

"Bring the girl to me," Graytorris demanded. "She'll be the

perfect bait for Daemus Alaric."

"Yes, Great Keeper. She's in the cells below. Von Lormarck sent her, and she arrived today." Jhodever bowed and hurried down the opposite side of the tower to a set of stairs to attend to his master's wishes.

"Zinzi, my witch," Graytorris said, "send word to the Black Vicar and the Moor Bog and tell them the time has come. He'll have his great cryptid in return for the service he promised. Tell him that we'll both share in its freedom. It's been imprisoned for too long."

Zinzi bowed and took her leave of the Great Keeper following Jhodever's steps.

Radu removed his hand from his mouth and breathed deliberately to slow his panting and heart. He was alone with the fallen Keeper. If he could summon the courage and move fast enough, perhaps he could end this while the cursed man was alone. But instead, he balled himself up and shook in fear.

Graytorris stood atop the remains of the Cathedral of the Watchful Eye despite not being able to see the destruction around him and appeared to take in the echoes of his deeds in the once great hall. He made his way to the Tome, clicking through the rubble, his obsidian staff leading him. The Tome once made all marvel at the open pages at night, sending a bright beacon of light into the skies over Solemnity.

Radu prayed it was a sight Graytorris would never see again. He mustered the courage to stand but remained in the shadowed nooks of the ruin.

Graytorris ran his hand over the cover, his head bowed low.

Radu stepped from the ruins and watched. *Had the pages of the Tome somehow comforted the fallen Keeper in his loneliness?* He watched the man steel himself and concentrate. Even from afar he felt the hale of the Keeper's magic emanating in the remains of the inner sanctum.

"Rrhon Talamare." Graytorris invoked, his head spinning in the throes of a summoning spell. "Leave the trail of Daemus Alaric. Return here to the cathedral and your next task."

A dark grin grew up fallen Keeper's face.

———✦———

PRECEPT RADU HUGGED THE wall outside the inner sanctum, and as silent as he could made his way to the entrance, just outside the observatory. Satisfied that Graytorris was trapped in the throes of his spells, he descended the endless cathedral stairs as fast as he could without appearing frantic or rattled. In silent desperation, he made his way through the campus, his old bones aching from the effort. He ignored the pain and the racing of his aged heart. In the distance, the cries of the slaughter had already begun.

"This is a good night to die, my old friend," came a voice from the shadows.

Radu slowed, his shoulders slumping. It was the voice of the High Watcher, Volcifar Obexx.

"Where are you heading?" Obexx asked, a quiver in his voice. "I saw you in the inner sanctum." He paused. "You know then who's returned?"

Radu didn't reply, nor did he turn to Obexx. Obexx was a trained warrior. He had no chance at his age, or in his condition.

He raised his face to the dimming sky, resigned to his fate. For a moment, he recalled Nasyr atop the Eye, charting the stars in the heavens, looking for signs from their Ancient. "Forgive me if I don't want to face my killer eye-to-eye. Is this what Erud wanted, brother?"

Radu sensed Obexx drawing closer.

"I don't know how you are going to do it but make it quick. For an old friend?"

He heard Obexx take a few more steps toward him. Radu repeated a final prayer to Erud.

Obexx's shadow rose against the wall, a knife's blade silhouetted in the moonlight. Radu dropped his head and awaited the death blow. He felt the man at his back, and then something dropped to his feet. He dared to glance down.

A satchel?

He turned to his friend, who offered a meek smile, his face pale. "Please forgive me," Obexx's voice shook.

"I forgive you." Radu's voice cracked.

"Save Daemus," Obexx whispered, "and save the priestess. Erud, please forgive me."

Obexx took a step back and before Radu could act, drew the keen edge of the blade across his own throat.

Radu blinked. He watched a thin red line appear across Obexx's neck, followed by a rush of red.

The High Watcher's arms weakened, and the knife slipped from his hand.

"Volcif—no," Radu muttered. He caught his friend as his knees buckled.

Obexx's mouth moved, but his voice failed him.

Radu's mind raced, trying to find a way to help a man he'd known for twenty years, but he knew in his heart there was no way to save him. "Why?" he whispered in desperation.

Obexx's eyes rolled, focusing on the satchel. With a feeble motion, he gestured with one finger to the bag. His strength failed and his arm collapsed by his side. With fading eyes, the men locked gazes in a few precious seconds they had remaining.

Radu held his friend tight, his hands covered in blood, until Volcifar Obexx's eyes went dark. He rocked with him in his arms for a moment, fighting the urge to scream, but he couldn't fight the tears welling in his eyes. He gently laid him on the ground.

The sound of running met his ears, and he knew what he had to do. And he had little time to do it. He emptied the satchel, finding a key he recognized. It was Obexx's skeleton key, one that would unlock all the doors on campus, including those in the Cathedral of the Watchful Eye. He pocketed it, a final gift from his friend—one who had returned to the faith before he departed for the Hall of the Ancients.

Radu quietly said a prayer to Threnody for Obexx and rose to find Caspar Luthic.

—✦—

HE MADE HIS WAY into the low Keeper cloisters and took a deep a breath before climbing the stairs to Daemus Alaric's old room. He knocked and stood back, staring back down the stairs to ensure that he hadn't been followed.

"Yes?" Caspar Luthic, Daemus's old cloistermate, called. Radu had taught them both since they'd crossed the cathedral's threshold ten years earlier.

"It's Precept Radu, son. I need to speak to you most urgently."

A few seconds passed before Caspar opened the door, brushing his disheveled blond hair from his face.

"Precept?"

"Come with me, Luthic," Radu whispered. "Stay quiet and in the shadows. Do not run no matter what you see or hear."

"I don't understand," the low Keeper replied.

"Shh, boy, or else we'll both be caught."

"Caught?" Caspar's soft voice sounded desperate, but he followed his precept down the stairs and out into the courtyard.

Radu didn't answer but proceeded as quickly as he could without attracting eyes. The two emerged near the stables where the Knights kept their gryphs. As he feared, the stables were guarded by two young initiates of the Knights of the Maelstrom.

"Stay back," Radu murmured. "Don't step in front of me."

Caspar nodded and stayed in the shadows, lurking between two buildings. Radu stepped from the alley and approached the guards, who both snapped to attention when they saw the precept.

"*Miego snausti plaukeliai,*" Radu began in the conjurer's tongue. He waved his hands in front of the hapless guards. Before they could sound an alarm, both slumped to the ground in a magical slumber.

Radu waved and Caspar hustled from the alley to the stable doors.

"What's going on?" Caspar repeated in a panic. "You're scaring me."

"You should be scared. Treachery is afoot."

"Treachery?"

"There's no time to explain," Radu already heard the sounds of the slaughter drawing closer. The Keepers were not ready. They'd been taken in the night by those they trusted. "There'll be blood here, but not for you, son. I'll sneak you to safety. Erud has called you to a higher purpose."

"What do you mean?" Caspar's eyes glazed in tears. His head jerked back and forth, looking for the origin of the violent sounds.

"Your powers of the Sight," Radu grabbed him by the shoulders, trying to regain his attention. "You're a clairvoyant, correct?"

"Yes. But my powers are lost, like the others."

"But you can enter people's minds, correct?"

"Sometimes." Caspar looked even more confused, if that were possible. "When it works. Why?"

"Can you do the same with animals?" Radu asked, recalling the way the boy had calmed the beasts only a few days before.

"I... I can," he replied. "I can calm them."

"You need to call on those powers now, Caspar." The two skulked into the stables and Radu quickly readied a gryph for Caspar to ride. With Caspar's help, he threw its saddle on along with a bag full of rations for the low Keeper and the gryph.

"I've never ridden a—"

"You'll learn on the way." Radu helped Caspar saddle one of the gryphs. "Talk to it like you do with the animals in class. Quickly, before we're noticed. Fly to Abacus and warn Daemus Alaric of what has transpired here."

"Daemus?" Caspar repeated.

"He's in grave danger. Graytorris has returned and is hunting for him."

"Graytorris?" Caspar gasped. "The fallen Keeper that you warned us about in class?"

"He wants to kill Daemus," Radu replied. "This is life or death, Luthic."

"Why does he want him dead?"

"I don't know yet, but I believe it's because he's the last Keeper with the Sight. He's the only one who can lead us from this darkness."

"I won't fail," Caspar promised.

"They have a woman—a young healer that Daemus knows—and they plan to use her to trap him into returning. A healer named Katja Seitenwind. You need to warn him. We must act before they know Daemus is on his way back with you."

"How will I find you?"

"Meet me in Solemnity, far from the cathedral and the campus so that nobody sees you. I'll have more allies there to help us. Now, go!"

Radu slapped the hippogryph on the rear and it galloped off with Caspar clinging to its neck, barely saddled and unable to control the startled beast. Radu took a deep breath as Caspar and the gryph escaped into the night sky.

"Travel with the speed of the Ancients, son." He watched Caspar Luthic rise into the night sky and disappear over the horizon.

CHAPTER TWENTY-SEVEN

"In vengeance, I am death."
—Graytorris, the Mad

GRAYTORRIS STOOD AT A crack in the cathedral's walls, listening to the faint screams rising on the wind from the campus below. The cries sounded like distant banshees wailing, foretelling of the death to come this historic evening. And each wail was but a piece of a larger opera sung tonight, heralding his triumphant return to the Eye. The Keepers would be no more.

Behind him, he heard booted footfalls and turned away from his personal concert hall. "Ah, First Keeper," the wretched man smirked, "I hear you've followed my commands?"

There was a pause, and then Jhodever's tremulous voice said, "It's done."

Graytorris understood the man's misapprehensions, but he didn't need to earn the approval of his puppet. "Are they *all* dead?"

"Yes, Great Keeper."

"Bring me Katja Seitenwind," Graytorris waved. He listened as Jhodever hustled off to fetch the imprisoned healer.

Zinzi appeared from the shadows. "The plan has been executed without flaw."

"Not quite," he replied. "The First Keeper of Castleshire still lives, and we haven't heard from the Disciples that escorted that old fool Amoss from here. They're several days overdue."

"Shall I try and scry upon them?"

"No." Graytorris turned back to screams. "Both men are too wise for such amateur tricks."

"Then what?"

"Steel yourself." Graytorris's lined face twisted. "We will need to make the young healer take us to the Crystal Well."

"As you command, Great Keeper." Zinzi's voice failed to hide a tremor of anticipation. Even though he couldn't see her, he knew his incantatrix was smiling. He turned back to the campus below and raised his arms to the sky.

"In vengeance, I am death!"

———✦———

"WHERE ARE YOU TAKING me?" Katja asked the brutish guards that led her from her cell in the middle of the night.

"Shut up and walk," came the grumbled reply from beneath the visor of a helm.

She'd been shaken awake and led across the campus toward the Abacunian elevator of the ruined cathedral. It was dark outside, and even darker in the cathedral's subterranean portals. She followed her guards as they ducked into a side tunnel that sloped underground, barely illuminated by torches ensconced on the walls.

The guards pushed her down the angled corridor and she stumbled, slowed by the shackles around her feet and wrists. She caught herself on the wall, escaping a nasty fall, but they grabbed her forcefully around the arm and pulled her to the end of the hallway.

The corridor emptied into a basement, where the yawning door of the damaged elevator awaited her. Two more guards helped her into the apparatus and closed a guide rail in front of them. She heard the crack of a whip nearby and the neighing of horses, and then the elevator began to rise. With the sound of mechanical groaning and the tensing of thick ropes above them, her eyes darted around in wonder at the machine that carried them.

She slipped, falling into one of the guards, who nudged her

away with his armored shoulder. Each floor passed at a snail's pace, and she soon lost count, but when the wall in front of her gave way to the open night sky, she found herself as high as a mountain. With part of the cathedral torn open to the sky, instinct took over and she slunk backward and leaned against the elevator walls.

The guards chuckled but didn't address her, and then the clicking of the elevator's gears came to an end. One of the guards reached out and knocked on an outer door, which was soon opened by the man that Katja had met in the courtyard. Jhodever stood before her, adorned in white and gold robes. He looked eager to greet her.

"Welcome, Katja Seitenwind." With beckoning hands, he invited her to step out of the elevator. "Oh, I see your shackles have cut you."

Katja looked down at her wrists and ankles and saw that her skin had broken in scrapes and tears from the metal. Then an uncaring push from one of the guards moved her out of the elevator and onto a drafty platform at the top of the cathedral. Katja ignored the cuts and looked out over Solemnity from the holes in the cathedral's walls.

Jhodever escorted her along a wide corridor with high ceilings and scorch marks on the remaining walls. They entered a large room that she immediately recognized from the description Daemus had given to her when they'd met in Forecastle. She knew she was in the inner sanctum, but the observatory he waxed poetic about was heavily damaged.

She saw two figures standing in the darkness. The only light, save for that of the stars above, came from a large mirror that had been placed at the rear of the ruined chamber next to a dais that had been damaged by fire.

"Remove her shackles," an unfamiliar voice rang from

beside the glowing mirror. The guard obliged and nudged her shoulder, forcing her to take a step toward the pair of silhouettes.

"Come closer." Jhodever waved, and after rubbing feeling back into her hands and feet, she followed him cautiously inside.

"I'm sorry for my earlier rudeness," Jhodever began. "We're grateful for your willingness to come all the way from Foghaven Vale to visit the cathedral."

Katja didn't correct him. The choice had been Von Lormarck's and not hers. She was a prisoner.

"Allow me to introduce you to Graytorris Kanaan, the Great Keeper of our sect." Jhodever stepped out of her way. "He's been waiting to meet you. And, of course, his incantatrix, Zinzi of the Moor Bog."

Katja fought to remain poised, calling silently upon her Ancient to help her to stay calm. But her chest felt heavy, and her stomach turned at the sight of Graytorris, the man Daemus had warned her about from his dreams.

The wretch stood up from a small desk, where a quill was levitating above an old, leatherbound book. The quill had been writing for the blind seer, but it hovered in stasis once he turned his attention to her. He stepped forward with the use of his black staff, moving within inches of her. The virulent smell of his necrosis attacked her senses as open lesions on his face leaked puss.

"Leave me," Graytorris ordered, waving a hand at his companions. "I want to be alone with her."

"Great Keeper, I—" Jhodever protested, but Graytorris just twisted his head, silencing the First Keeper.

"She's an acolyte of Ssolantress. If I'm not safe with her, I'm not safe anywhere."

Jhodever, Zinzi, and the guards bowed and crept away,

closing the door to the inner sanctum as they left.

"Please forgive my servants," Graytorris said. "They don't understand the power you possess and the blue aura of magic that surrounds you. I can't see it, but I can feel its unmistakable hale from here. They're learned servants, but they're not as familiar with your kind as I."

Katja nodded and then realized the man couldn't see her.

"Yes," she said. "They're forgiven, of course. But I need to ask you a question, Great Keeper."

Graytorris laughed and leaned onto his staff with one hand. "Such courage, always from the followers of Ssolantress." He lowered himself back into his seat with the other. "My presence doesn't frighten you?"

"Should it?"

"Yes." His grey lips cracked a despotic smile. "Yes, you should fear me. But please, Katja, ask your question. I'll be as honest with you as you are with me. Now, what is it you want to know?"

"Why it is that you've gone through so much trouble to bring a low priestess of Ssolantress here?"

The man paused before answering and sighed. "You have a kind way about you," he replied with a politeness she didn't expect. "I know you were brought here against your will. For that, I ask for your forgiveness."

Katja staggered over the sentiments. His apology seemed sincere enough. She thought for a second, and in silence, prayed to her goddess for guidance. None came. "I accept your apology. I go where Ssolantress needs me, and so I must be needed here."

Graytorris's mouth widened in a sickly smile. "Yes, you are needed here."

"Is it for your wounds?" she asked.

"I need to know where your Crystal Well is." Graytorris minced no words, his voice spitting from between his crooked teeth. The edge to his voice didn't escape Katja.

Yet he is being honest, as he said, she thought.

"All priests and priestesses of Ssolantress must make a pilgrimage to the Crystal Well." She spoke bravely, fighting the urge to turn and run from her newly freed shackles. "If we're worthy, the well appears to us. It's there that we learn to use its healing waters."

Graytorris raised his hand and reached out for Katja. She froze as he petted her blue hair and took his time feeling the outline of her face. He rubbed his fingers over the mark of her Ancient, which hovered just below her skin. It tinged light blue when he touched it.

"I can feel the mark of Ssolantress upon you. You *were* successful in your pilgrimage, Priestess."

"I was." It took everything she had to keep from looking away.

"Then you must know where it is."

"I do."

The man stepped away from her, guiding himself back to his desk with the clicking of his staff as it grazed through the rubble on the floor.

"I'm shocked by your poise and honesty," Graytorris admitted. "It's rare for a woman of your youth."

Katja tilted her head and looked at the fallen Keeper but didn't reply.

"I desire only honesty," the fallen Keeper said, "but fear can be useful. You're here not only to lead me to the Crystal Well, but you are here because Daemus Alaric will come for you. When he discovers you're my prisoner, he'll return to the cathedral in a vain attempt to save you, where I'll kill him…

and relieve myself of this curse."

Katja gasped at the notion and fought to maintain her composure as she absorbed the weight of Graytorris's words. Although she hadn't known the Low Keeper long, Daemus had been kind to her, and she didn't want to be the reason he was harmed.

"I don't wish to be involved in such a gambit," she insisted.

His eyeless face sneered. "Does it appear that you have a choice?"

A moment of tense silence passed between them.

"How did Daemus bring this curse upon you?" she asked. "Why do you blame him so? And how can you be so sure that Daemus will come for me? We only met each other once, and I can't be of such consequence to him."

"I saw it in *The Tome of Enlightenment*," he replied, pointing to the unwieldy book that lay closed atop a strange wooden pedestal.

"How can you see if your Ancient blinded you?"

"I haven't always been blind, Katja."

His voice was stern and poignant, but she sensed a distant tremble in it. She took a deep breath and paused. She understood his words, and then for some inexplicable reason felt compassion for her captor.

Ssolantress is answering my prayers, she thought. *The Blue Lady is with me.*

"May I address your wounds?"

Graytorris's head turned toward her in disbelief, a morose look etched upon his face. For a second, she thought he didn't know how to respond.

"Is your kindness real?" he asked at length.

Katja approached him with an air of caution and without permission. He didn't stop her. She reached carefully for the bloody mask that was wrapped around his face and gingerly removed it.

His cold but gentle hand touched her arm, and for a moment she expected him to ask her to stop. But instead, he relented and let her continue. She looked into the dark recesses of his skeletal eye sockets, where no eyes stared back. It was as if his eyes had been ripped away, and blood seeped down his sunken cheeks.

Without hesitating, she reached down and tore off part of her blue dress and cleaned his cursed eyes. Then she fashioned a new mask from what material remained.

"*Vindicarea ranii*," she murmured, and the blue light of her divine magic fell upon his face.

Graytorris winced at first then grabbed at his face. For a few precious moments, her spell seemed to lift his pain and stopped the bleeding. The pain in his face twisted from misery to hope. But the fleeting moments passed as the spell's hale dissipated, and she saw the familiar agony return.

"You tease me." His voice was laced with a tint of desperate sadness. "The blood won't stop." He paused. "It will never stop." He rubbed the new rivulets of blood that slipped from under his mask away with his fingers.

"Tell me about your wounds so I can better treat you. How did you lose your sight?"

Graytorris hesitated. "It's an old wound," he replied at length. "And it's not one I wish to discuss."

She stepped away from him and looked at the broken man as he slumped in his seat. "Why do you want to visit the Crystal Well?"

"The well heals, does it not?"

"The well heals wounds and diseases, but it won't wash sin away," she replied. He fell silent again. She could tell that her techniques had nearly exhausted the man. His fatigue wasn't from age. He appeared old and haggard in his physical form, but she sensed that he was younger than he looked. There was a determined strength about him, one that sustained him in his fight against a chronic pain.

"What's the nature of your other malady?" she asked.

He seemed surprised by the question. "How do you know?"

"I can smell it in your blood." She tried to sound calm, but she'd smelled this type of affliction in patients before. And without the powers of the well, they were doomed.

"It's my mother's disease." His voice was sullen and near emotionless, and a distance in his face told her he was visiting a memory of his past. "It's one that haunted her when she, too, was young. And now it haunts me."

"The well may be able to cure you of it." Her words were hopeful. "I can take you to the well, if that's what you wish. But I have a condition."

Graytorris cracked a half-smile. "You are in no position to negotiate," he reminded her.

"If the water heals you of your mother's malady, I only ask that you stop your pursuit of Daemus in return. However, your curse will likely be beyond the well's magic."

"I can't," he said, his tone both kind and feeble. "He and I have more to account for."

"Why do you want to kill him so badly? What could he possibly have done to you?"

"Erud has intertwined our fates." He pointed to the Tome.

"You saw your rivalry with Daemus in the Tome? That's why you must kill him? He must have been a mere child when you fell. Why would an Ancient such as Erud tie your fate to his?"

His head dropped and his mouth drew into an

anguished line.

Confused, Katja accepted his silence as his answer. "If you refuse to stop pursuing Daemus, I'm afraid I can't take you to the well. Daemus revealed his visions of you to me—one of you poisoning the Crystal Well. I knew you'd ask this of me. He told me so. I can't allow you to taint the waters of Ssolantress."

She stopped for a moment, stunned at her own brazenness, her own courage. She waited for her captor to respond.

The man laid back in his chair, one hand holding his obsidian staff, the other scratching at his face. Then he leaned into her. She tried not to show fear, but the smell of his breath and decaying flesh made her wince.

"If you don't take me then you, too, shall die," Graytorris muttered, pulling at his staff to rise.

Katja swallowed hard, but her mouth was dry. "Then I'll die."

"Jhodever!" Graytorris called, his spittle flying in her face.

The doors of the chamber opened, and the First Keeper re-entered the ruins of the inner sanctum.

Graytorris sat back into his chair. "Thank you, Katja Seitenwind, for your kindness and for attending to my condition. Jhodever, have her moved from the cells and placed here with me, on this floor."

"But Great Keeper—"

"And allow her freedom of movement. She won't be treated as a prisoner any longer. Feed her, let her bathe, and find her new clothes. Make sure she's comfortable."

Zinzi and Jhodever exchanged a quick glance.

"As you command, Great Keeper."

CHAPTER TWENTY-EIGHT

"A seed hidden in the heart of an apple
is an invisible orchard."
—Erudian Proverb

JOINED BY JERIC TUTTLE, Daemus and his party had ridden to Vorodin's Lair under the watchful eye of the knight castellan and twelve of his troops. At Bane's insistence, a citywide search was being conducted by the High Aldin. Wizards from the Horn of Ramincere, the school for Abacunian sorcerers embedded in the High Aldin, had been assigned the task of finding the Bone elf and his companion while Daemus and the princess entered the library.

As they progressed through Abacus, Bane's eyes weren't on the unique architecture and the vibrant city but on the rooftops and alleyways where the assassin might have been hiding. Even with Bane and Peacemaker at their side, Daemus felt their collective nerves standing at attention until they made the final turn into the city's piazza, the Calendula Esplenade.

The esplanade's grandeur overwhelmed them. The flat piazza was the heart of the city and took the form of a diamond that was overlaid by a square. The streetscape was perfectly bricked with dark, polished stone, with whisks of wispy marbling throughout. A mechanical fountain stood at the center of the esplanade, casting white plumes of fresh water several stories into the air, flanked by smaller, bubbling fountains that joined the dancing show.

The Faye Tree stood across from the fountain. It was a giant and ancient hollow oak, whose center contained a multi-level building that disappeared into its trunk. It had been much larger in Daemus's dreams, but it was unmistakably the place the half-ghost had led him.

The top of the library held a mechanical clock of sorts that could only have been found in Abacus. Its hands kept the time of day while massive star charts rotated along the outside, pointing to many of the constellations Daemus had learned about at the cathedral.

"This is what I saw in my dreams," Daemus affirmed. "We're supposed to be here."

"I've never seen its equal," Faux's eyes danced from marvel to marvel.

"How can this be possible?" Addilyn added.

"We may be here for several hours," Ritter said to Bane. "We aren't quite sure what we'll find, if we even find anything."

"I'll return, then." Bane turned to his troops. "I'll lead the effort to capture the assassin in the meantime."

Addilyn bowed to the knight castellan. "Thank you."

As the group entered the massive doors of the library, Daemus found scholars from around the realm, all studying, collaborating and learning freely amongst themselves. "Why doesn't the Ancient of Knowledge, Erud, have such a structure in Solemnity?" Daemus wondered aloud. "This place is unrivaled."

From the outside, the library appeared square, but once inside the doors, each library chamber seemed to have a shape of its own. Some rooms were small and private, while others contained vaulted ceilings. One room even contained a set of floating stairs made of books, and tall bookshelves created their own archways.

"Good day, fellow scholars," a voice said. Daemus spun to see a Dale elf with minty green hair, dressed in a spotless white robe. The man appeared to levitate inches from the floor and had a pleasant smile on his face. "You look lost. How may

I help you?

"Thank you, sir." Addilyn made a quick gesture of greeting. "But who are you?"

"I'm a Scion of Vorodin," the man explained. "Welcome to the library of Abacus. We Scions serve the library, and I'm here to help visitors find what they need. Now, what brought you here today?"

"We're here to see Vorodin." Daemus didn't want to waste any time. "The Athabasica has given us a key to enter the lair." The young Keeper produced the book key Anoki had given them and showed it to the Scion.

The Scion remained stoic but polite. "I'm sorry. I can't help you there. You must find the lair on your own. Use the key to enter, but I can't guarantee that Vorodin will reveal himself. He doesn't see many visitors."

"It's of grave importance," Ritter insisted.

The Scion shook his head. "I'm sorry. I'm required to decline assistance in that regard. I can help you in the library proper, however."

"Can you tell us which books my friend, Anselm Helenius, either read or checked out?" Tuttle asked.

"Again, I must apologize." The Scion floated nearer the alchemist. "Any research done here is a matter of privacy."

"But he was killed," Addilyn explained. "Right here in Abacus. We surmise it was for the information he found."

The Scion closed his eyes and pondered their request for a second or two. "Very well. Stay here. I'll return shortly."

The elf turned and floated off, mumbling a spell under his breath. Within minutes, he returned with a handful of books and scrolls. He placed the trove of knowledge on the table in front of Tuttle.

Daemus grabbed a handful himself and scanned the

spines. They included books on cryptids, tetrine, mythology, bestiaries, and, of course, rare Melexian tongues.

"This book was the last one he read." The Scion pointed at a book with gilded linings and Melexian script on its face.

"How do you know?" Daemus asked.

"We watch and guard all the knowledge here," the Scion went on. "We know all."

Daemus was grateful for the Scion's help, even if he didn't understand how this was accomplished. The rest of the group gathered around a table and Tuttle fixed his spectacles while Daemus opened the final book Helenius had read. The entire tome was filled with ancient writing in a language that was beyond them all.

"Allow me." Addilyn reached for the book. She whispered a short incantation and the tome lit up with a soft yellow hue, but after a few frustrating minutes, she relented. "My magics won't allow for a translation." She pushed the book away in frustration.

"Now what?" Blue asked, his tone thick with irritation.

No one answered, but each took a book and began to look through the pages. Daemus held one the mythology of the tetrine and other fanciful creatures, but he soon found it to be a dead end. He closed the cover and looked around the hall, disappointed.

His eyes affixed on the far wall, where he noticed a painting that intrigued him. While the others buried their heads in the musty texts, he stood and walked toward it for a closer inspection. As he drew nearer, he recognized the countenance depicted in the painting. It was the ghost of the man from his dreams in Flowerdown Syphen.

He rushed to the painting with a renewed energy and looked at the figure's face. There was no doubt it was him.

"I've seen this man in my dreams," he said, loud enough to draw the room's attention to him.

"Shhh," the Scion warned. "This is a library."

The group followed him to the wall where the plaque beneath the man read: Abacus Athobasca, Founder of the Scholar City of Abacus.

"He was the one who showed me the Faye Tree," Daemus whispered this time.

"Ya saw a ghost, kid?" Blue asked.

"Possibly," Tuttle answered. "Abacus Athobasca killed himself. It was an accident, I assure you. It was during one of his many experiments. There was an explosion and he... disintegrated. Not a trace of him left, save for dust on his laboratory floor. Some say that his ghost helps people from time to time. He was so beloved the founders named the town after him."

"And he visited you in your dreams?" Addilyn asked.

"Yes."

"What did he say?" Ritter pressed.

"Nothing." Daemus shrugged. "There was no sound. He escorted me to the center of the library, where we entered the tree. He just... showed me the tree."

"Which way did he take you?" Blue grunted, drawing the ire of the Scion. "There are a dozen halls."

"I don't know." Daemus looked around at the maze of corridors. "We just appeared there."

Ritter sighed, Blue growled, and Daemus felt the eyes of his friends upon him.

"Master Scion, are we allowed to inspect the painting?" Addilyn asked. "May we touch it?"

"Yes," he replied.

Ritter and Marquiss each grabbed an end of the painting

and gently lifted it from the wall. Tuttle spun the frame and looked for clues or a hidden back to the portrait, but neither he nor Ritter found one.

"Wait." Jessamy turned to Daemus. "You said that Abacus didn't tell you where to go but that he showed you, correct?"

"That's right."

"Then look at him," she replied. "Where's he guiding us?"

The young Keeper shrugged again. "I don't get your meaning."

"His eyes." She pointed to her own. "He's turned sideways in this portrait. He's looking up a grand staircase. He may be telling us where to go."

Daemus looked at the Scion, hoping for some validation to Jessamy's theory, but the elf's face didn't register the slightest of emotions.

"Perhaps he's guiding us to the lair from the grave with his eyes." Addilyn started to walk up the stairs.

"If this works," Marquiss turned to Jessamy, "I could kiss you."

"Not unless you want to look up at me from the flat of your back again."

"I don't mind," he quipped, before following the swordswoman up the stairs.

Daemus was the last to go, holding the key and looking back at the Scion, who was shaking his head and reaffixing the painting to the wall.

By the time he reached the top of the stairs, the group had already spotted a second painting of Abacus, this time looking down a long hallway. They continued to follow Abacus's eyes, with each painting leading to another in every second or third room. The uncertain trail led deeper and deeper into the never-ending library until they stumbled upon a corridor and open archway formed from the spines of a thousand tomes. The hallway had no shelves or tables, just floating books.

"The magical hale in this chamber is overwhelming." Addilyn searched the corners with her eyes. "We must be getting closer."

The group scanned high and low but found no more paintings.

"A dead end?" Marquiss guessed.

"Did we misinterpret this?" Ritter added. "Were we wrong?"

Daemus stepped past the group and approached the archway. Something familiar drew him to it, but he didn't know what. "What am I missing?" he murmured, looking down at the book key. Then he remembered the ghost of Abacus floating upside down, examining the spines of the books in his dream. He started to feel a rush of adrenaline, knowing he was about to solve the riddle.

"Here." He pointed to the floating archway. "In my dream, we floated upside down and he showed me the books sideways. I remember now."

He fumbled about for a few seconds, looking up at the arches, and then lay on the floor, reorienting himself as they had in his dream.

"What are ya doin', kid?" Blue asked. "Get up and help us out."

"You can't even read, Blue," Marquiss jabbed, but before another word could be spoken, Daemus shushed them down.

"Look," he said, pointing to a missing book in the floating archway. "I think I've found it."

The group turned and approached Daemus, all eyes looking up at the gap in the stacks.

"The key," Tuttle muttered, motioning for Daemus to hand it to Addilyn. The Vermilion slid the book into place, and as she did so, the books in the archway began to swirl. Book by book, one by one, the levitating tomes restacked around her. When all were in place, a door formed which resembled a singular, giant book cover.

Daemus rose in amazement and approached the door with Addilyn.

"Together?" Daemus asked.

The Vermilion nodded and with some apprehension, they both grabbed the cover and pulled. The animated cover swung open, and the breeze of outside air filled the hallway.

Daemus's memory returned him—this was the magical portal revealed to him in his dreams, the one Abacus Athobasca had led him to in his dreams. He fought back a smile, always expecting the worst, but he couldn't stop his lips from curling.

"This is it." His voice brimmed with confidence. "This is what he showed me."

"Daemus, wait," Addilyn cautioned, but the Keeper had already stepped across the threshold.

As he emerged on the other side, he found himself no longer in the library. In fact, there was no library at all. Instead, he stood outdoors and felt the warmth of sunlight on his face. He closed his eyes and breathed fresh air, clearing his nose of the smell of old parchment and leather-bound tomes.

The Faye Tree stood in front of them, gnarled and twisted from years of magical growth. It was the size of a large oak, hidden and protected in the center of the lair by the magics of the apparent mirage outside. The branches reached out like two arms hugging an invisible figure, creating a courtyard of grass and flowers in its grasp. The arms were pocked with open knots and holes, which created natural shelves and places to store books, scrolls, and the like.

Daemus turned to see the group appearing next to him,

one at a time, as they stepped through the door with a wispy flare of near-invisible magic. He smiled as the last of them appeared, Jeric Tuttle bringing up the rear. Tuttle coughed and stumbled, taking a moment to clean his glasses on his tunic to get a better look around. The doorway slowly closed behind them and then subtly disappeared.

The group wandered around in the courtyard, befuddled and lost.

"Is this Vorodin's Lair?" Ritter asked.

Daemus plucked at a branch. "Must be."

Addilyn stepped toward the Faye Tree. "It's *perfect*."

"It'd be perfect if it had a bar." Blue murmured. Marquiss laughed and pulled a flask from his haversack so that he and Blue could share a shot before tucking it away.

"Stop it." Faux glared at the pair, scolding them like impertinent children. "Enjoy the splendor of the chamber."

Tuttle wandered to the left and began poking around, his hands diving into the open knots in the tree limbs and fishing through the ancient works hidden within. Addilyn walked up to Tuttle and touched the tree.

"What are you doing?" Daemus asked.

"Checking to see if it's real," the Vermilion replied.

"Listen." Jessamy's raised finger quieted them.

Daemus heard the gentle chirping of birds from above, but they couldn't see them. The same was true of the babbling of a nearby brook.

"It feels... safe," Daemus remarked. "No black rose, no brewing war. It's the safest I've felt since leaving the cathedral."

Ritter approached the sacred oak. "Look."

Daemus peered over Ritter's shoulder and saw that the center of the Faye Tree had hollowed out with age, with room for several of them to step into its barky center. He glanced through several open knots and creases in the bark and found a small, natural staircase winding around the tree like a spiral flight.

"Ritter, here," he pointed, as the Longmarcher approached. The others followed, and he made room for them by stepping into the center of the hollow tree.

"Hello?" Daemus called out, hoping an answer would come. But none did.

"Where's Vorodin?" Addilyn asked.

"The Scion said he doesn't see everyone even if they find the lair," Ritter reminded her.

The group waited for a few more minutes and Daemus called out again. "He has to be here."

"I have an idea," Tuttle added. "Read the words on the parchment Helenius left for Addilyn." He removed the note from his waistcoat and handed it to Daemus.

Daemus nodded and unfurled the small scroll. He closed his eyes and concentrated, as he had in the Gatehouse. His white eyes soon glowed with the Sight, and he was blind to everything except for the Melexian verse. Again, his eyes read the note and his voice spoke the words in a tongue that wasn't his own.

As he finished the short recital, the lair fell silent. The birds stopped singing and the brook stopped churning. A perfect stillness hung in the air, as though time stood still. Daemus looked around in anticipation, hoping he'd piqued Vorodin's interest.

Moments passed, and then he heard the soft footfalls of someone descending the stairs inside the Faye Tree. A venerable Dale elf stepped from the sacred oak, his grey hair clinging to a slight tinge of mint green. His once-sharp nose had wilted and the lines in his face betrayed his age. He wore a faded green tunic, tied at his waist with a rutty hemp belt, and his shoulders were covered with a matching cape and collar that rode down his back to his knees.

"I haven't heard the tones of that ancient tongue for millennia," the man said in an inquisitive but friendly voice.

"Are... are you Vorodin?" Daemus asked. He approached him, his eyes wary but hopeful.

"Why has the Melexian tongue deserted you?" the man asked while taking stock of the group, squinting at them with his faded green eyes.

Daemus took another step toward him and handed him the scroll. "I don't speak the language, but I can somehow understand it."

The elf shuffled closer to him. "I *see* your eyes *see*." The man's eyes peered into Daemus's and the Keeper had to stop to register the words before answering.

"At times," he replied."

"It's never the right time—until it's the right time," the quick-witted elf smiled back.

"I have no control when the Sight comes to me, unfortunately."

Addilyn stepped closer to the pair. "Great sir, I'm Addilyn Elspeth of the Vermilion nation. We've traveled far to meet you. This is Daemus Alaric of the Keepers of the Forbidden."

"Your eyes read, and your voice spoke, but neither was you," the elf turned back to the Keeper.

"I don't understand."

The elf leaned uncomfortably close to Daemus, meeting him eye-to-eye. "Who are you, really?"

"I... I don't know what you mean, sir."

"I assure you—" Ritter tried to step in, but the elf interrupted him.

"I'm speaking to *you*, Daemus," the venerable elf leaned in, inches from the Keeper's face. "*Vorbesc cu tine.*"

Daemus didn't hear the Melexian tongue. Instead, he heard the translation: "I'm speaking to you."

He felt his eyes flare for a moment, and before he could respond, the other voice returned.

"*I'm Daemus Alaric of House Alaric and the Silvercroft Mountains,*" he replied in old Melexian. "*I was once a Low Keeper of the Cathedral of the Watchful Eye, but now I'm the last Keeper with the Erudian Sight in all of Warminster.*"

The man leaned away from him, his hand rubbing at his chin as he seemed to ponder the out-of-body response. The elf's eyes rolled back into his head for a second, and Daemus could feel the hale of the elven magic around him. Again, he felt secure and let the effects wash over him.

"What did you say?" Faux asked. "You were speaking in tongues again."

"I told him who I was in old Melexian," Daemus replied, looking at Vorodin, who was still caught in a conjurer's trance. After a few tense moments, the elf's eyes wobbled then focused on Daemus.

This time, he spoke in Warminsterian. "You're much more than that, Daemus Alaric."

"Are you Vorodin?" Addilyn asked.

"I am."

Addilyn breathed a little easier, an expression of hope returning to her. "We came here for—"

"Yes, I know why you came, Princess," Vorodin interrupted. "I can see the two-horned tetrine in your mind."

Addilyn leaned away and Daemus peered at her. She seemed uneasy with the thought that Vorodin had admittedly invaded her mind.

"You're not going to like the answers I provide."

CHAPTER TWENTY-NINE

*"The worst sin, before one meets
Threnody, is to not find peace."*
—Matron Persephone Rhowan

KATJA FOLLOWED JHODEVER BACK from her chambers, where she'd been resting. She couldn't sleep and had barely nibbled at the food she'd been given. The smell of Graytorris lingered in her nostrils and turned her stomach against it. She'd spent most of her time praying to Ssolantress, asking for guidance and safety for Daemus Alaric, but the echoes of the madman's voice resonated in her mind and interrupted her adjuration.

She decided to test Graytorris's orders that she may roam freely on the top floor of the cathedral, so she opened her chamber doors. No guards waited for her outside, so she stepped back into the inner sanctum. Her eyes adjusted to darkness in the room, but it was day. With the holes in the ceiling, she should have been able to see the blue skies over Solemnity for miles around. Instead, a foreboding and unnatural darkness pervaded the sanctum and what remained of the observatory.

Zinzi and Graytorris stood near the glowing mirror. It was the only source of illumination in the chamber. Even with her limited knowledge of arcana, Katja could sense the hale of a powerful magic emanating from the device from the corridor.

Jhodever bowed to the Great Keeper and turned to leave the room. Katja knelt and hid from him in the opened doorway. She quieted and watched him walk off. But when she turned back, Zinzi had snuck up on her, and now stood in her face with an unsheathed dagger.

The priestess raised her hands in peace. "I won't fight you."

"Come," the incantatrix ordered, motioning to her with the blade, "kneel in front of the mirror."

Katja did as she asked but began to slip quietly back into a reverie of prayer to her goddess.

Graytorris interrupted her entreaty. "This is your time."

Katja approached the mirror with Zinzi at her back. "I don't understand."

Graytorris pointed to the magical glass. "Concentrate on the mirror," he told her, pointing at the glowing surface. "Show Dromofangare where the Crystal Well is, and it will respond."

"I won't take you there," Katja reminded him. "As I said, I won't help you to carry out your vengeance on Daemus."

"I don't want to hurt you." Graytorris's tone changed, his voice now purring in a veiled threat. "But I will if you continue to ignore my commands."

"I'm not yours to command." Katja closed her eyes and prayed for strength, but before she could finish her prayer, Zinzi zipped the dagger across her back shoulder.

Katja screamed in pain, feeling the burn of the knife as it sliced through her flesh. Her warm blood trickled down her back and she grabbed at the open wound, awkwardly trying to stave off the bleeding.

Graytorris bent at the waist and whispered in her ear, "Concentrate, or more pain will come."

"I must pray for the well to appear," she pleaded, trying to remain calm. "It only reveals itself to a priest or priestess of Ssolantress when summoned. It doesn't exist as a place."

Graytorris swung his staff, catching Katja beneath her chin and knocking her to the floor.

"You're lying," Graytorris growled.

Katja tried to gather her thoughts and to sit back up, but

the blow had stunned her. She felt Zinzi grab the back of her hair and pull her to her knees. The witch held her face inches from the glowing glass.

The fallen Keeper's staff began to thrum, and his eyes closed in concentration. "See the well, Katja," Graytorris said, but this time his voice echoed through her mind in a magical rush of power.

She cocked her head against Zinzi's will and looked at the Great Keeper. Feeling the power from the staff reaching out for her, she gritted her teeth and resisted its effects. The first wave of magic wafted over her like a suggestion from a carnival barker, asking her to look into the mirror.

She resisted.

The second wave was more forceful, squeezing at her consciousness. Graytorris's voice reverberated in her skull, his commands growing louder with every word.

"Look… look… look!" his voice cried in her head.

She resisted again, closing her eyes and calling to Ssolantress for aid.

Then a second whack from his staff crossed the small of her back. She reared up and Zinzi's arm wrapped itself around her throat. Zinzi's elbow settled in the crook of her neck and Katja fought to breathe. Her mind raced away from the echoes in her mind as she struggled against the incantatrix's grip. She tugged at Zinzi's arms, but the witch sliced her forearms with the dagger each time she tried. There was more pain and no air. Her mind raced with the chaos of the invading voice, and she began to swoon. She called out for her goddess in silent prayer, but there was no reprieve.

"The well!" Graytorris's voice screamed in her head, this time booming loudly enough that she no longer noticed Zinzi's arm or keen blade. She felt her arms go limp, and her mind searched for Ssolantress one last time. Then memories of her ascension rushed back to her, replacing Graytorris's ceaseless shrieking. She felt the calm waters of the Crystal Well buoying her, the stillness of peace that Ssolantress imparted.

The stings on her back and forearms no longer hurt and the tightness around her neck had loosened. Had her Ancient finally heard her prayers?

Then her eyes opened, and she found herself face down in the rubble of the cathedral. The pain slowly returned to her limbs, and she inhaled. Dust from the floor rushed into her lungs and she coughed. When she sat up and wiped her eyes, she caught a vision of the Crystal Well glowing in the mirror in front of her. Her ears still rang from the fallen Keeper's magic, and her head pounded from Graytorris's commands.

The image was of a snow-covered mountain with a wooded rise at its base that contained a small lake. She knew the sight all too well. It was a memory she'd never forget. It was her place of ascension. It was the site of the Crystal Well.

"You've done well," Graytorris's voice returned, even though to sound was muffled in her ears.

She felt Zinzi's arms around her waist, helping her to stand. Her knees wobbled and she leaned into the witch to hold her up.

"The image is precise," Zinzi smiled to the Great Keeper. "Can you take us there?"

"Not through the mirror," he replied. "Without Traumefang on the other side, we'd be stranded there with no way to return. My staff has such magics, but the effects are... painful."

"I'm ready," Zinzi nodded.

"Hold the priestess," Graytorris ordered. "She comes with us."

"*Calatorie plana sumplimentara keliones,*" Graytorris

incanted in the conjurer's tongue. *"Papil domo putovanja."*

As his spell reached its crescendo, a flash of color and a wisp of cold air brushed against Katja's face. She heard a crackling rip and saw the breach of a magical portal in front of her, hovering only a few feet in the air. On the other side was the vision she'd had through the mirror, and the chill of the Silvercroft Mountains reached through the tear, startling her.

The three figures stepped through the portal and then the breach closed behind them with a second flash of prismatic color. Katja felt the rush of a freefall, her stomach pitting as she tumbled freely. She reached out for something to hold, but her attempt met with failure. She tried to scream, but her lungs couldn't expel any air and her voice disappeared in the rush of colors around her. Her descent sped and she began to flip over and over. It felt as if the portal was simultaneously choking and dropping her. Then she heard a second rip before she slammed hard into a bank of snow.

Katja gagged and felt the burning of the spell still crawling over her skin. Her eyes, blind at first, captured the white of the snow that broke her fall. Then her stomach let loose, and she vomited.

A moment passed and her senses returned, and she could hear voices around her. As she glanced up, she saw Graytorris leaning on his staff nearby with Zinzi kneeling beside him. She wrestled herself to her feet, just to fall back down again.

"Pick up the priestess," Graytorris ordered, and she heard the crunching of snow as Zinzi appeared above her. The incantatrix pulled Katja up by her bloody arm and forced her toward the Great Keeper.

"Come, Katja." Graytorris stepped toward the lake. "Bring forth the powers of your Ancient and summon the Crystal Well for me to bathe in it."

"I won't," she managed, struggling to speak.

"Then your life will end here," he snapped. "Bring her to the lake."

Zinzi pushed the priestess forward, kicking her legs out from her as she neared the shore.

"This is the view your precious Daemus saw of me in his dreams," Graytorris teased. He grabbed her face and made her look at the mountains in the distance and her feet at the water's edge, then pushed her head into the frigid waters of the lake.

The icy water shocked her from her stupor and her eyes opened wide in fear. Then a tug on her hair lifted her head from the lake. She gasped, the bony hand holding her fast, inches from the surface. Her wet hair fell into her face.

"He knew I was coming for him… he knew I'd find him. Oh, I've searched these long years for him. By involving you, he put your life at risk. Why do you hold out for him? Help me and I'll leave you here, alone but alive."

"I won't," she repeated, resigned to her fate. She wondered if he'd drown her in the icy waters or whether his witch would finish her with her blade. Either way, the results would be the same. "But without the power of the lake, you can't be healed."

"Where is your friend now?" Graytorris raged. "A world away on a fool's errand. He seeks answers to questions when it's too late to solve them. I ask you for the last time, Priestess. Reveal the healing waters of the Crystal Well!"

"She won't, but I will," a voice carried in from the distance.

Katja felt the man let go. She turned her head and brushed her wet hair from her eyes.

A woman in the blue robes of Ssolantress emerged from the woods and began to walk toward them.

"It's another priestess," Zinzi said to Graytorris, who couldn't see the interloper.

"Come any closer and your acolyte dies," Graytorris growled.

"I was sent here to help you," the woman replied. "Why would you kill her?"

"Who are you?"

"I'm Persephone Rhowan, the High Priestess of Ssolantress, and I've been told of your coming."

Katja smiled and exhaled a frosty breath in relief. Perhaps she wouldn't die after all. Her eyes met briefly with Rhowan's. The woman's steel-blue hair matched her eyes and lips like all that had ascended, but the mark of the Blue Lady on her face glowed with more intensity.

"You were sent here… by whom?" Graytorris asked.

"By Katja, of course" she answered. "She sent word to me through a messenger of House Alaric before she was taken prisoner. I've been awaiting your arrival for some time, Graytorris."

"Alaric," Graytorris growled.

Katja closed her eyes. Her prayers had been answered. Phineas Silvera and the Alarics had gotten word to the high priestess in time. She dared to breathe a sigh of relief.

"Why do you threaten a simple servant of Ssolantress?" Rhowan asked.

"I require the healing powers of your well," the fallen Keeper admitted. "I've seen my salvation here… written in the annals of *The Tome of Enlightenment*."

"The well can cure wounds and disease, but cannot rid you of your curse," Persephone warned. "That, Graytorris, you must remove on your own, through your deeds. You must make peace with Erud before the well's powers will work on you."

"Summon the powers of the well so I may bathe, or you and the girl will perish." He turned his staff toward the high priestess.

"There's no need for death in a place of full of life," Rhowan replied, and she approached the group, arms outstretched. The high priestess knelt by the lake and closed her eyes. Her hands warmed in the blue light of a healing spell. *"Konjurigung,"* she began in divine prayer, *"heilund brunnen speichern gracianus."*

With her hands aglow in a soft blue haze, Rhowan touched the surface of the lake, her prayers tapering off to near silence. Katja watched Graytorris's countenance grow anxious and impatient, but he didn't dare disturb the high priestess.

Soon the lake's surface glowed with the same blue hale of magic. The high priestess stepped back. "The Crystal Well awaits you."

Katja's eyes filled with tears, half in hope that the lake would heal the Keeper, half in relief that her holy mother was there to help.

Graytorris grimaced and handed Zinzi his staff. He staggered to the edge of waters, and as he approached the placid pool, his crooked frame knelt on the edge. He breathed heavily and appeared timid to Katja for the first time. She sensed reticence in the man.

He reached into the blessed waters first with his hands. The blue glow began to travel up his arms, slowly enveloping his body with the healing powers of Ssolantress.

Katja looked on in awe and wonder. She noticed the man had stopped shaking. His limbs went calm, and years of pain and morbid putrescence drained from him. Slow in his approach at first, he splashed his face with the healing waters and pulled the bloody rag from his skull. The blood had stopped draining and his eyes had returned to their rightful place.

"I… I can see," he muttered. "I can see!"

Zinzi looked at her master but didn't dare approach, so Katja slid her way over to help him. She looked up into his eyes for the first time, and he turned his gaze back from Katja to the reflection of himself on the water. As Katja joined him, she saw that the reflection in the glassy pool didn't show Graytorris. It was of a woman in the middle of her life, staring back at him.

Time stopped for them both, confusion running through her.

"Mother!" he yelled, overcome with emotion. His haggard frame fell into the placid lake, disappearing into the shallows.

The well's waters splashed onto Katja, and she felt the touch of her Ancient's healing hands. At first, it was warm and familiar, and reminded her of one of her own healing potions that she'd administer to the sick or injured. Then she saw the wounds on her arms begin to close and a rush of energy filled her limbs.

"Thank you, Blue Lady," she muttered under her breath.

She stood and stepped back, joining the two other women on the shore. Graytorris rose to the surface, his face still underwater. Years of blood and rot plumed around him in the waters, leaving a cloud of ugliness. But within moments, the water was clear again.

With a whirring motion, Graytorris emerged and stood only feet from the shore. His skin was healthy, his eyes bright, and his withered form gone. He appeared as a man in his early forties, his brown hair returned and a look of confusion on his face.

"Mother!" His voice rose and his hands scraped at the water's surface. "Please! Don't go! I... I tried to save you. I tried to find the answers."

Katja heard his words grow into incoherent ramblings and she turned to her high priestess, who was standing by, a stoic look on her brow. She turned back to the Great Keeper to see a middle-aged man, rejuvenated and restored. But as the water dripped from him, the maladies that had plagued him started to return.

"No!" he raged, splashing water onto himself like a petulant child. "Please, no!"

Persephone Rhowan said nothing as she watched him fight the inevitable.

"Help him," Zinzi urged, grabbing the high priestess by the robe and pointing the Great Keeper's staff at her.

"I warned him that I can't," she replied.

Graytorris fell to his knees in agony and wept, his cries echoing across the surface of the lake. "Help me, please!" he begged, joining Zinzi's chorus, but the high priestess shook her head.

Katja watched as the magic of the Crystal Well dissipated.

"Only you can help yourself," Rhowan advised.

The man staggered to the shore, crawling toward the high priestess. "I beg of you," he cried, tears turning to blood as his eyes slowly disappeared.

"Make peace with Erud." Rhowan cupped his face in her hands. "Once you do, Ssolantress will help."

His hand grabbed her robes and he tugged himself toward her through the snow. Prostrate, he kissed her feet. "Mercy," he mumbled.

Persephone looked to Katja and then bent to hug the man.

In an instant, Graytorris attacked her. Summoning the last vestiges of stolen power from the lake, he pulled the high priestess to the ground and crawled on top of her, pinning her to the ground.

"No!" Katja screamed. She moved to help, but she was rewarded with a swift strike of a staff to the back of her head by the charging Zinzi. Katja fell flat and lifted her head, trying to recover from the witch's move. She watched Zinzi hand Graytorris her dagger, which was stained with the healer's blood. It soon found its way into Persephone's ribs.

The high priestess cried out in pain as Graytorris twisted the blade, ripping it across her midsection. His bloody eyes dripped on the face of the dying high priestess as she writhed in anguish.

"If your goddess can't help me then damn her!" he yelled in Rhowan's face, his full weight nearly pushing the dagger through her and into the ground beneath her. "I'll lift my own curse," he growled, spitting blood onto the dying priestess. "*The Tome of Enlightenment* showed me how."

"No!" Katja cried. She tried to crawl away through the bloody snow, but the raging Keeper turned his fury to her next. She recoiled and tried to escape his grasp, but he caught her leg and pulled her to him.

"Daemus will come for your acolyte," he spat, still speaking to the high priestess. "And when he does, they'll both perish."

Rhowan's dying eyes flittered at Katja and she tried to speak, but blood oozed from her lips instead. Her body flailed one last time.

Graytorris leapt from Katja onto Persephone's body, leaning into her face. "Inches from the healing powers of your Ancient's waters," he teased and pointed for the dying priestess. "The well could save your life. Alas, you will never reach it."

He waited, a cold stare of empty eyes into the face of the high priestess until he was sure she was dead. When she drew her final breath, he kicked her lifeless body into the lake.

A plume of red mist rose around her, polluting the pool with a cloud of her blood. Katja began to weep, reaching for her high priestess, her body convulsing in a string of emotions that she no longer controlled.

"Master, what is your command?" Zinzi asked, her demeanor chillingly calm. "Daemus will come for her."

Graytorris struggled back to his feet, his resolve seemingly returned to him. "Let him. We'll be ready."

"Shall we return to the cathedral?" Zinzi asked.

"Once I recover," he replied. "When we return, retrieve the potion as planned. There's no hope for me. It's time."

CHAPTER THIRTY

"There's a peace that can only be found
on the other side of war."
—Anoki, Athabasica the Poet

VORODIN MOVED TO THE center of the courtyard in front of the Faye Tree. He sat on a curved bench that looked as old as he did. Addilyn took a seat next to him as the sounds of the birds and the babbling brook returned.

"I met a tetrine that spoke to me, mind to mind," Addilyn began, her voice tentative. "A mare with two horns. She imparted a vision to me of sorts. I suppose it was different from the visions that Daemus has. It felt like more of a memory, but one I hadn't experienced myself."

"And what did the mare show you?" Vorodin asked. His eyes were mild.

"One of her herd had been captured, falling under the spell of a man in dark robes. She arrived too late to stop it. I think she wanted me to help."

"There's only one tetrine that has two horns, Addilyn," Vorodin explained. "It hasn't been seen for several millennia, perhaps for as long as it's been since I've heard the ancient elven language of Melexis spoken aloud. Your story doesn't surprise me."

"What is she, then? And why did she reveal herself to me?"

"She's the mother of the tetrine and the first of her line," Vorodin stood for a moment and stretched his old bones, then walked toward the Faye Tree, taking a seat on one of its thick branches. "At least, that's what the legends tell us. She was the steed for Melexis herself before the goddess departed for the Hall of the Ancients."

"And she still lives?" Daemus asked.

"It's said, young Daemus, that she maintains some connection with the elven goddess—even to this day." Vorodin's brows raised, and he turned to the young Keeper. "Perhaps that's what you experienced, Princess. The mare's name is SamaraShay, and Melexis left her here, in the realm of Warminster, to tend to her tetrine in a place called the Andarynne Fields. The fields are not fare from here, just south of the Eternal Forest, near what's known today as Deadwaters Fork."

"I see," Addilyn's eyes widened in amazement.

"It is also why they often appear to elves," he continued. "They're known for delivering warnings to all, but more so to the Vermilion. The Vermilion are the first race of elves, as she's of the first line of tetrine. You, Princess, are linked from the heavens." He spread his arms and glanced up, then returned his gaze to Addilyn.

Addilyn's face stilled and her eyes intensified in recognition. "And that's why she showed herself to *me*?"

"You're a Vermilion princess," Vorodin continued. "You're next in the line of succession."

"Do her portents mean that Coronelle Fia will die?" Addilyn's face turned sour.

"No." Vorodin offered a friendly smile. "But you asked why she chose you."

"Then why did she reveal herself to me as far away as the Dragon's Breath Mountains?"

Vorodin stood and walked to Ritter, putting a friendly hand on his shoulder. "Usually, the tetrine appear where the crisis will be." His face became serious. "They foretell of the coming of great despair. In your case, Warminster's civil war, the calamity at the cathedral, and the kidnapping of one of her herd are all linked. And her warning tells us the true threat rises in the Dragon's Breaths, not in Foghaven Vale or Solemnity."

"What of the hidden conspiracy surrounding Thronehelm?" Ritter asked.

"Wars and struggles are common to Warminster, my dear Valkeneer," Vorodin explained. "Your family should know that more than most. But tell me this: what would make the leader of all the tetrine, one who hasn't been seen in thousands of years, appear in the Dragon's Breaths? Something greater than just a war, I'd wager."

"The cloaked man?" Addilyn guessed.

"Ah, now you've put your finger on it," Vorodin replied. "Why would one seek to steal a tetrine from her herd? How would they know where to find one of the most elusive creatures in all of Warminster and where it would appear at that exact moment?"

"To be honest," Addilyn said, shaking her head, "it clearly didn't want to be seen. The man used magic to lure it. But he seemed to know where it was and when it would be there. He was ready for it."

"The tetrine appear to us, not the other way around," Vorodin added, coaxing the group. "Think."

"Perhaps the man used magic to divine its location by magical means?" Daemus offered. "Some of our Keepers can use the Sight to find people or places by predicting future events. It's not so uncommon among us, but rare to the rest of the realm."

"What did the man look like?" Vorodin asked.

"It was night," Addilyn recalled. "He was cloaked, so I couldn't tell."

"What would someone want with a tetrine?" Faux weighed in, her hands on her hips.

Addilyn's shoulders raised at the question. "He rode away on it. He made it his steed."

"Who would hunt a tetrine to do that?" Faux went on. "Seems like a lot of trouble for a horse, albeit a special one."

"Helenius?" Blue suggested. "So the song goes."

"This wasn't Helenius," Addilyn replied.

"What about its horn?" Tuttle asked. "Isn't that the source of its magic?"

"Yes," Vorodin answered.

Addilyn lifted her gaze to old wizard. "But if he sought the tetrine for its horn, what purpose could the horn serve?"

"I believe Master Tuttle could answer that," Vorodin replied, staring back at the alchemist. "Your hold in your hands a book that your friend Helenius died to uncover."

Tuttle scrambled through his pack to retrieve the book on the tetrine that Helenius had used and that the Scion had retrieved for him. He flipped quickly through the pages, searching for answers.

"Helenius was on to something," Tuttle confirmed. "This book says the horn can be used for many things. It can be fashioned into a wand to enhance spells, a magical tip on a longspear, or as an ingredient in rare potions, including one that can be used by a necromancer to create a metamorphosis of some kind. The book offers few details on this change, so far as I can tell. I'll need to study it further."

"A necromancer?" Daemus lamented.

"Graytorris," Ritter said, despair dripping from his words. "Coronel Briar spoke of Graytorris using necromantic spells to create his Antlered Man."

"And Ghostwood," Daemus put in.

"Ghostwood sits in the Dragon's Breaths," Vorodin observed.

"What does it mean, then?" Faux asked. "Was Graytorris

the cloaked figure that captured the tetrine to steal its horn? Is the tetrine dead?"

"By the Ancients, I hope not," Addilyn replied.

"There's a mysterious cult, long-forgotten, that used to roam the Dragon's Breaths," Vorodin went on, his eyes now distant. "They worshipped cryptids like the tetrine, among others. They're known as the Moor Bog."

"Do they still exist?" Ritter asked.

"I don't know," the wise elf replied.

"In my visions," Daemus said, "I've always seen Graytorris emerging from the mountains, hidden by fog, and reaching for something behind me in the cathedral. When the Great Keeper told me of his curse, she said he was a child of Foghaven Vale. Perhaps the Mountains indicate the Dragon's Breaths, the fog is a sign of Von Lormarck and *The Tome of Enlightenment* is the item he sought to steal?"

A smile grew across Vorodin's face. "Yes, my Keeper friend. If Graytorris grew up in Krahe, he'd likely know of the Von Lormarck family. If he's stolen the Tome from your cathedral and needs the tetrine's horn for this metamorphosis, perhaps he also used his power of the Sight to foretell of the coming of the tetrine? If he knew he would someday need its horn, of course."

"So, you're suggesting that the fallen Keeper has sided with Von Lormarck?" Ritter asked.

"And the Moor Bog," Vorodin added. "It's possible that they wanted the tetrine as much as he needed the horn. And if a tetrine offers its horn freely, it will grow back. If it's taken by force, the creature will die. The Moor Bog would never allow such a fate for one of their *honored beasts*."

"Graytorris is cursed by my Ancient," Daemus reminded the group. "How does a horn help him?"

"He may be seeking to change his form as Tuttle's book suggests," Faux suggested. "From what you say, he's unhealthy and blind. This ingredient, along with others, may help him to achieve this change."

"What does he seek to change into?" Ritter asked.

"A lich," Tuttle mumbled aloud, his eyes still buried in the old book. He'd been fumbling through its pages while the others were debating. He removed his spectacles and cleaned them on his sleeve, seemingly unaware that he was doing so. His face was red, and he wiped his brow.

"A lich?" Faux asked, looking around at the others. "Aren't they just a myth?"

"A lich is a creature of death," Vorodin explained. "It's a form necromancers can take to sustain their lives indefinitely in undeath. It takes the skills of a powerful wizard and the right potion to poison themselves while maintaining enough power to rise again."

" 'The lich's potion must contain the ground horn of a tetrine,' among other elements," Tuttle read aloud.

The group took a moment for the gravity of their discoveries to sink in. Their eyes scanned each other for fear and doubt.

"If Graytorris is a great necromancer, why does he need the Moor Bog?" Daemus asked.

"The more important question is, what's he giving to the Moor Bog in return?" Vorodin replied. "If the Moor Bog has returned after these many years, what could a necromancer give them in return for the horn of a tetrine?"

"What could a cryptid-worshipping cult want?" Faux asked.

"That's something you must learn," Vorodin stated as a matter of fact. "But it appears that if we're correct, there may be a greater plot unfolding than we know."

"Would SamaraShay know?" Addilyn asked. "Perhaps she

could help. And if they've stolen one of her herd, we need to find her and rescue her lost stallion."

"SamaraShay revealed herself to you, Addilyn," Vorodin reminded her. "It seems obvious that she did that so you could gather the forces of Warminster to ward off the coming calamity. Only the Vermilion command the attention of all races."

"I've failed her, then." Addilyn's voice swirled with desperation. "We've been on the run and taking far too long to help her. What if the stallion is already dead?"

Vorodin gently turned Addilyn's gaze back to him with his hand on her cheek.

"Nothing is lost, child," he assured her. "This great battle has just begun."

"Is this a greater warning than any other they've given?" Addilyn asked, seized by the anxiety of the historic moment.

"Perhaps," Vorodin answered, "but I'd think she and her kind would have the powers to find and rescue one of their own. Remember, they travel where and when they want to."

ARJUN LAY NEXT TO Anoki, still dizzy from the impossible day he was having. Anoki's exotic perfume certainly wasn't helping matters. But it was a good feeling, and he couldn't believe his love dozed in his arms.

A knock broke them from their musings, and Millen Bane entered without pause, followed by another man. Anoki held a silken sheet about her to hide her nakedness.

"Forgive me, Athabasica." Bane turned his gaze away. "But the Knights of the Maelstrom are at the gates, looking for Daemus."

"And who's this?" the Athabasica asked, looking at the other man, clad in wind-worn armor.

The Knight bowed. "I am Danton Hague, Captain of the Knights of the Maelstrom."

"He comes in peace," Bane replied. "But the others with him do not."

Arjun sat up and reached for his katana at the edge of the pillow bed. He glared at the captain.

"I am not with the rest of my troops," Hague promised. "I am here to help Daemus Alaric. There's been an insurrection, Athabasica."

Arjun rushed to put his clothes back on while Anoki got dressed from behind a screen.

"We know of Daemus. What has happened, Captain? Tell me now," Anoki ordered.

"A man named Graytorris has taken control of the Cathedral of the Watchful Eye. He was excommunicated decades ago and has somehow returned to seize power and now seeks the return of the young Keeper. Although I travel with my aerie, I can't allow that to happen."

"Graytorris?" Arjun's eyes narrowed in rage. "We were sent here to stop him." He fastened his armor and slung his sword over his back.

Hague's gaze shifted to Arjun. "How do you know him?"

Arjun offered a slight nod. "Daemus has told us about the man from his dreams."

"Then we, too, are allied." Hague removed his riding gloves and stepped closer to Anoki. "I'm not part of the insurrection. Away from my ears, they label me a traditionalist. We seek to restore the true Sight to our cathedral, and we need Daemus to do it."

"Will your Knights not be suspicious of your absence?" Arjun peered into the man's eyes, looking for some clue of false intent.

"I told them that we are here in peace," Hague explained. "I told them an aerie of fifty gryphs and Knights from the cathedral landing in the center of a foreign town without warning would be seen as an act of aggression."

Bane's tone told the story. "I assure you, Captain, it would have."

"My second-in-command is not an accommodating man and already suspects my true intentions. I cannot stay long, but I did buy some time to warn you."

"What do you plan to do?" Arjun asked.

Hague looked to Bane. "Knight Castellan, follow me to the wall and announce that you will handle the search for Alaric. Tell them a force like ours isn't welcomed and to wait outside the city walls until you find the young Keeper."

Bane raised an eyebrow. "And when we don't *find* Alaric?"

"I will order the aerie to fly north away from the gates as a sign of peace," Hague continued. "For now. That should buy you enough time to get him out of the city."

"Ready your forces, Knight Castellan," the Athabasica ordered. "And summon the Horn of Ramincere to defend Abacus. I fear these men will betray their captain if this ruse fails."

The Knight Castellan bowed. "As you command, Athabasica."

"And the Keeper?" she asked.

"Safe, for now." Bane cocked his head in the direction of the library. "Still in Vorodin's Lair. I escorted him there myself."

The Athabasica leaned over and kissed Arjun passionately before slinging her sword across her back.

"Dashiel!" she yelled.

"Yes?" a voice replied from an adjacent room.

"Fetch me my old armor from the High Aldin. It's time to put down my quill and pick up my sword."

CHAPTER THIRTY-ONE

*"Her waters flow black, a toxin bubbling from
the cauldron of the sisters of Threnody."*
—Entry from the Diary of Anselm Helenius

DAEMUS PEERED OUT OF the front door of the library,
looking for the knight castellan. Instead, he found only two
guards left, waiting for them in the square.

"Where's Bane?" Faux asked.

"I'm not sure." Daemus scanned the piazza. "Perhaps there
was trouble?"

"If that were true, those guards would be standing inside
the library with us, warning us of danger." Addilyn slipped
down to a second window and looked to the rear of the library.

"Stay here." Ritter slid his way out through the doors toward
the guards. After a quick conversation, the Longmarcher
waved to the others, and they left the building to join him.

"The knight castellan was called away," Ritter said to the
group. "An aerie of hippogryphs bearing Knights from the
cathedral appeared at the gates. They demanded that Daemus
be turned over to them."

"Hippo-whats?" Blue Conney asked.

Daemus turned to his springheel friend and tried to
explain. "Hippogryphs are the flying steeds of the Knights of the
Maelstrom. They're winged horses. Well, part horse, part eagle."

"So how many gryphs and Knights are in an aerie?"
Marquiss asked.

"I don't know." Daemus looked to the skies for watching
eyes. "They must be here to help."

"Well, you do have the Sight," Addilyn offered. "I am
certain they want the connection of their Ancient returned

to their order."

"The guards said the Knights were prepared for battle." Ritter motioned in the direction of the Gatehouse. "Bane's been called away to address their captain."

Daemus's eyes rolled. "Battle? Ritter, are you sure?"

"Somethin' stinks," Blue said with a growl, "and in ain't my breath."

Ritter turned to the alchemist. "Jeric, if Bane is busy with them at the front gate, will you allow us to lay low at the Boiling Beaker until we receive word that all is safe? I believe Blue may be correct."

Tuttle nodded. "Of course."

"We'll escort you there," one of the guards offered. "And then we'll return to the Gatehouse and inform the knight castellan of your location."

Ritter started toward his horse. "Let's go, then. The longer we stand in the open, the greater the chance that we're spotted by the assassin."

The group mounted and rode at pace through the streets of Abacus with the Castellan guards leading the way. As they neared the Mistchapel Quarter, a shadow passed from overhead, and the young Keeper looked up to the skies. A single rider on the back of a gryph circled above. The guards pointed, and the group glanced up, into the sun.

"It's a rider from the cathedral." Daemus's voice was hopeful, and he urged his steed ahead into the Mephisto Quad and stopped in front of the Boiling Beaker. The gryph and its rider descended, and with a batting of wings, he and the others shielded their faces from the spiraling dust that washed over them. The guards at his side drew their swords but Daemus motioned for them to steady themselves. When the rider came to a stop, Daemus lifted his gaze to see his old cloistermate,

Caspar Luthic dismounting. He couldn't help but smile.

"Daemus!" Caspar called, running over to hug him.

Daemus's face contorted in confusion and happiness, and he returned the hug, his expression softening. "Caspar?"

"I'm so glad you are safe." Caspar stepped back and looked him over.

"How did you find me?"

Caspar pointed to his gryph. "Eyes of an eagle. We spotted you from the air. Precept Radu snuck me out and told me to find you in Abacus. The cathedral needs you."

"*Snuck you out?* Daemus's mood changed, and he bit at his lip, trying to steel his nerves for what may come next. "What happened? How did you get a gryph?"

"Radu and I stole him from the stables just before they locked the campus down." His voice was almost proud, then his tone changed and became serious. "I escaped, but he stayed behind."

"Escaped?"

"I don't know how to say this..." Caspar's countenance morphed, and he looked for a second at his feet before lifting his gaze to his friend. "Graytorris has returned. And he dons the mantle of the Great Keeper."

Daemus drew a deep breath. His heart sank and images of the haunted man from his dreams flooded back to him.

"H—how?" Daemus's voice quivered, and he swallowed hard.

Caspar stilled. "I don't know. But Precept Radu asked I bring you back to Solemnity. Those who follow Nasyr's teachings have been silenced."

"What of First Keeper Amoss? Does he live?"

Caspar winced. "Amoss was sent to replace First Keeper Jhodever of Foghaven Vale, who's now the First Keeper of the Cathedral.

"Jhodever?" Addilyn stole a glance at Ritter and Jessamy. "That explains much of what transpired at Thronehelm."

It had made little sense to the young Keeper in pieces, but before him Erud's message was clear. Graytorris's arm reaching beyond him in his nightmares, seeking vengeance on the Keepers, was all but complete. *He* was the last piece of the puzzle. He looked to his cloistermate, his countenance rigid. "We must stop him, Caspar."

"We should go inside," Ritter tilted his head toward the Beaker. "The assassin may be watching. The gryph's landing was not subtle."

The group dismounted and they entered the blue confines the Boiling Beaker. The two castellan guards remained outside and flanked the outer doors.

"I have something else to tell you," Caspar continued once they were inside. "Graytorris was aided by Baron Von Lormarck. He sent a kidnapped woman, a healer of sorts. She's being held prisoner in the cathedral. Radu told me that you know her."

"A healer?" Daemus muttered. He grabbed at his stomach as he reached the unsettling conclusion. "No—Katja."

"Who?" Blue asked.

"The woman who healed us in Forecastle." Faux threw a sisterly arm around Daemus's shoulder.

Daemus felt the attempt at comfort, but his head hung with guilt and a forlorn look crawled onto his face. He slumped into a chair. "It's my fault she's been taken. It's *always* my fault. Uncle Kester, Chernovog and Burgess… Delling, and now her."

"We can get her." Caspar approached Daemus and bent by him. "Radu has a plan to rescue her and take the cathedral back. Come with me and Syl. We'll fly back together."

"Who's Syl?"

"It's my gryph," Caspar replied with an innocent yet odd glance. "I named him after my old dog, Sylvain."

"You can't fly out of here," Ritter warned, stepping closer to the conversation. He appeared nervous. "There's an aerie of Knights from your cathedral here. They'll hunt you down in the air."

"How do you know this?" Caspar turned from Daemus to the Longmarcher and rose from his crouch. "Syl and I saw only clear skies."

"We can't stay here," Daemus insisted. "She needs us, Ritter!"

Ritter's dark eyes hardened. "The *realm* needs you. By going back, that's what he wants."

Daemus turned away and rubbed the back of his neck, trying to calm himself. The others broke into a muffled debate in front of him, but his mind had left their conversation, tumbling in fits of anger, guilt and disbelief.

"I can't stand around and let her die," he said at length, drawing an end to the discussion around him. "I must return for her. I must."

"We will." Faux leaned over Daemus, reassuring him. "But let's first get out of Abacus."

"What's that?" Marquiss pointed to the roof. Addilyn's elven ears twitched too, and then Daemus finally heard a sound growing in the distance. It was too far away to hear clearly, but it sounded like flags in a windstorm.

"By the Ancients." Blue walked to the storefront and glanced up as the guards outside came through the door and locked it.

"They're here," one announced through a muffled visor. "From the skies."

Daemus looked at the springheel, his face turning desperate. "It's the Knights of the Maelstrom." He shuddered as the deafening noise grew closer. "They've come for me."

The echoing of a hundred wings descended on Mephisto Quad as the gryphs circled to a crowded landing outside the Boiling Beaker. The windows shook and rattled in their sills and the door breathed harshly in and out against the vacuum created by the beating of their wings. Dust from the street splashed against the blue glass, pluming around the side of the Beaker. Tuttle held his ears and Daemus ducked behind a shelf.

The gryphs galloped to a stop, filling most of the Quad. Daemus could hear people scrambling away and voices calling to others to run.

"They must have seen my approach from the air." Caspar ran his hands through his hair, his eyes wide. "I left Syl in the open, too."

"What's going on?" Marquiss asked, inching his way closer to the front door and drawing his sword.

"Some of the Knights are dismounting," Faux said from behind a bench, her steel ready in her hand. "One of them's coming this way."

"Daemus, I'm sorry I led them here." Caspar began to shake, a hushed panic seizing him.

"No need to whisper, son." Blue turned to the Low Keeper. "They know we're here."

"It's Danton Hague." Ritter readied his bow from a corner. "I recognize him from the Caveat."

"Shh… listen." Addilyn held her hands out, signaling for the group to quiet.

The Beaker fell silent.

"Hague is telling someone he'll try and trick us into going peacefully." Her brow furrowed and her eyes peeked into the Quad. "He's explaining that he knows Daemus and that Daemus trusts him. I can also hear people calling for the Castellan."

"Thank the Ancients, but the Castellan better hurry." Ritter moved to the second level of the Beaker to get a sniper's view. "We can't handle fifty trained Knights on our own, let alone their steeds."

Hague approached the door while his Knights dismounted and fanned out, surrounding the building.

"I see your bow, Valkeneer," Hague called from outside. "And your sword, Dauldon. I come in peace. May I enter?"

"Throw down your sword and you may enter," Ritter called.

"I won't become a hostage." Hague raised his empty hands in a gesture of peace.

"Like Katja Seitenwind?" Daemus cried. "Your leader takes hostages. Why shouldn't we do the same?"

"I don't want any blood spilled," Hague called back. "Especially among friends. The cathedral needs you, Keeper."

"You can keep your sword," Ritter called. "But if you unsheathe it, you'll be the first casualty of this battle."

"Deal." Hague kept his hands wide and approached. "May I enter?"

"Slowly." Faux's determined face showed little room for mercy.

Hague opened the door and stood among the pointed swords and arrows. He scanned the room until he found Daemus. "They've come for you Keeper, but I'm here to help."

"We know what help you bring," Addilyn scowled. "I heard your intentions from across the Quad."

"The Beaker is surrounded, but I'm with you." Hague bowed to Daemus and took a knee. "Graytorris has taken the cathedral, but I came here to protect you. You're the only Keeper possessing the Sight. Erud blesses you, Low Keeper. I'm here as a sworn Knight of the Maelstrom—a loyal knight of Erud's endless knowledge. And you have my sword."

Daemus leaned away from the Knight. His eyes filled with

doubt, yet something in Hague's manner gave him hope. "I want to trust you. But how can I?"

"The Knights want to take you back to Graytorris, but I can't allow that." Hague's eyes were desperate. "We're going to have to fight our way out of here."

"Fighting is illegal in the city," Jeric murmured from behind the counter.

"Then it is time for us to become outlaws." Captain Danton Hague drew his sword and turned to face his own Knights.

———✦———

A TENSE MOMENT HAD passed, and Ritter watched through the second-floor window as Hague left the Boiling Beaker as planned and stood just outside the doorway.

"Do you have the Keeper?" one of Hague's men called from his saddle.

"Yes." Hague took a few steps toward the aerie of knights and gryphs. "But you can't have him."

"I knew it was only a matter of time with you, Hague," his subordinate answered with a scowl. He looked to the men at his flank. "Knights, it appears that our captain is a traitor. He's sided with the banished Keeper. Arm yourselves."

The sound of fifty swords hissing at once, as the knights unsheathed their weapons, sounded to Ritter like a serpent's tongue, warning its enemies it was about to strike.

"Surrender, Captain," the man ordered, pointing his sword from his steed.

Ritter closed his eyes and connected to Storm. The falcon twitched and Ritter opened the window. Storm flew out of the Beaker and into the sky. The Knights in the Quad glanced at it and then looked back at the captain.

Hague took a few courageous steps into the street, and he was soon flanked by Marquiss, Jessamy, Blue Conney, and

Jericho. Ritter drew the string of his silent bow and somewhere behind him, he felt the magic emanating from Addilyn's hands.

Hague looked back at the Beaker and cracked a half smile, and then his lips flattened into a defiant line when he looked back at his lieutenant. "I won't surrender."

The knight slipped off his saddle, the clanking of his plate mail echoing across the Quad.

"I've waited for my chance at you for a long time, Captain." The soldier raised his visor and sneered.

"Come, then Lorraine," Hague snarled. Then he signaled to Uriah and Jeric inside the Beaker and shouted, "Now!"

From the second story windows, Uriah Loring and Jeric Tuttle launched glass vials into the crowd of gryphs. The bottles cracked on the streets and exploded in flashes, releasing billowing smoke in all directions.

The aerie of gryphs screeched at the popping sounds, some lifting off or smacking into one another, trying to fly from the Quad. Several spooked gryphs launched from the square in protest, while others squawked and batted their wings, pushing the smoke in all directions. The force from their wings knocked several of the knights to the ground. Even Ritter had to duck when the force of their eagle wings rattled the windows in their casings.

He took a deep breath and spun Silencer, looking for his first target. The Quad filled with the obscuring mist, which persisted even in the face of the billowing gryphs. Uriah had said the magic would hold against the strongest of gusts, but Ritter hadn't believed it.

He glanced down to the street and watched Faux sneak out of the Beaker with Daemus and Caspar as planned, using the cover of the smoke to conceal their exit. He knew that the rest of them would be sorely outnumbered, but the Keeper's escape was of the utmost importance.

The first of the Knights charged in from the magical clouds of smoke, but Ritter unleashed his silent arrows, felling three Knights before they could reach Hague. The fourth Knight to emerge escaped the Longmarcher's aim and ran headlong into Hague's shield. Hague pivoted quickly and swung at the stunned Knight, cutting him to the ground.

From the corner of his eye, Ritter saw Jessamy wading into the fog, only for him to hear the scream of more Knights falling to her blade.

Blue Conney used the distraction to jump onto his war dog, and the two charged into battle. He heard the dog growling and tearing, followed by the sound of its teeth cutting through armor and the springheel's voice in a war cry as they dashed through the fog. Then another Knight emerged in front of him but was cut down by Marquiss's keen blade.

For a second, Ritter thought Hague had no one else to fight, but then he heard screaming from Hague's lieutenant, "The Keeper! Get the Keeper!"

Ritter turned to see a dozen more Knights chasing after Daemus, and the hurried flapping of giant wings sounded from above. Hague and his lieutenant met in a violent collision, shield bouncing off shield and swords clanging off each other's armor. Hague spun and managed to keep his feet. He coughed in the persistent smoke and raised his visor to get a better look at his assailant.

Ritter trained his bow on the lieutenant but knew he didn't have a clean shot. He was too close to Hague to risk it.

Hague's enemy circled like a hyena on the prowl and then leapt at him. Again, the two banged away at each other, only to dent shields and armor. Three more Knights emerged from the chaos and headed for them. The captain fell back into a low, defensive posture.

Ritter had to help.

He nocked an arrow and let loose, striking one Knight on the hip. The man cried and spun back into the fog. Ritter couldn't wait to see if he'd survived the shot and drew back on Silencer one more time. His arrow leapt from his bow and sliced through the second Knight's gorget, impaling the man in the neck. His target fell hard onto his knees, grabbing at the arrow, but the shaft had buried itself deep and the dying Knight could only swipe at the feathers before collapsing.

But the third Knight broke through their defenses and rammed into Hague's shield, giving his lieutenant time to strike. He wasted no time and slashed at Hague, finding an opening between his thigh and calf.

Hague screamed and pushed off on his good leg and connected with his second-in-command, knocking him to the ground.

As Ritter aimed to strike, a blanket of smoke from their alchemist allies rolled in, and he lost sight of the two men. He cursed, but Addilyn stepped up beside him.

"Irris Vohl!" she called in the conjurer's tongue, then exhaled. The simple act shattered the glass in the window, her hands crackling with a white-hot magical hale. She pointed at her target and the magic rushed from her palms, searing into the knight that had aided his lieutenant.

The Knight screamed as the evocation took effect, his armor warping and melting into his flesh. He tugged at the metal skin in a panic as steam rose around him but was too late. He fell flat, rolling and helpless against the scorching armor, until he stilled at Hague's feet.

The lieutenant used the moment of distraction to disengage, chasing after Daemus.

Ritter lowered his bow. His trollborn eyes tracked rivulets of blood racing down Hague's thigh. He knew the wound was mortal.

Ritter leapt from the window at Hague, even though it was too late. The captain slumped to the ground, a torrent of blood gushing from a gaping wound.

The Knights' captain fell to his knees, not bothering to react to the wound. He leaned on his sword, trying to hold himself up for long enough to see Daemus escape through the remaining whisps of the fog. His eyes darkened, and he mumbled a short prayer to Erud, then he collapsed.

"Captain!" Addilyn cried and reached to help, but the captain was gone.

A screech of terror echoed in Ritter's skull. His eyes, no longer his, left the image of the dying Hague and paired with Storm above. The shifting view nearly dropped him to his knees, but he'd never felt Storm's connection so intense.

He shook off the effect of the transition and his sight adjusted to the war falcon's. Circling above, his avian eyes fixed on the Quad below. Atop a nearby roof, his eyes trained onto two figures, one nocking an arrow for a shot below. It was the Bone elf!

Ritter realized he had no time to react. With a mental command, he sent Storm one thought: Attack!

The falcon descended with the speed of one of Ritter's arrows, diving at the Bone elf with no regard for itself. Ritter had stolen the falcon's instincts, controlling him with his mind while he watched the assault through Storm's eyes.

He saw the sniper draw down on their position, looking at himself on the ground. Before the Bone elf could take a shot, the assassin noticed Storm appear from the camouflage of the rising smoke and turned away. Storm's talons hit their mark anyway and it tore at the sniper.

The man cried out in pain as Storm ripped ribbons of flesh from his face. The falcon's wings batted against the man's head, struggling to stay aflight. Ritter could feel the feral attack, his blood pumping in time with Storm. His own hands clawed up, and he stood rigid, commanding Storm to kill… just kill!

The sniper dropped his bow to the rooftop and ducked, swiping blindly at Storm with his hands. At first Storm pressed the assault but the man's strength forced it to disengage. It flew out over the rooftop and looked back, where Ritter saw into the bloodied countenance of the assassin. Sitting next to him was the gray imp creature he thought he'd killed at the naval battle in Castleshire's harbor. The imp's face twisted in hatred, and it launched itself from the roof, chasing after Storm.

The break gave Ritter a few precious seconds to recover.

"Assassin!" Ritter yelled at Addilyn. He left the connection with Storm and pushed the princess toward the safety of an alley.

The others took Ritter's cue and darted away behind him.

He hugged the front part of the wall and looked at Addilyn, who pressed herself against another wall across the street from him.

"The Bone elf!" he cried, nocking one of his arrows. He tried to reconnect with Storm, but his mind was jumbled. He could hear the bird squawking in his ears but had lost his shared vision.

He looked up, trying to sight in the assassin from his position against the wall, but the man had moved. He scanned the rooftop but found nothing from his position. He drew a deep, calming breath and closed his eyes, concentrating on his connection with Storm.

Their shared vision returned, and he found himself peering into the black eyes of the imp. He nearly gasped and ducked away as if he was there himself but managed to stay connected.

Storm and the imp spun in a barrel roll, engaged in a in a life-and-death battle. The creature's talons slashed at Storm, tearing at feathers, but the war falcon squawked—and with its sharp beak, bit down on the imp's bulbous nose.

Ritter tasted the vile blood of the creature in his own mouth and heard an unworldly, keening scream in his ears as the creature let go of the war falcon. It hovered inches away, its dark wings beating, and its taloned hands grabbing at its gushing nose.

"Fly," Ritter commanded, and Storm broke away from the stunned imp, pushing off into the sky again. Ritter needed him to find the assassin but knew from personal experience the imp was almost as deadly.

Their combined vision held, the bird ascending and turning back, as the imp recovered and pursued. Ritter nocked an arrow, searching and hoping to line up a shot. He watched himself from afar, on the ground below, a disorienting view at best. His hands warmed with the magical hale emanating from Silencer. He pulled his string and let his arrow fly. The shot arced from his bow, and he watched through Storm's eyes as the arrow approached.

His aim was true and ripped through one of the creature's wings. The imp whelped in pain and spiraled down, its wing torn, and crashed onto the far rooftop. The wound smoked and crackled, as the creature writhed in pain.

Ritter commanded Storm to circle higher, gaining altitude, trying to stay away from the range of the assassin's bow. The man was injured, but not out of the fight.

From the remaining fog below, an arrow veered by Storm, close enough that Ritter swore he could see the black rose etched into its shaft. Hitting a rising target cloaked in a magical fog was a one-in-a-million shot, and the assassin almost had him.

Storm surged higher and looped away. But now Ritter knew where the Bone elf was. He'd revealed his new position.

Ritter nocked a second arrow and waited. He blinked and broke the connection with Storm to refocus on the elf. He was looking for the crown of his head peeking over the rooftop. He needed inches, not feet. But the assassin surprised him and stood up before running back to his original position. He wasn't ready for such a brash move, and his shot soared harmlessly wide.

"Run!" he cried to Addilyn, knowing that if the man passed the alley from the roof, she'd be exposed.

She turned to Ritter as he heard the shot. Addilyn winced as an arrow exploded against the stone building beside her, casting shards into her face. She ducked back and Ritter returned his gaze to the rooftop, but the man was gone.

"The store!" he cried. "While he's moving!"

He scanned for his target while Addilyn headed back for the relative safety of the Boiling Beaker. Jessamy trailed her, but then Ritter saw the assassin's shadow on the ground.

It was too late.

Somehow, he had made it from the rooftop to the street in seconds, perhaps through the same spell that had launched him from the walls of Thronehelm.

Ritter stared at the man, who stared back at him.

Time seemed to slow, as they both raised their bows in unison, arrows nocked and fixed on each other. Ritter didn't have time to cringe or to wait for the hot slice of the Black Rose's arrow cutting into him. His only thought was of Addilyn—and if taking an arrow to save her life meant she'd escape, so be it. He could die knowing he'd killed the Black Rose while saving his beloved.

Fair trade.

They both released their drawstrings, twin shadows of each other. In near synchronicity, the arrows leapt from their bows, speeding at their targets. Every instinct in Ritter told him to move, but he couldn't. Moving may cause him to miss. This shot was to be his last. He heard his father's voice echoing in his ears. *"May your arrows fly true."*

He waited for the arrow's sting.

In an explosion of metal and wood, their arrows collided in midair, shattering, and sending shards of broken shafts and arrowheads to the ground.

The two marksmen looked incredulously at one another for the briefest of moments, glaring at their own mirror images. Ritter swore he could feel the anger of the Black Rose reaching out for him from across the street.

The sound of rushing horses interrupted their standoff. Ritter and the assassin both turned to see a charge of two dozen armored men astride barded war horses roaring around the bend.

Ritter blinked. The Castellan had arrived.

Led by cries from the knight castellan, Millen Bane led a phalanx of soldiers, his magical golden mace held high.

Ritter felt the hale of Peacemaker's magic engulf him. A wave of warm serenity pulsed through his veins, washing away his instinct to fight. His eyes fixated on Peacemaker, glinting in the Abacunian sun, and he knew that somehow the strength of the mighty weapon was bringing the battle to an end. He lowered Silencer.

Ritter's gaze fell back to the assassin. At first, he wasn't sure if the Bone elf felt the mace's effects, but the Black Rose stood still, his bow held at his hip. He didn't reach for another arrow.

He turned, and Ritter could see the damage Storm had done to his ashen face. Even from across the street, he could see the hole through the assassin's cheek, the side of his jaw exposed with a row of teeth protruding through. It was as though he was staring at a decomposing corpse. Black blood trickled from his face.

The man appeared to fight the urge to raise his bow, struggling against the powers of the mace, but all he could do was glare at Ritter, boring venomous holes into his archenemy from afar.

"I'll take her from you," the Black Rose cried, gargling through a mouth full of blood. Ritter could see his tongue through the torn flesh of his face.

"This isn't over," Ritter called back. "I will hunt you until the end of days."

The Bone elf turned, a crooked smile appearing on his bloody visage, and ran down the alley, away from the effects of the mace. Away from Ritter's beloved Vermilion princess.

———✦———

DAEMUS RUSHED DOWN THE side alleys, losing his way in the winding streets of Mistchapel Quarter. Caspar followed a few steps behind while Faux had taken the lead. She turned down several side streets to lose their pursuers, but no matter how fast they ran, the Knights kept pace.

Daemus's lungs burned, and his heart pumped with adrenaline. He looked over his shoulders and saw a pack of Knights bearing down on him. He gritted his teeth and kept sprinting, his labored breathing nearly deafening out the sounds of the Abacunian streets. But he could still hear their armor jingling as they ran after him.

"They're gaining on us," he managed, but Faux ignored his warning and shot to the left and through an open door that led into a butchery.

"Wait for me!" Caspar cried, and Daemus grabbed his friend by the arm and tugged him inside.

He slammed the door and jammed it closed. The three

jumped over tables and skirted around corners, their boots slipping on the wet floor, which was covered with fat. Daemus could hear the rear door being kicked in and knew the Knights were still hot on their trail.

"This way!" Faux waved, and the three made their way into the front of the store, dashing past patrons and through the open door onto the main street.

Daemus pressed on, looking back, and catching a glimpse of the Knights behind them.

He ran blindly into the street, stumbling, almost knocking Faux to the ground. She'd stopped, frozen at the sight of their predicament.

They were surrounded.

Gryphs with riders in their saddles lined both ends of the street, blocking every conceivable exit. To their rear, armor clinked and clanged as their Knight pursuers drew closer.

"Stop, Keeper!" a voice called from the streets in front of him.

Daemus recognized the man as the lieutenant who'd quarreled with Hague in front of the Boiling Beaker. The man was bloodied but had survived the incident. He could only assume the worst for Hague.

He had no choice. There was nowhere to go.

Faux stood in front of Daemus, shielding him, and drew her sword. But they were in the middle of the open street. The Knights emerged from behind them in the butchery and stood only yards away.

"Put down your sword," the lieutenant ordered.

"Come and take it," Faux replied, undaunted.

The Knight jumped from his saddle and drew his sword.

"I shall," he grunted, and with a sarcastic smile and wink, he stepped toward her. Daemus noticed that the blade was slick with a black liquid. His first thoughts were of poison.

"Faux…" he warned, brandishing his mace.

"I see it." She dared not look back at Daemus, but as he approached, the other Knights dismounted and readied their weapons. They encircled the trio, offering no path of escape.

Faux lurched forward, but the Knight raised his hands, stopping the others from attacking.

The lieutenant grinned. "This one's mine." The rest of his troops relented and watched the two combatants size each other up.

Then they heard horses' hooves rounding the bend. Daemus turned to see Arjun and Anoki at the head of a makeshift cavalry charge, their swords drawn as they led two dozen guards of the Castellan.

He looked back to the Knights, who wasted no time engaging them. "Stop them!" the lieutenant cried, and the circle of Knights around Daemus turned away and charged at the onrushing guards from the High Aldin.

Steel rang in the streets, sounding like the doors to an open smithy, as the two waves of warriors crashed together. The gryphs turned to join their masters in the fight and galloped into the approaching lines of horses. Talons ripped through the chain mail barding of the horses while feathers flew as Castellan swords hacked into the gryphs.

A group of robed soldiers followed the horses into combat, their hands ablaze in a litany of spellcraft as they evoked attacks of spectacular magic. The hale of multiple mystical auras enveloped the street, their attacks focused on the hippogryphs. The creatures let out wails of pain and jumped back. Some took to the skies to escape while others were killed in their tracks. The muttering of the conjurer's tongue nearly drowned out the battle cries of the combatants, but Daemus didn't care.

His only thought was of escape.

"By the Ancients, who are they?" Caspar yelled. Daemus turned to see his friend struggling with a hand crossbow Blue Conney had given him at the Beaker.

"Just point it and fire!" Daemus hollered back over the din of metal on metal.

Caspar listened and discharged the weapon at an approaching Knight, its bolt piercing through his mail and dropping him from the saddle.

Daemus saw a second Knight coming at Caspar and jumped in front of his friend. The Knight's surcoat was on fire from one of the spells and he stumbled toward the Keeper, flailing uncontrollably.

Daemus closed his eyes and swung, connecting with the Knight's helmet with a gong and knocking him flat. Caspar breathed a quick sigh of relief as the giant shadow of a gryph fell over them.

"Look out!" Daemus cried. He dived to the ground as the gryph swooped by and landed, missing them by inches. He turned to swing his mace defensively.

"Daemus, no!" Caspar called. "It's Syl! It's my gryph!"

The two scrambled toward Syl, and the animal lowered itself, as if signaling for them to climb on. They darted for the gryph, but the lieutenant jumped in front of them. He shook his poisoned blade as if taunting them.

"You're going nowhere, Keeper, save for back to the Cathedral," he said. "Your fate awaits you."

Then a familiar voice rose from behind them.

"Daemus, get out of here." Arjun approached on foot, staring at the lieutenant.

Daemus looked at Arjun, whose gaze was steely and whose katana was already red with blood. The two men began to circle one another in an uneasy dance, gauging for weaknesses.

"You too, Dauldon." Arjun motioned with a dismissive wave of his sword, encouraging Faux to follow the Keepers.

"Arjun, I'm not—" Faux began.

"Go!" he yelled. Then he pointed to the lieutenant with the tip of his blade. "Let's finish this."

The two waded together, Arjun's katana in high guard as he connected with the Knight's blade. The poison splashed droplets of death on his face with the impact, and the two crossed swords again in multiple blocks and parries.

Daemus watched the battle from Syl's back as Caspar climbed into the saddle.

"There's no room for me," Faux said. "Just take off!"

"No!" Caspar said, leaning across to whisper in the gryph's ear. Syl let out an eagle's caw and one of the gryphs, no longer with its Knight, landed beside him.

"Get on!" Caspar demanded.

"How?" she asked, but she didn't waste time climbing into the saddle. The two beasts pushed off and leapt into the sky, their wings batting as they gained altitude.

Faux screamed in terror as the gryph lifted off, but she held on tight as they spiraled away.

"Where do we go?" Faux yelled. "What do we do?"

"To the cathedral," Daemus said over the rushing of wind. "To save Katja and the Keepers of the Forbidden."

ARJUN'S BLADE CUT AT the Knight's leg, but he countered with a low block and spun, clipping Arjun on the shoulder with his shield as he passed to the left. Lorraine was fast, nearly too agile for his armor, but the old captain of House Dauldon had a few tricks for him as well.

Arjun feinted right and came up against Lorraine's side,

only to spin back on the heel of his foot. The Knight took the bait and opened his stance. Arjun swiped inside the hollow of his shield and sliced at the man's forearm.

The Knight adjusted well, absorbing the blow and swinging down at Arjun's head. But Arjun twisted and flipped back into high guard, forcing Lorraine's venomous blade away with his own.

The two broke for a second, and Lorraine lunged at Arjun, lancing at his midsection. Arjun swept his feet back and swung his sword, connecting with the blade and barely keeping it from piercing through his armor.

The lieutenant wasted no time and spun himself this time, leading with a shield block and carrying the captain's blade up and away.

Arjun saw the next move and ducked from a wicked swing that cleared over his head. He recovered and rolled away into a crouch, holding his blade to the side to stop any counterattack. But the Knight kept coming and rushed in, his shield knocking Arjun flat on his back.

Arjun spun around, sweeping Lorraine's leg with his own and dropping him to the ground. They both rolled over onto their knees, but Arjun, armored only in studded leather, was quicker. He lunged forward.

His sword caught the top of the lieutenant's shield and careened past it. The tip slipped between his visor and his neck guard, sinking into Lorraine's throat. He could see the Knight's eyes widening in amazement at Arjun's speed, but then he fell to the ground, grabbing at the wound. Blood drained uncontrollably from under his visor, down the once white surcoat of the Knights of the Maelstrom.

Arjun took a breath and turned to face another when his left leg gave out and he fell to one knee. His eyes found Anoki, who was emerging from her melee and rushing to his side. He glanced down at his leg, which had gone numb. He'd been nicked by the toxic blade in the heat of battle. The poison from the sword had already started coursing through his veins. He hadn't felt the bite of steel or the sting of the poison.

He lifted his head again, his eyes struggling to focus and his ears hearing only the echoes of Anoki's cries as she rushed to his aid. Then everything swirled into blackness.

CHAPTER THIRTY-TWO

"In order for one's heart to open, it must first be broken."
—Illustra, the Ancient of Love

"URIAH!" RITTER SCREAMED AS he raced into the Boiling Beaker. "An antidote for poison! Now!"

The doors burst open as Tuttle struggled to lift the wounded Arjun by his shoulders while Marquiss hoisted his legs. Anoki and Blue Conney followed shortly thereafter. Anoki's eyes were wet with tears, which had turned pink from the blood that had spattered her face during the battle.

Ritter stood next to the springheel, who was tending to Jessamy and Addilyn's wounds but paid close attention to the chaos swirling around the captain. His first concern was Addilyn.

The old tinker lardal slid down the ladder from his perch on the second floor, where he'd been since the battle had begun.

"What kind?" he yelled.

"The wound is blackening," Tuttle cried. He hastened to turn the Beaker into a treatment room by clearing a few lab desks so they could lay the wounded captain on it. Different ingredients spilled to the floor with the pungent odor of an astringent mixed with moldy cheese.

"That doesn't help much," the lardal called, gathering a handful of bottles in the crook of his elbow, and rushing to the aid of the captain.

Uriah pushed his way past Anoki on his way to Arjun's leg. She stood there beside him, holding the wounded warrior's hand.

"Stay with me, my love." She squeezed his hand as though imparting some of her strength to him.

"Give him room," Tuttle urged.

"What is it?" Marquiss asked.

"Venom of the Abyss." Uriah shook his head.

"It's a potent poison," Tuttle explained, looking Anoki in the eyes. "You'll need to leave us. It's for your own good and for the captain's life."

"I'm never leaving him again," she declared.

Tuttle groaned and then turned to Uriah for help. "What do you need?"

"I need ambire," the lardal yelled. "Dissolve it in wine or water, whichever you find first."

"I have wine," Marquiss turned to rush away. "It's in the damned saddlebag."

"Water?" Anoki asked, her eyes searching desperately for the precious liquid.

Tuttle scaled the ladder to the second story and started rifling through the vials, barely reading the labels. Ritter and Addilyn scrambled to help, but Tuttle knew where to look. He found what he was looking for and slid down the ladder, hitting the floor in a sprint. He scrambled under the front desk and found himself a container of water, then darted back to Arjun. He poured water into a beaker and then turned to Uriah.

"How much?" Tuttle asked.

"I don't know," the lardal's bushy eyebrows raised, as he cut torn strands of leather from Arjun's leg.

"What do you mean, you don't know?" Blue barked.

"I don't know his weight, age, and physical condition," Uriah replied. "So, make it… half and half."

"What if you're wrong?" Marquiss asked, trying to help.

"Then he dies."

The group let out a collective groan while Tuttle followed Uriah's orders and poured the ambire into the beaker. It smelled of herbs, honey, and a splash of tobacco, countering the nostril-clearing aroma of the spilled beakers. He swished the contents together and then carefully placed the beaker in Uriah's hands.

"Now what?" Blue asked, impatient.

"We wait." Uriah sat back and wiped his brow with his puffy sleeve, stained with the captain's blood.

"Wait?" Anoki repeated, sounding panicked.

"The potion will take a few minutes to ferment," Uriah explained. "We'll apply it to his cleaned wound and cover it, repeating on the third, seventh, and eleventh hour. He must also drink the concoction. If we're successful, he'll live. But I'm not sure if he'll ever walk again."

Minutes passed like hours as the group huddled around their captain and friend. Uriah cleaned the wound, and then he cut it and used a contraption of tubes and suction to address the wound and clear it of any poison that hadn't entered his bloodstream.

When the time was right, he took Anoki by the hand and asked her to apply it with him. The Athabasica listened intently and then Uriah poured the substance onto a fresh dressing before the two administered the antidote.

Arjun didn't move.

"Hold his head," Tuttle ordered Marquiss, and then he retrieved a small funnel from the back of his counter. He stuck the funnel into Arjun's mouth and poured the ambire mixture down the captain's throat. Arjun coughed and gagged at the treatment, but Tuttle fought to make sure he swallowed every droplet.

Then they sat back, catching their collective breaths. A few tense and quiet moments passed, and Anoki stood above Arjun, squeezing his hand. She kissed his forehead, tears tracking down her face.

"What happened to Daemus?" Addilyn asked, breaking the uneasy silence.

"He escaped on the back of a gryph." Anoki looked to the Vermilion, recalling the battle while still attending Arjun. "They flew off with the Dauldon woman. I don't know where."

Bane appeared in the door of the Beaker and walked over to Anoki. His armor was dirty, and his surcoat torn and bloodied. Dashiel had been summoned from somewhere, and he joined the knight castellan at his hip.

"Athabasica, the city grieves with you." Bane removed his helmet and lowered his head. "We rounded up the remaining attackers and their unique steeds and are treating the wounded."

Anoki ignored Bane, her focus solely now on Arjun.

"I've called for the gates of Abacus to shut," Bane added, "and the Knights of the High Aldin will search high and low for the assassin. We checked the rooftop, but both he and his imp have disappeared. We didn't find a body."

"My falcon is searching for them, too," Ritter added, his mind now back on the Bone elf. "The imp has the power of concealment, but I'm not sure what powers the assassin has."

"When you feel safe, we'll escort you back to the Gatehouse for your own safety." Bane looked to Addilyn. Then he turned to Anoki and put a consoling hand on her shoulder. "We'll take Arjun back to the Gatehouse too, so he can convalesce."

"Summon the healer from the Temple of Ssolantress." Anoki's voice wavered, emotions choking at her. "We'll need all of his Ancient's power to help Arjun." Then she lifted her head and looked at Tuttle, who sat at Arjun's side. "I'm sorry for the damage to your store. I'll ensure the city pays for it. I don't know what I would have done without you." She started crying and leaned over to hug the motionless Arjun.

Tuttle didn't respond to her offer, but instead removed his

glasses and wiped them on his waistcoat.

"Princess Addilyn." Dashiel moved closer to the princess. "I'm afraid I'm the bearer of ill tidings."

Ritter's ears perked. "What else could be happening?" He swore in exasperation, spitting on the floor.

"What do you mean?" Addilyn asked.

"I know there is no good time for this, but we've received word that the baronies of Warminster are on the brink of civil war. The news arrived from Castleshire an hour ago." He held up a scroll that had been delivered by a messenger.

Ritter turned to Addilyn, and the two then looked to Jessamy. An unspoken conversation passed between them.

In truth, Ritter's mind was split. Daemus had left with no way to track him. He'd been their priority since they'd left Castleshire. But a war at home—one caused by the same men that sought Daemus—couldn't be ignored. The thought of not being back in Thronehelm or even the Bridge when war was at their door ate at him. Vorodin had told them about this despotic alliance of Graytorris, Von Lormarck, and the Moor Bog. He felt paralyzed, unsure as to how to act.

Tuttle looked at his new friends and approached Addilyn, whose head hung low. "I know you came here to find Helenius and his answers, but you've gained the knowledge you were seeking and must return to face those who started the war. I assure you we'll take care of Arjun."

Ritter looked at Anoki and the two exchanged a knowing glance.

"You need to leave," Anoki whispered. "Go."

"May I ask a favor of you?" Addilyn braved a question and Ritter blinked.

"Anything that's in my power will be yours." Anoki sniffed back tears and tried to gain some sense of composure.

"Allow us to take three of the gryphs that you have in custody. Sir Ritter, Jessamy, and I will fly back to Thronehelm, saving us weeks of travel."

"They're yours." Anoki waved to Bane and Dashiel to make it so.

"What about us?" Marquiss asked. "We can't leave him here alone, and I need to help my sister."

"It's your choice." Ritter approached his friend. "I can't ask you or Blue to come with the princess and me. You have Arjun to care for and Daemus and Faux to find."

"Then we'll stay," Marquiss said, as Blue Conney nodded beside him. "Once we find Daemus and Faux, and Arjun is healthy, we'll find you in Thronehelm."

Ritter visited with Arjun one last time before they departed. "Be well, Captain," he muttered under his breath. "I will ensure Daemus and the princess survive. Stay here with your love. You have earned the right to do so."

Arjun didn't stir, and Ritter patted him on the shoulder before turning to the princess. If his growing love for Addilyn could find the depth of feeling to survive a decade of loneliness brought by the ardors of duty like Arjun and Anoki, perhaps Ritter's feelings could survive the chasm of their cultures and one day be recognized.

Then Jessamy, Ritter, and Addilyn departed for their gryphs' saddles and the long flight back to Thronehelm.

———✦———

INCANUS SAT MOTIONLESS IN the cast iron bathtub, his dark eyes fixated on his reflection. Ritter's falcon had torn a hole in his right cheek, peeling the flesh away, leaving his tongue and upper teeth exposed. The pain, dulled by the Ophidian's potion, left him conscious as he insisted, but did nothing to repair his injury.

"I thought you said this would heal me," he growled, not turning away from his own watery image.

"In time, assassin," the combined voices of the Ophidian answered. "You will be scarred, but the wound shall close. However, we must steal you away. The Castellan and the Horn of Ramincere are seeking you. You are no longer welcomed at the Twin Snakes."

Incanus stood from the tub, his body now cleaned of the dirt and blood from the battle, but the impossible showdown with Sir Ritter of Valkeneer tumbled over in his head, again and again. He reached for his tattered armor, which some servant had done their best to clean.

"Master, she is correct," Skullam muttered, his own wounds ailing him. "We must depart. The Horn of Ramincere has a way of detecting me, even if concealed by my own magics."

Incanus cared little for escape. He had the Vermilion in his sights. His bow was drawn, his arrows loosed. Yet no skulls. No blood.

No revenge.

"Master are you—"

The assassin's reflexive reaction caught Skullam flatfooted, smacking the creature across the face, reopening the wound on his nose. The imp skulked away, a half-laugh mixed with a half-cackle escaping his mouth. He said no more.

"Here's your palmettes, whores." Incanus dropped a pouch of golden palmettes that he'd stolen from the carcass of Anselm Helenius. "Payment in full and then some."

"Thank you." One of the sisters reached for the coins. He didn't bother to turn to look to see which it was. "Now leave. And by the will of the Ancients, never return."

Without apology, Incanus slipped into his armor and waved for Skullam to follow. The imp, hobbled and grounded with injury, followed in silence by his side.

"Where did she go?" he asked as he walked to the secret entrance that spilled out into the adjacent alley.

"We heard she and the Longmarcher headed back to Thronehelm," the sister on the right said.

"On the back of a winged horse," remarked the other.

"You've lost her." They both teased together, their gravel voice grating to his ears. "Face it, Dru'Waith. She has escaped."

Incanus tilted his head and opened the door. Dusk had fallen, making their departure a bit more difficult for their pursuers.

"We shall see," he mumbled to himself as the doors of the Twin Snakes closed behind him.

CHAPTER THIRTY-THREE

"The face of despair appears invincible,
but in time, it always fades."
—Warminster the Mage

"WHERE DO WE GO from here?" Faux whispered.

"He didn't say," Caspar replied. "He just said he'd meet us here." The journey from Abacus to Solemnity took Daemus, Caspar, and Faux three days and nights on the backs of their gryphs. They'd been stifled by a rainstorm one evening, which was typical in the south during the Season of Long Nights. The town was dark, save for some ensconced lanterns that glowed through stained windows. The streets were bare, and there were no horses or dogs to be found.

Then Daemus noticed a hooded lantern as the door to a nearby stable opened, and then closed. He stopped for a second and waved to the others. They glued themselves to the side of a granary. Faux disappeared into the shadows while Daemus and Caspar slid behind her.

The door opened and closed a second time.

"A signal?" Faux asked.

Daemus shrugged.

"Stay here." She guided the two Low Keepers with her hand to stay close to the wall. "I'll find out."

She ducked from the cover of the shadows and skulked toward the mystery light in the stables. Within a minute, she'd returned.

"It's your precept," she said with a smile, her eyes alit. "He wants us to join him in the stables."

"Why's he there?" Caspar asked.

"He's hiding."

The three hustled across the street and made their way through the cracked stable doors.

"By all the Ancients, you've returned," Radu whispered, his voice struggling to control his excitement. "Erud hasn't truly abandoned us."

"Precept, what's happened?" Daemus asked as he hugged his old teacher. "How in Erud's name did you know how to find us?"

"I can feel you." Radu glowed with hope. "When you came close, I felt Erud's presence return. The Ancient of Knowledge blesses us all."

Daemus knelt next to the precept. "What do we do?"

Radu looked to Caspar. "Son, do you feel the presence of Erud now that you are around Daemus? Do you have the Sight back?"

"I'm not sure." Caspar's eyes dropped and his face tightened as if he was concentrating. "I've been with Daemus for the last three days, but I've never had the powers that he has. I'm more of a clairvoyant, visiting people from afar. And I can whisper to animals, like Syl."

"Syl?" Radu asked.

"The gryph we stole." Caspar pointed back the way they came. He struggled to hide a smile. "His name is Syl."

Daemus looked Radu up and down. "Why are you wearing a Disciple's robe?"

"Mine was bloodied." Radu's gaze hardened. "But Volcifar Obexx helped me to escape before he died—in the service of our Ancient."

Caspar eyes narrowed at the thought. "I thought he led the insurrection."

"He did, in part, but he returned to the fold when Graytorris arrived. He saw the error in his ways."

"What of the cathedral?" Daemus asked. "What of Katja?"

"There was a great and terrible purge," Radu explained, his voice tremulous. "The Disciples and Knights carried out Graytorris's vile orders and slew every Keeper on campus. They even sent assassins out on gryphs to kill those that didn't return for the conclave. I'm afraid your classmates are dead—except for those who escaped or converted. They now follow Graytorris, only to save their skins."

Daemus slumped and wrapped himself in his arms, his eyes drifting from Radu, seeing only the faces of his former classmates, teachers, mentors, and friends. He ran his hand through his disheveled hair and caught himself drifting from the conversation.

"Daemus?" Radu shook him by the shoulder. "Don't you see? We have hope now that you've returned. I prayed and waited for a sign, and then I felt the presence of Erud. When the Knights, the Disciples see you, they'll know the protectorate can be redeemed!"

Daemus's face turned resolute, thinking only of the worst. "Katja first. I must save her."

"Radu shook his head. "I don't know what they did with the healer."

"Would she be in the dungeons?" Faux asked.

"We have no dungeons." Radu stepped to peer through the open doors to make sure they hadn't been followed. "Just a few holding cells. I was there before I escaped, but she wasn't among us."

"If he wanted to bait me into returning, he'd keep her close," Daemus surmised.

"At the cathedral?" Radu asked. "It's a big building. If she's there, how will we find her?"

The four sat in silence for a minute, occasionally raising

their eyes to look at each other.

"What of your clairvoyance?" Radu asked Caspar. "Has your Erudian gift returned or not?"

Caspar shifted as he mumbled, "I... I don't know."

Daemus took his friend by the elbow, a strained smile returning to his face. "Please try. You can find her for us."

The young Keeper sat back and exhaled. He looked unsure. "I don't want to let anyone down. My gifts were some of the first to fade."

"You controlled Syl," Daemus reminded him, injecting a bit of false confidence in his words. "You even convinced the other gryph—"

"Rolf," Caspar mumbled.

"You named the other gryph?" Faux asked.

Caspar shrugged. "He named himself."

"Never mind that." Daemus tugged at his friend. "You convinced *Rolf* to fly Faux in the heat of combat after his rider was killed. If you can use your gift to do that, you can certainly do this."

Caspar sighed. "I'll try." He sat back and closed his eyes.

Daemus had only seen Caspar using his gifts sparingly in the past. Unlike Daemus's oneiromancy, Caspar told him he would find the power of Erud swirling within him, almost welling up whenever it wanted. When it did, their Ancient revealed objects, actions, or even people, appearing somehow removed from space and time. He could see and sometimes hear them in his meditative state, and yet other times when it came uncontrolled, he'd see it at random moments, attacking him like a seizure.

A few tense minutes passed. Caspar's frame didn't flinch, and his breathing had grown so shallow that it was hard to discern whether he was even alive. Then he gasped, opened his eyes and lurched forward, trying to reorient himself.

"Caspar?" Daemus reached for his friend. "Did you see anything?"

"I saw you," Caspar managed, his eyes unfocused. "You were with... me."

"I'm with you," Daemus replied, trying to sound reassuring.

"No." Caspar shook his head as he began to recover. "I saw you in the high spire of the cathedral. I hovered above you, but you were there."

"I don't understand."

"I saw you find the blue woman." Caspar's face contorted, and his gaze rose, unfocused.

"The blue woman? Then you've found Katja?" Daemus glanced at Faux, and they both exchanged quick smiles.

"She's near the observatory." Caspar pointed as if she were in the stables with them. His voice tapered into delirium. "Oh, how I would have loved to have seen the observatory and inner sanctum before the starfall. To view it... in this way... is—"

"Caspar, lay here," Radu said as he knelt to lower the Low Keeper to the ground.

Caspar's eyes swirled, seeming to emerge from his state. He looked at Daemus. "Did I do it?"

"Yes, you did well."

"How in the name of the Ancients will we get there?" Faux asked Radu. "You said the place has become a fortress."

"I have a key," the precept explained, handing the pouch to Faux. "It will open any gate on campus, including the cathedral's. It belonged to Obexx, who gave it to me for just such a purpose."

"And the Knights?" she asked, her brows raised in doubt. "They aren't just going to let us pass by."

"I have some thoughts on that." Radu's curious finger tapped at his temple. "The Knights change guards every two hours at the front gates. They've been doing it the same way since I was a Low Keeper. I think I can distract them long enough for you to sneak by."

Daemus shook his head. "They'll recognize you." His face begged for a different plan of action. "Everyone in Solemnity knows you."

"I want them to." Radu cracked a half-smile. "I'm a fugitive on the run. A choice prize for a novice Knight pulling night duty, I'd wager."

"What if they catch you?" Faux asked.

"You get Daemus to the top of the cathedral," Radu replied. "Don't worry about me."

"What should I do?" Caspar asked.

"Go back and fetch the gryphs." Daemus pointed outside. "Bring Syl and Rolf here and wait for us to get back with Katja. We'll escape on their backs. If we don't make it, fly far from here. But don't go home. They'll come looking for you there."

"I can't just stand by and do nothing," Caspar complained.

"Someone has to get the gryphs." Daemus hugged his friend. "You are our means of escape. You saved my life in Abacus. I'll never forget that."

"I'll meet you back here," Radu offered, trying to calm Caspar. "We will hide here together and wait for Daemus to return with the healer."

"There won't be enough room for five people on two gryphs," Caspar reminded them with a shake of his head.

"I won't be going with you," Radu explained. "My duty is here."

"I don't understand." Daemus turned and faced his precept, his eyes widening with the thought of leaving Radu behind.

"I must fight this insurrection," Radu replied. "But you need to escape until we're ready to face the fallen Keeper. And that time is not now."

Daemus took a deep breath and hugged his teacher, knowing inside what Radu was trying to say. Radu wasn't coming with them. He was going to likely die here, another friend, sacrificing himself for the cause. His stomach turned but his thoughts returned to Katja.

"We need to get going," Faux urged. "Darkness is our friend."

She reached into a pouch on her belt and produced an even smaller bag. She poured something out in her hands and rubbed it on her face, turning it black as pitch.

"What's that?" Daemus asked.

"It's burned cork," Faux explained. "It blackens your face and makes it easier to disappear in the darkness."

She handed the bag of dust to Daemus, who rubbed some on his face and hands, darkening his skin to a sable grey.

"And you just happened to have some?" Radu asked.

The rogue smiled at the old precept. "I'm no Knight in shining armor. I do my best work in the shadows."

RADU RODE ALONE THROUGH Solemnity, passing the last row of houses before arriving at the campus walls. He'd brought a borrowed horse from the stables, and Caspar had calmed the horse with his newly restored powers, a strange form of animal empathy. The steed was as silent as he was. He knew the gates were always open and the Knights on guard were young and inexperienced. He smiled to himself. He could take advantage of that.

He peered out into the darkness and saw two figures softly illuminated by the flickering glow of torches ensconced outside the gate. He nearly laughed. Plenty of shadows for Faux to do her work, he thought. But first, he had to hold up his end of the bargain. He urged the horse forward and edged his way into the clearing, then made his way toward the Knights. One came out to greet him, halberd in hand.

"Sorry, Master Disciple," one of the Knights called out. "We must stop anyone entering or exiting at this time of night. First Keeper Jhodever's orders, I'm afraid."

Radu lowered the cowl of his cloak, revealing himself to the two young sentries. "I have money," Radu offered, glancing down at his satchel. "I won't be long." He knew it was a blatant ploy to bait them. Too much for them to ignore.

"Hold, sir!" The other Knight stepped from the wall and raised a hand in warning. "You're no Disciple. Lieutenant Lorraine warned us you may try and return."

Radu acted the part. He shot them a surprised look and reared his horse. The two guards scrambled in their approach and moved toward him, their halberds held high.

"Stop!" one of them yelled, but Radu wasn't going to wait around for reinforcements to come. He turned the horse and galloped along the side of the wall, opening a wide lead on his pursuers, then turned back into the town. He could hear the men chasing after him; the ruse had worked. Now he could only hope that Faux and Daemus had been able to use his diversion to sneak inside.

"FOLLOW ME," DAEMUS WHISPERED to Faux as they crept through the unguarded front gate. "I know the way."

The two snaked through the darkness, staying close to the walls and the places where the starlight wouldn't betray them. As quiet as they could, they made their way to the mouth of the Cathedral of the Watchful Eye. The grandiose staircase that climbed to a pair of red double doors was intriguing, but too conspicuous.

Instead, Daemus waved to Faux and pointed to a bay entry, a small ramp that sloped down into the back of the cathedral used to deliver goods and wares. He knew it well, as he and the other initiates had spent hours in the sweltering heat of the Season of the Rose moving heavy boxes in and out. He knew it would be empty and that no one would be guarding it at that time of night.

The sunken entrance led into a small warehouse and storage area, and Daemus and Faux found it full of crates and barrels, but empty of people.

Daemus pointed, and the two darkened figures made their way through the basement and took a flight of spiraling stairs that emptied onto the first floor of the cathedral.

"Only thirty-six flights to go," Daemus joked, but his attempt at humor was lost on Faux.

The two peered into the expansive foyer of the cathedral. It towered several stories in all directions, each hall marked with its own grand archway, stained by time. Opulent chandeliers hung from the vaulted ceilings, their flames extinguished, save for one. Its candles flickered in the great hall, caught in the breeze from a damaged window. Shadows danced and Faux smirked. Even Daemus knew it was perfect conditions to sneak by unnoticed.

The platform to the central elevator stood empty and unguarded ahead of them, but Daemus knew better. He fought the urge to trap himself inside it and led Faux to the main staircase. They began a patient climb to the top, clinging to the sides with every turn, avoiding even the slightest of sounds and cautiously putting each floor behind them.

Twenty-one, Daemus counted. *Twenty-two.*

The slow ascent was torturous on his legs. Unaccustomed to the climb and in no great physical condition, he stopped more than once to catch his breath and let his muscles rest. Each time, Faux crept ahead of him to the next floor and waited for him to push through the pain.

Twenty-nine. Thirty.

As they rounded the bend to thirty-one, Daemus and Faux heard a whisper from the hall ahead of them.

"Daemus, is that you?" the voice asked.

Faux drew her sword and pointed it at the robed woman in front of them. Half-petrified, Daemus rooted himself between the stairs and grabbed at his mace. Then he looked up into the eyes of First Keeper Portia Brecken. They held their stunned gaze for what seemed an eternity.

"I won't harm you," Portia assured him, trying to relieve the tension with a smile, but Faux closed in, evening herself with the woman and shooting a sideways glance at Daemus for instruction. Daemus stayed Faux with his hand and turned back to the First Keeper.

"I knew you'd come," Portia whispered, raising her hands. A tear appeared in her eye and her voice wavered. "I was stirred from my sleep by our Ancient. I felt an aura of peace for the first time since—" She stopped herself, and then stared into Daemus's white eyes. "I sense Erud in you. Like never before."

Daemus looked her in the eye, his voice steady. "I just want the healer."

She nodded. "I'm a friend to Radu. He convinced me that you'd return."

"If you're a friend of Radu's, why aren't you dead?" Faux's tone was both stark and accusatory. "Or on the run? You sleep comfortably in your bed while he hides and scrounges for food and safety? You're no friend of his." Faux stepped closer to her, steel flashing in her hand.

"I'm ashamed of my cowardice," Portia admitted, bowing her head. "But Erud's light had left me. I know what I need to do now to keep it from extinguishing again. Let me lead you to your healer, young Keeper. She's on the highest floor, but it's guarded."

"How can we trust you?" Faux asked.

"You'll never gain access to the inner sanctum without me," she replied. "Graytorris, Jhodever and a witch await you there, along with a contingent of Knights. They know you're coming, but not when."

"Are they awake?" Faux asked.

"Yes. Graytorris is preparing for some sacrament. I can get you to the inner sanctum safely, but from there, you're on your own."

"I'll trust you, First Keeper." Daemus stepped closer to her. "On the lives of our friends. How do we do it?"

"Follow me," Portia lifted her gaze and took the lead climbing the stairs.

Faux turned to Daemus and the two shared a glance. He knew Faux didn't like his impromptu agreement, but he didn't think he had a choice.

The three ascended the last few sets of stairs together. Daemus fought back memories of the last time he'd climbed them. He could still see visions of Amoss, Kester and Nasyr huddled by the Abacunian telescope the night of his expulsion. Now, he returned.

It had come full circle.

He knew the door opened onto the observatory, where the ancient Tome rested on its pedestal—and where Nasyr had sent him down. It had been the longest walk of his life, leading to the quickest of departures. It had also been where his Uncle Kester had come to take him home in shame, and where he'd learned the story of Graytorris and his fall.

Thirty-four.

Daemus felt a cold gust of wind in his face. The top of the tower was nearby.

Thirty-five.

The smell of charred rubble and damp soot invaded his senses. They were twelve steps from the once-proud pinnacle of their religion, which now stood in ruin.

Thirty-six.

First Keeper Brecken stopped them before they arrived at the top. "Your healer is locked inside a room on the far side of the inner sanctum."

"We can take care of that." Faux reached into a small pouch around her waist and produced Obexx's key.

"Beware," Portia warned. "She's wounded. Her stay hasn't been a kind one."

Daemus said nothing but gritted his teeth, clutching his mace even tighter.

"How do we get by the guards?" Faux asked. "How many are there?"

"There won't be any left when I'm done," Portia replied.

Before Daemus could react, Portia blinked and drew a hard breath. She stepped out into the ruins of the thirty-sixth floor followed by the rushing feet of armored guards approaching.

"*Irris... Ohren... Stille...*" came the words from Portia in the conjurer's tongue.

Daemus's eyes widened as her spell took effect, and the space in front of them wavered, vacillating like heat rising from a desert mirage in the Killean Desolates. His ears went deaf with Portia's magic. A shimmering burst of light surprised him and set the ruins of the inner sanctum alight. Daemus reached to cover his eyes for a second but when no one charged at them, he peered around the corner to assess their situation.

Portia's first wave of attack collapsed the guards to the ground, their screams of agony silenced, the clangs of their smoking armor muted as it scattered to the floor.

"Now," Faux mouthed.

The two dashed across the top floor. Daemus jumped over debris and fallen timbers to rush for Katja's room. His feet carried him faster than they ever had before, and he nearly ran up Faux's back.

A second volley of Portia's hushed assault glimmered behind them, and he could see flashes of magic dancing along the crooked walls as he ran. He knew reinforcements must have arrived, but his thoughts were only of Katja. He made the bend to her chamber first and when they turned the corner, their hearing returned.

"Out of range of her spell?" Faux dared to say aloud as she removed the key from her pouch and handed it to Daemus, who fitted the key in the lock and opened the door.

As the light from the battle flickered in the room, Daemus saw a thin figure sitting up in the bed. Long blue hair fell about the woman's face as she rose, startled by the opening of the door. His eyes found hers, which widened in surprise.

"Say nothing," he said, rushing to her side while Faux guarded the door. "I've come for you."

Katja smiled, her tears betraying her feelings. He reached out to embrace her, and the two held one another for the briefest of seconds. It was all they could afford, but if that was to be their last embrace then Daemus would have traded his life for it twice over.

He pulled her out of bed, and she grunted in pain. His eyes scanned her, and he saw the wounds Portia had warned about. Rage filled his heart and the anxious fire that overtook him at the Battle of Blood Ridge flooded back to him. He struggled to remain calm. Her escape had to be his only concern.

"I'll help you," he said, a gentle look in his eyes. "Hold on to me."

"Hurry." Faux closed the door all but an inch to allay suspicions. "It looks as if the battle is over."

"I can walk," Katja whispered softly in Daemus's ear.

He looked into her affectionate stare. He knew for the first time in his life that he was in the exact place he needed to be.

"Let's move," Faux urged, and slid out into the hallway. "Is there another way out?"

"One way in," Katja said, "one way out."

"Of course," Faux replied, shaking her head and pressing herself against the far wall, trying to make herself small. The three crept back toward the stairs.

"They knew you were coming for me," Katja whispered.

"I know," Daemus nodded. "But I had to."

When they reached the corner, Daemus glanced at the smoldering piles of armor in the hall where the guards lay dead. A spear had found its way into Portia's stomach, bringing the skirmish to an end. No one had survived but her spell of silence persisted.

"This is our chance." Faux turned to run down the stairs.

Daemus heard her, but his white eyes had wandered. He stared at the closed doors to the observatory. He knew his nemesis was inside, and if they'd known he'd come, why hadn't they emerged to stop him from escaping?

He closed his eyes for a second, flashing back to the time when Faux had asked him to use his powers willingly, instead of waiting for signs. He took a deep breath and focused inward. He could hear Faux's voice tapering off as he disappeared into the spiraling world of his wakened oneiromancy.

When he opened his eyes and looked at the door, he could see through it to the other side, where the witch was in the throes of her spellcraft. Jhodever stood near the closed Tome of Enlightenment, preparing for the ritual sacrament that Portia had described. His ethereal gaze wandered and fell upon the scarred figure of Graytorris. He took the measure of the cursed man, his demon from his dreams. He was so close.

Graytorris's crooked frame rose to attention and his gaze fell upon the other side of the door. The fallen Keeper's eyeless sockets stared back in the direction of the Low Keeper, and Daemus knew he had made a mistake. His scrying had alerted the madman of his presence, just as it did in his nightmares.

"Daemus," Katja's voice interrupted the Low Keeper's reverie and his eyes returned to him.

"I can't leave," Daemus stared at the healer, wanting to run, but Erud had shown him a different path. He knew their destiny awaited them through the double doors. His gaze shifted between Faux and Katja, who were staring back at him. "It's a trap. We can't escape through the cathedral. The Knights and Disciples await us below. Our only way out is through those doors."

"Through *those* doors?" Faux repeated. "Graytorris the Mad and a ruined tower lie through there, and that's our way out?"

"Yes," he said, confident in his Erudian Sight for the first time. He approached the closed entrance to the observatory. "The key, Faux?"

"Your eyes showed you that?" she asked, her voice tainted in disbelief.

"They showed me the way home."

"What do we do when we go inside?"

"The Tome must be opened. Then the knowledge of Erud will reveal itself."

Faux withdrew the key, her reluctance evident, and handed it to the Keeper. "I don't understand the Ancients," she complained, softly drawing her sword.

Katja crouched behind Daemus and whispered a quick appeal to Ssolantress, asking her to watch over them and to protect them from harm.

Daemus felt the warm glow of the healer's hands on his shoulders and his fear left him. Erud wanted them there, regardless of the outcome. He didn't see all, but he saw enough. He stepped into Portia's radius of silence and approached the door. Then he slowly turned the key.

The doors to the once-hallowed observatory cracked open. The wind from the cold night air snaked through the Eye's pocked openings and ruined roof. The expanse of constellations, studied by countless generations of Keepers, hung overhead. But the absence of the Tome's light was pronounced, leaving only the dimness of the starry night. The Tome, their sect's most precious connection to Erud, sat atop the tree pedestal, closed to the realm.

"You!" Graytorris cried as he turned. "You dare come! Come for *me*?"

Daemus ignored Graytorris's rambling and sprinted to *The Tome of Enlightenment*. He leapt onto the short dais and lunged for the tree pedestal, but Jhodever's coveting hands beat him to the artifact.

"Guards!" the witch yelled, from some dark recess of the room, but before she could move toward Daemus, Faux lunged and cut her off.

The witch dodged Faux's blade with an unexpected twist and reached to her belt, brandishing a weapon of her own. A small, moon-shaped sickle gleamed in the starlight, and she crouched low to avoid a second swing. Then she sprung to the attack with a swing of her own, but Faux's ready blade caught the crescent of her sickle, deflecting it to the side.

Graytorris spun, scowling, and reached for his staff and muttered in the conjurer's tongue, *"Fonces noir whyrren!"* With a furious wave of his hand, dark globes launched from his palm, exploding at the feet of the warring women. They both fell to the ground, dazed.

Daemus reached and took hold of the diamond-shaped Tome. Jhodever's grip was strong, and the two tugged at it, spinning from the dais. Daemus struggled to maintain his balance against the taller man and felt his hands slipping from the book. He gritted his teeth and kneed the First Keeper, landing a lucky blow to his groin. As Jhodever groaned and buckled, Daemus tore the book from his grip and smashed the Tome into his face, crushing his nose.

The two parted, the Tome falling to the ground between them. Jhodever fell backward and grabbed at his face. Blood seeped between his fingers as he hid his crooked nose. He crumpled to the ground in a heap, fighting to recover.

From the corner of his eye, Daemus saw the fallen Keeper pointing the crown of his staff at the artifact.

In the conjurer's tongue, Graytorris called out, *"Flutur per te levitas!"* A wild magical hale issued forth and the Tome levitated from the floor. "Is this what you've come for, Alaric?" he gloated as the Tome floated toward the decrepit man. "It's lost to you, as it's lost to your false Ancient, Erud!"

Frightened but undeterred, Daemus rose to his feet to confront him. "Why have you stolen this?" Daemus shouted as he carefully approached the man, uncertain what he'd do with the relic. "You blame our Ancient for your curse, but it's you who's at fault. Your sins are unforgivable!"

"I've blinded your sect by sealing the Tome, as your Ancient blinded me," Graytorris growled. "And it's now a time of reckoning."

"You've brought this world to the brink of war," Daemus yelled. "Vengeance for a mistake you made?"

"On the contrary, Alaric," Graytorris crowed. "*You* are the prize."

The fallen Keeper turned his staff from the Tome to Daemus, the book falling to the floor. The staff's dweomer shifted and enshrouded Daemus in a forceful hug, lifting him from the ground. He squirmed as he tried to peel away, but realized he was caught in Graytorris's inescapable grasp. He writhed in agony as the invisible energy pulled him toward the fallen Keeper, his toes scraping against the marble floor until he floated face to face with Graytorris.

"I am no prize," Daemus muttered, still fighting the power of the spell.

The madman peered blindly in Daemus's eyes, their vile and angry sockets oozing blood.

"You have my eyes!" Graytorris screamed.

The wretched man's spit spewed forth as his contorted form convulsed with vengeful anger. The strength of his fury was reflected in the crushing grasp that held Daemus fast.

Daemus couldn't breathe and he could no longer speak. His mind raced in pain and confusion. Part of him had heard Graytorris but the pain of his spell prevented any cogent thought.

"Erud punished me and granted a blind, innocent child my Sight," Graytorris bellowed. "The last image I saw in the Tome before my vision burned away was of me killing you... and lifting this curse!"

Daemus fought unconsciousness, his fate sealed. His lungs had nearly collapsed, and his head dangled backward, looking up at the night sky.

Then a searing light radiated from behind him, so bright that he could no longer see. He heard Graytorris wail in pain and agony as the rays washed over him. The staff released him, the forceful grasp around his body dissipating in an instant. He fell to the ground and gasped for breath. Then he covered his eyes and looked back at the source of his salvation.

Katja stood up, holding the great Tome open, its power

shining like a beacon and bathing the cathedral in Erud's white light. Daemus, however weak, smiled as he felt Erud's touch on his face and the warmth of the Tome's magic filled the chamber. Then he heard the beating of familiar wings above, the incessant sound he'd heard for three days and three nights on his trip to Solemnity. It was the unmistakable sound of descending gryphs, and he looked through the ruined ceiling of the Eye. Caspar and Radu flew through the opened ceiling and landed in the cathedral.

Radu slid from his gryph and stepped into the open ruins of the Eye. "We meet again, Graytorris."

Graytorris whimpered something inaudible for a second, pulling himself from the ground with his staff. His blinded skull refused to peel itself away from the light. He stammered something and tried to shield himself with his hand.

Jhodever, recovered now, dived from the dais and tackled Katja to the ground. The healer squealed as his weight fell upon her, her head striking the stone floor. Her eyes rolled away, and she fell limp, dropping the Tome. Its divine bindings closed once more. The room fell back into darkness.

"Katja!" Daemus called, jumping toward her, but his effort was greeted by a swift punch to the face from Jhodever.

Daemus rolled over with the impact, grabbing at his jaw and bloodied countenance. His eyes flickered, stunned from the blow, but he dug deep inside himself. He was desperate. Pain could wait.

He lunged back at the First Keeper, grabbing at his feet and pulling him to the ground. Jhodever fell with a thud, letting out a feeble moan. Daemus crawled over him and grabbed at the Tome, but Jhodever's long arms intercepted the move and twisted, their arms intertwining with each other as they rolled to the edge of the broken cathedral walls.

Jhodever freed his hands, managing to wrap his fingers around Daemus's neck, started strangling him. "You've failed, Alaric!" His bloody face grimaced as he squeezed.

Daemus pulled at Jhodever's arms, trying to dislodge them, but the man was stronger and had leverage, straddling him. He punched at his elbows with his fist, but the move didn't work. Jhodever had him.

Then the charging of talons and horse hooves raced toward him, the familiar sound of a gryph's sharpened claws scratching at the stone floor echoed in his ears. He smiled through his bloodied lips as he saw Caspar and Syl riding to his aid.

Jhodever looked up, releasing his grip for the slightest of seconds, and Daemus watched as Syl's two foretalons impaled the First Keeper through the chest. The First Keeper howled in anguish, blood bursting from his mouth with the force of the blow. The gryph lifted his body and tossed the First Keeper through the hole in the wall, his last screams tapering away as he fell to the campus below.

Katja screamed behind them, and both Daemus and Caspar turned back to help. Daemus felt the power of Graytorris's staff filling the Eye again, holding Katja hostage with its grasp. The magic dangled her over the broken parapet as Graytorris's skeletal face turned back to Daemus.

"Surrender, Alaric," Graytorris demanded, "or I drop the healer."

"Don't!" Daemus cried. "I... I'll gladly give my life for hers."

"Daemus, no!" Radu yelled, stopping short of Graytorris. Daemus knew that if the precept attacked, Katja would fall. "You can't! You're the light in this darkness!"

Daemus fell to his knees and looked at the fallen Keeper. "I'm yours if you set her free."

"Gladly," Graytorris replied, releasing Katja from his

power. She fell and screamed, plummeting from the cathedral's open ceiling.

Daemus watched her tumble toward the campus below. "No!" he cried, his arm partially raised in a futile attempt to catch her. A helplessness like he'd never felt before clutched at his heart, his mind swirling in desperation. Not her, not another.

Then a blur swooshed past him, and his eyes finally caught up to Caspar and Syl. The pair dived facedown from the parapet, racing after Katja.

Daemus rushed to the opening, every fiber of his being ignited in adrenaline and fear, but before he could reach the ledge, the dark hale of magic from Graytorris's staff enveloped him again.

Air rushed from his lungs as the mystical force squeezed the life from him. His mind fluttered, wild thoughts fighting against the pain. As his bones bent and body contorted in the air, the quiet acceptance of his fate washed over him. Instead of fighting, he prayed. Prayed to mighty Erud that Caspar and Syl had caught up to Katja. Prayed that his friend Faux would survive his ill-begotten plans. Prayed for the Keepers, hoping that Radu and Portia were correct—that his return would somehow restore their faith. Maybe in his death, the protectorate would rally and defeat the man from his nightmares. Perhaps he'd be held to his promise during his first embrace of Katja—his life forfeit for hers.

A sudden howl of pain reached his ears, and the force that held him disappeared. He fell back to the floor, gasping for air while holding his sides. For a moment, he thought his senses betrayed him, but his blurry eyes glanced up to see Radu standing above a fallen Graytorris, his sword wet with the fallen Keeper's blood. Graytorris squirmed on the ground, his staff lying next to him, trying to stave off the blood that leached from the wound Radu had left in his abdomen.

Radu stared at the fallen Keeper. "I should have done that when we were back in Ghostwood."

"Kill him," Graytorris groaned and began to cackle, looking to the walls of the parapet.

Daemus managed to turn, his senses keen to the sounds of scraping claws above the wind.

Climbing one claw at a time, the monstrous frame of the Antlered Man joined its master on the roof of the cathedral.

Radu staggered away from the creature, his eyes glued to the cryptid. The bowing antlers of the beast lowered; its head cocked in the precept's direction.

Graytorris smirked, his mouth oozing blood. "Let me reintroduce you to your old friend, Rrhon Talamare. The man you left for dead when you ran from me in the woods all those years ago. He won't do the same to me, I assure you."

"Daemus," Radu cried, "save yourself!"

Daemus felt Faux's arms pulling him to his feet. He wasn't sure what had happened to the witch, and he'd lost track of Faux during his own battle, but he welcomed her help.

"Get to the other gryph!" she yelled.

Daemus had other plans. "The Tome!" he shouted to her, staggering his way back to the ancient book that lay on the floor near the parapet. His ribs ached and it hurt to breathe as he inched toward it.

Graytorris's gurgling voice rose in protest. "Dromofangare!" the madman called. "The Laurentian Labyrinth!"

Daemus spun and glanced into the glow of the mirror that hung upon the wall. The polished surface, which had once reflected the battle, now featured a moving sky above a giant, walled labyrinth.

From his knees, the fallen Keeper aimed the crown of his staff at *The Tome of Enlightenment,* and it lifted from the ground, only a few feet from Daemus's grasp. "You'll never possess it again," Graytorris sneered, casting the book into the mirror's lighted surface.

Daemus stretched for it, but the Tome crashed into the image on the reflective face and fluttered away, disappearing into the depths of the labyrinth. He cried out, nearly chasing it through the mirror before Faux tackled him to the ground.

Graytorris slumped to the floor, a satisfied grimace growing on his face. His staff fell from his enfeebled grasp and he lay prone, cackling and clutching at his wound.

"Go!" Radu yelled, and the old precept stepped between them and the encroaching Antlered Man.

"Daemus, we have to go!" Faux tugged him away. "We can't defeat it like this."

"No more," he begged, "please, no more." Blinded by tears and rage, Daemus hobbled with Faux and jumped on Rolf's back. He glanced back at his precept, dwarfed in the shadow of the Antlered Man's frame, and pleaded to Erud for help.

"I am sorry, old friend." Radu stared at the cryptid and raised his sword. "I should have fought with you. I shouldn't have run. Please forgive me."

The creature crept to within inches of Radu and lowered its osseous maw. "Clawk! Clawk! Clawk!" The beast flexed and spun its skull, knocking Radu's sword from his hand and boring its antlers into his chest, skewering him.

Radu cried in horror, and when the beast raised its head, Radu's flailing body lifted from the ground, caught in the spiked antlers. Dangling and struggling Radu fought against the inevitable. His arms tugged at the tines and his legs kicked and bucked, but the beast's remaining eye watched the life slowly drain from the precept's body. With a whimper, Radu went limp.

"Clawk! Clawk! Clawk!" The cryptid raised its taloned hands and rendered Radu's corpse in front of Daemus and Faux.

"Radu!" Daemus cried out. His gaze met with the Antlered Man's and the creature charged. He felt the gryphs wings flap and its foreclaws push off from the floor. He screamed at the cryptid who ran beneath them, but he and Faux circled away, escaping from the dark scene beneath them.

CHAPTER THIRTY-FOUR

"In death, I am vengeance."
—Master Mortus

"THE POTION IS READY, Great Keeper," Zinzi said. "It's time."

Graytorris turned his head to meet the motion he'd detected when she'd entered the ruins of the inner sanctum. He'd almost rendered her unconscious with his spell during the battle, but Zinzi was as resilient as he. His hand clutched at the bandage she'd tied to his stomach to treat the sword wound.

"Yes." He forced the feeble word through a hoarse cough. "The choice is no longer mine."

"We must hurry." Zinzi helped him to his feet, and he groaned in pain. "I've prepared the parapet."

The pair disappeared through the broken portal and made their way to what remained of the stairs that led to the once proud Eye of the Cathedral. He followed her presence, searching in the darkness with the tip of his staff. Soon, he felt the cool midnight air on his face as he left the confines of the ruins. He knew he had little time left.

Graytorris climbed atop a stone slab that was exposed to the elements, created for him by the Fates when his spell swarmed the Eye with fiery meteors, decapitating the great tower. Dark clouds boiled above him, a necessary conjuration from his most recent spell. They grumbled as if the Ancients themselves were bearing witness to Graytorris and the deed to come.

He stumbled through the stones that were strewn atop the parapet and leaned on his staff against the howling winds high above the campus grounds. His strength waned with every passing moment and his tattered cloak fluttered like a weary flag that had seen its share of life and blood. It barely clung to his wretched body.

"Let us begin."

In unison, he and Zinzi chanted the vile notes of their necromantic incantations, and he soon felt the familiar pulse of magic in his veins. He fought through the pain for the sake of the spell, and their voices grew from faint whispers on the winds to near-deafening tones as their final reverie hit its throaty crescendo. As they concluded, Graytorris's voice trailed off into silence, his emotionless visage staring in anticipation. The time had finally come.

"The vial," he asked.

The incantatrix handed him the potion and it glowed bright orange for a moment, imbued with the strength of their combined spellcraft. His ossein fingers worked carefully to uncork the potion until he felt the waxen seal crack. He drew a deep breath and then swallowed the contents with reckless abandon before dropping the vial from the stone parapet to the distant courtyard below.

Zinzi's gasp reached Graytorris's ears, and once he'd finished consuming the liquid, he leaned on his staff to balance his bony frame against the headwinds. Thunder rolled above him and even in the darkness of his sightlessness, he could sense the flashes of angry lightning above.

Within seconds, the potion began to take effect. He twitched violently and dropped his staff, his hands grasping at his burning throat. He choked, fighting for air that he could no longer inhale.

He muttered indiscernible words, lost on the high winds, his voice now damaged and devilish from the potion's effects. Lightning crackled from cloud to cloud, and his mind whirred like a dervish in the cursed sands of Gelvar's Gorge.

His knees weakened; his bones burned with an infused ache from his own concoction. Then he felt the searing fire of lightning as it struck his outstretched hand. The pain lasted but a second.

Fear raced through his maddening mind. In synaptic bursts of lucidity, he wondered if the potion had worked, but the pain won, wracking his body until he collapsed on the stone. He felt his heart slow. Between fleeting beats, his last moments of clarity flirted with the mirage of time, bending back in desperation to when his heart had still been beating.

His body let go and his consciousness released itself from the shackles of mortality, violently kicking against the inevitability of death. He'd called upon the Ancient of Death one final time, as she tortured him from the Hall of the Ancients for this blasphemy.

ZINZI TOOK A FEW cautious steps back into the castle and out of the wind, trying to hide from the grisly scene. Her master had fallen to his knees, choking and dying, before slumping over onto the cold, dark stone of the cathedral's exposed Eye.

A moment passed, then another and another.

Graytorris's body lay motionless on the parapet. A cold rain wept from the storm clouds, baptizing the exposed ruins with its chilling waters.

She gathered her courage and took a few steps onto the stone slab, slowly approaching her master. Then she bent and carefully turned Graytorris's crooked form toward her, his lifeless corpse offering no resistance.

Terror and confusion gripped her, and her mind raced with endless possibilities, none of which would be acceptable to the Black Vicar, her true master. What had gone wrong? Her preparations had been precise. She'd left no room for error.

She took a few nervous steps toward the edge of the tower and turned back to Graytorris for one last glance. She wondered if returning to the Moor Bog as a failure was preferable to flinging herself from the Eye and ending the dishonor. She looked down at the darkened ground below and her chest grew heavy. She closed her eyes, inhaling her last breath and beginning to lift her foot.

She'd made her choice.

Then she heard a crackle of bone behind her. Her gaze returned to the corpse, which was twitching and contorting with electric life.

The potion had worked.

A fiendish smile returned to the witch's countenance, and she stepped away from the edge of the cathedral.

Graytorris's body twitched once, and then again. His charred skin began to crumble from him as his corpse rubbed against the stone until only the ecdysis of a snakelike shedding was left behind.

The flesh underneath had darkened from the heat of the lightning, and his blood vessels popped like logs on a fire. Their contents oozed onto the stone, hissing like droplets of acid and melting away the remnants of tissue from his corpse.

Zinzi's mind leapt and recoiled at the same time as she watched in reverence as the dread creature she'd helped to create began to rise. Graytorris's skeletal remains reanimated, one sluggish bone at a time. The creature looked like a fawn standing for the first time, but soon stronger and more coordinated movements followed.

The metamorphosis was complete.

"Graytorris, you've been reborn!" Zinzi cried. Tears welled in her eyes as she fell to her knees and bowed to the lich in front of her.

The creature's skull crepitated, bone scraping against bone as his fleshless face turned to her. The threadbare blindfold he'd worn for nearly twenty years slipped to the ground, revealing shadowy, eyeless sockets. A distant flame of ghostly light burned in the back of his skull, flickering in the holes.

"Graytorris is no more," the lich decreed, his voice raspy and sounding as if two souls lived inside him, speaking as one. "We are Mortus."

Zinzi stood still, unsure how to respond.

The lich didn't seem to care and ambled away from her. His new eyes, lit in necromantic flame, looked across the horizon at the dark skies. Mortus tilted its head with a sudden motion, popping its skeletal spine into alignment. Its jaw dropped, tearing at the remaining sinew before relaxing into its eternal mask of death. A cackle arose from somewhere within its bowels.

"Time will never be my enemy again!" it decreed in an insubstantial, ghastly voice.

Mortus raised its hand again, drawing lighting from the clouds above. The surge heated the parapet and Zinzi squinted and turned her head from the white-hot light.

"In death, I am vengeance," it muttered.

Zinzi recovered and with caution, lowered her hands from her face. She glanced down and in the grounds of the cathedral ruins, she saw hundreds of torches and covered lanterns dotting the ground below like a swarm of mating fireflies. Even from their height, tense voices lifted from the crowd to her ears. The spectacle of the storm and lightning strikes had drawn out the whole of the Divine Protectorate of Erud, and the blurry faces of Graytorris's old sect were looking up at him.

Mortus approached the edge of the parapet and turned to the Antlered Man, which lurched back like a howling wolf. It clawked in pride.

"My brothers and sisters," Mortus called in an inhuman voice that pierced the night sky. "It is our time."

A chorus of cheers rose from the rabid sycophants.

"Let us show the whole of Warminster the light of Erud," the false prophet continued.

Ovations of acceptance carried up in the midnight air as thunder rattled the remaining windows in the cathedral.

"May the light of Erud shine upon them all, blessing those who follow in our new path and blinding those who oppose true knowledge," Mortus shouted. "Follow me, your new master, your new Great Keeper, and I will show you the magics that will bring you eternal life."

ABOUT J. V. HILLIARD

BORN OF STEEL, FIRE and black wind, J.V. Hilliard was raised as a highlander in the foothills of a once-great mountain chain on the confluence of the three mighty rivers that forged his realm's wealth and power for generations.

His father, a peasant twerg, toiled away in industries of honest labor and instilled in him a work ethic that would shape his destiny. His mother, a local healer, cared for his elders and his warrior uncle, who helped to raise him during his formative years. His genius brother, whose wizardly prowess allowed him to master the art of the abacus and his own quill, trained with him for battles on fields of green and sheets of ice.

Hilliard's earliest education took place in his warrior uncle's tower, where he learned his first words. His uncle helped him learn the basics of life—and most importantly, creative writing.

Hilliard's training and education readied him to lift a quill that would scribe the tale of the realm of Warminster, filled with brave knights, harrowing adventure and legendary struggles. and help his people.

He lives in the city of silver cups, hypocycloids and golden triangles with his wife, a ranger of the diamond. They built their castle not far into the countryside, guarded by his own two horsehounds, Thor and MacLeod, and resides there to this day.